LOVE IS MURDER

THRILLER 3

Edited by *New York Times* Bestselling Author

SANDRA BROWN

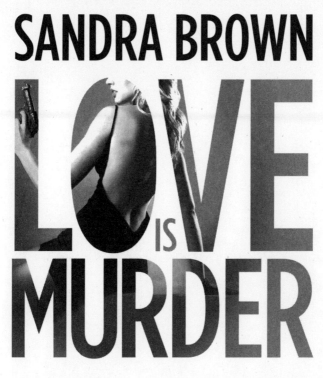

LOVE IS MURDER

Including original stories from bestselling thriller authors

LORI ARMSTRONG • JEFF AYERS & JON LAND
BEVERLY BARTON • WILLIAM BERNHARDT • ALLISON BRENNAN
ROBERT BROWNE • PAMELA CALLOW • LEE CHILD
J.T. ELLISON • BILL FLOYD • CINDY GERARD
HEATHER GRAHAM • LAURA GRIFFIN • VICKI HINZE
ANDREA KANE • JULIE KENNER • SHERRILYN KENYON
DIANNA LOVE • D.P. LYLE • JAMES MACOMBER
TONI McGEE CAUSEY • CARLA NEGGERS • BRENDA NOVAK
PATRICIA ROSEMOOR • WILLIAM SIMON • ALEXANDRA SOKOLOFF
ROXANNE ST. CLAIRE • MARIAH STEWART • DEBRA WEBB

MIRA®

Recycling programs
for this product may
not exist in your area.

MIRA®

ISBN-13: 978-0-7783-1344-1

THRILLER 3: LOVE IS MURDER

www.Harlequin.com

Printed in U.S.A.

First Printing: June 2012
10 9 8 7 6 5 4 3 2 1

On Thursday, April 21, 2011, Linda Jones and I lost our very dear friend Beverly Barton; it hurts so much to realize anew every day that her laughter has been stilled forever, and yet in a way, it hasn't. Her voice and her laughter live on in the words she wrote. Beverly loved the romance genre. She loved writing about love, and threw herself into her work with unbounded enthusiasm. I remember her emails to us when she was invited to join all these talented writers in the *Love Is Murder* anthology, how happy she was, how excited about her story "Poisoned." So here's to you, Beverly. We love you. We miss you. And, damn, you could write!
—Linda Howard

CONTENTS

FOREWORD FOR LOVE IS MURDER

Before I could read, my parents read to me, so I don't recall a time in my life when I wasn't losing myself in fictional worlds. On Mother's and Daddy's knees, I cultivated a passion for make-believe. I grew up with books as a staple and libraries as a second home. Reading was my favorite pastime as a child, and it became an addictive habit I never outgrew.

I can't remember the first romantic suspense novel I read. It might have been *Rebecca* by Daphne du Maurier, or perhaps one of Mary Stewart's classic blends of mystery and romance, or Victoria Holt's sweeping, gothic tales. I read and reread them. They left me enthralled and wanting more…largely because so few authors were writing what we now call romantic suspense.

But those who did write in that vein, though few in number, wrote it well and had an enormous impact on my professional future. They entertained me, but I also learned from them and continue to try to live up to the standards they set. Helen MacInnes and Evelyn Anthony come to mind. Charlotte Brontë's *Jane Eyre*.

One of the best cornerstone novels of the genre was Ken Follett's *Eye of the Needle*. On the surface one could say that neither these authors nor their books have anything in common. Not so. They contain terror tinged with romance. Or is it the other way around? That depends upon the writer, but both elements are in their work.

Romantic suspense is a combination of genres—and the mix is *potent*. Mysteries are puzzles that tease and test our minds. We experience an adrenaline rush from the high-stakes plots of thrillers. Romances remind us of the eternal power of love, honor and self-sacrifice. Stories of romantic suspense offer the best of all these. They give readers an exciting and emotional thrill ride that engages the mind, the heart and all the senses. Merging a rocky romance with a fast-paced thriller makes for a story that crackles with electricity.

The element of love ratchets up the stakes for the characters. It intensifies their motivations, increases the tension and heightens the suspense. When a person one cares about—lover, spouse, child—is in jeopardy, all else ceases to matter. Failure isn't an option. When what one stands to lose is the person most dear, terror is made manifest. But so are determination and courage.

This then is the essence of good storytelling—an individual overcoming incredible odds to save a loved one from peril. This is what makes romantic suspense satisfying on multiple levels.

And, lest I begin to sound too lofty, let's face it—danger can be a turn-on.

Love Is Murder is an anthology of short stories penned by some of our most popular romantic suspense authors. In addition, the anthology features stories by writers better known for their thrillers, but who often incorporate into their books the relationship layering that is the trademark of traditional romantic suspense.

Also included are three stories that were selected from more than sixty blind submissions—D. P. Lyle's vigilante story "Even

Steven"; Jim Macomber's domestic abuse tale "Execution Dock"; and William Simon's riveting, high-stakes kidnapping "Spider's Tango." I'm overwhelmed by the quality of all twenty-nine stories and hope you enjoy reading them as much as I did.

Inspired by the above-mentioned writers and others, many talented authors today write in this expansive genre that has diversified to include historical settings, the forensic sciences, police procedurals, the military, the justice system, espionage, the supernatural and plots ripped from the headlines. The variety offered by romantic suspense is vast, and so is the array of storytelling talent contained within this anthology.

It is with a great deal of pleasure that I introduce these stories written in a genre which might not have a *lengthy* heritage, but certainly an impressive one. I'm proud to be included.

~ Sandra Brown

DIAMOND DROP
ROXANNE ST. CLAIRE

*Sexy, naughty, savvy and fun, this story has quick,
smart dialogue and a fantastic twist. —SB*

In spite of the cacophony under the marble dome of Antwerp's Central Station, Donovan Rush heard the distinct tap of high heels about ten feet behind him. The main terminal echoed with a hundred different languages and shook with the shrill whine of high-speed train brakes on the platform levels, but the music of that familiar feminine drumbeat reached his ears and slowed his step.

The footsteps grew closer, preceded by a whiff of peppery perfume, a whisper of a silky sleeve, a subtle clearing of a woman's throat…and she passed him without a glance.

But he stole one, and then stayed two strides behind her just for the fun of it.

Mahogany waves clipped in a careful French twist revealed a slender column of a neck, squared but narrow shoulders casually draped in a bloodred scarf. Hip-hugging black leather pants molded to a heartbreaker of a backside then tapered over long, lean thighs.

And then there were the noisemaking shoes. Five inches if they were a centimeter, platforms, open toes and little silver buckles that he'd like to unfasten with his teeth.

Deadly.

Too bad he'd only be in Antwerp for the brief hour it would take to pass security at the Beurs voor Diamanthandel, meet with the client's sightholder, take delivery of two million dollars worth of rough-cut diamonds and get back on the Thalys for the return trip to Paris.

There was no time for lovelies clad in leather. Especially when his boss had sent a text from New York just moments ago reminding him that the client for this routine diamond drop, Boisvert Jewelers, was run by a CEO who evidently did not tolerate tardiness. Lucy Sharpe had ended her brief text with three simple words: don't be late.

When the owner of the Bullet Catchers—and queen of understatement—issued a warning like that, no one who wanted to keep his job with her elite security firm would dare disobey. Especially not because he was, uh, sightseeing.

The woman in front of him slowed almost imperceptibly, glancing to her left, then quickly pretending she hadn't.

Donovan did the same, noticing a man outside a café entrance, a cell phone to his ear, but his gaze on the leathers, as well. That made him human, since Donovan would guess that most male eyes in the terminal would take the same trip his had.

But the highly trained bodyguard in him noticed the woman's hesitation, the change in her heel-to-toe tempo and the aura of awareness that shot up around her.

She shifted to the right just as the man ended his call. When he took a single step forward, she turned on one of those spikes and beelined in the opposite direction.

The heels clicked into a trot.

The gold-embellished station clock read twenty-one minutes to ten. Donovan had been doing the Antwerp diamond drops long enough to know he needed twelve minutes to clear security at the

Bourse, and two minutes to cross the cobblestone street that led there. That left seven minutes to follow his instinct…and a woman who'd just upped her speed from purposeful to petrified.

The man hustled toward her, small and spare and quick on his feet, smoky gray eyes locked on the lady, one hand in the pocket of a loose-fitting jacket.

With the reassuring weight of a Glock under his sport jacket, Donovan kept his attention evenly divided between the two people. She took a sharp left toward stairs leading to the upper level train platforms, snaking her way through the crowd with a quick burst of speed.

She paused once to glance over her shoulder, her gaze locking on Donovan's for a split second before she looked away. At the top of the stairs she blended in with a pack of travelers on the train platform, but Donovan kept sight of the ruby scarf.

So did the other man, who attempted the same maneuver up the stairs, but didn't nail it as gracefully as the woman. His failure let Donovan get right behind him and stay there.

Leather lady was on a tear now, running down the platform as the scream of the next high-speed train reverberated through the second level's glass-domed ceiling. She spun around, giving Donovan his first chance to really see her face.

Normally, he'd register the contours of beauty, the appeal of every feature from a whisper of a widow's peak to a shadow of a cleft in her chin. But this wasn't normal. That expression of raw, ripe terror was not normal.

The man had her in his sights, then reached deeper into his pocket, shifting his weight like he was bracing to fire.

Donovan pounced. An arm to the throat, a knee to the thighs, and the guy was down and done.

"Hey!" He tried to thrust an elbow, but Donovan twisted the offending arm and locked it into a position of paralyzing pain. Certain he was immobilized, Donovan peered through the wall of the gathering crowd as the train doors zipped open.

A red scarf fluttered as its owner darted on board. Holding on to the door, she leaned into the light to look straight at him.

"Thank you," she mouthed and then disappeared into the train.

Donovan released his captive and stood slowly.

"What the hell?" the man croaked with a heavy British accent, pushing himself up and whipping around to Donovan.

Donovan stepped back and held up his hands. "Sorry. Had you confused with someone." He turned to leave, but the man grabbed his jacket.

"What's your fucking problem, mate?"

"Excuse me." Donovan brushed the hand off and glanced at the clock above the platform. "I'm late for an appointment."

● ● ●

"You are free to enter, Mr. Rush." The last of three security guards handed Donovan his clearance papers with an officious nod, his heavily accented English flawless. "Monsieur Pelletier is waiting for you at table fourteen."

Donovan tucked his paperwork in the breast pocket of his sport jacket and entered the double doors to the main room. Sunshine poured through a hundred skylights, built for the express purpose of giving the jewel traders the best possible natural light.

Dozens of tables flanked a center aisle where men sat in small groups, face-to-face, nearly every one wearing a jeweler's loupe, examining stones.

A middle-aged man sat alone at the far end of table fourteen, a black velvet cloth spread with an array of cloudy white diamonds in front of him. He looked up as Donovan approached and stood, no smile on his angular, harsh features.

Donovan slipped into the space behind the table, reaching out his hand in greeting, introducing himself. "I'm delighted to welcome Boisvert Jewelers to the Bullet Catchers client roster," he added.

"We understand your company provides the finest security couriers in the business."

"You understand correctly," Donovan assured him, gesturing toward the diamonds. There was no time for small talk if he was going to make the train back to Paris and meet the client's timelines.

"This is what I've selected for you to deliver," he said. "I know the CEO of Boisvert to be a connoisseur of excellence. I've no doubt these diamonds will meet the highest standards."

There were at least forty sizable stones, many that would be cut to make two or three multicarat diamonds. Pelletier had probably spent the past three days poring through hundreds and hundreds of rough-cut rocks delivered from Africa and Australia, his job as a sightholder to be the "eyes" for the parent jeweler back in Paris. A parent company with deep pockets, if they could manage this purchase.

"You've chosen well," Donovan said. Although it wasn't his job to pass judgment on the diamonds Pelletier had purchased; his job was to safely deliver them to the Parisian jeweler whom he worked for. On *time.* "Is the paperwork complete?" If Pelletier had filled it out ahead of time, they were in luck.

The man slid a packet toward Donovan. "Yes. I'll need your signature in all the right places, while I pack this parcel and sign off on what you've taken."

The transaction was so standard, Donovan barely looked up from the pages he had to sign, flipping through each with just a cursory glance, until Pelletier pulled a cell phone from his pocket to take a call.

"Excuse me," he said softly before launching into rapid French. Unable to follow the foreign language spoken that fast, Donovan continued to sign, until a note of alarm in the other man's voice made him look up.

"Is there a problem?" he asked softly.

Pelletier just held up one finger. *"Très bien. Merci."* He hung up. "That was the CEO of Boisvert Jewelers."

"Really."

"We have an issue that I am obligated to bring to your attention. There has been a credible threat to this diamond delivery. Apparently, the details were leaked."

"By whom?"

He shook his head, unable to hide disgust. "The CEO's assistant. She's been arrested and detained, but we don't know how secure these diamonds will be between Antwerp and Paris."

"I have them," Donovan said, scooping them into a red velvet pouch that would fit in his jacket pocket. "So you can assure Boisvert management that they will be quite secure."

The other man looked relieved, but dubious. *"Très bien, mais…* a word of advice, Monsieur Rush?"

"Don't be late?"

"Trust no one," he replied. *"And* don't be late."

• • •

He didn't alter his travel plans. Whoever was tracking this diamond drop would assume that an experienced—and forewarned—courier would choose a different form of transportation back to Paris. But getting to the airport or renting a car would cause unnecessary delays and play right into a thief's expectations.

Instead, Donovan slipped back into the train station, and purchased a new Comfort One ticket on the high-speed Thalys to Paris using different identification. He boarded the first car the moment the giant red wedge-shaped train blew into the station, before most of the other passengers had even reached the platform. Strolling the length of the train, he memorized the face of every passenger already on board since Amsterdam or Rotterdam.

Under the guise of a traveler looking for the most privacy and comfort, he perused nearly four hundred seats in a dozen connected cars, including the bar and café, and every lavatory. And he had no doubt where he would sit.

The last set of glass doors whisked open with an automatic vacuum that responded to the slightest pressure. This small compartment seated only eight, with two rows of seats facing each other, separated by a narrow aisle. Well protected, away from most passengers, and with a single entrance that he could watch every minute of the hour and a half trip to Paris, it made the perfect place to detect a thief.

But, shit, someone had beat him there. He could see the top of dark hair, not quite tall enough to extend above the orange headrest, facing the back seats. No matter. He drew his weapon. He would convince the passenger to leave.

But the person shifted positions to cross a foot into the aisle. A foot wearing a platform peep toe with an unforgettable silver buckle.

Trust no one.

Especially damsels in distress and leather. There were no coincidences in this business; his experience as a Bullet Catcher taught him that. She identified him this morning, got a good look at him and no doubt had the Boisvert informant tell her what train he'd be on.

Of course, he could simply turn and take another before she even saw him.

But that's not what Lucy Sharpe demanded from her men. She wanted to impress the new client? All right, then. He'd deliver the diamonds *and* the thief. On *time.*

He cleared his throat. "May I join you?"

"I was hoping you would." A sultry and feminine American voice answered.

He came around the seat back, his gun drawn, but not yet aimed at her. Let her know he had it and wasn't afraid to use it. "Although I'd prefer not to have to kill anyone who's chasing you on the way to Paris."

"On the contrary." She lifted amber eyes and met his gaze, not even a flicker of surprise. "You've done your good deed for the day."

"So this is no coincidence?" Not that he thought it was for a moment.

Her lips widened in a sexy smile. "I was on the platform and saw you get on board. I decided you were the type of man who would choose the back compartment for…privacy."

"So you're just riding the rails for fun today."

She shrugged. "I did have to take an unexpected trip to Rotterdam, thanks to you giving me that chance to escape, but I easily made it back here on a return train. Going to Paris?"

"I am."

"Then we'll travel together." Her smile was warm. No, *hot*. And inviting. "That guy is gone now, so you can put the gun away."

Not a chance. "I prefer to err on the side of caution." He took the seat across from her—the one he would have taken anyway, because it allowed for a direct view through the doors and into the next car—and kept the pistol in his hand, resting on the seat next to him.

"I'm Claudia Greenwood," she said.

"Donovan Rush." No reason to lie. Obviously, she either knew exactly who he was—in which case he'd either kill her or deliver her to the authorities at the Gare du Nord in Paris—or she really was just a beautiful American on holiday or business in Belgium. Not too hard to guess which. "And who was your pushy friend in the station?"

She exhaled a breath of disgust. "A bad choice from my past."

Yeah, right. "A woman who looks like you involved with a guy who looks like that? C'mon, I might be big and ugly, but I'm not dumb."

"You're quite big—" she let her gaze slide over his shoulders and chest "—but you are *definitely* not ugly. Sadly, I wouldn't be the last woman who got swayed by an impressive…bank account. What brings you to Belgium, Donovan?"

As if she didn't know. "Business."

"Business that requires you to carry a gun?"

"It is Antwerp," he said, as though that explained it. That *would* explain it to a diamond thief, which, he'd bet the entire pouchful in his pocket, she was. "And you?"

"Business, as well." Her fingers flicked the end of her scarf. "Fashion accessories. I'm headed to Paris for a trade show."

"Then we have a whole hour and a half to get to know each other." And to see just how long it would take for her to make her move.

She settled back into her seat with an alluring smile. "I can't imagine a better way to spend my time."

● ● ●

He had to give the woman a lot of credit. She never dropped character, chatting about clothes and fashion shows, her apartment in New York, her small business. All the while, the train careened through the autumn-washed fields of the Dutch countryside, bridges and farms a blur in Donovan's peripheral vision. No one entered the compartment but a conductor checking tickets after they'd stopped in Brussels, and neither of them made a move to hit the restroom or get a drink for a full hour.

But thirty minutes outside of Paris, she finally got down to business.

"I really owe you a debt of gratitude for your assistance this morning, Donovan."

"Not at all. You seemed like you were in trouble."

"I don't suppose you'd let me take you to lunch when we arrive in Paris."

"I'm sorry. I have an appointment."

She gave a hopeful smile. "Dinner?"

"I'm leaving for Rome this afternoon."

"Oh, how can I thank you for what you did? I mean, you really saved me. How did you even notice what was happening?"

"I'm observant," he said, letting his gaze drop from her glossy lips to her silky scarf to her leather-clad legs. "For instance, I noticed your sexy shoes."

She smiled, raising one foot toward his left hand. "You like them?" She set the heel in his palm playfully, allowing him to cup the buttery leather.

"You wear them well."

She straightened her leg a little, which made his hand slide up to touch skin. "I can unwear them, too."

Ah, so she was going to use sex to get the diamonds. As appealing as that strategy was, it almost made him laugh with its unoriginality.

"That won't be necessary," he said, circling his fingers around the fine bones of her ankle. "Nice thought, but not necessary."

She leaned forward, a gap in her creamy silk blouse revealing the curve of her breast. Lifting red-tipped fingers, she toyed with the loose knot of the scarf, giving him an even better view of her cleavage.

An announcement in French almost drowned out the slither of silk over silk as she drew the scarf along the collar, sliding it off.

"We have less than thirty minutes," she said softly, the light and message in her eyes unmistakable. "I can use them to…thank you."

She let the scarf hit the floor. Her knees would be next, he surmised. One minute and she'd be kneeling in front of him, unzipping his pants…reaching into his jacket pocket when his eyes closed in pleasure.

Really, the oldest trick in the book.

She reached up to her hair clip in a move that pressed the thin material of her blouse against luscious breasts.

"Do you mind?" she asked in a sultry voice.

"Not at all."

Auburn hair cascaded over her shoulders, assisted by a slow shake of her head. The halo of soft curls made her delicate features even more attractive, and ratcheted up his already high trouble alert, sending an unwanted bolt of heat into his lower half.

No doubt about it, Claudia Greenwood was a pro.

But she surprised him; instead of dropping to her knees, she leaned back, lifted her other leg and set her shoe on his lap.

"So you really like my shoes?"

He was still holding the left one, his hand running up and down a velvety calf under the leather pants. "Very much. That's what I noticed about you."

She gave him a dubious look. "Not my leather pants?"

"I heard your heels behind me."

"And that sound turns you on?"

"A little," he admitted. He thumbed the little buckle in response, swallowing against a dry throat and willing his cock not to react to the proximity of her other shoe.

He had a thief by the ankles and he wasn't about to let his dick get in the way of taking her down.

"So, you're a shoe guy." She glided one platform sole over his thigh. His cock stiffened some more but his brain wasn't bloodless. He calculated exactly how far that greedy foot was from the diamond pouch in his jacket pocket.

Far enough that he could snap her leg in two before she got anywhere near it.

But it wasn't the diamonds she tucked her toes into. She wiggled her toes and shot a little fire into his balls.

"Spread your legs, Donovan," she whispered, her fingers closing over the edge of her seat as she added pressure by pushing her feet into his groin a little more. When he obliged—he had to see how far she'd take this—she pulled her other foot out of his grasp and set it on his leg. "Watch what my shoes can do."

"I'm not worried about your shoes." He surreptitiously slipped his index finger on the trigger of his gun while her stilettos bracketed his erection. She released her grip on the seat to finger the button of her blouse and opened it to reveal more creamy cleavage.

"You shouldn't be worried about anything. Just take your reward for being a Good Samaritan." She wet her lips and let her eyelids shutter, the leather of her pants skimming over his legs as she worked the shoes up and down the erection tenting his trousers.

"Close your eyes," she told him. "I'll do all the work."

He just smiled and dropped his head back, pretending to follow her orders but ready for her to slam a heel into his balls. She'd be dead before the pain hit his brain.

She stroked harder, faster…and touched her breast with a sensual sigh. He waited, ready…but she seemed intent on pleasuring him.

The first announcement of the arrival at the Gare du Nord filled the compartment, the French barely drowning out the thump of blood in his head. It was time to end the party, sadly. He lifted the gun.

"Party's over, Claudia. Pack up. You're going to the French police."

"What?" She paled, her feisty feet suddenly still. "Why?"

"Because I'm taking you in."

Confusion darkened her features. "For what?"

For a moment, he almost believed her. Then he laughed. "You're

very good, Claudia, but I'm better. I've been in this game too long."
He leaned forward, lifting both her ankles in one hand to set her
feet on the floor. "I like you, so I don't want to shoot you. When
we pull into the Gare du Nord, we're going straight to the French
police."

Her jaw completely unhinged. "What the hell are you talking
about?"

"I'm talking about…" Was it possible he was wrong? No. This
couldn't be a coincidence. "Your effort to charm, mesmerize and
foot fuck me."

"Look, I'm sorry." She started buttoning her blouse with trembling fingers. "I'm not some kind of a hooker. I just was…fooling
around." Her voice hitched with a very believable crack. "Please, I
didn't know it was against the law. *Please*."

Doubt crept into his head. His instinct was rarely wrong. But
was it possible this really was no more than a chance encounter?

"I know what you want," he pressed.

Her golden-brown eyes flashed like flames. "I don't want anything," she insisted. "I was being…nice. And, evidently, stupid."

Was it possible he was completely wrong about her? He had to
find out. He had to know. She was so intriguing, so beautiful, and
so in the right place at the wrong—

The door swooshed open and a conductor barged in.

"We've already had our tickets punched," Donovan said quickly,
shooing him out.

The man's hand slipped from beneath his uniform, drawing a
pistol he instantly aimed at Claudia's temple.

Over her shocked shriek, he made his demand. "Give me the
diamonds or I'll splatter her brains all over this compartment."

●　●　●

Either she was in the wrong place at the wrong time or she was
a hell of a good actress because blood drained from Claudia's face,

her eyes popped wide, her next breath trapped in terror. All very…
convincing.

"Please…" Her voice was no more than a croak. "Give him what
he wants."

The Glock was still secure in his hand. But if Donovan so much
as lifted that pistol, this woman would be dead. And while that
wouldn't bother him if she were a plant and part of the ruse…it
would piss the hell out of him if she were an innocent fashion ac-
cessory buyer on a trip to Europe.

"Pick the gun up with two fingers and throw it into the aisle,
Mr. Rush, or this woman will die."

She might anyway, and she obviously knew it. Claudia's eyes
brimmed with fearful tears, a plea for her life emanated from every
cell.

"The gun," the conductor repeated, as calmly as if he were asking for his ticket.

Was her life worth two million in diamonds? Not if she was in
on this…but if she wasn't? He couldn't risk it. He slid the Glock
down the aisle between the seats.

"Now hand me the bag. And if you have another gun in that
pocket, she will be dead before you can produce it."

She whimpered and the man's Walther pressed a bloodless spot
in her temple.

Okay, what were his options? To give up the diamonds, and possibly his life. To make a surprise attack that would cost hers. Or…
to trust this woman to work with him.

"The diamonds are hidden in her shoes," Donovan said. "I transferred them there."

The conductor's eyes narrowed as he dropped his gaze to her
feet. "Where?"

"They're hidden in the platforms." Which would make a perfectly creative and logical place to smuggle diamonds.

"Take them off her," he ordered.

Donovan crouched into the space between the two seats to un-buckle her shoe. As he did he looked up to silently communicate with her. Her gaze shifted to the gun with a slight question in her eyes.

Working as one, they could get this guy. If she really was... *innocent*.

Torn between warring instincts, his fingers caught the silver buckle and slid the leather strap through, the shoe sliding off in his hand.

"Give it to me," the man demanded.

Once more, he shared a look with her, boring into her lioness's eyes, searching for...trust. He saw something there, enough to take a chance.

Donovan reached up to hand over the shoe, deliberately holding it far enough away so the other man had to bend to get it. As he did, Donovan pitched the shoe toward the glass door, the weight making the auto-suction whip the door open. In the split second the man followed the path of the shoe, Donovan dived for his gun.

The man fired, but Donovan heard the bullet ricochet. Claudia dropped to the ground with a cry.

When the man launched at the shoe, Donovan grabbed his leg, pulling him down with one hand so they both landed on Donovan's Glock. He had the gun in his hand, but the other guy pounced, wrestling and rolling as Claudia cried out again, scurrying to her feet. As she leaped over the two men, she scooped up the shoe and threw herself toward the door, making it slide open again. She was gone in an instant.

"She took the fucking diamonds!" the man said, scrambling to get up and run after her.

So she *wasn't* in on it. Now he had to protect her or this guy would kill her for sure. Donovan tried to pull him down by the leg, but the man fell on top of him, crushing him with his weight. He had complete advantage and a gun pointed directly at Donovan.

"Bye-bye, bodyguard." He took a breath, just about to pull the trigger when a deadly five-inch heel smacked the man's face, shocking him enough to let Donovan shove him off.

Instantly, Donovan flipped him over and got his own Glock in the bastard's belly, looking up long enough to see Claudia in the doorway.

"Thank you," she mouthed.

Without bothering to retrieve her shoe, she disappeared into the next car and let him finish the job of taking down the thief.

• • •

Even with the side trip to the French police station, it was 2:59 p.m. when Donovan arrived with the bag of diamonds at the Paris showroom of Boisvert Jewelers, a few doors away from the Plaza Athénée. Lucy had texted her congratulations and informed him the client was most pleased.

Getting there on time would just be icing on the happy guy's cake.

"*Bonjour,*" he greeted the receptionist outside the management offices. "I'm Donovan Rush with the Bullet Catchers. I have an appointment with Monsieur Boisvert."

She smiled. "*Oui?*" There was amusement and admiration in her eyes. "We have heard of your heroics on the Thalys, monsieur. *Une moment, s'il vous plaît.*"

He glanced at his watch as the receptionist disappeared behind a set of double doors. If she hurried, he'd make it.

Four minutes later, she emerged. "You may go in now, Monsieur Rush." She held the door and he walked past into a large, dimly lit empty office. No one was here? After all the warnings to be on time?

"Excuse me?" he said to the thin air. "I was told I had a meeting in here."

"You're late, Monsieur Rush." Very slowly, the executive chair facing the window turned, revealing...a woman.

He just stared at her, processing everything. The mahogany hair. The crimson scarf. And a heart-stopping smile of pure sex and... authority.

"Claudia Greenwood?"

"Claudette, actually. And you should study your French, Donovan." Her accent was thick...and natural.

Green wood...*bois vert.* Of course. "You're the CEO of Boisvert Jewelers." It wasn't a question; it didn't need to be. "Why?"

"We often test new couriers. The run-in at the train station was a test of your observation skills." She pushed the chair back. "You passed."

"And the foot massage?" He lifted a brow. "A test of my concentration skills?"

"Yes, but..." A soft flush rose to her beautiful cheeks. "I let my attraction to you take that a little too far."

Actually, not far enough, and the attraction, he couldn't deny, was mutual. "And the attempted theft?"

Her expression grew serious. "Unfortunately, that was no test. There was no real threat that we knew of. You were told that so we could monitor how you handled such a situation. But, when it happened? It was real. And you were impressive."

Holding her gaze, he approached her desk as she stood up. "I believe I have something of yours," he said, reaching into his jacket pockets.

"It better be worth two million dollars."

He held out the red velvet pouch. "It is. And this—" he reached into his other pocket and slid out a sexy high-heeled shoe "—is priceless when you consider it saved my life."

"You saved mine first, so we're even."

She reached for the shoe, but he tossed it to the floor and let the diamonds drop with it. "No we're not," he said. "I haven't had a chance to thank *you*."

He pulled her into his arms and backed her up to the desk to lay her down right on top of it.

"Now?" Her question was a breathy whisper in his ear.

"I wouldn't dare keep my client *waiting*."

COLD MOONLIGHT
CARLA NEGGERS

Only a writer as gifted as Carla Neggers could use so few words to convey so much action and emotional depth. —SB

Ryan "Grit" Taylor felt snow melting in his right boot. He didn't feel whatever snow might be melting in his left boot because he didn't have a left foot, or any of his left leg below the knee. In the year since he'd lost it in a firefight in Afghanistan, he'd learned to manage with a prosthesis…even in the Vermont snow, even while looking for Marissa Neal, the eldest daughter of Preston Neal, the vice president of the United States.

It wasn't a Navy SEAL mission. It was a Charlie Neal mission, Charlie being the youngest Neal, a sixteen-year-old meddling genius and the missing Marissa's only brother. The Neals had arrived in tiny Black Falls, Vermont, last night for a long weekend in the early-spring snow. Charlie had popped out from behind a tree fifteen minutes ago, when Grit had gone to look for Marissa, thinking she might be making a snowman. Now he wasn't sure what was going on. Charlie had a tendency to overreact.

He also had a tendency to be right. He was worried about his sister.

The Neals weren't Grit's responsibility, but Charlie knew how to give the Secret Service the slip and had done it before. Marissa probably knew how but she was the eldest of five, a history teacher, responsible, mature…pretty. Had she just wandered off? *How?*

What if something was wrong?

"My life didn't used to be this complicated," Grit said.

Next to him in the snow, Charlie shook his head. He wasn't wearing a hat, and his hair seemed even fairer in the early-evening light, with a half foot of fresh spring snow on the ground and clinging to every branch, twig and pine needle in the Green Mountains. "You're wrong," Charlie said finally; he was confident that way. "Your life was complicated even when you were fighting in Afghanistan. It only seemed simpler then because you were a member of a special operations team that worked under a chain of command, with a clear mission."

"Still am, still do."

Charlie paused on the snow-covered trail. His face was pale, much paler than it should have been given the cold temperature and the pace he'd been maintaining. "Do you have a clear mission now?"

"Keep you safe. Find your sister. Keep her safe. Get you both back to the Secret Service."

"What if Marissa's already—"

"Don't go there, Charlie. It won't help."

Without comment, Charlie resumed walking. He and Grit both wore boots, not snowshoes or cross-country skis. There were no other prints in the snow. They rounded a sharp curve shrouded with evergreens. Elijah Cameron was there, as grim as Grit had ever seen him—which was saying something, since Elijah, a Special Forces soldier, had been in the firefight in the Afghan mountain pass the night Grit had lost his lower leg. Black Falls was Elijah's hometown. He'd always wanted to come home.

Black Falls wasn't Grit's hometown. Too cold.

"Marissa Neal's in trouble," Elijah said, never one to ease into a conversation. He glanced at Charlie, then shifted his Cameron-blue eyes back to Grit. "I spotted her up on the trail. Then out of the blue some jackass decides to shoot at me sniper-style."

"You were hit," Charlie said, wide-eyed as he took in the blood on Elijah's shoulder.

Elijah shrugged. "I'm good."

Grit knew better than to argue with him. "Where is Marissa now?"

"There's a ski chalet not far from here. She's probably heading there to hide, try to get hold of the Secret Service. She's got about a ten-minute head start on you." Elijah glanced at Charlie. "You, too." He turned back to Grit. "One of them is hurt. Her or the guy who's after her.

"Blood trail?" Grit asked.

Elijah gave a curt nod. "Intermittent."

Grit didn't respond. Charlie's instincts had been on target, not for the first time. Elijah's presence had to have distracted whoever was after Marissa. Elijah had gone for an afternoon walk in the mountains he knew so well, maybe to think about his upcoming marriage to Jo Harper, a Secret Service agent and another native of pretty Black Falls, Vermont. He and Grit had become friends during the past year, but especially over the winter, when they discovered a network of killers had set up shop in Black Falls. The killers were now dead or in prison.

Whoever was after Marissa Neal would be soon, too.

"Let's go," Elijah said, teeth clenched.

Charlie Neal was shivering, more from fear than cold, Grit thought as he looked up at the clear Vermont sky. "A nice day for maple sugaring, and here we are again." He sighed at Elijah. "I thought you said Vermont was one of the safest states in the country."

"It is."

"Yeah. Just not Black Falls. Not lately."

Charlie stood between Elijah and Grit. "What do we do now?" Charlie asked.

Grit took charge. "Elijah will get you back to the lodge. I'll find your sister."

"Not a chance, Grit." Elijah's voice was low, uncompromising.

Most people would be intimidated. Grit wasn't. "I'd take you with me if I could, but you know I can't, Elijah. You have a bullet in your shoulder."

"Graze."

"Take Charlie. The Secret Service must be all over this thing by now. You can fill them in." Before Elijah could argue further, Grit added, "We're wasting time."

Elijah was an experienced soldier and knew how to set aside his emotions and do what the situation demanded. "You're not armed, Grit. Neither am I." He glanced back through the woods, then shifted again to Grit. "It wasn't supposed to be that kind of day."

"I'll grab a big rock or something," Grit said, half-serious. "I'll be fine. Go."

Charlie was close to hyperventilating, his lips purple, the skin at his jaw splotchy. He looked younger than sixteen. "I have a gun."

Grit sank deeper into the snow, the ground underneath soft, beginning to thaw. "Figures. Is it loaded?"

"Yeah. Of course. I wanted to be prepared. Just in case, you know?"

Elijah had the weapon out of Charlie's hand and into Grit's in two seconds flat. A Browning 9 mm. It'd work.

"It's not mine," Charlie said without a hint of defensiveness.

Elijah held up a hand. "Stop right there. Don't tell us anything we don't need to know."

"I won't get arrested. It's a legal weapon."

No doubt Charlie could cite the appropriate Vermont and federal laws—or make them up as he went along—but a look from Elijah and Grit silenced him, which wasn't easy to do.

Despite his bullet wound, Elijah clapped an arm on the boy's shoulders. "Come on. Let's get out of here." Elijah winced as he lowered his arm. "I've been shot, you know. I need a damn doctor."

"The bullet didn't hit any major organs or veins or arteries," Charlie said. "You'd be dead by now if it had. How's the pain?"

"Not as bad as the pain of listening to a kid with a 180 IQ yap at me."

Elijah's teasing seemed to energize and steady the teenager as they headed down the path, around the curve. Elijah glanced back just once, his expression grim, penetrating, as if he wanted to beam his strength and determination into Grit. Grit wished he could. He'd figured out early on in life—long before his SEAL training—that he wasn't Superman.

He ducked past a hemlock and saw blood, still bright red, splattered in the white snow. For a split second, Grit thought he could smell it, then realized that was a memory of a long, violent night a year ago—and the memory of the smell of his own blood.

You can do this mission.

He swallowed at the sound of the familiar voice close to him, as clear and calm as it had been that night in Afghanistan. As real. "Hey, Moose. What are you doing here?"

You're in love with Marissa Neal.

Grit's throat tightened. It was true. He was in love with Marissa. It'd started when he'd first met her last fall, just for a few seconds. He'd been chasing hired killers. Charlie had been trying to help on the sly. Marissa had been starchy, annoyed with Grit, annoyed with her brother. Understandably. With the network of killers finally dealt with, she and Grit had been spending time with each other the past month.

"Yeah, Moose. I'm in love with her."

But Michael "Moose" Ferrerra wasn't there in the Vermont snow. He was dead, killed in action on a bad night last year in a remote Afghan mountain pass. Grit gripped the 9 mm and averted his eyes from the blood.

He had no illusions. He knew he was alone, and he knew the Secret Service wouldn't get there in time. He had to find Marissa on his own.

• • •

Marissa Neal shoved a heavy butcher-block island in front of the back door of the unoccupied ski house where she'd taken refuge, but immediately pulled it back to the center of the kitchen. She didn't want to barricade herself in the kitchen after all. She wanted to be able to run out onto the snow-covered mountain if the man chasing her found her here.

Unless he's already in the house…

She gave herself a mental shake, refusing to let her fear take control. She'd checked for footprints and signs of a break-in before she'd smashed the door window and slipped into the house herself.

She was breathing hard, but she was no longer dripping blood. She'd torn her hand on a broken branch and had managed to tie her scarf over the cut. It ached, but she ignored the pain. Her thick leggings were soaked and cold from her trek through the snow. She'd fallen twice—maybe three times. Once in the house, she'd pulled off her gloves and hat but was careful to stuff them in her jacket pockets, in case she had to flee. Hypothermia was a risk… but the immediate threat was the armed man who'd shot Elijah Cameron. She'd gotten a glimpse of the shooter. Enough to know it was a man but not enough for a description—to know who it was.

Marissa tried to focus on what she had to do now. To figure out her options.

I'm not a Cameron. I don't know these woods. I don't know where this place is.

The house was at the top of a dead-end dirt road. How far was she from help? Marissa tried to keep unanswerable questions at bay. Forcing back panic, she kept moving, digging through the drawers and cupboards for anything she could use for self-defense. Knives, bottles, rags, chemicals. She'd already grabbed a gas can from the attached one-car garage.

Elijah's a combat veteran. He knows what to do.

Even wounded, he'd find a way to get help to her. He'd spotted her above him on the trail and yelled for her to run, giving her a chance to get away—to get here.

Going to him hadn't been an option.

Marissa quickly assembled her potential weapons on the floor by the table. She was avoiding windows, wanted to be prepared if the shooter came after her. She paused, peering down the dark hall that led from the kitchen. The house didn't look as if anyone had stayed there all winter, but the driveway was plowed, the walks shoveled. The owners must have hired a local groundskeeper. Maybe whoever looked after the place would come by, help her.

Except why would they if they'd already been here after yesterday's snow?

Marissa reminded herself that her sisters and brother and parents all were safe. She was a high school history teacher, the eldest of five. It didn't matter that her father was the vice president. She was no more important than the next person.

"Marissa. You okay in there?"

Grit. She recognized his soft, low voice and felt her knees buckle as relief washed over her. She wasn't alone anymore.

And he wasn't the shooter. Not Ryan Taylor, Navy SEAL.

"I am, Grit. I'm here."

He came through the back door, moving with an agility and smoothness that had surprised her at first, given his disability, but now she had come to expect. He was one of the finest men she'd ever known. He was also witty, sexy, ultracompetent and as incorrigible in his own way as her little brother. Except she didn't think of him as a brother. Not even close. Right from the start, even when he'd annoyed her, Marissa had been attracted to him.

"Damn, it's dark and cold out there. Springtime in the frozen North."

Marissa bit back a smile and tears at the same time. "If you can figure out I'm here—"

"So can the guy who's after you."

She studied him for half a beat. He was dark-haired, wiry and quiet, with a quick wit and a steadiness that often took people by surprise. He'd told her he was a mix of Creek and Scots-Irish, a kid from the swamps of the Florida Panhandle who'd always wanted to see the world.

"He's not after me." Her voice was a hoarse whisper as she realized what she was saying was true. "He's not my enemy or my father's enemy, or a Cameron enemy. Grit..." She took a breath. "He's after you."

Grit shrugged. "Even better. Why's he after me?"

"Because you're here. He lured me out here because he knew you'd come after me. It's so clear to me now, Grit. Elijah was a surprise. That's why he shot him. But I could teach yoga in Black Falls for all this man cares. He wants you, Grit. Who is he?"

"I don't know," Grit said, the moonlight catching his dark eyes as he turned to her. "You're sure about this?"

She didn't hesitate. "Yes."

He gave her a small grin. "That Neal intuition at work. You okay? The blood—"

"A scratch. It's nothing. I'm fine. The shooter wanted me to think Charlie was getting himself in trouble again. I see that now. I fell into his trap. I thought I could help. I thought..." Marissa didn't finish. "I'm not a prisoner of the Secret Service. I've always cooperated. I've never stepped a toe out of line."

"Unlike Charlie."

"He looks up to you and Elijah."

Grit didn't respond. He turned the solid wood kitchen table on its side, then slipped an arm around her waist. "Get behind here. Stay low."

Marissa crouched on the floor behind the table. "What about you?"

"No worries." He surveyed the array of materials on the floor, giving no indication of what he thought of them. "We're dealing with a professional. It's not easy to get past the Secret Service, even for your genius little brother. It's sure as hell not easy to get the jump on Elijah Cameron."

"It was a near thing. I was startled, and I fell and cut my hand. Elijah was farther down on the trail. At that point neither of us had any idea someone was up in the woods with a gun." Marissa stopped abruptly, felt the blood draining out of her face. She pushed aside the rush of thoughts and nodded to a wall phone. "There's a landline, but it's turned off. There's no cell service. Are you going to search the house?"

"No. If the shooter's hiding in here, he'll find us. We're good right where we are."

"You're armed," Marissa said, noticing that a pistol had appeared in his hand.

"Thanks to your brother. This isn't Charlie's fault. It's not your fault. It's the responsibility of this shooter. Period."

"If you have an extra gun—"

"You can shoot?"

"I've never fired a weapon, but how hard can it be?" She gave him a faltering smile. "Point and pull the trigger."

Grit squatted next to her. "I need you to keep doing what you've been doing." His voice was steady, as if he were telling her about what he'd cooked for dinner. "Stay calm and keep an eye and ear out."

"You know what this man's going to do, don't you?"

Grit didn't answer, but Marissa knew that she was right. The man who shot Elijah Cameron wanted to kill Grit Taylor.

The cut on her hand ached and she felt blood again seeping into the scarf she'd tied around the wound. "The shooter's in the house, isn't he?"

"Tupelo honey," Grit said with the barest of smiles.

"What?"

With his free hand, he brushed his bare knuckles across her cheek. "When things get rough, I think about tupelo honey. My family makes tupelo honey at home in Florida. Best stuff in the world. What do you think about? Teaching history?"

"Living a normal life," she answered without hesitation.

"No such thing."

"Black Falls has had a rough year, but I love it here. It's so beautiful, and I love the people. I love the Camerons, the Harpers, the café, the lodge." Grit was still and quiet, but Marissa could see the focus and intensity in his dark eyes. "I'd like to try tupelo honey one day. Do you want to go back to Florida?"

"To visit. I don't fool myself into thinking I could live there again."

"I'm sorry, Grit. You shouldn't be here…"

"Do you want to buy a place up here in snow country?" His dark eyes leveled on her. "If you do, I'm game. I'd chop wood and tramp through snow for you. Any day of the week."

"Grit…"

He winked at her. "It's okay." Then he called into the hall. "Hey, ace. I know you're in here. Let's talk."

A beat's silence. "I knew you'd come, Grit. You're so predictable."

The shooter's voice was deep and controlled—and close, not five yards down the hall. Marissa realized Grit must have known he was there. She hadn't noticed a shadow, heard a movement, the sound of any breathing but her own.

"That's right, Grit," the shooter said, "I know it's you."

Marissa gulped in a breath. *It's Brian.* Grit was frowning at her, and she said, "It's Brian Fenton. He's—"

"He's a private military contractor," Grit said. "I know him."

"I had dinner with him a few times before the election. A lot of contractors do good work."

"Fenton did, too, back then. Now he's wanted by the FBI and who knows who else."

"Ah, Grit, Marissa," Fenton said. "It's good that you remember me."

Marissa raised her voice above a whisper. "I thought you were out of the country."

"I wish I were."

"I can get you out," Marissa said. "It's easy. Pack up. Let's go."

Fenton gave a low laugh. "Even if you were telling the truth, Marissa, Grit won't let me go with you. Will you, Grit? You'd insist on going, too, and you'd slow me down with that missing leg of yours."

"Nah, the leg's fine," Grit said. "It's the cold that gets me, although I think I'm getting used to it. Scary thought. You ever try tupelo honey, Fenton?"

"What? What are you talking about?"

"My friend Moose would have liked you before you dishonored yourself with your illegal side deals. You had your own private black market going. I found you out, Fenton. You were selling weapons, supplies, parts, whatever you could get your hands on. Think of the hardworking people doing a job—"

"I'm just as good as you are."

"You were. Then you decided to cross the line, and now you're a loser. If you don't give up, you'll be a dead loser."

"Put your gun down, Grit. Give up, and I'll let Marissa go."

Marissa shook her head, adamant. "He won't."

Grit gave her a slight nod but spoke to Fenton. "It's not my gun. I didn't come to Black Falls armed. Why would I? You meant to kill Elijah but you screwed up. You gave away your position a split second before you fired. That gave him all the time he needed to give Marissa the head start she needed to get away from you, and to keep you from getting off a second shot. Now he's going to land on your head any second."

"He's messed up. He's not doing anything."

"You don't know Elijah. He isn't seriously injured. You can still get out of this, Fenton."

"What, put my weapons on the floor and come to you with my hands up?"

"That'd do it."

"I know you're trying to last long enough for reinforcements."

"Or I could shoot you before they get here."

Marissa reached for a rudimentary Molotov cocktail she'd made just before Grit had arrived, using a slender glass bottle, the gas and a flour-cloth dish towel. She whispered, "Every history teacher knows about Molotov cocktails."

Grit grinned at her. "Look at you."

She handed him the bottle. She was surprised at the steadiness of her hands. "One thing before…" *Before what?* She decided it didn't matter. "I love you, Grit."

"Marissa—"

"Let me finish. I started falling in love with you last November when you returned Charlie to school after he went AWOL the first time. He trusts you, and you trust him."

"I don't trust Charlie. He's a kid."

"You trust his instincts, his mind. You and Elijah gave him attention when we were all too distracted and busy to notice he needed to feel as if he mattered."

"So you fell for me because I wasn't a jerk to your brother?"

She smiled in spite of her fear, or maybe in part because of it. "I also thought you were attractive in an understated manly way."

He grinned suddenly. "That can't be bad, right?" He kissed her lightly on the mouth. "That's just for starters. I love you, too, babe. With all my heart and soul. I'm going to tell you how much I love you every day for a very long time, but right now is it okay if we deal with this crazy son of a bitch?"

Marissa knew they had no choice. She could hear Brian down the hall.

The lights went off.

He was coming.

Grit leaped up, moving with speed and precision. The suddenness and force of his assault seemed to suck the air out of the immediate vicinity.

Marissa didn't breathe. Everything happened fast. There was nothing slow-motion about it. She saw the flash and heard the explosion, smelled the smoke of a Molotov cocktail. Brian yelled, and then came two shots…and silence.

"It's okay, Marissa." Grit's voice, gentle, calm. "It's over."

Brian Fenton wouldn't kill Grit, or her brother, or Elijah—or her.

She lifted her head and focused on the man she loved, standing in the moonlight.

● ● ●

Three hours later, the Camerons had a fire roaring in the big stone fireplace at Black Falls Lodge and pancakes and sausages fresh off the griddle for Grit, Marissa and a handful of Secret Service agents, who were marginally less tense and irritable than they had been after their very long night. Charlie Neal showing up at the lodge with a wounded Elijah Cameron…leading them to Marissa Neal at a remote ski house with Grit and a dead Brian Fenton.

"Fenton left a note," Elijah said. "He blamed the SEALs for ruining his career after they caught him running his own black market, and he blamed you specifically for stealing Marissa from him."

Grit dribbled hot maple syrup—what he'd been told was first-run syrup—onto his pancakes. "Kill two birds with one stone, except Marissa dumped him long before I came into the picture."

Elijah pointed at Grit's forkful of pancakes. "What do you think? Is real maple syrup better than tupelo honey?"

This from a man in a sling from a gunshot wound. Grit figured that was why he and Elijah got along. "Different. They're both good. Are you and Jo going to have to postpone the wedding because of your shoulder?"

"Not even for a minute."

Charlie Neal squeezed past a Secret Service agent and sat by the fire. "I think it should be a double wedding. You're going to ask Marissa to marry you, right, Grit—I mean, Petty Officer Taylor?"

Grit ate his forkful of pancakes. The syrup was damn good. He sighed as he put down his plate. "You know, Charlie, just because you think something doesn't mean you have to say it."

"I'd like you as a brother-in-law. Two of my sisters are dating real dicks."

"You haven't told them that, have you?"

"I don't know. Maybe."

Elijah laughed. "You're a piece of work, my friend." He nodded to Grit. "Go. I'll keep Charlie out of your hair for ten minutes."

Grit walked into the dining room and over to the windows, where Marissa was gazing out at the view of a snowy meadow and, in the distance, snow-covered mountains. He found himself experiencing phantom pain for the first time in months, as if to remind him that Marissa Neal could say no.

She turned to him and smiled. "I love the smells of the fire, maple syrup—and apples. I think someone's baking pies."

"Marissa…"

"I know you have to go back to Washington. Your work at the Pentagon awaits."

"It can wait a few more days. I knew you were on school vacation this week." He stood next to her, tried not to show her the pain he was in from a leg he'd lost so long ago—it felt like a lifetime. "What were you thinking about?"

"All the reasons we should be together. There's only one that matters. I love you, and I want to spend the rest of my life with you. What were you thinking?"

"All the reasons you should say no."

"You have more reasons not to ask than I have to say no."

Her comment took him by surprise, but that was one of the things he loved about her. She was unpredictable, totally herself. "Name one."

"My family. I'm a history teacher. I don't know how to use a gun. I don't want to know."

"You make a mean Molotov cocktail."

She waved a hand in dismissal. "As if you wouldn't have done that yourself."

He caught her hand midair and held it between his. "Marissa Neal, I love you and I want to be with you forever. I don't have a lot to offer."

"That's right, you don't. I've seen your apartment. Rats, Grit. Rats." Her eyes sparkled with humor, but she couldn't maintain it and flung her arms around him. "Yes, yes—yes, I'll marry you, Ryan Taylor. Anytime, anywhere."

"I think we have an audience."

"Good."

He swept her into his arms. The phantom pain was gone, and he saw Moose out in the meadow, laughing as he turned, his back to the lodge, and walked through the undisturbed snow.

One day Grit would tell Marissa about his friend Michael "Moose" Ferrerra and the good life he'd lived.

One day he'd tell their children.

He smiled and saluted as Moose disappeared over the mountains and into the blue Vermont sky.

POISONED
BEVERLY BARTON

*What a great hook! How could you read
the first sentence and not continue? —SB*

I've been poisoned!

There could be no other explanation for what had happened to her. The recurring nausea, the horrific abdominal cramping, the blurred vision, the dizziness and mental confusion were a result of poison. It had been a deliberate, premeditated murder attempt. She had lived in fear for such a long time, watching her back, playing it safe, afraid to trust.

Apparently her drink had been doctored. Why hadn't she been more careful? Had she been a fool to trust Jed Merrill?

"Olivia? Olivia…"

His voice came from far away, as if echoing through a long tunnel. Where was he? How close? Could she escape before he found her?

I have to keep moving. Must get away. I can't let him catch me.

Darkness surrounded her. She couldn't see where she was, let alone where she was going. But she couldn't stop long enough to get her bearings. If she slowed down, he would catch her. He was close. She could hear his approaching footsteps. She could almost feel his hot breath on her neck.

Suddenly flashes of light zipped past her. Car headlights maybe? They had been moving fast, revealing nothing, not giving her a clue about her location.

For the life of her, she couldn't remember leaving her apartment, had no idea how she'd gotten here, wherever the hell here was.

Winded and exhausted, Olivia paused long enough to suck in some deep breaths. Easing backward, hoping to hide in the murky shadows, she encountered a solid wall behind her, firm and yet giving, as if the surface was padded. She couldn't stay here for long, just another minute at most. If she lingered, he would catch up with her. What would he do to her? Shoot her? Strangle her? Break her neck with those big, powerful hands that had only recently caressed every inch of her body?

Damn you, Jed Merrill. Damn your black-hearted soul. I trusted you. I believed you really cared.

Why was he following her? He had already poisoned her, hadn't he? She was probably dying. If she couldn't find a way to get to a hospital soon, someone would find her dead body lying in the ditch. Maybe that was why he was coming after her, in order to dispose of her body once she was dead. He could toss her in the river or in the landfill or bury her somewhere out in the woods.

"Olivia, can you hear me?"

Oh, God…oh, God. Jed was talking to her, his voice distinct, close, as if he was standing right beside her. With trembling fingers, she felt all around her, floating her hands in front of her and then on either side. Nothing. No Jed. No one. Just black emptiness.

And then he closed his hand around hers. For a split second, she didn't move, didn't breathe, and couldn't make her body obey her mind's commands.

"No," she cried as she jerked her hand free of his gentle hold.

"Olivia, honey, don't fight me," he told her, his baritone voice Bourbon smooth and dripping with Southern charm.

Without hesitation, she turned and ran. Her legs felt as if she had heavy weights around her ankles. Tired. Listless. Her lungs aching. Her heartbeat wild. Tears trickled down her cheeks, dripped off her nose, and moistened her parched lips. She had to stop again, just for a few minutes, to catch her breath, to regroup, to figure out where she was and how to get to the nearest hospital.

Lights appeared again, closer, dimmer, nonthreatening. She moved toward them. Streetlights? She had to be careful, had to weigh the odds, had to decide if going out into the open was worth the risk. But what if she could find someone to help her, someone driving by or walking by, someone who could call 911? If only she could remember how long ago it had been since she had drunk the champagne and ingested the poison now killing her by slow, painful degrees.

Think, damn it, think. Try to remember.

She and Jed had been celebrating. He had brought the champagne with him. She had prepared dinner. No…she hadn't had time to cook. She had picked up takeout on her way home from work. Had they eaten first, before Jed opened the bubbly? Yes, she thought they had. Vague memories of the two of them sitting on the floor in front of the fireplace, the food spread out on a tray, drifted through her mind. The jumble of memories and odd thoughts drifted through a hazy fog as if her mind wouldn't allow her to see clearly.

What were we celebrating?

Olivia stumbled, barely managing to maintain her balance, and then continued running.

She remembered Jed making a toast, could see him smiling, could feel his lips against hers. His taste lingered, stronger than the taste of the champagne. Had she been given a promotion at work? Had he? No, she didn't think so. Had one of them been given a pay raise? Won an award?

She shook her head.

Dalton!

Oh, my God, that was it. Dalton was in jail. The fact that he was behind bars was reason enough to celebrate.

How long would it take for his case to come to trial? Weeks? Months? Years? Until she testified and he was convicted, she would be in danger. He couldn't allow her to live, to testify against him.

Olivia stumbled again, the earth beneath her feet slick and damp. When she looked down, she couldn't see her feet, only the wet pavement glistening with iridescent moisture created by rain and oily road sludge. She didn't recognize the street, couldn't identify a single building, but she could hear the hum of motors and the drone of faraway voices.

"Help me…please, somebody, help me."

"Olivia." Jed's voice surrounded her, coming from every direction, but she couldn't see him.

Why was Jed trying to kill her?

Wasn't it obvious? He was on Dalton's payroll. A dirty cop. No, please, God, no. Not Jed. Not the man she loved, the man she trusted. But what other explanation could there be? Jed had poisoned her. And now he was following her, waiting for her to die so he could get rid of her body.

Barely able to stand, her throat dry, her limbs heavy with exhaustion, she struggled to make her way across the street toward the well-lit building. One you-can-do-this trudging step at a time, she pushed herself to keep moving. The cold nighttime rain pelted her face and soaked through her clothes. As she reached the double glass doors of the building and reached out to grab the door handle, a bone-rattling chill shook her from head to toe.

The pain in her belly hit with brutal force. She doubled over in agony as sour bile rose up her esophagus and coated her mouth with a bitter metallic taste. Her stomach tightened. She retched several times before the poisonous gold liquid spewed out of her mouth and coated the concrete sidewalk. As the pain subsided, she managed to stand up, her pulse drumming wildly in her ears. She was sick. She was cold. She was wet.

With an unsteady hand, she reached for the door handle and pulled on it.

Locked.

No, please. It can't be locked. I have to get inside. I need help. And I need it now.

She jerked on the door handle again and again before giving up and pounding on the door with weak, trembling fists.

"Please, somebody help me."

No response. No one was coming to help her. She couldn't stay here. She had to keep moving. She needed to go to the hospital, needed to be there now if she had any hope of surviving.

Call for help!

Dear God, why hadn't she thought of that before now? Standing under the canopy over the building's entrance so that she was temporarily out of the rain, she searched her pockets for her phone. Where was it? She usually kept it in her purse, but she hadn't brought a purse with her. Had she left the phone back at her apartment?

Olivia gazed through the heavy downpour and tried to figure out exactly where she was. If she was only a few blocks from her apartment, why was everything around her so unfamiliar? She couldn't possibly have run far enough to have left her own neighborhood. The darkness combined with the rain made everything look different. That had to be what was wrong. In the daylight, with the sun shining, she would know exactly where she was. Her apartment was only blocks from downtown Florence, Alabama, and a stone's throw from the UNA campus. Although it was the middle of the night, surely someone was out and about, someone would drive by soon, someone would hear her cries. But Florence was a typical small Southern city where on a weeknight most good folks were in bed this time of night, not out prowling the streets, not even the college students.

Realizing how vulnerable she was there in front of the brightly lit building, Olivia ventured out into the rain. Her brisk walk turned into a slow run as she made her way up the sidewalk and turned onto a gloomy side street. Her gaze hampered by the relentless downpour, she didn't see the sidewalk café until she stumbled over a metal chair. Barely managing to stay on her feet, she grabbed the back of the chair to steady herself. A twinkling neon light in the café window cast multicolored flashes of illumination across the sidewalk and the half-dozen black metal chairs and three small glass-and-metal tables.

She had to stop. She couldn't go any farther. Olivia chose a chair in the corner and dragged it to the most obscure area of the outdoor café that she could find. Halfway hidden behind a huge potted plant and partially sheltered by the building's overhang, she slumped down into the chair. Bracing her elbows on her knees, she leaned over and supported her pounding head between her open palms. She massaged her throbbing temples with her fingertips.

How had she gotten herself into such a horrible predicament? Olivia Lynn Warren had lived an uneventful, vanilla, white-bread life. A good girl from a good family, an honor student, graduated magna cum laude, paid her taxes, went to church, obeyed traffic laws, had never even gotten a speeding ticket.

Cramps twisted her belly as nausea threatened. She needed a bathroom. She needed to rid her body of the poison. Unable to stop the flow of tears, her emotions raw, Olivia leaned her head back against the brick wall behind her and took several deep breaths. The nausea subsided, at least temporarily, and the gripping pain in her belly eased up enough so that she could bear it.

Olivia tried to remember that night—weeks or months ago—

when she had been in the wrong place at the wrong time and witnessed a murder. From that moment on, her life had been an upside-down whirlwind of disaster, Jed Merrill the only good thing that had come out of so much bad. But now, Jed had turned against her. He had poisoned her.

Why couldn't she remember? Had the poison affected her brain?

But she hadn't forgotten everything. She remembered some things, mostly bits and pieces. And the things she did remember seemed to be all mixed up together, making it difficult for her to form a correct timeline.

Olivia remembered Amber Carr. Amber had hired their decorating firm to redo her living room, dining room and perform an extensive kitchen remodel. Olivia had been fresh out of college, a first year resident with the firm, and eager to prove herself. From the moment Mrs. Carr had walked into Downtown Interiors and spotted Olivia, the two had hit it off like a house afire. Amber had been only a few years older than Olivia and they found they had a great deal in common…except for Amber's husband, a wealthy businessman twenty-five years Amber's senior. Everyone in Florence knew Dalton Carr, one of the areas few multimillionaires.

If only she hadn't stopped by the Carr's home that Friday evening. But Amber had been eager to see the swatches for the draperies and Olivia's boss had been eager to please her wealthiest client. When she arrived at the lakefront mansion, Olivia had found the front door wide open and upon entering the marble-floored foyer, she'd heard loud voices. Amber was screeching at her husband and he was bellowing obscenities at her.

Why didn't I just turn around and leave before they knew I was there?

When Olivia heard the first shot, she hadn't recognized the sound, but when Amber had screamed, "No, please, Dalton," Olivia had acted on impulse. She had dropped the material swatches, frantically raked through her purse for her cell phone and had been unable to catch her bag as it slipped out of her hand and plunged down on top of the swatches. She had dialed 911 as she'd run toward the sound of Amber's pleading cries. Just as she reached the entrance to the downstairs master bedroom, Dalton Carr had fired another shot. Olivia had stood there, frozen to the spot, unable to move or speak as Dalton stood over his wife and shot her for the third time, that time at point-blank range.

As if sensing her presence, Dalton had turned and stared at Olivia, and then pointed the pistol directly at her. The 911 operator's voice had come in clearly on her cell phone, clear enough so that Dalton heard the woman. Olivia had turned and run back through the house and out onto the driveway. But before she could reach her car, Dalton Carr had come out of the house, gun in hand, and almost caught up with her as she fled. Her car keys had been inside her purse in the Carr's foyer. She'd had no choice but try to escape on foot.

Olivia moaned as the memories of that night bombarded her foggy brain. Dalton had chased her. He had shot at her. But what had happened after that? Why couldn't she remember?

Hunching over, cuddling herself by wrapping her arms around her wet, aching body and bringing up her knees, Olivia huddled in the dismal corner as she prayed for someone to help her.

She had prayed that night, too, prayed for someone to save her from Dalton Carr.

Jed had saved her.

"You were my hero that night," she had told him later.

Unlike tonight, that night she had kept her cell phone with her. While running away from Dalton, she had spoken to the 911 operator. She had told the woman what had happened and that she was being chased by the killer. She had run for her life, pleading with God not to let her die, hiding in the darkness, afraid to breathe.

"Miss, you're safe." His soothing voice had calmed her. "We have Mr. Carr in custody. He can't hurt you."

She had looked up into the most striking blue-gray eyes she had ever seen and instantly believed the man who was lifting her up and into his arms. Apparently, she had passed out then and when she came to hours later, she had found herself in a hospital room, Jed Merrill sitting at her bedside.

"Hello," he'd said. "How are you feeling?"

"Okay, I guess."

"Do you remember what happened?"

She had nodded. "I—I ran from Dalton Carr after I saw him kill his wife. He chased me. I stumbled and fell. My knees hurt and—" She had lifted her right hand and encountered a large bandage over her left shoulder. "He shot me!"

"The bullet went straight through and the doctors say there won't be any permanent damage."

"You were there, weren't you? You're the one who saved me."

He had shrugged. "I found you hiding in the bushes on the lawn of a house about three blocks from the Carr home. I followed the blood trail."

"Who are you?"

"Sorry, I should have already introduced myself. I'm Lieutenant Jed Merrill with the Florence Police Department. I'm heading up the Amber Carr murder investigation."

Days later when she had been released from the hospital, Jed had taken her home and explained that although the Florence P.D. didn't have the resources to assign someone to guard her 24/7, he planned to make sure she was safe.

"Dalton Carr is out on bond until the trial," Jed had explained. "He hasn't made any threats against you. Guess he's too smart for that, but you need to be careful and take every precaution. I want you to know that I'll do my level best to keep an eye on you."

The sudden roar of a truck passing by on Court Street, a block away, brought Olivia from the past to the present. How long had it been since that day when she'd been released from the hospital and found out that her life was still in danger? It couldn't have been that long ago, not if Dalton Carr had yet to be tried and convicted of his wife's murder. But for some reason, it felt like years ago. That wasn't possible. If Dalton had hired Jed to kill her that had to mean she hadn't testified against him yet.

Shivering from the cold March breeze whipping around her damp body, she hugged herself tightly as she scanned the area in every direction. The rain had let up and was now only a misty drizzle. She needed to get up and start moving, to keep running. It was only a matter of time before Jed found her. He was good at tracking, good at figuring out what the other guy was going to do, good at his job as a police detective.

And he had been a good friend to her. Her protector. Her lover. She loved Jed. And he loved her.

No, it was all pretense on his part. He doesn't love me. He poisoned the champagne. Did he? Are you sure? Maybe the poison wasn't in the champagne. But if he didn't poison me, who did? And why is Jed chasing me?

Are you sure Jed is the man hunting you?

Yes, she was sure because she recognized his voice, the only voice she could hear out there in the wet, foggy darkness.

Olivia forced herself up and onto her feet. Simply standing was a monumental task. She swayed, dizziness spinning her head. Somewhere nearby a dog barked and then another farther away answered the first one's howl. In the eerie silence that followed, she heard footsteps again, faint at first, and then coming closer and closer.

Struggling with every step she took, she moved away from the shadowy corner of the café and inched her way along the buildings until she reached the entrance to the alley. A streetlight shone dimly into the backstreet, giving her a semiclear view, enough to see that if she entered the narrow passage, she wouldn't be trapped. The alley went straight through and came out on the other side. Keeping close to the wall, she crept silently along the paved path until she reached a large Dumpster blocking her way. The stench of garbage assailed her senses and once again nausea threatened. Holding her breath until she slipped past the full Dumpster, she managed not to vomit.

Winded, her sides aching, every muscle in her body rioting, Olivia paused halfway into the alley, pressed her back against the damp stone wall and listened. The sound of her labored breaths echoed inside her head. And the distinct tapping of footsteps drew nearer.

Dear God, he was in the alley behind her. What was she going to do? She couldn't run, could barely walk. If only she had some way to protect herself.

She had taken the self-defense classes Jed had insisted on and she had kept the small handgun he had bought for her and taught her how to use. But the gun was locked away in her apartment and if he caught her, she didn't have the strength to fight him. If she hadn't been poisoned…

Why would Jed have signed her up for self-defense classes if he hadn't wanted her to be able to protect herself? And why would he have bought her a pistol and given her lessons at a local firing range if he had been planning to kill her? It didn't make any sense.

"I love your hair," he had told her as he had lifted a strand and wound it around his finger.

"I'm not a natural blonde, you know. I was when I was a child, but underneath this expensive dye job, it's a mousy brown."

He had laughed and kissed her. "Anything else about you fake?" He had caressed her, skimming his hand over first one breast and then the other, running his fingers down across her belly and cupping her mound with gentle possessiveness.

"What do you think?" she had teased him.

"I think everything else is one hundred percent real, but before I make a definite decision, I believe further investigation is in order."

That had been the first time they had made love, the night she had realized she was madly in love with her knight in shining armor. They hadn't said I love you then. Not until months later.

Months? How many months?

"Olivia," he called to her.

It was Jed's voice. He was the man in the alley behind her, the man who had been chasing her.

You love him. He loves you. You trust him. You know he would never hurt you. Listen to your heart. What if the poison had been in the food? What if someone at the restaurant…? No, that doesn't make any sense, either.

"Jed," she cried out to him. "Help me, Jed. I'm so sick. I've been poisoned."

She crumpled down onto the damp pavement, drew her legs up and bowed her head as she waited for Jed. Was he her rescuer, her true hero? Or was he her killer?

"I'm here, honey. Everything is going to be all right."

She could make out only a man's silhouette as he approached, but the moment he took her hand in his and she felt the tender strength of his touch, she closed her eyes and sighed. He took her in his arms, lifted her, carried her, held her close.

"Poisoned," she repeated. "Hospital."

"Hush, Olivia. Hush, sweetheart. Just relax and rest. You're going to be fine. I promise."

Jed Merrill kept his promises. Always. He was a man of honor and integrity. He would never hurt her. Why had she ever thought he had poisoned her? It was the champagne. He had brought a bottle of expensive Dom Pérignon. She remembered he had opened the bottle and poured the bubbly wine into their glasses.

"Here's to us, to our future together."

She'd been so happy. They had been celebrating something important. But what?

Somehow, someway, someone had poisoned her. The only person she knew who wanted her dead was Dalton Carr. Without her eyewitness testimony, the D.A.'s case wouldn't be as strong and there was a chance Dalton would be found not guilty.

"Jed," she managed to whisper his name.

"Don't talk. Just rest."

"Poison. Who?"

Jed didn't answer her. But she could hear him talking to someone else. She couldn't make out what they were saying. Who was he talking to?

Oh, God, she was sleepy. So sleepy. Was she dying?

I don't want to die. I want to live. I'm young and in love. I have my whole life ahead of me. Jed and I are going to get married.

A shudder racked Olivia from head to toe. Gentle hands lifted a blanket up and over her, tucking it around her shoulders. She sighed as sleep overcame her. Her last coherent thought was the memory of Jed proposing, her accepting, him putting a ring on her finger, and then popping open the champagne.

They had been celebrating their engagement.

● ● ●

Olivia woke to morning sunlight winking through the partially closed blinds at the double windows. She stretched languidly, but paused midstretch when she realized just how sore her body was, from throat to rib cage to abdomen. And then she realized she was not at home, not in her own bed, and she wasn't at Jed's place, either. Glancing around the room, scanning the pale walls, the tiled floor, the IV bag hanging beside the bed, and the hustle and bustle of people outside her half-open door, Olivia knew she was in the hospital.

What was she doing here?

She had been sick, so very sick. Had someone really poisoned her? Had she run from her apartment? Had Jed chased her through downtown Florence? Had he saved her, brought her here to the hospital?

Olivia found the buttons on the remote that controlled her bed and lifted the head of the bed into a sitting position. Looking down at herself, she found she was wearing the ever-fashionable hospital gown and the IV was hooked up to a needle in her left hand. For the first time in hours—maybe days—her mind was clear and her memory intact.

The door swung open and Jed, carrying a foam cup filled with hot coffee, came into her room. The moment he saw that she was awake, he rushed over to her, set his coffee on the bedside table and eased down next to her.

"Good morning, beautiful," he said. "How are you feeling?"

"Like I've been hit by a Mack truck," she told him.

"Not a Mack truck, just a wicked bout of food poisoning."

"Food poisoning?"

"Apparently the takeout you picked up for our dinner took you out. Or possibly something you ate for lunch."

"You're okay, aren't you?"

"I'm fine because we didn't eat the same thing. I ate beef. You ate chicken. And I didn't eat any dessert with the cream sauce. Honey, don't you remember waking up around two o'clock with severe vomiting and—?"

"Yes, I remember now. I started vomiting and had diarrhea. I had chills and a fever and a horrible headache."

"I finally managed to persuade you to let me take you to the E.R. around eight o'clock yesterday morning. We were lucky. You were only slightly dehydrated." He glanced at the IV bag and then back at Olivia. "It was killing me to see you in so much pain."

"Jed, I—I must have had some crazy dreams or something. I didn't run away from you, did I?"

"You couldn't have run away if you'd wanted to, honey. You were really out of it." He caressed her cheek. "Hell of way to end our engagement celebration."

"How long have I been in the hospital?"

"Almost twenty-four hours. You've been asleep most of that time, coming to now and then, and talking crazy."

"You've been here the whole time, haven't you?"

"Where else would I be?"

She leaned into Jed, placing her head on his chest and wrapping her arms around his waist. He embraced her carefully. "Did I accuse you of poisoning me?" She tried to laugh, but couldn't.

Jed kissed the top of her head. "You kept saying something about poison, but then you mumbled a lot of gibberish."

"Dalton Carr is dead, isn't he?"

Jed cupped her chin and lifted it so that she had to look up at him. "You were having a nightmare about Dalton Carr? Oh, Olivia, I'm sorry. I thought you had moved past the horror of what happened to you back then."

"I thought so, too." She tried to smile, but the effort failed. "I testified, didn't I? He was convicted of second-degree murder. That was nearly two years ago. And he committed suicide in jail before he could be transferred to prison."

Olivia closed her eyes and clung to Jed, shivering as the memories exploded inside her. In her drug-induced sleep, her mind had combined various aspects of her life—her near-death experience the night Dalton had tried to kill her, the fear she had lived with until after the trial, her relationship with Jed that had grown slowly from friendship into passion, their engagement celebration and her battle with food poisoning.

Opening her eyes, she gazed up at Jed. "I love you. And I'm sorry that in my crazy dreams I thought you had poisoned me."

He lowered his head and kissed her. Sweetly. Gently. "You had a difficult time trusting anyone after what happened. Even me. Maybe this was your subconscious way of working out the last of your trust issues and completely letting go of the all-too-real night-mare Dalton Carr put you through."

Maybe Jed was right. Maybe it had taken being poisoned—even if it was food poisoning—to cleanse her mind and heart from the fear and distrust that had poisoned her life for the past few years. Now she truly was free. Free to move forward into the future with the man she loved, the man she knew she could trust completely.

SPEECHLESS

ROBERT BROWNE

This story, written in first person, beautifully expresses universal insecurities about love, loss and trust. Expect a twist! —SB

The only reason I was there was because of my mother.

I had always trusted David implicitly and couldn't quite believe that I had let myself be talked into doing what I was doing. I am, after all, a grown woman, and this was bordering on high school behavior. I'd felt silly about it from the very beginning and had hesitated more than once before finally punching the key on my computer to print out my boarding pass.

Yet there I was, six hours later, on a cool Wednesday night, sitting in a rented car several hundred miles from home, watching the entrance to the Traveler's Inn in Los Angeles, with the keen obsessiveness of a stalker.

Maybe I didn't trust David as much as I thought I did. Or maybe it had nothing to do with him at all.

It was my mother's fault.

It always is.

And who could blame her? The woman had been through two nasty divorces and thought of the male species as a contaminated breed. To her mind, *no* man could be trusted. Especially if they had yet to produce a ring or even utter the word *marriage.*

They were all barely a step above animals, whose need to seduce just about anything with legs would always take precedence over a committed relationship. Even one as committed as David's and mine.

Mother barely knew David, but that didn't stop her from judging him, or complaining about the shiftiness of his eyes. Something I'd never noticed myself. I'd always thought he had beautiful eyes. A startling blue that was one of his main attractions.

So *why*, then, was I there?

I won't try to explain the mother-daughter dynamic to you. I don't think there's a psychologist on earth who can come within a hairbreadth of unraveling its complexity. But if you're a woman and you have a mother—and I think most of us do—it doesn't really *need* to be explained.

You just *know*, don't you?

Bottom line, I was there simply because I wanted to get the nosy bitch off my back. I wanted to prove to her, once and for all, that she was wrong—*dead wrong*—about the man I loved.

Unfortunately, things didn't quite turn out the way I thought they would.

● ● ●

As a sales rep for a small, struggling software firm, it was part of David's job to travel. He left town at least once a month and I wasn't ashamed to say that I missed him like crazy. If you've ever watched that show about the people stranded on an island after a plane crash, you'll remember the tall, athletic blond guy who looks like a surfer slash underwear model slash soccer player.

That's David.

Well, not *really*—but that's pretty much what he looks like. And because of this, I'd be lying to you if I said I never worried about other women.

When I first met David in a bar in Boise, I was so intensely attracted to him that I immediately invited him home for the night. And what a wonderful night it was. So I'd never had much trouble imagining that other women might be compelled to do exactly the same thing. And if they did, and David were to succumb, I knew they wouldn't be disappointed. He had a way of using his hands that was quite unlike any man I'd ever been with.

Then there was his kiss…

Well. Let's just say it didn't take much more for this particular girl to see fireworks. After years of struggling with what I'd always thought of as sexual inadequacy, I discovered in that one night that it wasn't *me* who had the problem. It was all the selfish, fumbling brutes I'd been with prior to that.

So while I'll freely admit I worried about other women, what I *never* worried about was David himself. He once told me that his father, whom he loved dearly, had been an extremely strong believer in fidelity and had passed that belief on to his son. David claimed he had never in his life cheated on a woman and never would. It simply wasn't in his DNA.

Was he protesting too much? Am I?

Maybe.

What I was about to see certainly made me wonder.…

● ● ●

She couldn't have been more than twenty-three or -four, giving me a good six or so years on her. You could see those years—or lack thereof—in the firmness of her body. The kind of firmness that, once you reach a certain age, no amount of exercise in the world can achieve. You try and you try, but you just can't get those years back. Which is why you feel so threatened by those who are still reveling in the glory of youth.

Like her.

She was what my father had always called a *humdinger*. He had said this openly and often, which no doubt contributed to my parents' divorce. The comment was usually targeted at someone tall and high-breasted, with a waist you could almost fit a single hand around and an ass that provoked either envy or scorn in every woman it passed.

And *this* girl certainly would have made Daddy's list.

Normally, I wouldn't have cared. I don't often sit around pining over my lost youth, and I like to think that I could probably hold my own on that website *Hot or Not*. But the fact that this girl was climbing out of the passenger seat of my boyfriend's rented car gave me pause. To put it mildly. She wore a tight-fitting business skirt and a blazer that accentuated the fullness of her chest, and for all intents and purposes she might as well have had the words—if I may be so crude—FUCK BAIT stamped across that ass.

Another term of my father's.

Needless to say, I wasn't happy watching as David handed the keys to the hotel valet, then followed the woman inside. Something sour began to roll around in my stomach, and as a person who's prone to throwing up at the slightest provocation, it was a miracle I didn't hurl all over the steering wheel of my forty-dollar-a-day Hyundai.

Somewhere in the back of my brain, a single phrase kept tumbling around like socks—or maybe *rocks*—in a dryer:

Mother was right.

Mother was right.

Mother was...

Shit.

A moment later the lobby doors slid closed, and I knew I had no choice but to follow the winsome couple as I quietly prayed that what I was witnessing was completely innocent. That I was merely victim to my parental unit's constant and unrelenting skepticism.

The girl was probably David's assistant, Kim—and, if so, I immediately understood why he had never introduced her to me.

He'd been sparing me the heartache of knowing what a knockout he worked with every day.

Uh-huh. That was it.

Sparing me.

Unlatching my seat belt, I once more staved off the urge to vomit, then climbed out of the car and headed toward the hotel entrance. I was about to either make a fool of myself or see a relationship I cherished come crashing down around me.

● ● ●

Whenever he traveled, David made a habit of texting me his room number once he checked into a hotel. He carried one of those smartphones with a battery that lasted about thirty-five seconds, so he was constantly turning it off when he didn't absolutely need it. Texting me was his way of assuring me that he was always available, via the room phone, should I need to contact him. I had received that text the moment I stepped off the plane at LAX and had the number burned into my brain.

When I got to the lobby, there was no sign of my prey. It was well past the dinner hour, but I took a quick peek into the hotel's restaurant and lounge before heading for the elevators.

They were nowhere to be found.

The big question in my mind was whether they had gone to separate rooms or were now getting comfortable on my boyfriend's bed. There was the possibility, of course, that they could have gone to *Kim's* room—assuming that's who the girl was. But if David wanted to stay available to me to avoid any suspicion—just in case I should happen to call—then it made more sense that they'd...

What the hell was wrong with me?

There I was, already assuming the worst. I had long thought that I had somehow managed to beat back my mother's rampant misandry, yet I was quickly proving that I was just as cynical as she was.

I got off the elevator on the fourteenth floor, wondering what I'd do once I reached David's room. I imagined myself knocking on his door and lowering the pitch of my voice, saying, "Housekeeping" or "Room service," as if I were a character in some bad romantic comedy. But when I reached it I simply stood there, staring at it, suddenly not wanting to know the truth.

Then I heard a woman's laughter.

I couldn't be sure if it originated from David's room or the one next door, or even across the hall, for that matter. My sense of direction when it came to sound had always been faulty. All I knew was that a woman had laughed and it was a playful one, and in my mind, I could see that perfect female body stripping down to the nethers as the man I loved reached up from the bed and cupped her heaving breasts in his palms.

I suddenly wanted to be anywhere but there.

Five minutes later I was back in my rented car, thinking the worst and not knowing quite what to do about it. I was tempted to call my mother, but I knew that would be a huge mistake. The last thing I needed right now was an *I told you so* from her.

I sometimes thought she would prefer that I'd never find a man worth loving. That anyone I hooked up with was some kind of threat to our relationship. That I needed to be just as miserable as she'd been all her life, so that she would always have someone to commiserate with. Someone who understood just how worthless the male species really was.

There was a kind of desperation in that need that had always unsettled me. My mother was a lonely, bitter woman, and the thought that I might one day wind up exactly like her sent chills up my spine.

I couldn't let that happen.

Wouldn't let it.

And just as I had nearly convinced myself that I should trust my boyfriend, as I always had, and assume that the implications of what I'd seen and possibly heard had merely been the product of thirty years of parental indoctrination, the lobby doors slid open and David stepped outside, hurriedly handing a ticket stub to the valet.

Surprised, I checked my cell phone clock and saw that nearly an hour had passed—an hour that had seemed like minutes. I watched David intently, wondering if the lobby doors would open behind him and deposit Miss Wonderbod at his side.

But then his car came and he tipped the valet and climbed behind the driver's wheel. He seemed to be out of sorts, as if he'd gotten sudden bad news, but I couldn't for the life of me imagine what it would be. He had no family to speak of, and any urgent calls would most likely have come from *me*.

A moment later, he was on the road and I quickly started my engine and followed him, feeling more like a stalker than ever.

●　●　●

Following a car isn't as easy as it looks in the movies. Especially at night. I could count at least three times I'd mistaken the wrong set of taillights for David's and it was a miracle that I managed to find him again each time.

Twenty minutes into the drive, he took the turnoff toward the airport. He hadn't taken a bag with him, and I had to wonder why he was headed this way, unless perhaps he was scheduled to pick up a colleague and was worried about arriving late.

Then he surprised me again by suddenly pulling to the side of the road. I couldn't very well pull up behind him, so I zoomed past, craning my neck to catch a glimpse of him behind the wheel.

I could be mistaken, but I swear he had his face buried in his hands.

What the hell was going on?

I had the urge to circle back and find out, to ask what was troubling him, but that would only expose me for the jealous idiot I was. Not something I was ready to cop to.

Nearly frozen by indecision and shame for even following him in the first place, I instead kept driving on, thinking enough was enough.

I soon found myself pulling into the airport rental car facility, ready to turn in my Hyundai and catch the next flight home. As much as I wanted to comfort David, I knew I couldn't. And if something was wrong, he would eventually tell me.

I had to believe that.

As it turned out, however, the revelation came not from the man I loved, but from the morning news.

• • •

There's something surreal about seeing a part of your life on TV. You feel as if you've been launched into a dream—or nightmare, in this case—and everything around you has that gauzy, slightly out-of-focus feel.

I had always used the television in my bedroom as an alarm clock. At precisely six forty-five every morning, it popped on, whether I liked it or not, bringing my favorite cable news network into my home, my favorite morning news anchor cheerfully chirping on about some national disaster or public tragedy. Usually that meant an earthquake or a bank robbery or train crash or, more often than not, a political or celebrity scandal. But that morning the news was considerably more personal than I had expected it to be. It took me a moment to wrap my head around exactly what was being reported.

A photograph of David hammered it home. They'd lifted it from his Idaho driver's license and it didn't even come close to doing him justice—an insignificant observation in the scheme of things.

My favorite reporter's voice was droning on, saying something I didn't quite understand until I forced myself to focus.

"…after the body of his colleague was discovered in his hotel room by the night maid. The maid said she had received a call for fresh towels and was shocked to find another guest, Ms. Kim Gallagher, lying naked on Mr. Atlee's bed, the victim of an apparent strangling. Los Angeles police aren't talking, but a source close to the investigation claims that Ms. Gallagher's death may have been the result of a sex game gone wrong."

There are no words to describe how I felt at that moment.

Do I really need to?

I sat on the edge of my bed just staring at the TV, hoping I'd wake up and find David lying next to me, that crooked smile of his asking me what the hell I was dreaming about.

But, of course, that didn't happen. Instead, I watched news footage of my boyfriend being arrested in the lobby of his hotel. Apparently, he hadn't gone to the airport after all. Had turned around and gone back to the Traveler's Inn and soon found himself confronted by a phalanx of uniformed and plainclothes police officers.

He didn't resist arrest. Just stood there, looking stunned, as they cuffed his wrists and escorted him away.

And I didn't speak to him again until after the trial.

● ● ●

I did, however, speak to my mother. More or less.

My favorite cable channel was in the midst of looping the arrest footage for about the hundred and forty-seventh time—the phrase "sex game" repeated ad infinitum—when my phone rang and that piercing nasal whine filled my right ear.

"Oh, my God," she said. "Oh. My. God. Tell me it isn't true. Tell me I'm having a terrible, terrible nightmare."

I don't know why I answered the damn thing. I'd known it would be her. And the last person in the world I wanted to talk to was mommy dearest. But for reasons that will always escape me, I had grabbed my cell phone by the fourth ring, and now I not only had to find a way to respond, I had to do it in a way that somehow didn't make me sound as humiliated as I felt. Humiliated by David's betrayal and by the dreaded realization that the woman on the other end of the line had been right all along.

I was devastated, no doubt about it, but I'd be damned if I'd show it.

Not to her.

She would be sympathetic, of course. I knew that. She would try to soothe my wounds, as she always had. She would do everything she could to protect me from further harm.... But behind it all, hidden just beneath the surface of every word and deed, she would be gloating. Every syllable she uttered would be laced with that *mother knows best* tone that she had perfected over the past thirty years.

Both she and I were victims, simply because of our gender. No man could ever be trusted and we ladies had to stick together if we wanted to survive. Love and happiness were elusive, unrealistic goals if we depended on the opposite sex to provide them for us. Any woman who thought she had achieved the fairy tale was a deluded fool, just as I—and she—had been.

But I didn't want to believe that. I didn't want to believe what I'd had with David was a lie. Even with the evidence staring right at me, a part of me thought that there had to be a mistake. That, in our case, the fairy tale *was* true.

How was it possible that I could be so easily duped? Surely David couldn't have been *acting,* could he?

And surely I wasn't *that* stupid.

Was I?

Everything I saw on my television screen told me I was. Everything I'd seen with my own eyes. Heard with my own ears.

Whether it had been an accident or a premeditated act, my boyfriend was both a philanderer and, yes, a murderer. There was simply no way around that fact.

And I had been there, right outside the hotel, when it happened. God save me.

My mother was still chattering away in my ear, her voice full of alarm, and I know I said something in return, but I couldn't tell you what it was.

I had stopped listening to her. Put her on mute as my mind reeled, a cacophony of thoughts swirling inside my brain with such ferocity that I could barely contain them, feeling them build and build as if an orchestra were trapped in there, playing the final crescendo of a dark, discordant symphony.

Then, clicking off the phone midwhine, I went into my bathroom and spent the next fifteen minutes hunched over the toilet bowel.

No point in holding back now.

● ● ●

"Thank God you answered," he said. "I was convinced I'd never talk to you again."

"I almost didn't," I told him. "I'm still not sure why I did."

The trial was a month past and a verdict and sentence had been handed down. David had been found guilty of Voluntary Manslaughter and would be spending the next fifteen years in a California penitentiary.

I hadn't attended the trial. Had no desire to. There had been some talk of calling me as a witness, but nobody except Mother knew that I had flown to Los Angeles that day. They hadn't even bothered to check. And after sending a Boise P.D. liaison to interview me, the prosecutor decided I had nothing substantial to contribute to the case.

I was, after all, simply the grieving ex-girlfriend who had been completely clueless about her boyfriend's extracurricular activities. I wanted nothing to do with David. Didn't care if I ever saw him again, and couldn't wait for the news media to get tired of the case and leave me alone.

By the time the verdict was read, David and Kim and their disastrous sex game had become little more than a footnote as the news moved on to bigger and better scandals. And a month later, I doubted that anyone could remember either of their names.

None of which had kept David from calling me. His phone privileges seemed to be on a set schedule, and every Tuesday and Thursday afternoon he left a message on my voice mail, begging me to come see him. To let him explain what had happened. That what I was seeing on TV was not the truth. Not even close.

It killed me to hear his voice. To know he was in such pain. But I dutifully erased each of the calls and went on with the business of trying to put my life back together, despite the nagging desire to believe him. Unless he was the world's greatest liar, the sincerity in his tone was hard to ignore.

Mother moved in with me. A temporary situation, she said, until I got back to my old self—although I had to wonder which of us would determine exactly when that moment had arrived. She was using every weapon in her passive-aggressive arsenal to let me know that she was the expert here, and I had a sneaking suspicion that I might never be rid of her.

Then, on a cold Tuesday afternoon, while Mother was out getting her hair done, my phone rang, and after a long moment of indecision, I answered it, knowing full well who it would be.

"It's so amazing to hear your voice," he said. "You're all I've been able to think about."

"Leave me alone, David."

"I've missed you, babe. You don't know how much I—"

"Please," I said, "you need to stop calling me. I've got nothing for you anymore."

But if I was honest with myself, that was a lie. This brief conversation alone had sparked something inside me. Something intangible. Irrational. I suddenly felt giddy and alive again, the way I had always felt when I was around David, Mother be damned.

"Come see me, babe. Let me explain. I didn't do what they say I did. I swear on my father's grave that everyone has it wrong. Including you."

The invocation of his long-deceased father didn't come lightly. I knew this. David had cherished the man, and despite what he had been convicted of, I honestly didn't think he'd use his father to convince me of his innocence, unless what he was saying was absolutely true.

It took a while longer, but he finally convinced me to come to California for a face-to-face. If nothing else, it would be a chance for me to finally purge myself of him forever.

To let him know just how much he'd hurt me.

That was worth a trip, wasn't it?

● ● ●

I left the next morning, while Mother was still asleep. My overnight bag had a broken latch, so I took hers from the hall closet, filled it with a change of clothes and some toiletries, then left a note on the fridge and headed for the airport.

She wouldn't be happy with this decision, but I didn't care.

I had to do what I had to do.

Several hours later I sat at a table across from David, staring into those beautiful blue eyes. Not shifty at all. Not in the least. He was shackled and wore an orange jumpsuit, and I'd felt my heart break the moment I stepped into the room and saw him sitting there.

He looked smaller than I remembered. Beaten down. But the weight he carried didn't seem to be the weight of a guilty man, and I found myself once again wanting to believe that there'd been some mistake.

I guess that was what I was there to find out.

"I wasn't having an affair with Kim," he said. "There *wasn't* any sex game. Everything between us was strictly business. I won't deny I found her attractive—who wouldn't? But my heart was always with *you*, babe. Always will be."

Normally I would have melted about then, but I resisted. "Why don't you get to the not-killing-her part?"

"That's just it. I was set up."

"Oh, please, David."

"I *swear* it's the truth. We met with a client earlier in the day and had just come back from shopping."

"Shopping?"

He hesitated. "We went to a jewelry store. Kim helped me pick out a ring."

I was confused. "For what?"

"It was supposed to be a surprise," he said. "And the one we chose was perfect. It was already your size, so I bought it on the spot."

I felt my heart kick up. "What are you saying, David?"

"I was planning to ask you to marry me."

The words thrilled me, but at the same time I suddenly felt wary, thinking this was a ploy to get me on his side. But the David I knew would never resort to such a tactic.

Then again, the David I knew wouldn't be shackled to a chair.

"After that, Kim and I went to our rooms—separate rooms—and all I wanted to do was hop in the shower, then take a long nap."

And that's exactly what he did, he told me. The first part, at least. He'd thrown his clothes on the floor, then gone into the bathroom and stepped into the shower, taking a long, hot one, as he always did. He figured he'd been in there at least twenty or thirty minutes, and when he finally toweled off and stepped back into the room, he found Kim lying on the mattress. Naked.

It had taken him a moment to realize that she was dead. And

when he did, he panicked. Threw his clothes back on and fled the hotel. Headed straight for the airport, planning to get out of L.A. on the next available flight. But then he realized how stupid that was. That only a *guilty* man would run. So he returned to the scene of the crime.

"A lot of good it did me," he said softly, staring at his hands. "I didn't kill her, babe. Someone else put her body in my room. And I never called the night maid for more towels. I think whoever did is the *real* killer."

"But why, David? Who would do that?"

He shook his head morosely. "A jealous boyfriend, maybe? The sonofabitch took the ring, too. Snatched it right off the dresser. I'm not sure if Kim was dating anyone, but maybe he was convinced we were having an affair and followed us to the hotel."

I felt a twinge of guilt. The idea obviously wasn't beyond the realm of possibility. But before either of us could say anything more, the guard came over and told us our time was up.

As they escorted David toward a doorway, he said, "You've gotta help me, babe. You have to find out who Kim was involved with. My attorney was supposed to try, but I think he—"

The door slammed shut before he could finish. I sat there, wondering if I should trust my instincts and believe the man I loved. Because that much hadn't changed. I still loved him. Fiercely. I couldn't help myself.

I knew David had appealed his conviction, but the chances of him winning that appeal were slim. He needed new evidence, evidence that would support his side of the story.

The question was, where would I find it?

Little did I know I'd had it with me all along.

● ● ●

Jealousy comes in many different forms.

I can't begin to understand the workings of the human heart

and mind, or the lengths to which some people are willing to go to protect what they cherish or desire, or to satisfy their own egos and sense of self-worth. People kill for the most mundane reasons, and I suppose everyone has a breaking point.

I was a late check-in at the hotel, planning to spend the night and visit David again before heading back to Boise. Despite the short stay, I made it a point—as I always did—to unpack my overnight bag before settling in.

Or, I should say, my *mother's* overnight bag.

After I neatly folded my clothes into a dresser drawer and re-moved the small toiletry kit I'd brought along, I noticed something bulging slightly in an inner pocket of her bag.

Curious, I reached in, grabbed it.

A small square box.

And as I pulled it out and saw what it was, a sudden chill swept through me, dread doing somersaults in my stomach. With shaky hands, I pried the lid open and stared down at a beautiful diamond engagement ring.

The ring David had bought for me.

And as luck or fate would have it, my cell phone bleeped at that very moment. I dug it out of my purse and answered it.

"It's about time you picked up," she whined. "I can't believe you could be so stupid. How can you let that murderous bastard get under your skin?"

I stared down at the ring. "Don't mother. Don't even try. I know exactly what you did. I've got the evidence right here in my hand."

And for the first time that I can remember…

…my mother was speechless.

LOCKDOWN
ANDREA KANE

*Two occasions: a wedding and a honeymoon.
They should be memorable. But Kane's characters
never bargained on this. —SB*

It was times like this that Claire Hedgleigh hated her
psychic gift.

Her best friend was about to get married. The chapel was alight
with anticipation and joy.

But all Claire could sense was darkness. Dark energy. Filling the
room. Hovering over the fairy-tale setting.

Why?

Not because of the marriage. This time Kim had gotten it right.
Her first marriage had been a disaster. She and Ted Benton had
met in college, fallen wildly in love and eloped to Vegas when Kim
was a sophomore.

Huge mistake. Kim was wealthy, accustomed to the finer things
in life, and not about to give them up. She was also bright, ambitious and—within three years—a junior VP at the major advertising firm on Madison Avenue where she worked. Ted was a middle-
class, nine-to-five kind of guy. Wanting a traditional life. Pissed
off when he didn't get it. And how did he react? By slacking off at
work. Spending his time watching football and drinking beer.

Kim's pregnancy was unplanned. But Sam had arrived, healthy, happy and all boy. Ted was terrific with his son. Then again, it was easy to be good with a child when you were still one yourself. He and Kim had tried to make it work. It hadn't. They'd called it quits last year, when Sam was two. Things had plummeted downhill after that. An acrimonious divorce. Full custody for Kim when Ted drank his way to the unemployment line. And limited visitation rights after he started showing up late, drunk or not at all.

This marriage was different.

James Coleman was an ideal match. A wealthy investment banker, he loved Kim *and* respected her for who she was—a materialistic workaholic, just like him. They were both committed to their professional futures, and gladly accepted the personal sacrifices those futures entailed. It had taken an exhaustive amount of juggling to find two weeks they both could make this wedding and honeymoon happen.

And now here they were, tying the knot in a beautiful wedding chapel nestled in the gardens of Maui's most elegant luxury resort hotel, the Punahou Lani.

So why couldn't Claire shake the dark energy that seemed to surround them?

The beautiful strains of Pachelbel's *Canon* began, filling the walls of the elegant chapel. The guests all turned, craning their necks to see the bridal gown that Kim Hewitt had chosen to begin her second, far more suitable, marriage.

Smoothing the folds of her custom-made ivory silk dress, Kim linked her arm through her father's and made her grand entrance. Her gaze flickered over the guests to James—who was grinning broadly—to Sam, who had successfully made it down the aisle, stern in his all-important job of ring bearer. Other than wriggling around with his pent-up three-year-old energy level, he was being a trouper.

Claire, Kim's longtime friend and maid of honor, stood beside

Sam, fondly ruffling his hair and keeping him rooted to one spot. The bridesmaids clustered on the other side of the dais, watching Kim glide her way to her future.

The bride was only feet away from the groom and a new life when it happened.

The outside chapel door burst open. A man wearing a ski mask and gripping a handgun exploded into the sanctuary. He locked the heavy door behind him, simultaneously holding up his weapon, and aiming it straight at the dais.

Everyone screamed.

The gunman ignored it.

Keeping his sights on the crowd, he strode over to the inside chapel door—the one Kim had just entered through that connected the chapel with the ballroom wing—and locked that one, as well. He turned in a slow panoramic sweep of the room, the pistol tracking each person.

"Everyone—get down," he ordered in a rough, gravelly voice that pierced the shrieks of fright. "Throw all your purses and cell phones on the floor and push them away from you. Then put your hands in front of you where I can see them. Anyone who plays hero, dies."

Immediately, everyone sprang into panicked action, the women struggling over their formal dresses and high heels, the men groping in their pockets. Kim's father pushed his daughter to the ground and shimmied his cell phone out of the pants pocket of his tuxedo before joining her. Claire dropped her bouquet and pulled Sam against her, cradling him protectively in the folds of her gown as she drew them both down to the floor.

Within two minutes, the entire roomful of people were on their knees and the aisle was strewn with designer handbags and Black-Berry phones.

"Now stay still. I'll come to you. If you move before I tell you to, you'll be shot."

The masked gunman unzipped his duffel bag and walked to the rear aisle before making his way methodically forward. "All valuables in here. Jewelry, wallets, money clips—everything. Not a word. Just do it. Fast."

He waited while the terrified guests complied, the men tossing in their wallets, money clips and watches, while the women fumbled with their necklace clasps and earrings. While his instructions were being executed, the gunman snatched up the cell phones and expensive purse contents, shoving them in the duffel bag until everything had been collected. And "everything" was a lot. The Hewitts and the Colemans were both wealthy. So were their friends.

"Please," Kim managed in a quavering voice, hearing her son's quiet sobs. "You have everything you came for. Please go. Don't hurt us."

His hard glare bore through her. "I'm going to unlock the outside door," he announced to the group. "When I do, I want all of you to get up and get out of here. You have thirty seconds before I change my mind. But the bride and the boy—they stay."

"What?" Kim's father's head shot up. "Why would you want them?"

"Shut up and do what I say," the gunman snapped. He waited for Kim's father to nod. Then, he turned the gun on Kim. "You stay down," he ordered. "And you." He pivoted until the gun pointed at James. "Get out with the others."

"I'm not leaving Kim or Sam," James stated flatly, half rising to a crouched position on the dais.

"Then you're dying in front of them both." A gloved index finger moved to the trigger. "Your choice."

"Please, James—go," Kim whispered to him. "I don't want you to die. And Sam is already traumatized. We've got to protect him."

With reluctant acceptance, James fell silent, giving a terse nod.

"Good." The gunman swung the duffel bag onto his shoulder and retraced his steps to the outside door. He turned the lock and flung it open. "Go," he commanded.

Everyone scrambled to their feet and there was a mass exodus out the door. Kim's parents had to be shoved out by James, who was muttering, "It's the only way to keep them safe. We'll get help."

The reverend was the last one out. He hesitated in the doorway, turning to scrutinize their abductor's masked face. "Let them go," he said quietly. "The little boy is practically a baby. He doesn't understand. Please. Show some mercy."

"I am. He's with his mother. Now get out. Your being a man of God won't stop me from putting a bullet in your head."

The silver-haired reverend turned, gazing sadly at Kim. "God be with you," he murmured. "I'll do what I can." He clearly didn't mean just prayer. Judging from the speed with which he moved, he was en route to notify the authorities.

The gunman locked the door and turned, expecting to see only the bride and her little boy in the chapel.

Instead he also saw a slim, blonde woman on her knees beside the child, shielding him with her body. He was weeping and clinging to her.

"What the hell are you doing here?" the gunman demanded. "Didn't you hear me say to get out?"

"I heard you," Claire replied in a soft, calm voice. "But I'm not going anywhere. This is my godchild. I'm staying with him and his mother."

Through the slits in his mask, his eyes bore through her in disbelief. "You're staying," he repeated, a bitter note creeping into his gravelly voice.

"Yes." Claire gathered Sam against her, simultaneously giving Kim a hard shake of her head. She could sense that her friend was about to leap up and grab Sam. "Don't," she instructed Kim, never shifting her gaze from the gunman. "Ted would never hurt his son."

"*Ted!*" Kim gasped. It was a statement, not a question. Kim had spent a lifetime exposed to Claire's talent. She no longer questioned it.

"Take off the mask," Claire urged. "Sam is already scared to death. At least let him know that it's his father doing this. Not some masked monster." Irony laced her voice.

Ted muttered an oath and yanked the ski mask over his head. "Damn you, you freak," he ground out, teeth clenched, pistol aimed at Claire. "It's too bad for you that you decided to play heroine. Because *you're* expendable. If we don't get out of here before the cops show up, you'll be my human shield. You're a psychic, so you know I'm dead serious. I want Kim and Sam. Not you. So, if it comes down to it, I'll take my family and let the cops put a round of bullets through you."

• • •

With one hand, Sloane Burbank Parker squeezed the water out of her hair, letting it trickle down her bikini-clad figure. She continued walking along Kalhui Beach, sand beneath her bare feet, her fingers linked with her new husband's. Twelve out of fourteen days of a dream-come-true honeymoon.

Soon to be followed by twenty-two weeks of FBI training at Quantico.

"Beautiful, isn't it?" Derek murmured, following her gaze and watching the sun shimmering its last rays of the day on the serene waters. He brought Sloane's hand to his lips. "We could just forget to go home."

"Tempting." She smiled. "But forget it, Special Agent Parker. You're no longer going to be the only one in this relationship who works for the Bureau. I'm coming back with a vengeance."

She'd been sidelined with a career-threatening injury for two years. Two years too long. Now she was coming back, retraining and raring to go. Her wedding and honeymoon had been incredible. But in a few days it would be time to go home and live life.

Derek was chuckling at her reply as they walked across the chapel lawn toward their room.

His laughter was short-lived.

A crowd of white-faced people rushed across the gardens, bumping into each other and nearly colliding with Sloane and Derek in an attempt to escape from…something. They were dressed in formal attire, an obvious indication that they'd come from an event at the chapel. They were also clearly terrified.

Instinctively, Sloane put out her arm and stopped one woman, who jumped a foot in the air at the contact.

"I didn't mean to scare you," Sloane said.

"You've got to run," the woman replied, struggling to get away. "He's got a gun."

"Who's got a gun?"

A fearful silence.

"We're with the FBI," Sloane announced quickly. "Tell us what's going on."

The woman sucked in her breath. "You're FBI agents?"

"Yes."

That calmed the woman down enough to elicit a response. "A man with a ski mask broke into the chapel during the wedding ceremony. He held us at gunpoint and demanded all our money and our jewelry. He's still in there, holding hostages."

"Is anyone hurt?" Derek demanded, abruptly switching from new husband into special-agent mode. "How many hostages?"

"Two. Kim and her son, Sam. I don't know if he hurt them. He made us all go, but kept them."

Sloane and Derek exchanged quick glances. She was already

reaching into her tote bag and pulling out her BlackBerry. "He took your phones?" she surmised aloud as she punched in 911.

"Yes..." The woman covered her face with her hands. "I can't believe this is happening."

"Who are Kim and Sam?" Derek asked, while Sloane reported the situation to the Maui County Police Department.

"The bride and her little boy."

"How little?"

"He's three. He was sobbing his heart out when we left." The woman broke down and began to weep.

"Try to calm down," Derek said in a soothing tone. "Tell me who you are."

"Marge Hewitt. I'm Kim's aunt, her father's sister."

"Okay, Ms. Hewitt, we're going to get them out."

"How?"

"My wife is a hostage negotiator. She'll get the right people here, and do what needs to be done."

"The police are on their way," Sloane announced as she ended the call. "Their precinct is about four minutes up the road." Sloane turned to Derek. "Find security," she instructed. "Have them seal off the building and clear the grounds. I'm sure the hotel has established a phone tree. Have management activate it. This way, all the guests who are in their rooms or in the dining rooms can be advised to stay put. No one will be able to go in or out, so the danger will be isolated."

"Done." Derek was already on his way.

Sloane gave Marge Hewitt a questioning look as a small group of the wedding guests began gathering around them. "Did I hear you say you're the bride's aunt?"

A nod. "Marge Hewitt."

"This gunman—did he give you any indication that this was personal? Or why he chose to keep Kim and Sam in particular?"

"It's not just Kim and Sam," a dark-haired man in his late thirties interrupted. He turned to Marge. "Claire's in there, too. The reverend said she was crouched behind Sam and never came out."

"Oh, no." Marge squeezed her eyes, then opened them to make a quick introduction. "This is James Coleman, the groom. James, this woman is an FBI agent."

For an instant, the groom blinked, taking in Sloane's petite size and bikini-clad figure. Then he looked up and met her gaze.

"It's true," Sloane assured him. "I'd show you my credentials, but clearly I wasn't on duty. I'm on my honeymoon." She extended her hand. "Special Agent Sloane Burbank." She realized it would be several months before she could truly use that title again. But, in this situation, it hardly mattered.

"I apologize, Agent Burbank," James said, shaking her hand. "I'm a mess."

"Understandable. And no apology necessary." Sloane gave him a questioning look. "Now, who's Claire?"

"Kim's best friend. The maid of honor. She's also Sam's godmother. So she's very protective of him. She probably refused to leave."

At that moment, a uniformed Hawaiian patrol officer strode over to join them. "Agent Burbank?" he asked.

"That would be me." Sloane turned to the earnest young man.

"I'm Officer Kahanu. Two detectives and our command officer should be here momentarily. Our command officer already contacted the Maui FBI, and our tactical unit is ready to be dispatched. What's our status?"

"Three hostages and an armed gunman." Sloane frowned. The FBI Resident Agency in Maui consisted of two agents. Not great odds for what she needed. "Do any of your detectives have hostage negotiation training?"

"Two. Also, one of the FBI agents here is also trained. We're small here, but we try to be prepared."

"Good," Sloane said with grim relief. "Because one of the hostages is a three-year-old boy. We'd better find a way to talk this offender out."

She watched as Officer Kahanu raced back to meet his command officer. It would take them a couple of minutes to get here. In the meantime...

Her gaze slid to the outside door leading to the ballroom hall—which connected directly to the inside entry to the chapel. Security would be locking that door down any second.

Someone needed to be on the inside, barricading that door and communicating with the offender, working simultaneously with the lead hostage negotiator. Someone with training.

With a quick glance around, Sloane sprinted over and let herself in.

It only took a few seconds to get oriented. Then she crept down the hall to the door that separated her from the chapel—and the hostage scene.

• • •

Inside the chapel, Ted held the gun on Claire and reached out his other hand to Sam.

"It's okay, buddy. It's Daddy. Come on over here. You, Mommy and I are going through the inside of the hotel. I know a secret entrance. We'll leave through there."

Sam cringed against Claire and whipped his head from side to side. "No."

"Don't be afraid, buddy," Ted continued, a muscle working in his jaw. "I'm not going to hurt you or Mommy. I just want us to go where no one can keep us apart."

"You said Claire might die." Sam didn't release his grip on Claire's gown. "Are you gonna shoot her?"

A hard swallow. "Of course not. I just said that so your mommy would remember how much she loves us."

"What about Claire?"

"Claire will be fine. She'll just stay with us until we leave the hotel. Then she'll say goodbye and go home."

Sam's lower lip began to tremble. "I don't want her to say goodbye. Can't she come, too?"

"No, Sam," Ted said, trying to keep his tone steady and gentle. "I only have three plane tickets. And enough money in this duffel bag to take care of you, me and Mommy. No one else."

Kim noted the frenetic look in Ted's eyes, heard the familiar tremor in his voice. Wondering how much he'd had to drink, she chose her words carefully. "Put down the gun, Ted. You're scaring Sam. How do you expect him to believe what you're saying when you have that pistol aimed at us?"

Ted half lowered the gun, but not enough so that Kim or Claire could charge him and try to snatch it away.

"I'm going to our son," Kim told him quietly. "Maybe I can calm him down. That will be to all our advantages."

"Fine." Ted half waved the pistol. "But don't just calm him down. Convince him. We're running out of time."

"I'll do what I can."

Kim and Claire exchanged glances. The clock was ticking. And no one seemed to be around to help them.

● ● ●

Within the next five minutes, Detectives Ignaccio and Silva had joined their on-scene command officer. Then came the Maui County SWAT team, and FBI Special Agent Fitzpatrick, who was the acting primary negotiator. EMT had also arrived, should they be needed. The area surrounding the chapel and the connecting wing were sealed off and surrounded. Just outside of that, of course, was the press, who smelled a story in the air.

Derek had just returned to the scene. He scanned the entire area, seeing no sign of his wife.

"Have you seen Agent Burbank?" he asked James.

The groom shook his head. "Not in the past few minutes. Last I saw her, she was standing over there, near the chapel corridor."

Derek's gaze made a quick sweep of the area. But the gesture was perfunctory. He knew exactly where Sloane was.

He whipped out his BlackBerry. His wife's would be on silent. He punched her number.

She answered on the first ring.

"You're inside the chapel wing," he stated flatly.

"Right outside the chapel door," she whispered back. "Is everyone there?"

"Yup."

"Good. I need to speak to the primary hostage negotiator. Tell him I'm acting as a third party intermediary. Then find out everything you can on the bride's ex-husband, Ted. He's the offender."

"Sloane, I know how good you are," Derek replied. "But you're in there without a gun, without backup and practically without clothes."

"All the better. I'll look less threatening. Please, Derek. The guy isn't even sober, and he's desperate. We'll debate my decision later."

"Fine. Just be careful." Derek lowered his phone and signaled to Special Agent Fitzpatrick. In as few words as possible, he explained the situation.

Fitzpatrick took the phone. "Ms. Parker?" His tone was as pointed as his form of address. "This is Special Agent Fitzpatrick. Based on your husband's explanation, the child and his mother aren't in immediate danger."

"But the maid of honor is," Sloane replied. "If the offender knows you're out there, he might act irrationally and kill her."

"I realize that. I'll try to talk him out."

"You'd have to get a throw-phone in. That would tell him the FBI is here, which would freak him out. He might shoot Claire before even opening the door. Please, let me try first. I can take a more personal approach."

"And maybe get yourself killed in the process."

"That won't happen. Give me ten minutes. If I can't make headway by then, you can take over."

A reluctant pause, during which Sloane could hear Derek saying, "She's damned good, Fitzpatrick. Give her the time."

"Fine," Fitzpatrick said. "Do it."

● ● ●

Sloane waited until Derek had filled her in on everything he'd learned about Ted Benton, plus an interesting tidbit about the suddenly quite intriguing Claire Hedgleigh. Then, Sloane turned off her phone and took a deep breath. Things were getting heated inside the chapel. Sam was crying. His mother was comforting him. And his father was losing patience—fast.

"Get over here, Claire!" he shouted. "We're getting out of here."

"How?" Claire asked. "I'm sure they've sealed off all the hotel entrances by now."

"I mapped out a route through the basement. The door locks from the inside. I know what I'm doing." A bitter laugh. "You've always thought I was an idiot. But I'm not." He didn't wait for an answer. "Now let's go. We're walking out the inside door. And you're walking in front of us. My gun will be aimed at your head."

Judging from the proximity of his voice, Sloane estimated that Ted was about halfway across the chapel. She wasn't sure if Kim and Sam were with him, but she wasn't taking any chances.

She knocked. "Mr. Benton?"

There was a flurry of motion from inside. "Who's there?" Ted demanded. "And how do you know my name?"

"A few of the guests recognized you," Sloane said calmly.

"They've called the authorities. I wanted to talk to you first. My name is Sloane Parker. I'm a guest here at the hotel."

"And why would I talk to you?"

"Because I used to work for the FBI. I've seen situations like yours. And I understand what you're going through. I want to help you all get out safely."

"Well, that doesn't look like it's gonna happen. Especially if the cops and the FBI are on their way."

"You want your wife and son with you, is that right?"

"They're my family, so, yeah."

"You love them very much. You want to protect them. Am I still on track?"

"Uh-huh."

"Do you really think that holding them in a locked room with a gun in your hand is the best way to keep them safe?"

A pause. "I just want to get us out of here."

"I understand that. And I believe it can be done. But not at gunpoint." Sloane heard Sam's sobs. "Your son sounds frightened. Can't you let him wait in the hall while we talk this out?"

"You'll turn him over to the police," Ted stated flatly. Angrily.

"No, I won't. The outside doors are locked. He'll stay right here and wait. The only problem is that he'll still be scared. He'll want his mom. So why don't you let your wife and son both come out? You can talk to them through the door and make sure they haven't moved."

Sloane could hear his wheels turning.

"Is this a trick?" he demanded at last.

"How can it be?" Sloane asked. "You're still holding Claire. I'm not about to jeopardize her life by grabbing your family and trying to run away."

"You're not gonna jeopardize your own life, either. I'm sure you're armed. And you're playing games to keep me talking till the cops get here."

"First of all, I'm not armed. I told you, I'm no longer FBI. And why would I play games? To put all of you in danger? That would be counterproductive."

Pausing, Sloane moved to the next step.

"You're the one with the gun, Ted. I'm just a regular person who believes that families should be together. If you don't believe me, unlock the door and check for yourself. I'm wearing a bathing suit and an open shirt. In two seconds you'll see I'm unarmed. If I'm lying, you can shoot me. If I'm not, send Kim and Sam out and take me instead. You'll have two hostages to bargain with."

Another silence.

From inside the chapel, Sloane heard Kim implore, "Please, Ted. I won't do anything stupid. You and I both love Sam. Neither one of us would risk his safety with gunfire. At least open the door and see if the woman is legit. We'll stay back until you're sure."

"And if she is?"

"Then Sam and I will wait right outside the door. You can keep calling out to check if you don't believe me. And when all this is over, you and I will talk."

That seemed to catch him off guard. "You'd actually consider going with me by choice?"

"Like I said, we both want Sam to be happy. And if you're willing to go to such dramatic extremes…how could I not be open to what you have to say? It all depends on what happens when you talk to this person."

Good girl, Sloane thought silently. She glanced at her watch. Five minutes to go.

"What do you say, Ted?" she asked. "Will you do this for your family? Let me in so we can talk."

"And when the cops show up?"

"I'm former FBI. I can talk to whoever's in charge. They'll listen to me. And they won't put my life in danger. You're a lot safer if they know you're holding me at gunpoint than you are if I'm standing out here in the hall."

"Fine." That obviously prompted his cooperation. "Stand behind me," he ordered his ex-wife and son.

A rustle as they complied. Sloane took that time to drop her tote bag and snatch her BlackBerry, changing the ring status from silent to loud.

"I've got a gun on Claire Hedgleigh," Ted announced to Sloane through the door. "So if you try anything…"

"I won't."

A hard click, and the door opened a little—enough so Ted could scrutinize Sloane, and Sloane could see the woman Ted grasped before him, his pistol pressed to the side of her head.

"Turn around," Ted ordered.

Sloane pivoted slowly, hands raised, so he could see she had nothing to use as a weapon.

"Why do you have a BlackBerry?"

"To talk to the FBI and tell them to hold their fire. I'll put it down as soon as I'm inside. I won't touch it unless you let me."

That seemed to satisfy him. He angled his head slightly. "You two wait outside," he told Kim and Sam. In one motion, he flung open the door, pushed his family out, and yanked Sloane in. He slammed the door shut, then leaned past her and flipped the bolt.

"Put down the phone," he commanded Sloane. He waited until she'd complied. "Now talk. My plan was to take my family and get away before the cops got here. Now this bitch—" he jabbed Claire's forehead with his pistol "—screwed everything up. How do I get out of here without killing her?"

"To begin with, you think about your wife and son." Sloane was assessing him as she spoke. He'd been drinking, but he wasn't drunk. He was average height and build. With her skills in Krav Maga, she could take him easily. All she needed was the right opportunity.

"You're not a killer," she continued. "You proved that by releasing the guests. Plus, your son is obviously fond of Claire. How do you think he would react if you shot her? He looks up to you. You're his dad."

That caused a slight softening of his jaw.

"Let me negotiate with the FBI," Sloane suggested. "I'll convince them to hold off while you reunite with your family."

"And then what? They'll storm the place and take me away the minute I'm not holding you and Claire at gunpoint."

Sloane drew a slow breath, as if she were struggling with a big decision. "If I were still with the Bureau, I'd say yes. But I'm not. And, like I said, I think families should be together." Another pause. "I assume you have an escape route?"

Ted nodded.

"Good. Then use it. That phone is going to ring any second. At that point, I'll know the agents are in place. I'll keep them talking. You take your family and run. I'll buy you enough time to get away. In return, you leave Claire and me here, unharmed. Fair enough?"

He scrutinized her warily for a long time. "Yeah," he said at last. "Fair enough. But I'll be taking my gun with me. So if you decide to change your mind…"

"I won't." Sloane's gaze flickered to Claire, hoping against hope that what Derek had just told her about the clairvoyant was true. If there was ever a time to pick up on life-or-death energy, now was it.

Claire gave an almost-imperceptible nod.

At the same time, Sloane's phone rang. No surprise. Her ten minutes were up.

Quizzically, she looked at Ted, waiting for permission.

"Get it," he directed.

She squatted slightly, reaching behind her and groping for her phone. On cue, Claire whimpered as if in pain and sagged. Reflexively, Ted's head snapped around toward Claire.

In two lightning-quick strides, Sloane was on him. Simultaneously, her arm came up and she turned sideways so the trajectory of the gun would miss her if Ted took a shot. With her right hand she grabbed the top of the gun's barrel while her left hand came up under the slide and grip, completing the trap. She snapped the gun up and back, intentionally breaking Ted's trigger finger.

He gave a scream of pain and released Claire, who darted away the instant she was free. With Claire out of danger, Sloane yanked the gun from Ted's hand, moved back and rotated the weapon until it was aimed directly at him.

"On the floor," she ordered. "Slowly. Hands behind you."

"You lying bitch!" he managed, clutching his throbbing hand.

"I said get down. *Now.*"

Her laser stare convinced him. He did as he was told.

"Claire, answer my cell," Sloane instructed, walking over and straddling Ted from behind, shoving the gun in his back as she grabbed his wrists. "Tell Agent Fitzpatrick I've neutralized the offender. His team can take it from here."

● ● ●

Derek made his way through the crowd, pulling Sloane to him as he gave a relieved but exasperated sigh.

"Only you," he muttered, wrapping his arms around his wife. "A honeymoon hostage negotiation at gunpoint. I don't have to tell you how many Bureau rules you broke."

Sloane leaned back, her lips curved into a teasing smile. "I'm not back at Quantico yet. So breaking the rules doesn't count. Only the outcome does. I'd say things turned out right."

"And *I'd* say you're going to age me before my time."

A twinkle. "I know a way to keep you young."

"Yeah, me, too." Derek shot her that sexy grin of his. "Shall we get back to the honeymoon, Mrs. Parker?"

"Lead the way, Mr. Parker."

SPIDER'S TANGO

WILLIAM SIMON

*The premise is brilliant. When I realized what
the conflict was, I thought, "Oh, my God!" It's scary
on numerous levels. —SB*

Here's a piece of advice you won't find in any manual, leaflet, monograph, self-help book, or national talk show: when an agent with the FBI's Violent Crimes Unit opens an email, then spends the next ten minutes vomiting in the men's room, *do not under any circumstances* lean across the desk and look at the screen...

● ● ●

At 4:00 a.m., the FBI's Cyber Crime Division looks like any other office space, despite the inventive imaginations of Hollywood screenwriters. Computers and computer equipment dominated the floor, but it's hardly the high-tech toy-land television would have us believe.

"What's going on?" I asked as I walked in, Visitor badge clipped to my hastily snatched laptop bag, after receiving an abrupt cell phone call from the man standing in front of me.

"Kidnapping," Jeff Keyes, the Special Agent in Charge of the office replied. "Missing child."

My nerves twisted. Missing children were the worst.

"You have the manpower to handle that," I said, referring to a time not so long ago when the CCD consisted of individuals who could turn a computer on and not much else.

We came to a stop in front of a double cubicle. Four monitors connected to four computers, their screens flashing with data. A woman with ash-blond hair was there, her fingers flying across the keyboard.

She paused and stood.

My heart kicked into an off-key but sincere version of the *William Tell* Overture. I couldn't help smiling.

"Supervisory Special Agent Elizabeth Canton," Jeff said. "Nicholas White."

Her eyes flashed. "Nicholas."

"Beth, it's nice to see you."

"You've met?" Jeff asked.

Beth looked at him, then back to me. "I knew him when his last name was Bianco," she said. "He's my ex-husband."

Jeff's eyebrows shot up. "I didn't know you'd ever been married."

"For about three hours," I said before Beth could reply. "In college. It was a long time ago."

"Elizabeth's the Behavioral Analysis Unit Coordinator out of Quantico," Jeff explained. "She was here yesterday, giving a class." He broke off and nodded his head at a younger man who walked in. "This is R. P. Bristol, Violent Crimes, recent transfer from Washington.

"Nicholas is an outside consultant," Jeff told them both. "The Bureau uses him for, uh, special incidents."

"I've heard your name," Bristol said to me as we shook hands. "One of your cases is textbook at Quantico."

Beth rolled her eyes, turning back to the screens. Something I couldn't quite decipher played across her face as she pretended to ignore me completely.

The tension in the air between us was hard to miss. She was

probably struggling with the urge to leap over the cubicle and have her way with me.

As the song says, that's my story and I'm sticking to it.

"We've narrowed the video feed to the city, but no farther," she said, all business. "Running through a tri-proxy, and from there it's random. The Vesuvius, Buckingham's and Altair's, all three hotels offer free wireless. Then it all rotates again. It hasn't landed long enough to grab it."

A crude map of Las Vegas came on-screen. A red line kept moving, breaking off and starting over, an electronic Mobius strip.

On the left monitor a photograph came up on-screen, a posed school photo.

"The victim?" I asked.

"She and her parents came through the city yesterday, on the way to visit grandparents. As near as we can tell, the abduction occurred this morning, around 2:00 a.m.," Beth said.

The child's face rang a bell, but I couldn't quite place it.

"Thirty minutes ago, this showed up on the internet," she said.

I looked at the screen.

The little girl was in a Winnie the Pooh sleeper, sitting in a chair. The video quality was excellent. A wide leather strap held her in place.

She looked so tiny, so terrified.

The focus shifted to reveal an adult, height indeterminate, dark pants, white dress shirt and a full-face Frankenstein monster mask.

"Step right up!" he crowed as the features of the mask remained frozen. His voice was distorted but understandable.

"For auction tonight," he continued. "One fresh young thing, guaranteed! Opening bid is forty million dollars! Think about it," the creature went on. "For a mere forty million, you can own everything! Absolutely everything! You control it all, baby, all! If any police are watching this, don't waste time trying to get a voiceprint. You won't get a thing."

"The website didn't exist until half an hour ago," Beth said. "The video plays, the address changes. Plays again, another change."

An agent yelled into the room, "It's happening!"

A television screen in the conference room showed an empty conference room waiting for people to arrive. "Nicholas—" Jeff turned to me "—this is closed circuit, direct link from Washington, eyes only. You understand?"

I nodded. On the screen, a distinguished-looking man came into the room, his eyes raw from lack of sleep. Or from crying.

I realized why I had almost recognized her, and glanced over at Jeff.

He nodded and whispered, "His granddaughter."

A voice came over the speakers. "Ladies and gentlemen, the President of the United States."

● ● ●

"'Any attempt to invoke the Twenty-Fifth Amendment, she dies,'" the President read from a sheet of paper in front of him. "'Any anything, she dies.'"

"What's the Twenty-Fifth Amendment?" someone in the back asked.

"The President has the ability to remove himself from office if he deems it necessary," Beth explained.

Jeff stepped closer to me, his voice dropping even lower than before. "Her name is Angela Frazell." Jerking his head at the screen, he continued. "His daughter married some big-shot financier."

"I remember now. It was a big society wedding, lots of press. What about the Secret Service?" I asked.

"Three agents assigned to the family are dead. The Service is looking to drink this guy's blood when they get their hands on him."

"What's he trying to do?" I asked, jerking my thumb toward the other monitor.

"He's selling her," Jeff told me. "To the highest bidder."

At my puzzled look, he continued. "This isn't a child-porn thing," he said, referring to past incidents we'd worked on together. "He's gotten bids from al Qaeda, Red Brigade, Afghanistan and Beirut."

"Terrific." A terrorist group holding the president's granddaughter hostage.

"I spoke with the director personally—she classed it Code Black. You were my first phone call."

Code Black was Bureau slang for *Gloves Off.* It was a major step for an organization that prided itself on following the rules.

"Thanks. I think."

"We're good…you know that. You helped put together the Cyber Crime Division at Quantico," Jeff said. "But this is beyond words."

Agent Bristol was in front of a computer screen. "We've got an email, guys," he said as he clicked the mouse before anyone could stop him. "It's headed 'If You Think I'm Kidding.'"

Bristol turned pale, his eyes bulging. Making an odd noise in the back of his throat, he flew out of his chair and sprinted for the men's room.

No one said a word.

I've done a few stupid things in my day. According to Beth, doing stupid things is a specialty of mine.

In the interest of maintaining my status as Idiot of the Year, I leaned over and looked at the screen.

● ● ●

This is evidence, I told myself, using it as a mantra. This is data, nothing more. Only evidence. This is just evidence.

I jammed my hands into my pockets so no one would see them trembling.

The little girl in the photo wasn't Angela.

She'd been someone, though.

Beth slid into the seat Bristol had vacated so abruptly, smothering her own shock.

"Print it out," I said. "Headers, route info, everything. Get one of the tech guys in here and freeze that computer." I was aware she knew procedure, but I couldn't seem to stop talking.

She glanced at Jeff. "For the interim," he said softly, covering his own emotions, "in this area, if it comes from Nicholas, it comes from Almighty God. Okay?"

She nodded, and a couple of mouse clicks later, she handed me the papers.

I took the last page, the one with the photograph on it, and without looking deliberately fed it into a nearby shredder.

I just needed a copy of the email to work from, and had no desire to see that image again in this lifetime.

What was left was:

From: 2clvr4u@whitehorehouse.gov
Subject: If You Think I'm Kidding
Date: October 31, 5:25:47 AM PST
Received: from xm 2120.in.gotcha.com
(xm2.in-fec.whodaman.iamyerdaddy.com([218.41])

Bristol came back, looking embarrassed.

No one said a word about what had happened.

"He's clever," I said. "It says 'whitehorehouse' instead of 'whitehouse.'"

"Which means?" Beth asked.

"He's routing all over the place, but skilled enough to do his own headers," I told her. "He's making all this up in the original email. By the time it reaches us, it's so scrambled there's no telling where it came from."

"Anything else?"

"He's having fun, being cute," I said. "He wants us to know he's smarter than we are, there's nothing we can do. His kung fu is better than ours. We can use that against him."

I headed for a private area. "I need a secure network line," I told Jeff over my shoulder. "No firewall, total isolation. I need room to move."

Beth followed me. "You're on to something."

"Maybe, but not enough to go into it yet."

She leaned against a desk, folded her arms and looked at me. Almost as tall as me, stunningly beautiful, cheekbones that could cut diamonds. "Nicholas, right now, I'm willing to listen if you tell me it's invaders from Mars."

"How did we get here?" I asked her as I set my case on the table.

"What do you mean?"

"Last time I saw you," I said, unpacking my laptop, "you were going to be an actress."

She bit back a laugh. "I was an actress. Two straight-to-video slasher movies. Victim Number Four in the first one, the Unsuspecting Wife in the second."

"Have to start somewhere."

"No nudity limited my options," she said. "I realized it wasn't for me, so I went back to Virginia, finished law school and applied to the Bureau."

"No nudity?" I echoed. "I don't recall you as the shy type."

Her cheeks reddened. "You were an exception. In a lot of ways." She stared at me for a moment, and then said, "I transferred to Quantico a year ago. Here I am."

"Older yet wiser, one assumes."

She neatly turned the tables. "And you? When did you change your name?"

"The day we signed the papers, I came back for a bit. If your last name's Bianco and you call Vegas home, people jump to wrong conclusions," I said as I powered up the computer. "Moved to Houston a while back. I came back this week on vacation."

"Just happened to be here?"

"Pretty much, yes. Ironic, isn't it?"

"Are you married?" she asked, ignoring my comment.

"One broken heart per lifetime is sufficient, thank you."

"Nicholas…"

"I'm sorry, that was out of line," I said. "Ancient history."

Silence hung between us for a moment.

"You've done well," she said. "I'm surprised we haven't crossed paths before."

"It's a big Bureau," I replied, not looking at her. "I've had some luck."

"I'd say better than 'luck,'" she said. "You're famous."

"Damn, I was going for infamous."

"They talk about you around here like you walk on water. Jeff said you're one of the best cyberslingers he's ever known."

"One of?" I repeated. "Can you imagine that?"

She shook her head slowly. "You haven't changed a bit."

I turned to face her. "How about we talk about this over dinner before you go back?"

"Don't waste your breath, Nicholas," she said firmly. "We are not getting back together after all this time."

"Never even occurred to me." Innocence personified. "Dinner. Nothing more."

"We'll see."

I didn't look at her as I connected the secure line to the laptop. "He's hopscotching on their systems and bouncing the signal around on a VWAN."

"In English?"

"Sorry," I said, covering both subjects. "Virtual Wide Area Networks communicate over the same line, but each one is a separate and distinct entity."

"Like that movie last year?" she asked, mentioning a popular film where a glamorously beautiful FBI agent had her life invaded by a serial killer. In the movie, the bad guy controlled her home, car and life via the internet. What I remembered most about that movie was laughing a lot at the technology.

"Sure. Like the BAU has its own G-5 to fly from case to case," I said, referring to a weekly television series where a team of stunningly attractive "profilers" has a private jet at their immediate disposal.

She laughed. "If we leave the office, we practically hitchhike."

"Be nice if life worked the way it does in the movies."

She said nothing for a moment, then, "What are you thinking?"

"Buckingham's and Altair's are a few hundred yards apart," I said, working the keyboard. "The Vesuvius is the point of the triangle. Ask Bristol to work that."

"Why him?"

"He's embarrassed."

"He just became a father," she said. "I think he's reevaluating his career choice." She paused. "You were pretty calm."

"I've seen worse."

"Worse?"

"How long have you been with the BAU?"

"Two years."

"Then you know it can be an ugly world out there."

She didn't reply directly to that. "Anything else?"

"An IV line of coffee would be good."

She smiled. "As I said, you haven't changed one bit. I was going to find some myself. Still take it black?"

"Please."

I saw her put her hand on Bristol's shoulder, lean down and

speak to him. When she walked away, the color was coming back into his face.

I brought up a program that wasn't supposed to exist, and launched it. The tracer lines formed on the screen.

Someone shouted from the other room. The video feed was active again.

Angela sat quietly, the fear in her eyes reaching through the screen. The kidnapper was now wearing a full-head Count Dracula mask.

Good, I thought. He's cocky enough to play with us.

He picked up the microphone again. I got closer to the screen. No wires.

I turned back to the desk, lost in thought.

"What is that?" Beth asked as she set a cup of coffee on the desk, looking at my screen.

"I call it Piranha."

"And it does what?"

"Hunts. Like piranha up a river."

Agent Bristol came into the room, holding a sheet of paper. He handed me a printout. "One of the other guys has been tracing IP addresses and the physical locations," he said.

I took a quick look at it. "Give all this to SAC Keyes," I said to him, handing it back, "and get some agents down there. Contact the network admins of those hotels. We'll need their help. You go with them."

"Me, sir?"

"You. I want someone I can count on ramrodding this."

Bristol looked at me for a moment. "Yes, sir."

"No need to call me *sir*," I said. "I'm not your boss."

"I realize that," he said as he left the room.

His words hung in the air for a moment.

Beth turned to me. "That was nice of you."

I shrugged it off. "He's not the first guy who booted over a photo like that. He won't be the last. The day you stop being sickened is the day to get out."

"I sent it to Quantico to see if they could identify it," she said.

The Justice Department keeps a running database of obscene and violent photographs confiscated over the years. If there was a match, they could solve an old case.

Or they'd be forced to open a new one.

I started yet another program. "He's wireless."

"We know that."

"We also know things most people don't. A wireless device, like a camera or microphone, is a device we can find."

"You can do that?" She sounded like I was telling her there really were invaders from Mars involved in this.

"Connecting via wireless shows up on a scan of said network. He's piggybacking off three we know of. We should be able to isolate this down to a few hundred feet."

She said nothing.

"The problem is," I continued, "I've got to catch him in progress."

"Okay. And?"

"He's rerouting every time." I paused for a moment. "Can we get a screen in here? It would help if we could see it real time."

Beth didn't waste time asking questions, just walked out to arrange it. She came right back. "Five minutes."

"What was in his last message?"

"Bidding is now at three hundred million dollars, traced to a cybercafé in Kabul."

"Better and better."

"Sometimes," she said, "this is a game of patience."

"Sometimes, people die while we're waiting."

She didn't reply.

• • •

Bristol and his team were now within shouting distance of the area we'd identified, waiting for the signal that would send them into action. More than fourteen hours since Jeff had called me.

Just give me one shot, you sick bastard. Just one.

As if he heard me, the screen in the room came to life. Angela looked okay physically, but the fear in her eyes was a tangible thing, so tangible it reached into my chest and squeezed.

It was a Wolfman mask this time.

Hang on, baby, I told her in my mind. *We'll find you. I promise.*

"Pay attention now, people!" he crowed through the voice distorter. "Bidding is now two billion dollars. That's BILLION. Auction is ending shortly, so get your bids in now!"

He rattled on. I tuned him out and frantically smacked keys. I had one good shot at finding him, if that. One.

A flash of light, a flicker, and it was on my screen.

Beth was waiting, encrypted radio in her hand.

"Fremont and Main," I told her. "Close to the Gold Dust Saloon."

She paused. "How solid is that?"

"Ninety-nine point nine." She relayed the information to Bristol.

Jeff came into the room. "Did we get him?"

"I think so." I stood. "Let's go."

"Go where?" Jeff asked.

"There."

They both got quiet. Very quiet.

The authority in Jeff asserted itself. "Nicholas, you can't do th—"

"Don't waste my time." I held up my car keys. "I go with you, or I go on my own. Either way."

Jeff hesitated a moment longer, then called to get a car.

• • •

The Downtown Experience was in full swing.

The after-work crowd was around, heading for the bars and nearby clubs. Tourists gawked and gaped at the flashing neon above them. It was a far cry from what I remembered growing up, but what was not?

Jeff nodded his head as we got out, and Bristol walked over from where he'd been standing, trying to appear relaxed.

"Unless we can do a floor-by-floor search of these buildings, we're screwed." Bristol's frustration was apparent.

I let my eyes roam everywhere and nowhere, drawing in all the information I could. I didn't know what I was looking for, but I'd know it when I saw it. She was here, she had to be.

I just had to find her.

Jeff turned. "Bristol, you're with me. Beth, you and Nicholas look around. Discreetly. We don't want to spook this guy."

Beth linked her arm through mine, instantly turning us into a couple out for a stroll. Her touch went through me like a jolt of electricity. In reflex, I shoved the old memories away and concentrated on the task at hand.

We walked along, pretending to be noticing nothing but each other. There had to be an answer, there had to be.

We walked down one side of the street, crossed at an intersection, then back. All three hotels were within line of sight. I smiled to myself as we walked past where the Sunset Theatre used to be. I'd spent most of my youth in that movie house, watching films so atrocious drive-ins rejected them.

I stopped.

"What?" she asked.

"Do you still smoke?"

"No. Why?"

"So I'm not standing here doing nothing," I said.

Sandwiched between Altair's and Buckingham's, two of the older hotels, was a small alleyway. Off to the side, an almost-hidden doorway to an office building. If you didn't know it was there, you'd never see it. It looked like a remnant from the 1950s, which it probably was. A sign posted read Second Floor Loft Available.

I tried the front door.

It opened.

Beth grabbed my sleeve.

"Nicholas, we can't just barge in there."

"*You* can't." I smiled at her. "I'm not an FBI Agent. Just a private citizen."

"Dammit, Nicholas."

"Just a look-see, I promise."

"Christ, no wonder Jeff warned me about you."

"As if you forgot," I said as I entered the small lobby. Three floors. The first and third floors listed a small law firm and a dentist, respectively. Lights were on in both offices; people were still there.

I headed up the stairs to the empty second floor. Beth started to say something unladylike, then reached under her jacket and drew her service pistol. Her left hand held the encrypted radio she'd brought from the office. "Turn that down," I whispered as I went up the stairs. "If you hear anything, call the cavalry and charge."

I took off my safari jacket and slightly tore my shirt pocket. A couple of pens I'd stuck in there flopped down, held in place by their clips. I wished I had a pocket protector and some ugly eyeglasses, but I was improvising.

The hallway was a little better lighted than I'd hoped, but the point of no return was in the rearview mirror now. I stopped in front of the big steel door on the second floor and knocked.

Knocked again, harder.

There was faint, very faint, shuffling inside.

I whammed the door as hard as I could in an effort to provoke a response. Social Engineering for Dummies 101: make enough noise, human nature will respond.

A voice from inside growled, "Yeah?"

"Frass mublenore, sir, I need vam moments of your time." I deliberately made up nonsense words and slurred my speech, making it impossible to understand.

"Fuck off."

A little girl's life was at stake, and I was betting one hell of a bluff on an empty hand.

"Ah, sir, please. My sobbs tells me I have to get my zumblekoms up. Frashawanna, I won't leak five numblety of your time."

"I said get lost!"

"Sir, if I can treak to you, I'll keep my bojalam," I said, putting a whine in my voice. "Mlease."

Silence.

"Sir?"

More silence.

"Sir?" I tried again, pounding on the door. Enough noise, and anyone in the building would get curious. He couldn't afford curious neighbors.

Come on, I thought, *open the door and send the pain in the ass away. Come on. You're human. Everyone else is stupid, beneath you. You're superior, do it just to get rid of me. Come on, one little click.*

Silence.

I thought I'd blown it. A small panel in the door suddenly slid open, startling me, and a pair of eyes glared out. I tried to look as inoffensive as possible, slouching my shoulders, forcing my stomach out.

The man who opened the door looked average in every possible way. Stare at him for an hour, you couldn't describe him a minute later.

"What?"

I lowered my voice and mumbled more nonsense, fumbling for a moment. "I'm busy," he said.

"I understand that, sir, and I appreciate your time," I said as I tried to see inside without being obvious. "If I could just...."

There was a slipper on the floor. A child's slipper.

With a cartoon tiger on it.

Winnie the Pooh...

And Tigger, too!

Sometimes, the most outrageous gambit pays off.

"I asked you a question," I heard him say. "Who the hell are you?"

My foot lashed out in a heartfelt and sincere effort to blast his testicles through his nostrils. "I'm Van Helsing, Monster Boy!" There was a satisfying *thud* as my foot connected.

Behind me, I heard Beth sprinting up the stairs, barking orders into her radio. The guy landed on his back, in a fetal position.

Checking my conscience for any shred of mercy or compassion, I found none. "Are you here alone?" I asked.

Tears ran down his face as he glared at me. I lifted my foot again. "Are. You. Here. Alone?" I repeated.

He managed to nod in the affirmative. I hoped it hurt.

Beth came charging in, gun drawn, with a glare a blind man could translate as "You *better* be right." She disappeared around a corner, and it got quiet.

The guy tried to get to his feet, both hands cradling himself. I put my foot on top of his hands and pressed to hold him still. He still tried to get up. I leaned down, aimed carefully, and hit him as hard as I could with the heel of my hand between his eyes while my weight came down on his crotch.

He screamed nicely.

A barrage of footsteps sounded up the stairwell, getting closer.

Jeff and half the team blew past me. Bristol stopped and looked down at the man I had pinned with my foot, just as we heard Beth's voice.

"Dear God."

No one in the room moved.

Her footsteps echoed down the hallway toward us.

I didn't realize I was holding my breath until my lungs started cramping.

Beth came back out from wherever she'd been.

In her arms was Angela Frazell.

Alive.

Angela looked at all of us, then at the man being none too gently yanked to his feet and handcuffed. Taking a breath deep enough to make her little chest puff out, she bellowed, "YOU LEAVE ME ALONE!"

Alive and mad as hell.

"He will, honey," Beth said. She carried her out the door and down the stairs to where other agents were waiting.

I waited until I was sure the two of them were gone before I turned back.

"The people you work for murdered three federal agents," I said to the handcuffed man. "You've been taken into custody by federal agents." I paused, my eyes never leaving his. "I'm willing to bet you'll resist arrest along the way."

Bristol took in the disheveled state of the guy, turned his head slightly and winked at me. "Looks like you were forced to defend yourself," he said.

I kept a straight face and replied, "I'm lucky to be alive."

I turned and walked down the stairs.

● ● ●

Jeff was doing a flawless impersonation of a man about to have an aneurysm and coronary occlusion simultaneously over my behavior, but Angela's presence on the return trip made him play nice. I knew I'd hear about it, eventually.

I also knew the Bureau would call me again if they needed to.

In the backseat, Beth was whispering to Angela and soon had her giggling just like a four-year-old should.

Jeff parked, and the three of them headed for the glass doors. I took two steps toward my car before Beth's voice stopped me.

"Nicholas?"

I turned and looked at her. She handed Angela to Jeff and came toward me. Jeff carried Angela through the glass doors and inside.

"I'm sure the president would like to speak to you," she said.

"Sorry, Beth. Not my kind of thing."

She looked at me closely. "This is—"

"I was never here," I said, interrupting her. "'Supervisory Special Agents Elizabeth Canton and R. P. Bristol, under the direction of Special Agent in Charge Jefferson Keyes V, handled this extremely delicate matter and achieved a safe resolution.'"

"You sound like a press conference."

"Probably won't *be* a press conference. This will be classified beyond words."

She thought that over, nodding.

"You'll have to be debriefed."

"More like de-boxered, but whichever you'd prefer."

The red bloomed in her cheeks.

"When do you go back to Quantico?" I asked.

She didn't take her eyes from mine as she considered her answer. "Settling all of this? A week, maybe ten days," she said.

"What a coincidence," I said. "That's how long I'll be in town."

She glanced around the garage. We were alone.

She wrapped her hands in my jacket lapels and pulled me close. Next thing I knew, her kiss was long and insistent.

"Do you have any idea how sexy you are when you save the world?" she asked when she pulled back, a bit out of breath.

I waited until my vision refocused before I answered her. "I didn't save the world. Just one little girl."

"To-may-to, to-mah-to," she said.

"Now then," I asked, coughing slightly to clear my throat. "About that dinner?"

"What's the old saying?" she asked, pressing closer. "Why don't we talk about it over breakfast?"

She ran her fingers under my collar while I pretended to consider it.

"You FBI agents are so evasive," I said.

"Does that bother you?" Her fingers began to creep into my hair.

"Not a bit," I replied. "But I thought we weren't getting back together."

Her fingers climbed higher. "Persuade me."

I was doing an admirable job of keeping my voice level. "How do I do that?"

"Oh," she said with a mischievous look in her eyes. "I'm sure I'll get the thrust of your argument...."

NIGHT HEAT

LAURA GRIFFIN

*For as long as there have been myths, rescue has
been a favorite theme. The knights these days just
wear a different type of armor. —SB*

Manila, The Philippines
2200 hours

Petty Officer Mike Dietz peered through the high-powered binoculars and knew there was a high probability that the woman in the low-cut black cocktail dress was going to die.

Unless he did something soon.

That is, unless Mike and his *team* did something soon. Barely an hour ago, the eight-man squad of Navy SEALs had been summoned away from a practice op in Manila Bay for an all-too-real rescue mission at the American ambassador's house. Still damp with salt water, the SEALs had arrived, geared up and reviewed their orders. Now they were ready to kick some ass. But while a bunch of bureaucrats debated exactly how and when that ass would be kicked, Mike and his teammates were left to simmer in the hot Manila night with their fingers itching on the triggers of their M-4s.

"What's the word, Dietz?"

Mike turned to look at Lieutenant Junior Grade Derek Vaughn, who was set up on the balcony beside him with a sniper rifle. The house behind the ambassador's had become a makeshift command post for tonight's operation.

"Still waiting on Quinn," Mike said, referring to their commanding officer, who was at this moment on the phone with Washington.

It was midmorning right now in D.C. and the guys in charge were probably seated around a conference table, sipping coffee and debating options while a young American woman's lifeblood drained out of her.

Mike gritted his teeth as he gazed through the binocs again. Jill Whitfield was pale, slender and had long dark hair that fanned out beneath her on the cobblestone patio. Since the initial attack, she'd been playing possum—and doing a damn good job of it—while feeding information to Mike's team through a cell phone hidden somewhere on her body. Smart girl, she'd realized that in the wake of the siege, the local embassy would be flooded with phone calls, so she'd directed her SOS to the American embassy in Bangkok, which had verified her identity and patched her through to Mike's commanding officer. She'd been providing info ever since, all the while surrounded by dead bodies and live terrorists.

And these tangos weren't the warm fuzzy kind. According to the team's latest intel, they were ACB, or Asian Crescent Brotherhood—a ruthless batch of extremists that made al Qaeda look like a glee club. They operated out of the Southern Philippine island of Mindanao, where just last month they'd captured and beheaded no fewer than thirty missionaries who'd wandered too close to one of their training camps. The missionaries' bodies—only—had been dumped on the outskirts of the island's largest city, and every female among them showed signs of brutal sexual assault.

The radio in Mike's ear crackled to life.

"Witness confirms four tangos, I repeat, *four* tangos, now stationed on the north patio door."

Mike shifted the binoculars until he saw the terrorists. Like the others, these guys were armed with AK-47s, Tokarev pistols and hand grenades.

Mike was ready to move. This was just the sort mission the SEALs of Alpha Squad had trained for: neutralize a band of heavily armed terrorists, rescue civilian hostages and defuse any bombs reportedly on the premises. No problem—it was textbook. But the chances of this op having a textbook outcome had been diminished by the fact that a number of those hostages—possibly including the ambassador himself—were already dead, along with the four armed marines who had been guarding the compound.

Sweat trickled into Mike's eyes, but he blinked it away. He kept his breathing even, his heart rate steady. But despite his cool demeanor, every muscle in his body itched to leap down from his observation post, scale the fence, and get Jill and every other civilian in there out of harm's way.

Mike studied her again through the binoculars. Jill Whitfield worked at the embassy as the ambassador's scheduler and had been one of two dozen guests at his poolside soiree. Out on that patio, she was getting paler by the minute. The terrorist patrolling the backyard had passed by her three times now, and evidently the puddle of blood under her body had convinced him she was dead or at least neutralized—and he couldn't be far from wrong. By the size of that puddle, Mike knew Jill probably needed a blood transfusion to have any hope of surviving.

Mike wanted to go in now. *Ahora.* But he wasn't in charge of the plan here, which involved waiting until 0200 hours, at which point Alpha Squad would slip into the compound through a hidden side gate and take the enemy by surprise.

But that was nearly four hours away. Jill didn't have four hours. She might not have four minutes.

And yet her lips were moving. Despite whatever injuries she had, she continued to whisper into that phone. Was it hidden in her bra?

Under her hair? Mike didn't know. But he *did* know that if the terrorists figured out what she was doing, she was dead. Period. And she had to know that. Mike had seen a lot in his twenty-eight years, and not much impressed him. But this woman risking her life to get his team intel sure as hell did.

"Okay, listen up. New plan."

As his CO's voice came over the radio again, Mike traded looks with Vaughn. The sniper could see Jill through his rifle scope, and Mike could tell he was impatient, too.

"Thanks to Harden, we've got the camera up and running," the commander said, referring to the smallest member of their team, who possessed the highly useful ability to slip through enemy lines and install surveillance equipment. "We've got six confirmed tangos in the backyard and another four in the house, all huddled around the so-called 'secret' entrance to the ambassador's panic room. We're guessing at least one to two armed tangos inside the room itself—" static interrupted the words "—and civilian guests. We've also got eight confirmed dead."

Eight dead. Same as an hour ago. Mike watched Jill's motionless body. He desperately hoped she'd stay alive long enough for him to get her out of there.

"So that's twenty-one friendlies, including the ambassador and his wounded staffer, and at least twelve enemy targets. I just got off the phone with Washington, and they've given us the green light. That's the good news. Here's the bad."

Mike's hand tightened on his weapon.

"Some of these guys are wearing bomb vests," Quinn said. "We've confirmed two so far. The tango in with the ambassador is said to be wearing one."

Shit, this was a suicide mission, just as they'd feared. Not good for the ambassador. And definitely not good for Jill.

"You know the plan," the commander said. "Now let's get this done."

• • •

Jane had never paid much attention to the smell of blood before, but right now it was all she could think of. It had pooled beneath her on the pavement. It had dried in her hair. The stench of it filled her nostrils and attracted flies that swirled around her with their ominous buzz.

Jane blocked out sound and smell and thought instead about her mouth. She longed to lick her lips. She longed to inch herself over to the pool and suck down about a gallon of water. But she knew she couldn't move. She couldn't bat an eyelash. One twitch while any of those men was watching and she'd be dead.

Jane's heart pounded at the thought, but not nearly as hard as it had pounded during the initial attack. There had been a loud *bang*—like a thunderclap—accompanied by a burst of smoke. Next thing she knew, she was on her stomach beside the pool with a god-damn bullet in her leg. She'd started to push herself off the ground, but then everyone around her had gone down in a hail of machine-gun fire, and she'd made an instant decision that her best chance of survival lay in pretending to be dead.

She wasn't sure how much longer she'd be pretending.

The backs of Jane's eyes stung with tears, but she willed them away. After withstanding an hour of agony, how pathetic would it be if she blew her own cover with some stupid tears?

Buck up, Janey!

She thought of her brother Josh's gruff impersonation of their grandfather's voice. Their granddad had been a Green Beret and had admonished them from an early age that crying was for girls. Forget that Jane *was* a girl—he'd made it clear tears wouldn't be tolerated, no matter what the injury or how many stitches it entailed.

Stitches. If only it were that minor. Jane was pretty sure she needed surgery for this one. Her leg burned from the bullet wound. But oddly, even more painful was the gash in her arm from where she'd fallen on a shard of china. At the time of the first explosion, Jane had been holding a plate piled with fancy hors d'oeuvres that the ambassador's chef had adorned with little American-flag toothpicks. She'd been nibbling on a bite-size sausage when she'd heard a commotion and glanced over her shoulder as the first grenade exploded. At least, she'd thought it was a grenade. Looking back now, she was pretty sure it had been a flash-bang—an explosive designed to stun, not kill. It was one of the few indicators Jane had that her captors didn't intend to kill everyone here, and she was clinging to it desperately. These terrorists wanted at least some live hostages—such as the ambassador, who was holed up with them now in the vaultlike room designated for emergencies.

The tropical heat seemed to press down on her as she lay there, motionless. A bead of sweat rolled down her forehead. She prayed the tangos wouldn't see it. To take her mind off the pain in her thigh, she penned a postcard to her brother in her head: *Weather's here. Wish you were beautiful.* It was an inside joke that would bring a smile to his face. And she'd sign it, *I love you. –Janey.* The last part was uncharacteristically sappy, but it needed to be said because if Jane didn't make it out of here alive, Josh would blame himself. Both of them knew that Jane was here, indirectly, because of him. If not for her older brother's example, she might be married right now, possibly even a mom, instead of the globe-trotting adrenaline junkie she'd been since her twenty-fifth birthday. Jane needed Josh to know she didn't blame him—she loved him. And she didn't regret for a minute following in his footsteps, even if doing so ended up getting her killed.

That the best you got, J? Her brother's voice echoed through her head, thick with contempt. *You mean to tell me that's it?*

No, that wasn't it. She felt dizzy and nauseated, but she still had some fight left in her.

Boots clomped on the other side of the patio. She heard the rapid-fire exchange of Bisaya, the language of the southern islands. She knew the dialect well, having studied it for years now, just as she knew what all their jargon meant. These guys were Asian Crescent Brotherhood. She'd been following the group's movements for months and had been one of the first agents to get word that they were gearing up for a "big event." At the time she'd intercepted this important bit of intel, Jane had no idea the "event" in question might directly involve her.

If, in fact, it did. Was storming the ambassador's residence their main play, or just their opening act?

Jane needed to find out. There were some other things she needed to do, too, and she had to keep her senses sharp. No giving in to fatigue. Or fear. Or that numb, tingly feeling that threatened to overtake her...

Buck up, Janey!

She forced herself awake. She listened to the footsteps fade and risked opening her eyes, just slightly. The ambassador's swank reception had started at dusk, but it was dark now except for the tiki torches surrounding the pool. They'd seemed so festive earlier when she'd been chatting with other expats and sipping on her rum and Coke. Jane's gaze shifted to the skirt of her dress, which she'd bought just a few weeks ago. At five-nine, Jane towered over all of the women in this country—along with most of the men— and she'd had to go to a European store in Hong Kong just to find something in her size. It had cost half a month's pay, but she'd rationalized it as a well-earned splurge after a grueling two-year tour that had almost come to an end. Her official stint as the ambassador's "travel liaison" ended tomorrow.

If she lived that long.

More boots on the concrete. They made the circle around the pool. They moved behind her, paused. Jane held her breath.

And then the world exploded.

● ● ●

Pop! Pop! Pop!

A triple burst of explosives accompanied Mike and his team as they poured through the gate.

Pop! Pop!

More strategically placed stun grenades went off on opposite sides of the pool, throwing the scene into chaos. To the enemy, it would seem as though they were being attacked from all sides and by an army, rather than an eight-man team.

The terrorists at the patio door, who'd been clustered there stupidly for twenty minutes, went down in the first rash of gunfire. Another appeared at the glass and was picked off by a perfectly placed shot from Vaughn's rifle fifty yards away.

Spurred into action by all the commotion, Jill Whitfield started to sit up and caught the attention of a tango inside the house, who opened fire with his machine gun. She tried to lunge away, and Mike threw himself on top of her, pressing her into the concrete.

"Stay down!"

He looked over his shoulder in time to see his teammates eliminate the shooters. Mike jumped to his feet and grabbed Jill by the arm, pulling her behind a giant stone planter on the far end of the pool. She stared up at him with wide, startled eyes as he yanked out his field kit and immediately got to work on her bullet wound.

"Are you Quinn?" she asked, and the sound of her voice brought a punch of relief.

"I'm one of his men—Petty Officer Mike Dietz, U.S. Navy." He took a moment to search her face. Porcelain skin, deep brown eyes. She was even prettier up close.

Mike glanced over his shoulder. He needed to be inside, helping rescue the ambassador and the other civilians, but he couldn't leave this girl out here like a sitting duck. They didn't need her getting snapped up as a bargaining tool by some terrorist. He looked back at her. Sweat beaded on her upper lip and her pupils were dilated.

"I'm Jill Whitfield. My leg—"

"I know." Mike pressed a ready-made bandage over the wound, and she yelped with pain. "Sorry, gotta get this on you. You feel faint, ma'am? You've lost a lot of blood."

She blinked up at him, maybe not understanding the question.

"This is my last day," she said as he secured the bandage. "I'm supposed to be on the beach in Cebu tomorrow, sipping mai tais." She smiled slightly, and he decided she was getting loopy from blood loss.

"What'd you do to your arm?" he asked. Her slender white arm was streaked with red, and he turned it over to reveal a deep gash just beneath her elbow.

"China," she said breathlessly. "Think I got some of the official State Department dinnerware in there."

Mike glanced to his right at the destroyed buffet table, where food and dinner plates had crashed to the ground.

"Dietz! We need you!" a voice barked into his radio.

Shit. Mike handed her a bandage. "Think you can do your arm?"

She mumbled something he couldn't hear. Mike's gaze dropped to her cleavage and he had the answer to that question about the phone. A little silver cell phone poked up from the black lace of her bra.

"Dietz!"

"Don't move," he said. "I'll be back. Put that bandage on and keep your head down."

"Wait!" She grabbed his hand, and the panic in her eyes made him want to ignore the rest of his mission.

"I'll be back," he repeated. "I promise."

She squeezed his hand and nodded at his side. "Can you spare that nine?"

Mike glanced down, surprised. She wanted his nine-mil? Damn, she was terrified, and understandably so. He jerked the gun from the holster and wrapped her hand around the grip. "You ever shot a pistol before?"

A faint smile. "I grew up in West Texas."

Well, okay then. He braced his hand on her pretty bare shoulder. "Don't shoot anyone in jungle camos, all right? They're the good guys. I'll be back to get you in two, maybe three minutes tops."

She nodded, and Mike's heart twisted as he grabbed his machine gun and stood up to leave her.

"Be careful," she said.

He sprinted inside, where he found several of his teammates clustered around the door to the panic room.

"Locked," one of them said.

"Where's Jones?" Mike asked.

"Roof, just like we planned."

Mike eyed the carnage around him. He counted ten dead tangos, which meant one to two in the panic room with the ambassador. One of his teammates was hunched over a body, quickly defusing the bomb vest. Good news, it hadn't been rigged to detonate when the wearer was killed. Bad news, there was one more vest unaccounted for.

"Where's everyone else?" Mike asked.

"We're trying to find out."

"Yo, we got eyes!" one of his teammates called from down the hall.

Mike rushed to the security room, where Petty Officer Greg Baynes had managed to restore video surveillance.

"Shit, only two in the panic room," Mike said, surveying the grainy video image. "Ambassador and a guard. Looks like he has a vest on."

"Here we go! Hostages!"

Another TV monitor came to life, showing a blurry black-and-white view of what looked like a utility room, where men and women in party attire were squeezed in like sardines.

"Utility room, northwest corner," Mike said, remembering the floor plan. "I'm on it. And we got orders to save this one for inter-rogation."

"I'm with you," Baynes announced. Then to the others: "You two wait for Jones to blow the panic room from up top, help get the ambassador out of there."

There was a trapdoor on the ceiling, and the plan was to blow the lock with C4, then quickly take out the tango and rescue the ambassador. It was a risky plan, but Mike knew the men on the job were up for it.

"Let's go." Mike rushed for the utility room, an image of Jill Whitfield's frightened brown eyes still stuck in his mind. They reached a corner, and Mike pushed away the image. Time to con-centrate.

He signaled Baynes, who was behind him. Three, two, one. Mike burst around the corner and dropped the guard with a well-placed shot to the hands. His weapon clattered to the floor, and then he fell on top of it, howling in pain. Baynes shot him with a Taser until he was unconscious and quickly cuffed his injured arms behind him.

Somewhere above them, a loud pop. A burst of machine-gun fire.

"Tango down," Mike said into his radio, then pounded on the door. "U.S. Navy! Stand back!" With a sharp kick, he popped the door open. A crowd of terrified-looking dinner guests stared back at him.

Mike turned to Baynes. "You okay to lead them out? I need to get the civilian on the patio."

"Go."

Mike sprinted back through the house, which now smelled of acrid smoke from all the flash-bangs. He rushed through the back door out to the pool—

She was gone.

Mike stared at the puddle of blood. He followed the streaks of it leading behind the concrete planter. A cold feeling of dread gripped him as his gaze followed the red trail from the patio inside the house.

Did someone have her? Had they missed a terrorist? Mike darted down the hallway, reviewing the floor plan in his head. This was the bedroom wing of the residence. Two bedrooms, an office, then the master suite.

Mike stopped short beside the office door, where he heard fingertips on a keyboard. He readied his weapon and peered around the corner....

And discovered Jill seated at a computer, frantically typing an email. She whirled around and reached for his pistol. "God, you scared me." She put the Sig back on the desk and clutched a bloody hand to her throat. "I thought you were one of them."

"If I was you'd be dead right now." He crossed the room in two strides. "Come on. We need to get you to a hospital."

"I just have to get this message out."

She turned back to the computer, where she was sending something that looked like a full page of numbers. An encrypted file.

"You need medical attention."

"I need to get this message out. This computer's been compromised."

Mike blinked down at her. This was no embassy "staffer." He wanted to ask her who the hell she was, but there wasn't time.

Pop!

They glanced up in unison as something exploded on the roof.

"That's us, breaking into the panic room," Mike said. "Last terrorist should be neutralized by now."

A staccato of gunshots. Mike's radio came to life again.

"Twelve tangos down." It was his teammate in the security room. "I repeat—shit, we missed one! I can see him on video screen. He's in a room! Dammit, where is he? He's got a vest on!"

"Clear the house!" the commander's voice cut in. "Get the hostages out! Go, go, go!"

Mike yanked Jill out of the chair.

"Wait!" She reached for the mouse and clicked something just before he lifted her off her feet and threw her over his shoulder in a fireman's carry. She squealed and pounded on his back as he raced through the door and down the hallway, darting his gaze around for the missing terrorist.

"I wasn't finished!" she protested, but he ignored her, propelled forward by the certainty this compound was about to get blown to bits by some fanatic with a death wish. Mike found himself in a foyer and rushed to the double front doors. Locked, of course.

"Hold on!" He gripped the backs of Jill's thighs against his chest as he gave a powerful kick. The doors burst open. He charged through them. He saw a yard, a gate, a flash of sirens. He heard the *whump-whump* of an approaching chopper.

Mike raced for the gate. A great boom shook the earth and hurled him to his knees.

Cebu Island, The Philippines
One week later

Jane lay on the hot white sand, letting the waves and the rum soothe away her aches and pains. Her cheeks stung from the sun, but she didn't care. In fact, she felt grateful. A touch of sunburn only confirmed that she was alive, when just days ago she'd almost lost her life. Twice. Make that three times, if she counted being crushed by two-hundred-pounds of hardened Navy SEAL, as Mike Dietz had fallen on top of her to shield her from the blast. The weight of him on her and his hands on her face, her neck, her body, making sure she was okay—it was a memory that had helped her through her hospital stay. She had a feeling it was a memory that would help her through more rough moments for years to come.

Jane reached for her drink and took a long gulp. The fruity sweetness cooled her throat as she thought about Mike. Didn't it figure that after years of constant work and no personal life, she'd meet a man who was just as much of a globe-trotting adrenaline junkie as she was? They didn't have a chance together, which was why, when she'd collected her personal items at the hospital and discovered a number programmed into her cell phone alongside the words *Call Mike,* she'd smiled at the irony—just before pressing Delete. And then she'd blinked back a tear of regret, because her granddad was right and crying was for girls.

Jane's skin cooled abruptly as a shadow fell over her. She opened her eyes to see an enormous man blocking out the sun. She shoved her sunglasses to the top of her head and gazed up at him.

"Hey," she said.

"Hey."

"What are you doing here?"

"Heard they have good mai tais."

He sat down beside her in the sand, and she turned to look at him. He wore a T-shirt, board shorts and flip-flops, and he looked like a carefree young American kicking around the islands, just as she did.

His gaze skimmed over her bruised-up body and settled on the bandage wrapped around her thigh.

"Can you get it wet?" he asked, and she noticed his eyes were the same color as the sea behind him.

"Not yet. But I can wade up to my knees."

His attention moved over her body again, and she started to get self-conscious.

"I look like hell, I know."

He met her gaze. "That's not what I was thinking."

She smiled and sat up, resting her arms on her knees.

"I've got some leave," he said casually, looking out at the water. "Thought I'd try and meet a beautiful woman." He turned to face her and held out a hand. "I'm Petty Officer Mike Dietz, U.S. Navy."

She hesitated a second before taking his hand. She didn't do this very often. "Special Agent Jane Hollister, CIA."

"Jane, huh?"

"Yep."

He pulled her hand closer and kissed the back of her knuckles, where she had a nasty scrape. She smiled as something warm and happy flooded through her.

"And you're CIA?"

"Yep."

He smiled back at her. "Now that, I believe."

B.A.D. MISSION
SHERRILYN KENYON

I knew I was going to enjoy this story when, on page one, the protagonist asks, "Who needs killin'?" —SB

There were only two reasons the man on that Ducati motorcycle had just rolled up Sam Garrett's gravel driveway this morning—he wanted Sam to interrogate or terminate a target.

Or door number three...both.

Sam didn't do extractions.

He lifted a rag off the engine of his '78 IROC Camaro and wiped his hands. Had to be serious for Joe Q. Public, Director of Bureau of American Defense, to ride all the way from Nashville to South Texas through a scorching heat wave.

And after Sam had retired his black ops equipment two months ago.

He and Joe had reached an agreement. He'd thought.

Joe peeled out of his dusty riding suit, dropped his helmet over a mirror on his bike and walked over to Sam. He swiped a hand over brown hair slicked back in a ponytail. "Tell me again why you live fifty miles from civilization?"

"Don't like salesmen...or surprises." But Sam had known who was coming up his drive the minute Joe's bike tripped a security beam. Sam pulled two beers from an ice chest next to his boots and handed one to Joe. "Who needs killin'?"

The most powerful man in B.A.D., an intelligence agency the world knew nothing about, opened his beer and downed a long slug. Joe let out a sigh only a cold brew could earn. His gray T-shirt and jeans were soaked with perspiration.

Joe's deep voice resonated with quiet power. "Not a killing, yet. An interrogation and possible termination."

That's one thing Sam and Joe had in common. Get to the point. Sam had learned long ago that Joe had a reason for everything he did, like who he sent on a specific mission. "They cut off your phone service, or you just like ridin' in full gear when it's hotter 'n hell?"

Joe shrugged. "Couldn't do this over the phone. Had to know if you'd have a problem interrogating—or terminating—someone aligned with the Fratelli de il Sovrano if—"

"The Fratelli? Hell, no…if I was still active, which I'm not." Sam ignored the itch to take down someone allied with the number-one enemy of the United States. The whole damned world. A secret group with more money than five billionaires combined and plans to destroy this country so they can create a New World Order.

Give me a break. Call a snake by his name. Just a damn bunch of dangerous terrorists.

"You didn't let me finish," Joe continued.

"That's because I'm not interested. We had a deal."

Joe nodded. "If you still want to pass when I'm done, I'll put Retter on it, but the target is your ex."

Sam chuckled with wry humor. "Not a problem. Tell Retter to have at it. I don't have an ex-anyone. Never been married. You know that."

After another swig of beer, Joe wiped his mouth with the back of his hand. "Ex-girlfriend."

"None of those, either." The women in Sam's life had come and gone faster than days in a week, which suited him just fine. He'd tried to settle down once right after high school with Danielle, but she'd had her sights set on bright lights and a corporate life. He wore ragged Levi's and she wore the latest Dior...from what he'd heard. Hadn't seen her since...

Joe shook Sam out of the past with his next statement. "Our file shows that you had a relationship with this woman."

What the fuck? Sam didn't blink, thinking. Where was Joe going with this? "If you mean I slept with some female who turned out to be a skank traitor, I didn't know it and I assure you she didn't know who I was or what I did." Sam maintained his slouch against his black car while every muscle along his back locked tight at the insinuation. He asked softly, "You trying to accuse me of something, Joe?"

"Hell, no. You were still in Colton, Texas, when you dated Danielle Burton."

Sam stood away from the car. Danielle a traitor? Absurd. "Your intel's faulty. You got the wrong woman." The Danielle he'd known was the best thing to ever come out of that spit-in-the-road town they'd grown up in.

She was a damn genius. Went to fucking MIT.

Joe gave another halfhearted shrug. "So you're still not interested?"

Sam didn't rile easily, but sending Retter after Danielle could do it. "This is bullshit. That girl's as much a traitor and working with the Fratelli as I am an astronaut." He hated airplanes.

"That girl's twenty-eight, went to MIT on a full academic scholarship and—"

"Is in the aerospace program," Sam finished for him. So Joe did have the right woman. Didn't mean she'd sold out her country. "She had two brothers killed in the military and a grandfather who was a decorated general before he died. She works to protect this country, Joe." Least that's what Sam believed from the tabs he'd kept on her over the past ten years.

What guy in his line of work hadn't checked up on an old flame?

"I read her file." Joe sounded resigned to a miserable task. "Her R & D in that field is how she hit our radar."

"Who dropped the dime on her?" Sam had all kinds of free time now that he was out of the business. Enough time to visit the person trying to smear Danielle's good name.

"I wouldn't be here if the intel hadn't come straight from our Fratelli informant."

Few things could take Sam's breath like hearing those words.

B.A.D.'s informant inside the Fratelli was exceptional and her information had never been wrong. She was some woman known by only one of their agents who constantly put her own safety at risk to sneak information to B.A.D. She'd prevented the Fratelli from killing thousands of innocent citizens more than once.

Nothing else could more thoroughly condemn a person than a warning from that informant.

Even Sam had to consider the unimaginable at this point.

"Danielle resigned from Cybertine Aeronautics two days ago. Our informant said Zydus Engineering has been courting Danielle quietly over the past month. They offered to buy a weapon design from her and she finally agreed. Zydus is a front for a Fratelli operation suspected of stealing U.S. weapons technology. We've had our ears to the ground on Zydus for a while and this is the first real break we've had. But her deal with them is far worse than selling standard weapons technology. She's giving them plans for a satellite-directed laser weapon."

Sam snorted. "If that's the case, Danielle's not just a traitor but a scam artist, too. There're plenty of satellite laser designs, but nobody's come up with a way to power the damn things." The Danielle he'd known had been a sexy, straight-as-an-arrow egghead he'd fallen for back when they'd been study partners.

"Rumors surfaced in Cybertine Aeronautics over the past month that she'd designed a compact laser weapon and a supportable power source. Our informant has proof that Zydus and Danielle reached an agreement."

Sam considered several possible scenarios and pointed out, "Selling plans to another company this way is unethical, and possibly illegal, but not necessarily treason if Zydus is building the weapon for the U.S."

"True, but according to our informant, the Fratelli will construct and launch this weapon in Russia. Danielle will be paid by funds wired to an offshore account."

A sick ball of disappointment fisted in Sam's stomach as he waited for the rest.

"Danielle is presenting her design to Zydus tomorrow at 9:00 a.m. and, as a show of good faith, she's handing over a component that's a key piece of the designs. I need Danielle coerced into taking a flawed set of plans into that meeting with Zydus and to wire her so you can listen in. And you've got to tag that component with a transmitter."

"You think she's going to hand over a phony design knowing the people she just screwed will come for blood the minute they figure out they were scammed?"

"She might as well. The Fratelli intends to fly the plans and component to Russia the minute that meeting is over."

Sam had always been fast at adding two and two. "They plan to kill Danielle after the meeting."

"That's why you—or Retter—may not have to terminate this target."

Which was how Sam ended up moving silently through the hall-way of Danielle's hoity-toity hotel in Salt Lake City two hours before her meeting. Zydus headquarters was five miles away in an eight-story building and the Fratelli probably had Danielle's hotel room under surveillance. Fratelli security would be watching for someone who looked like an operative entering the hotel this evening. Sam doubted they'd notice a man in jeans, an oversize blue Western-cut shirt stuffed to give him a gut and a weathered Stetson that blended in with all the other cowboys running around Utah. After reaching his room, he'd changed his boots to soft-soled shoes and swapped the Western shirt for a black T-shirt.

Would Danielle even recognize him?

What had happened to the woman he'd known?

One way or another, he was getting answers out of her tonight. Joe had shown him damning proof.

Upon reaching her suite, Sam breached the door too easily, which sent unease slithering along his neck. The only security had been the hotel's top-of-the-line key-card protection. Ambient moonlight filtered through window sheers into the living area.

He paused, listening in case she had someone in the bedroom with her.

Wouldn't that just suck? It'd been ages since he'd talked to her, but that didn't mean he wanted to see her naked with another man.

Once he'd reconned the living room and ruled out listening devices, he crept into the bedroom.

He'd been prepared to contain her once he'd determined she was alone.

He hadn't been prepared for Danielle sleeping naked except for panties.

She'd curled up on top of the covers, lush curves turned toward him with one arm draped over her breasts. The room smelled soft and inviting.

Hesitation could mean death in covert situations, but Sam had lost the ability to move. Danielle sure as hell wasn't a girl anymore.

Not with that body. Tousled auburn hair fell across her shoulders. Same pert little nose she'd turn up at off-color jokes, same soft lips that had driven him crazy, but the skinny legs she'd used to peddle an old bicycle around town had shaped up nicely.

She made a noise that shook him out of his stupor.

Sam moved to the bed, extending a hand to cover her mouth....

The hand Danielle had tucked beneath her pillow lashed out.

With a six-inch knife blade aimed at his balls.

He jumped back.

She came alive, snatching up a brass lamp she threw at him.

Sam dodged the lamp and rushed her, grabbing her knife arm and slamming her facedown on the bed with him on top.

She kicked and yelled, "Let me go!"

He had an iron lock on the wrist of her knife hand but she was jabbing him with the other elbow. "Stop it or I'll have to hurt you."

"Like that isn't the point of this," she snapped and started to scream, "Hel—"

He finally got his hand over her mouth, shutting her up. "Settle down, dammit. I'm Sam Garrett."

Her kicking feet lost power and dropped. She was breathing hard against his fingers. The minute she lowered her guard, he slid his hand from her mouth to her throat.

She asked, "What are you—"

He applied pressure to an artery in her throat, cutting off her words. She bucked and fought him...then went limp.

He could use limp right now. For years, he'd dreamed about her naked in bed with him, but not like this.

• • •

Danielle stared at the man sitting across from her. Sam Garrett.

This couldn't be Sam. Not the one she'd once loved. Well, it could be since he had wolf-gray eyes like Sam's and he had sand-colored hair like Sam's and a beefed-up version of Sam's muscular build.

"Are you listening to me, Danielle?" Sam asked.

"Hard not to since I can't cover my ears." She gave a pointed look at the zip ties he'd used to bind her to an armchair. The fact that he'd wrapped washcloths around her wrists first didn't earn him any credit or that he'd dressed her in a T-shirt and jogging pants.

He'd broken in and overpowered her, too.

"You're in serious trouble."

She lunged and fell back. "I'm in serious trouble. You're the one committing a crime."

He scratched his ear the same way her Sam used to do. "We know about the deal you cut to sell the laser weapon and power source to Zydus."

Disappointment flooded through her. "So you're here to get the plans for your people."

He gave her a wary look. "That's right."

She made a sound of disgust. "What happened to you, Sam? You're the last person I expected to go bad."

"Me? I'm not the criminal."

"You break in here to steal the laser plans for a third party and that doesn't make you a criminal? Then what are you?" Besides the man who just crushed memories she'd held close to her heart for years.

"Let's back up. I'm not here to sell plans to a third party. I'm here to prevent that weapon from ending up in the wrong hands."

She considered the possibility that she might have made a tactical error in planning for today's meeting. "Who do you work for? The government?"

"In a way. All I can tell you is that I'm with a covert intelligence agency that supports U.S. national security."

"And I'm supposed to just believe you? Got any ID, a badge, something?"

"You're smarter than that, Danielle. You really think undercover operatives walk around with ID?"

"CIA can't operate on U.S. soil and FBI—"

He cut her off. "We're not an alphabet agency. Think of us as Operatives Without Borders. All that matters is that my agency does have the jurisdiction to be here and an obligation to hand you over to the authorities, who will bury you so deep in the prison system you'll disappear forever."

Her brain stalled at his harsh warning and skidded out of control at the part about going to prison. She wouldn't have agreed to be the front person for this meeting tomorrow if getting arrested had been on the table. But she still wasn't sold. "If that's the case, why haven't you arrested me already?"

"Because we need you to follow through with meeting Zydus."

Now she was thoroughly confused. "You want me to give the plans to them?"

"Not exactly. I'll explain everything in a minute, but first I want some answers."

The quiet sincerity in his voice reached inside her to brush against her heart. Of all the times over the years she'd missed him, this week had been the worst. A few men had come and gone in her life, but none like Sam. He was the one person she had wished to have in her corner this nerve-racking week. Her best friend and lover at one time who would have understood why she had to take this risk. "What do you want to know?"

• • •

"Why are you doing this? What happened to you?" Sam asked Danielle, words struggling past the misery clogging his throat. She hadn't even tried to deny her complicity. "Why would you sell a weapon to terrorists?"

"Whoa, buddy." Her blue eyes rounded in surprise. "You think… you think… I can't believe…" She balled her fingers into fists. "You dog! You think I'd sell weapons technology to a terrorist? Me? Or is this some game you're still playing to get these plans?"

He wanted to believe her, but couldn't risk making a mistake, not with so many lives at stake. "Why were you selling plans you developed at Cybertine to Zydus? That's still a criminal offense, especially with Cybertine having a defense contract."

She didn't respond except to continue looking at him as if he'd destroyed something precious to her.

"It's time to come clean, Danielle."

Her chest moved with a deep breath. She swallowed and her eyes were shiny. Ah, hell. She'd never been one for tears except when she'd lost her brothers and cried on Sam's shoulder. Both times. Was she in deeper trouble than he imagined?

She finally spoke in a low voice hoarse with emotion. "You know me. You know how much I've lost in defense of this country. How can you believe I would do anything to help terrorists?"

How was it that she was the one tied up, but he was the one who felt guilty as hell? Or had she become a damned good actress over the years? "I'm still waitin' to hear your side."

"I'm not selling secrets. I'm here to catch the person who is stealing our research."

That's the kind of lie he would tell if he were in her shoes. Sam studied her every move, facial expression, sound of her voice, trying to determine if she was feeding him fiction or the truth. The first thing you learn as an operative is that everyone lies.

His heart argued for Danielle, but he trusted his gut when it came to decisions.

She raised hurt eyes to meet his. "My team is in charge of R & D for a laser power source, but only for the U.S."

"We have proof *you* are selling the plans yourself, not your team."

"You want to hear this or not?"

He'd forgotten her cute snippy side when she was interrupted while arguing a point. "Go on."

"We've been hunting a leak at Cybertine for a while. I came up with the idea about letting a rumor on my power design slip out. When Zydus contacted me with specific details I knew it had to be someone on my team. My boss and I agreed to keep all this between us until it's time to call the FBI. I agreed to meet with Zydus in person when they said their contact inside Cybertine would join us."

She made it sound so real. Sam hit the crossroad moment of believe-her-or-not. "What exactly is supposed to happen at today's meeting?"

"I'll give a PowerPoint presentation on the laser weapon and power source designs. Plus I brought them a component the size of a smartphone that they think is an important part of the prototype."

"Is that component real?"

"Yes, but no one will be able to construct a laser power source with it."

Believing too easily was dangerous. "Why not?"

"Because I left enough out of the plans that they'd need me to build the actual product."

That's when the possibility she was telling him the truth sank in. "You came here to act as bait?"

"Pretty much." She shrugged.

He went to his feet. "Are you crazy? Don't you realize what would have happened when they found out you sold them phony goods?"

She gave him a look that suggested he was simpleminded. "Their engineers will need a day or two to figure out the flaw. The minute I get out of their building, I'll contact my boss who will call the FBI with all the details so they can take over. We have a plan."

Sam slapped his hand over his eyes, so pissed he was vibrating.

When he removed his hand he told her, "This is not corporate espionage. The real people behind Zydus are the most dangerous in the world, worse than any terrorist bunch you can imagine. They plan to kill you after the meeting."

Her face turned ashen. "What? You're serious about terrorists."

"Yes, dammit." He still couldn't just go on her word even if his gut had ganged up with his heart in favor of her innocence.

"Do you believe me, Sam?" When he didn't answer, she mumbled, "I don't know how to convince you I'm telling the truth...."

Then she went silent.

He cut his eyes to her. "What?"

She had that serene look she used to get any time she had a solution to a problem. "I know one way to convince you. I hope."

"I'm listening."

"I'm telling the truth. Scout's honor."

Those last two words took him back through the years to when they both had wanted to be in the Scouts, but no one in their little town would organize a Scout group, let alone allow them to be in one together. So he and Danielle sent off for Scout information and practiced the skills. They agreed to be secret members and go camping when they grew up.

"Sam, I'd rather die than sell those plans to terrorists."

There was a point when you had to make a decision and he made his.

He believed her. But proving her innocence would be tough. Joe had sent him because Joe figured that knowing Danielle's weaknesses Sam could get answers quicker. If Sam pulled Danielle from this meeting she would be put somewhere by his agency where he'd never find her again and have no way to help her. Much as he hated it, she had to go to this meeting for any hope of proving she was not a traitor.

He produced a knife.

When she gasped and reared back, he said, "I believe you."

"Thank goodness. What about the meeting?"

"Give me a minute." Sam cut her loose then called Joe and caught him up. When Sam suggested pulling Danielle, Joe said, "We can't do that. Heard Vestavia's attending. Danielle set all this in motion. If she backs out now it'll look like she's protecting Vestavia from exposure. Can you prove she isn't?"

Sam hung up and wanted to slam his fist into a wall. Vestavia had once been in DEA under a different name then disappeared and surfaced later as a key man in the Fratelli. B.A.D. would turn a city upside down to catch him. Sam had one option that might save Danielle. He said, "You have to make the meeting."

She stopped rubbing her wrists and stood up. "Do they still plan to kill me?"

"Yes."

Her legs folded.

He caught her before she fell. She gripped his arms, her face soft and open like the last time he'd held her close. She'd kissed him like there was no tomorrow, which turned out to be true because she'd left the next day before he could tell her about the ring he'd picked out. He'd known with that kiss he couldn't keep her from leaving.

She was shaking now. "This is what I get for trying to do the right thing."

"I'm not going to let anything happen to you."

A tear slipped down her smooth cheek.

Ah, hell. He kissed her just to calm her down, or so he told himself. She held back for a second then opened to him, loving him with her lips the way she had back before she'd been offered a full scholarship and he'd left for the military. He was breaking all the rules for his line of work, but Danielle was in his arms again.

Damn, he'd like to keep her there.

But even if everything went right and he got her out alive, she'd have to answer to the FBI.

They still might arrest her.

One hurdle at a time. When he lifted his head, she opened her eyes. If he could just put her somewhere safe, but the Fratelli were too careful to do a hit at Zydus. Sam would be close enough to step in if they tried.

"Sam, I—"

"Save it. We're short on time and I can't let personal feelings interfere." And he needed to focus on protecting her. "We'll talk after this is over. Get showered, and then I'll put a wire on you and explain how we're going to do this."

• • •

Twenty minutes later, Danielle stood in the middle of the living room with nothing on from the waist up except her bra, but Sam didn't seem to notice. Based on his all-business attitude that kiss hadn't affected him the way it had her.

She'd been right to leave for MIT after high school. Sam hadn't asked her to stay or come to see her. He'd joined the army. Getting irritated all over again, reliving the hurt, she snapped at him, "I'm ready, if you haven't noticed."

"Oh, I noticed," he muttered then proceeded to tape a small transmitter on her abdomen below her breasts.

He was quick and efficient. At one time he hadn't been in a hurry when he touched her.

She waited silently as he went through the drill one more time on how she was to present the PowerPoint, agree to anything they offered and exit the building to a taxi Sam would prearrange.

She asked, "How do you know the taxi will wait on me?"

"Because my people will be behind the wheel."

His people. Whatever he did was dangerous. How long had he been an operative? Since he'd gotten out of the army? She'd heard from a friend back home that Sam had been in Special Forces. And that he hated to fly.

She smiled to herself. A superagent afraid of flying.

"Let's go," Sam told her and headed to the door.

"Where will you be?" She couldn't squelch the panic in her voice.

He turned around, took one look at her and came back across the room. Lifting his palm to her cheek, he said, "I'll be listening to every word and close enough to keep you safe. Scout's honor."

When she reached the sixth floor of the Zydus building, Danielle met a businessman called Vestavia whose hard face and steely eyes gave her the creeps. When she asked about giving a presentation package to the other two men in the room, Vestavia said, "Not necessary. One's security for the plans and the other is my helicopter pilot."

Security to transport the laser component and engineering plans immediately to the international airport? Would that give Sam time to get into place?

● ● ●

Sam hurried up a flight of stairs in the Zydus building, listening to the meeting transmissions the whole time. He'd entered through the employee garage with an ID badge and a car Joe's people had procured that morning. When Sam reached the sixth floor, the meeting was almost finished.

Slipping into a utilities closet, he watched through a slim opening.

Danielle's voice came through his receiver. "Is there anything else before I go, Mr. Vestavia?"

"Not yet."

Sam breathed again, glad he'd been right about nothing going down here. Or so he thought until Vestavia said, "My men will escort you and the plans to the helicopter."

"Why?" Danielle asked with a tremor in her voice. "I gave you everything."

"You said you'd like to work with us. We have a facility in Russia. My associates are waiting on the plans. You can walk their engineers through any questions. We'll talk next week."

What the fuck? Sam seethed as Vestavia, one of the most wanted men in the world, stepped from the conference room heading toward the elevators, away from Sam. Two men exited next with Danielle between them, her face as white as the blouse beneath her herringbone suit. The guy on her right, who was built to wrestle professionally, had a .45 automatic in a shoulder holster. The skinny one had to be the pilot.

Go for Vestavia or Danielle?

Sam didn't have to think about it, but he didn't want her caught in cross fire.

Once Vestavia disappeared inside the elevator and Danielle passed Sam's hiding spot with her escorts, Sam followed her. At the next corner, he saw the trio heading for the stairwell door. Sam had one shot and couldn't miss. He pulled out his knife and let it fly. The blade struck the bodybuilder in his neck. He dropped to his knees.

Danielle, bless her, rammed one of those deadly elbows into the pilot's gut. Sam reached her next and slammed the pilot's head into the wall. He stepped over the muscle guy and yanked Danielle to the stairwell. "Gotta go."

"Where?" She kept pace with him as he raced up the metal steps.

"The roof. Cameras are all over the building. We've got maybe three minutes until security reaches us." He shoved open the door to the roof, where a helicopter sat in the middle of a circle. He pulled her toward it.

"What're you doing?" Her voice shrilled with panic.

"Get in and buckle up." He lifted her up on the passenger side then ran around and jumped into the pilot's seat. "Put on the head-set."

"Can you fly this?"

He started flipping switches and grinned at her. "I rode in one once. Can't be that tough." He'd battled his fear of flying by learning how to pilot a helicopter. The rotors caught air as a bullet pinged the fuselage, but Sam had Danielle's side of the chopper turned away.

She shouted in his headset. "The pilot has the evidence we need to nail these guys. He'll get away."

"No, he won't." Sam looked down at the ground surrounding the building where sport utilities and armed agents swarmed the property. "My people are here."

"What about Vestavia?"

"Don't know if he escaped. He's hard as a greased lizard to catch." Sam glanced at her as he banked away from the building. "But I got news on the way here that your boss contacted the FBI when he couldn't reach you. He told them what you were doing so you've been cleared of any charges."

Smiling with relief, she leaned over. Love shone in her eyes. "Where does that leave us, Sam? Am I going to lose you for another ten years?"

He took one look at the woman who had walked into fire based on trusting him and said, "How 'bout we take that camping trip?"

She kissed him and said, "As long as there's just one sleeping bag."

DEADLY FIXATION
DIANNA LOVE

*I adore the city of Savannah…but this story reveals
a side of it I've never explored! With incredible imagery,
Love has created not just another Savannah,
but another world. —SB*

Devon Fortier eased forward through pitch-black passages

where death waited for foolish humans in Savannah, Georgia's forgotten underground.

He was neither foolish nor human.

Deep voices growled up ahead in what had once been a rum cellar. The argument echoed off the packed-dirt walls that seeped water. Dank odors of rot, urine and unearthly creatures clogged every breath Devon inhaled.

Creeping closer, he made out three shapes hunched around something on the ground that cast an orange glow across the trio of predators. Two were ten feet tall. One had scaly skin and the other had pointed ears that curled up to his bald head.

Trolls.

Devon's informant looked to be spot-on about some black market deal going down with trolls in this coastal city.

The third figure appeared to be a human male of average height. But he was probably a glamour-concealed troll.

Whatever those three had pinned down snarled, "Let me go, you stinkin' vermin!"

Devon sighed, recognizing the voice. He ought to let the trolls continue.

A fourth-generation leprechaun and pawnbroker, Coldfinger had just enough majik to be dangerous. A sick piece of work the world wouldn't miss.

But Devon's oath as a Belador meant he had to protect everyone—even slimy bastards with the integrity of a jackal—if those trolls decided to chow down on orange fast food.

He moved closer for a better view.

Curly-ears held his prey in place with a four-toed foot as wide as a briefcase. He shook his head at Coldfinger. "You think faerie dust is gonna cut it? That you can screw us?"

Trading faerie dust was illegal, but a petty infraction of VIPER laws. Not enough for Devon to risk his skin arresting three carnivorous beings. Besides, this didn't fit his profile of a major VIPER operation.

Beladors served as one of the enforcement arms for VIPER, an international league of warriors that protected the world from supernatural predators...like trolls.

"How dare you accuse me of scamming," Coldfinger whined in a voice bloated with insult.

Devon rolled his eyes. How could someone with no conscience be insulted?

All the trolls started yelling, threatening to dismember Coldfinger.

Baldy bared his fangs. "We got you the scrying dish. Where's the spell?"

"You lying 'chaun."

Devon used the cover of their voices to close thirty feet between him and the argument.

Coldfinger's voice tiptoed up an octave with fear. "Calm down, I got it. I got the Noirre Fixit spell."

Oh, hell, no. Noirre majik definitely fit the profile of his investigation. Devon had no choice but to take all of them to headquarters now...*if* they didn't kill him.

Trolls were a nasty bunch who ate their opponents, which left no evidence and made it hard to try them in a Tribunal court. Devon could attempt to call in Belador reinforcements, but he had faulty telepathic ability at best, especially underground. No worries. He might have gotten shorted in the telepathic department, but his other gifts were just fine.

Besides, lowering his personal shields to call Beladors would blow his element of surprise.

Murdering trolls had no business getting their hands on Noirre majik, especially a fixation spell that could freeze a person long enough to do harm. As the deadliest of black majik, Noirre carried a high penalty for dealing, even death.

Human law enforcement didn't know VIPER or supernatural beings existed. Handling trolls, leprechauns and Noirre fell to agents like Devon.

He paused. Most trolls wouldn't touch Noirre since few of them were powerful enough to control it.

Ah, hell. Could these be Svart Trolls?

Only if the gods really wanted to piss on Devon's day.

The Swedish term for black, *Svart* Trolls were preternatural black ops mercenaries.

Reaching over his shoulder, Devon slid his short sword from the leather sheath attached to his back.

Bullets only annoyed Svarts.

"Did you think I wouldn't find you, Lambert?" a throaty female voice called out from the other side of the trolls.

Devon stilled. No way.

He leaned right to see past the criminals. One look confirmed he had the worst luck ever handed out in this world.

Joleen Mac, a pain-in-his-ass bounty hunter whose four inches of black lace-up boots boosted her height to just under six feet. Viper-tongue-red lipstick accented lips that could sink a man to his knees when she smiled—or issued a deadly spell. Black hair flashed past her shoulders, two long braids slicing down the side of her face. Scary as she was gorgeous, Jo worked for Dakkar, a rogue mage who ran a bounty-hunter operation. VIPER allowed Dakkar freedom of movement as long as Dakkar's hunters didn't interfere with official missions.

Like this one. Devon's recon mission just turned official with Noirre being traded and Svart Trolls congregating. But he needed backup on this and had no way to reach anyone from down here.

Lambert, the troll in human glamour, grinned. "Jo, baby. Good to see ya. We got business?"

"You could say that." Joleen stepped close to the group. A tangerine glow washed across her loose-hanging rawhide coat, saddle-brown leather vest and jean shorts. She held a compact weapon with a short, squat barrel built to shoot two-inch-thick rounds that could kill a demon.

Devon had seen that weapon once before.

She pointed the muzzle at Lambert. "You're coming with me."

The two big trolls stared at her with bright yellow eyes and green saliva dripping from their lips. They growled low with menace.

"No, he's not." Devon stepped from the shadows and dropped his personal shields, allowing his power to radiate. Call it male arrogance, but he wanted the first shot at intimidating the trolls… and he liked the way Jo's cheeks flared with color when his power brushed across her skin.

"Stay out of this, Devon," she warned in a voice spiced with French influence.

"Alll-right, now we're talkin'," Coldfinger said, enthusiasm bubbling. "What say we all go topside, grab a brew and discuss this like sociable folks."

Joleen kept her weapon trained on her quarry, but ignored Coldfinger's bravado, pinning her gaze on Devon. "Lambert's behind a contract killing of a Connecticut witch."

Coldfinger howled. "You trolls tradin' stolen goods?"

Lambert said, "No, she's lying." He sneered at Jo. "I ain't goin' with ya."

"Yes, you are," she said without a hint of concern.

Devon sighed. "No, he's going with me."

Jo shifted the weapon toward Devon. "We're having a communication breakdown. That could be dangerous."

"You don't want to threaten *me,* Jo," Devon warned. "I caught them dealing Noirre. Makes this VIPER business. Lambert's got to face a Tribunal. That's the law."

All the trolls swung around to look at Devon.

Coldfinger howled again and glowed bright as a warning beacon. "You idiots. He's Belador. Heard everything you said. Stinkin' morons."

Jo asked Devon, "How can this be a sanctioned operation?" Her gaze shifted, scanning quickly before a smile teased her lips. "Where's your team? VIPER doesn't send their people in without backup. Doesn't want them *hurt.*"

She was goading Devon over how she'd used that same weapon to kill a demon hanging on his back the last time they'd met.

He owed her and she was calling in the debt.

But he couldn't pay up right now. "I have orders to pick him up." Big lie. "Let's work together this time. You cover them and I'll call in backup."

Her eyebrow arched sharply in a saucy smirk. "What gave you the idea we were negotiating, Dev? Lambert's mine. You can have the other two and the orange toad."

"You can't prove nothin' without Lambert," Coldfinger yelled.

Not technically true, but if Lambert was running a Svart Troll op Devon needed him most of all.

Lambert inched a step away.

Jo swung her weapon back at him. "Let's go."

Hellfire. Devon could use her help, but he'd just have to contain them without her. "Sorry, Jo, but VIPER laws take precedence over bounty orders. I'm taking them all in." He turned to Lambert and bluffed about using telepathy. "I've already sent word to VIPER for backup. Resisting will only make it worse when you face the Tribunal. You three, facedown on the ground next to Coldfinger."

Intelligence gleamed in Lambert's eyes. He shrugged and turned to his two giant sidekicks. "Sorry, guys, I know I said this would be a quick job. Guess there's nothing to do but...*kill them!*" He ducked and the huge trolls roared to life.

One giant rushed Devon and the other one dived at Jo.

A flash of green light burst through the room. Some kind of stun grenade? That wouldn't stop a Svart.

Devon swung his sword in a high arc. The blade sang with sentient power, but a second flash of light from Jo caused a strobe effect that threw off his timing. He slashed across the troll's arm and dodged the snap of fangs so close to his neck that his hair stood on end. Losing an arm didn't slow the bellowing monster whose armhole spewed murky-colored blood that smelled like sewage.

These ornery things were hard to kill. The next swing of his Belador sword severed baldy's head. It bounced away...the only sound in a sudden brittle silence.

Not good.

Devon walked over to where chunks of troll lay scattered around Jo. So the flash had been a high-bandwidth laser? He glanced at a slender barrel camelbacked onto the demon blaster, then at the ground where Coldfinger had been. *Had* being the operative word.

Glowing yellow-orange embers sizzled on the dirt floor.

"Any chance that means you got him, Jo?"

"No. That's residue from Coldfinger's body being held still too long. He escaped with Lambert." She stood ten feet away with her blaster hanging from a shoulder sling and hands propped on her hips. "They'll have made it to where the tunnel dumps into the river by now. What a krikin' mess you made of this."

"Me? You're the one who wouldn't keep this simple." He turned on her and moved forward with each word.

"Stop right there."

Not a chance. Nothing intimidated this woman.

He couldn't decide between wringing her stubborn neck and kissing her. Like that adrenaline-pumped kiss they'd shared the last time they'd survived a bloody battle. Was she thinking about that kiss? "With a little cooperation, we'd have hauled in all four and gotten you a nice fee for helping."

"I don't work for chump change...or VIPER." She raised her weapon and shoved it into his chest. "And if you get in my way again, there won't be enough of you left to feed a gnat."

That'd be a "no" on her thinking fondly of their last kiss.

This woman had unusual hunting skills. And based on what he'd seen, a little majik. She could be a witch. When you moved in a world where a broad spectrum of majik was the norm, identities were tough to nail down without information.

Jo might find Lambert faster than Devon could pull together a team. He had to cut a deal for any hope of stopping Svart Trolls from accessing that Noirre spell. "I get that Lambert was your bounty, but—"

• • •

"Not *was*. Is my bounty," Joleen said, setting Devon straight. Which goddess of fate had the twisted sense of humor to stick Devon Fortier in her path again? Blond strands fell loose from where he wore his shoulder-length hair tied back. Those dark hazel eyes were flecked with gold and seemed to maintain a perpetual anytime-is-playtime look.

A look that could make a woman do asinine things.

And make tactical errors. Like kissing Devon after their last unplanned meeting. She should shoot the cocky Belador just for interfering again.

"We can work out the money on this, Jo."

"It's not about the money or I'd charge you double and be done with this. I have quotas. I'm behind and need to hand in Lambert by tomorrow afternoon or Dakkar will cut me loose." That could not happen. Dakkar was the sole person who could keep her identity secret. And he would. For a price. She couldn't lose this gig or allow Devon to ruin it for her.

"What's the big deal on this troll, Jo?"

"He's not just a troll. Lambert is the bastard son of a Svart Troll and a black witch. He's slippery. I've been tracking him for days." She glanced past him. "Where's your team?"

He gave a half-assed look over his shoulder. "Should be here soon."

Liar. "You didn't call anyone." She let her weapon swing down and under her coat. "I got a bounty to pick up."

Sliding his sword into the sheath on his back, he said, "Then we better get rolling."

"Don't make me tie you up, Dev."

His grin ignited with lust. "We don't have time for that, but I like the way you're thinking."

One round from her demon blaster and he'd be little Devon pieces. Tempting. "I'm not joking."

His sigh accused her of being as much fun as rain at a picnic. Tough. She *had* been fun at one time in her life, but someone had stolen that life.

Devon scratched his whisker-darkened jaw—as unshaven as the last time she'd seen him. Did he never shave? "Here's the thing. Based on what you said about Lambert, he'll use that Noirre spell if we don't stop him."

"Don't see how theft is my problem." She beat down her surge of conscience. Nobody would waste that spell for simple robbery.

"Theft? That's a Noirre Fixit spell. Most fixation spells just freeze a human for a minute, but Noirre could be much worse."

Could be? Damn him. She couldn't let this Belador go off thinking that. "If it's Noirre, it's not *just* a fixation spell that freezes someone long enough to rob them."

Devon crossed his arms, waiting.

She cursed herself. Why couldn't she be like Dakkar's other bounty hunters who put their own needs first? "A Noirre Fixit spell will freeze everyone within twenty feet of another person hit by the spell. The freeze will last approximately two minutes, but when it dissipates, the memories of every person affected or watching the spellbound area will be wiped clean. They'll continue as if nothing had happened."

Devon's words came out slow and tight. "I can't share all my intel, but it's looking like Lambert has a team here for a hit. Now that I know about his ability and this spell, I'm thinking his target is involved with the St. Patrick's Day Parade tomorrow."

"Trolls wouldn't risk exposure in a crowd that big," she argued. "VIPER would send death squads after them."

"But as you just pointed out, this spell comes with a memory wipe. If Lambert pulls this off, VIPER will have nothing to use as evidence."

She asked, "Why this parade?"

Scratching his head, Devon stared off, thinking. "My informant thought the trolls were here to glamour their way through the crowd to steal gold, but I ran all possible scenarios and found out an Ansgar descendant is studying art here. She's in the parade. Six members of her family are joining her tomorrow, including the matriarch who goes nowhere without wearing her solid gold Celtic choker—"

"That holds the power to their entire Fae family." Joleen got it.

"Right. I blew it off before, because the Ansgars always travel with security. But now I'm thinking the Svart Trolls are after the choker and/or the family members for someone else. I'd like to know who's behind this, but with Svart involved, my bet is an enemy of the Ansgars. If that's Lambert's target and he pulls this off, war will erupt between powerful adversaries. The human world won't be a safe place for anyone."

Dakkar would be furious if she had any perceived part in that happening, since shielding nonhuman existence from humans was part of Dakkar's agreement with VIPER.

Pushing hair off her face, she hissed out a steam of air. "How many people show up for this parade?"

"Close to half a million." Devon hit her with a hard look. "And with the memory wipe, nothing would stop those trolls from snacking on a child, who would then end up on a milk carton."

Playing hero was Devon's job, not hers, but she wouldn't allow innocent people to be hurt. "Here's my deal. I help you get the spell and you give me Lambert."

Hesitation played through Devon's face. "I'll do what I can, Jo, but I don't make promises I can't keep. I'll give you Lambert if I can and *if* he doesn't die in the process."

A dead Lambert was of no use to her. She either gambled on throwing in with Devon or locking him in a rum cask while she hunted Lambert alone. But if she lost Lambert she'd have to live with the guilt for anything he did *and* face Dakkar empty-handed. "I'm in, but no promises either on what happens when we find Lambert."

She expected him to agree or argue, but he just lifted the hood of his fleece jacket over his head, covering the sword handle, and led the way out.

After backtracking with Devon to the exit point beneath the Pirate's House restaurant, they emerged on Broad Street. A balmy March sun had daffodils blooming and tourists crowding cobblestone streets along the historic district. She fell into step with Devon, who led the way to Coldfinger's pawnshop on the outskirts of Savannah in an area abused by age. Spiderwebs covered steel-barred windows on shabby buildings and the homeless loitered on the sidewalks.

Joleen mused, "Would have expected Coldfinger to be in a finer part of town."

"Not with clientele that shies away from crowds and humans to do their business." Once they'd left the dense pedestrian traffic in the city behind, Devon had picked up the pace. Now he slowed to enter a wooden shack of a building.

She followed him in, allowing her eyes to adjust to the sudden darkness. Sunlight filtering through holes in the walls and ceiling danced over musty piles of clothes and a filthy mattress.

Did Devon know where he was going?

He slowed and gave a signal for silence.

She drew her weapon though she'd prefer to use the wand she kept hidden along with her mage identity.

Devon eased up to the side of a closed door with light sifting out from the bottom and tried the knob. Locked. He shifted in front of it, put his boot up and kicked. Rotten wood shattered.

Joleen shook her head, muttering, "What is it about boys and kicking in doors?"

• • •

Devon took in the hideous scene against one wall of the pawn-shop. Coldfinger was dead, frozen with his remaining arm up in defense and his face contorted with a scream of fear. Devon wrinkled his nose at the scorched sherbet-ice-cream stench.

Jo pointed at a pile of half-chewed orange glob that might be Coldfinger's upchucked arm and smirked. "Looks like Lambert tested the spell on Coldfinger. Trolls have a weak stomach for leprechaun, eh?"

Devon let the rare humor in her voice pass without comment. He had to contact Tzader. As the Belador Maistir over North America, Tzader directed a large portion of VIPER's force.

Jo must have picked up the track of his thoughts. "If you're thinking of calling in backup, you better reconsider unless you want Lambert to use the spell on VIPER agents, as well."

She had a point, but he knew that wasn't her real concern. "You're just worried VIPER will pick up Lambert before you do."

"True, but what if you call in agents, and he unleashes the spell? Svart Trolls got any old scores to settle with Beladors?"

"I've thought about that, but even with my intel I can't just assume it's only a hit squad and that he's only after the Ansgar family. We have to cover more area than that. *And* we're not sure how long the spell will last now that Lambert is using it."

She hissed something that sounded like a curse. "That type of fixation spell that can be used in volume has a short shelf life. The spell must be contained in a way Lambert can release it as needed, but he wouldn't have wasted activating it unless he planned on using the spell again within twenty-four hours. Even if you call in VIPER, you still can't prove Lambert took the Noirre spell from Coldfinger *and* you put your teams at risk."

Hellfire, she was right and he believed she knew her stuff with spells. He'd love to find out exactly what Joleen was. She didn't fit the usual gutter profile of Dakkar's bounty hunters.

She nodded at Coldfinger. "That was a message for anyone who tries to cross Lambert. The spell's probably been working about twenty minutes because we've been here half that and Coldfinger's blood has started congealing."

Devon glanced over his shoulder. "Got what he deserved for dealing Noirre with a troll." He swung his gaze back to her. "Any ideas on how to find Lambert?"

She pondered her answer too long, as if debating once again on how much to share. "He'll likely position himself in a safe place to use the spell. He won't risk being with the other trolls in case something goes wrong or VIPER rolls in."

Devon had to contact Tzader, but without Jo knowing or she might disappear. And beyond needing her help, dammit, he didn't want that. "Our best use of time is figuring out the most advantageous place for Lambert to release the spell tomorrow morning."

Anyone watching Jo would think she might just be staring off as she processed information, but Devon could feel energy building that had to be coming from her. Energy she worked to keep contained.

What was she? Besides hot and dangerous?

Her lavender-blue eyes fluttered back to life, and that oddly interesting gaze met his. "You know the parade route for tomorrow?"

He lifted his smartphone up for view. "I can pull up everything we need. It starts on Abercorn Street near Forsyth Park."

"Then that's where we start." She walked off and Devon let her lead the way.

What man wouldn't want to follow something that fine?

He also took the opportunity to text Tzader a message. Not much for typing to begin with, Devon just punched in: Call me.

As one of the stronger telepaths in the Beladors, Tzader could reach across two hundred and fifty miles from Atlanta. His rumbling voice entered Devon's mind. *What's up, Dev?*

Devon answered, *Have a situation we need to handle carefully. A troll got his hands on a Noirre fixation spell.*

How'd that happen?

Devon explained about his investigation to this point. He finished by saying, *Lambert got the spell from Coldfinger.*

You bag the leprechaun?

No. Lambert tested the spell on him.

Joleen glanced back at Devon with a questioning look about his lagging behind. He smiled and held the phone sideways as if busy working on the parade route that he already knew.

She shook her head and kept walking.

Tzader said, *Call me when you contain Lambert. I'll send a team to transport him.*

If only it was that easy. Devon added, *One problem. I'm pretty sure Lambert plans to use the spell during the St. Patrick's Day Parade.*

Why?

Devon went through how the spell functioned, adding, *Got some help from a bounty hunter. She knows her stuff.*

She?

Hellfire. Tzader wouldn't like this. Devon said, *Joleen Mac.*

What's she doing there?

This is where things got tricky. Devon wasn't sure how any of this would play out, but he still owed Jo big-time and didn't want her marked as a VIPER target for interfering. *Jo was hunting one of the trolls. We intercepted the deal in progress at the same time. She's agreed to help.*

After a brief silence, Tzader said, *I'll bring in every available agent by tomorrow morning.*

That could be risky without knowing where Lambert plans to release the spell. If the team is too close they could be compromised.

We'll stay a hundred yards away. You find Lambert.

The connection died just as Devon reached Abercorn Street.

Jo waited for him on the sidewalk. "Lambert wouldn't be down here on the streets even with a Svart team. He'd be up there." She pointed to the rooftops.

"Then that's where we're headed."

By the time Devon had walked Jo across every rooftop on the parade route, twice, Jo finally agreed with Devon on the best place to expect Lambert to show. On the way back to hunker down on top of a building next to the one where they expected Lambert, Devon picked up a succulent meal from the Sapphire Grill for a rooftop picnic. He'd like to squeeze some information out of Jo, but pulling gold out of a troll's fist would be easier. And she sounded exhausted from tracking Lambert for two days.

Plus, too many questions might snap the thin commitment of this short-term alliance.

When she finished eating, Jo frowned. "Lambert won't arrive until he's ready to unleash the spell...unless he comes by early to scope the location."

"Agreed."

"You got first watch," she ordered and leaned back, closing her eyes, not waiting for his agreement.

● ● ●

Seven hours later, crowds packed the sidewalks on each side of the parade walk below.

Jo stepped up beside Devon and looked over the edge to the lower roof of the next building. "You sure about this?"

"Sure about the location or making that thirty-foot leap?"

"The jump." She straightened and faced him. "Is making death-defying leaps another boy thing like kicking in doors?"

Devon lifted his hand slowly and rubbed his knuckles along her cheek. "I won't let you get hurt."

She cocked an eyebrow at him. "I'm not the one in danger of breaking a leg."

"So you can fly?" He'd like to see just what kind of power she had.

Marching band music and crowds cheering surged from a distance. The thick of the parade would be right below them in another couple minutes.

"Where's Lambert?" Jo wondered out loud.

"Right here, Jo baby," Lambert said from behind them.

Dammit. Right idea, wrong rooftop.

Devon noted how Jo still leaned her arms on the short wall but moved her fingers inside her jacket and slid out a short stick before turning around. "Big mistake to use that spell on us, Lambert."

"That's what Coldfinger said." The glamoured troll held a glowing pocket watch in one hand, thumb resting against the clasp, ready to pop the cover.

Devon questioned if a field of kinetic power shoved at Lambert would do anything against the Noirre majik controlled by that watch, but he started to lift his hands.

Jo sighed and whispered, "Don't."

Did she have a way to stop the troll from freezing them or a plan to snake her bounty out from under Devon?

Decision time. He couldn't stop Lambert for sure and his gut said to trust her. He whispered, "Okay."

Lambert asked, "Any last words, Jo?"

She smiled. "Never assume all opponents are equal."

"They are when I hold this. Admit it. I beat you." Lambert lifted the pocket watch.

Devon tensed, fighting the urge to use his kinetics.

Jo moved so quickly Devon barely caught the motion. In the microsecond that Lambert's thumb moved to the clasp release, Jo pointed a pencil-size length of carved wood at him. It lengthened as she rattled off a chant.

Power met power halfway between Lambert and Jo.

The backlash of energy hit Jo and Devon. He caught her arm

just before she'd have flipped over the wall and used his kinetics to shove them forward.

When the power cleared, Lambert stood frozen with a mask of shock.

What the hell? Devon stared at Jo. Wizard? Mage?

Jo walked over to Lambert. "He didn't get a direct hit of the Fixit spell when it back-lashed. Might not hold him long."

She snapped a titanium neck shackle on Lambert who roused, muttering, "Bitch."

Devon clubbed the troll with his elbow, knocking the slimy bastard to the ground. Once he had titanium handcuffs on Lambert's wrists, Devon smiled, ready to offer Jo a celebration meal.

Then lost his grin.

She held the closed pocket watch that was still loaded with the Noirre spell.

Ah, hell. "Don't, Jo. If you freeze me long enough to snatch Lambert, I'll have to report you…oh. Guess I won't remember."

"No, you wouldn't."

With powers like hers, what was a woman like Jo even doing with Dakkar? Then Devon got it.

Jo was hiding from something or someone.

She walked over to him, hand extended, offering the watch. "I would never use the dark arts. Just wanted you to know I *could* have."

His chest eased with relief. He took the watch from her and shoved it in his jacket pocket. "Fair enough. Lambert's yours."

Her voice lit with suspicion. "What about VIPER?"

"I contacted Tzader last night."

That narrowed her eyes. "Figures."

He shrugged. "My duty to protect comes first. I'm telling Tzader that you single-handedly got the Noirre spell back and once I had that in hand, your bounty took precedence."

Surprise brightened her exotic gaze. "Why would you...?"

"Not bring in VIPER? Because then I'd have to tell them about your powers." He smiled. "Your secret's safe with me."

Appreciation relaxed the delicate muscles in her face until she paused. "So you're going to let me just walk away with Lambert?"

"Not exactly." Devon stepped closer and slipped his fingers into her hair. He gave her a chance to back off as he lowered his head, but she lifted up and met him halfway with a kiss of pure torment.

Sinfully sweet and without a chance of satisfaction.

She nipped his lip before stepping back, eyes sparking with challenge. "You think giving me Lambert pays off saving your hide from that demon."

"I know better." He didn't want to wipe out that debt too quickly or he might not see her again. "There's always next time."

HOT NOTE

A Detective Shelley Caldwell Story

PATRICIA ROSEMOOR

Rosemoor seamlessly packs a lot of information into the first paragraph, effectively setting the stage, then plunges the reader straight into this captivating story. —SB

Though the night's storm abated, wind still blew in powerful gusts, chopping waves of lake water over the corpse facedown on Oak Street Beach. Dawn had barely broken when an early-morning jogger had called it in. I hadn't been sleeping, but—worse—my cell phone blasting had torn me out of Jake's arms... and he'd been using his best vampire moves on me. Now as Detective Mike Norelli and I surveyed the scene, an evidence technician snapped photos.

"Nifty swimsuit," my partner said of the dead man's charcoal-striped suit. "Gotta get me one of them."

"Yeah, Norelli, as if someone could pry open your wallet."

"So I'm thrifty."

I snorted and crouched down near the corpse. "No wound that I can see."

"Just like the other two."

I was thinking the same thing. Earlier in the year, two other men had washed up on beaches, the first on the south side of Chicago, the second farther north. I shot my gaze to the corpse's feet.

I could still see an indentation where his body had disturbed the sand as waves off Lake Michigan had pushed it to shore.

The evidence tech backed off, so I searched the dead man's pockets and produced keys and a wallet, which I handed to Norelli.

"Just like the others," he repeated as I stood. "Not a robbery."

"What are the chances of three fully dressed men walking into the lake and drowning?"

I didn't believe in coincidence.

Furthermore, I was getting bad vibes. My inner alarms clanged.

Not again. No reason to believe anything woo-woo was involved.

As Norelli checked the wallet, I signaled the team. The EMTs rolled the corpse onto a stretcher, giving me a clear shot at the dead man's face, which was contorted with what looked like ecstasy.

I gasped.

"Neil Larson," Norelli and I said in unison.

He looked up from the driver's license. "You psychic or do you have X-ray vision?"

Actually, I *was* psychic, at least with my twin, Silke, and recently with Jake, but no way was I going to admit that. Not *another* departmental evaluation for me, thank you.

"Yeah, Norelli. Like I know you recently had pasta with marinara sauce."

He narrowed his gaze at me. "Last night. How did you know really?"

"The tomato stain on your lapel."

"I meant the victim."

"I recognize him," I said. "Larson Gallery, River North. He's the owner. *Was* the owner."

"You travel in those circles?"

"Not everyone parks in front of the television with a beer."

I'd met Neil Larson through Jake. The gallery represented Jake's photographs, and he and Neil had become friends. But the last thing I wanted was to bring Jake into this. If Norelli started investigating *his* background…

Sensing an observer, I whipped around to see a thin, elderly black woman in cropped pants and a T-shirt too big for her, feet in sandals repaired with duct tape. Clutching a full black plastic garbage bag, she was all wide-eyed. I wondered if she'd been on the beach the night before. She ducked her head and started to shuffle away, but I quickly caught up to her.

"Wait a minute. I'm Detective Shelley Caldwell." I flashed my star. "Do you know the man who drowned?"

She shook her head and avoided my eyes. I sensed strong emotion.

Fear.

"If you saw something, you need to tell me. What's your name?"

"Harriet."

"Well, Harriet, can I buy you breakfast? All you have to do is tell me what you saw."

Harriet considered the offer. Hunger trumped fear because she pointed to a bench. "I was sleeping there until the noise woke me."

"What kind of noise?"

"Singing."

"The victim?"

"No, a woman. Scary, that one." Her attention shifted to the body bag being loaded into the ambulance. "He be walking into the lake after her."

My pulse thrummed. Now we were getting somewhere. "Did the victim say anything to the woman?"

"Nope. Acted real weird. All happy but weird."

My mouth went dry. "Tell me more about the woman."

She did.

Chills crawled straight up my spine.

• • •

"Neil is dead?"

Jake wore a stunned expression, the black diamond in his right ear and nothing else. He'd gone back to sleep while I'd been on the job. Mornings weren't his thing unless a little something-something was involved as it had been when my cell phone had gone off. We spent our nights together not sleeping when I wasn't held hostage working a homicide.

"It's another woo-woo case," I added.

"How so?" He pulled on a pair of very brief briefs.

No more eye candy for me.

I told him about the homeless woman's story. "When she said Neil was acting weird, that's when my alarms went off."

"Neil didn't do drugs. He didn't even drink other than an occasional beer."

"Harriet said a woman standing in the shallows was singing seductively and it lured Neil into the lake. They both went under, but only she came back out."

"Hunh."

Jake's intent expression made me reach out and run a fingertip over the scar that was nearly hidden by beard stubble. But when the gleam in his eyes spelled sexual interest, I pulled my hand away and went into the kitchen to open a can of tuna for the cats. Sarge and Cadet came running at the sound of the can opener.

Swiping a hand down their backs, I left them to find Jake getting dressed. Triple-time speed. Normal for him.

He asked, "What about those other men who drowned?"

"We never found witnesses and the M.E. declared both suicides."

"Someone must have seen something. We need to find them."

My blood pressure crept up. "*We?* This is *my* case, Jake. *I'm* the cop here."

"Neil was my friend."

"You can't get involved. You're not a cop."

"Don't you mean I am a vampire?"

"No!"

He wasn't exactly a vampire anyway, though he'd inherited certain abilities—his mother had been turned by a vampire while pregnant with him.

"Bull. You don't want me involved in your life—"

My irritation was growing by the moment. "What are you talking about? You *are* in my life!"

"When it's convenient for you."

A variation on a familiar argument. I cared for Jake and he knew it. I wanted to protect him. Jake wasn't one to hide his abilities—increased speed, strength, vision, hearing. And a psychic connection with me that had saved my life. He'd never taken anyone's blood, but if others knew about his abilities, they might try to destroy him out of fear.

"I don't want to argue, Jake."

"Neil was my friend. Did you get a description of the woman?"

"Harriet said she had long blond hair that looked silver in the moonlight, and real feathers covered the shoulders and arms of her gown so that it looked like she had wings."

"Sirena."

"You know her?"

"Neil started seeing her several weeks ago. Took me once."

"Saw her where?"

Ducking my question, Jake said, "I got weird vibes, couldn't figure out what bothered me, but something did."

"When this Sirena came out of the water, Harriet closed her eyes and pretended she was asleep for protection. She peeked a minute later. No woman, but a big bird was flying away. That killed her credibility as a witness for Norelli, but I got real bad vibes myself. So…Sirena what? Her last name."

He shrugged. "No clue. But I know where to find her tonight. I'll take you."

I wanted to tell him to stay out of this, to give me the information and leave the investigation to me, but from past experience, I knew it was no use. When Jake's mind was set on something, even I couldn't change it. In the meantime, I had to get my butt to the office before Norelli sent the bloodhounds after me.

"I wanted to let you know about Neil myself, but I have to—"

"Go back to work," he finished for me, stepping closer. "I know."

My pulse flickered to life as did various other parts of my body. I placed a flat hand in the middle of his chest. He smiled in response. A knowing, hot, come-hither smile.

And yet, he said, "I'm not trying to stop you."

"The hell you aren't."

The way he looked at me played havoc with my insides, made them melt a little.

He picked up a lock of my hair, twirled the mahogany strands. "Wear something sexy tonight."

"To interview a suspect?"

"To keep me happy."

Keeping Jake happy was essential if I didn't want to lose him.

But right now murder was my priority.

And so for the next ten hours, I kept my mind off Jake and on the potential victims. I worked with Norelli, did whatever he asked me to do, tried not to feel guilty about keeping what I knew from him. Telling him about Neil's link with Sirena meant telling him about Jake, something I wouldn't do.

At least not yet.

For once the hours dragged. I brought up the reports of the other victims. I studied their photos. A Northwestern professor, Bobby Russo, sat in a wingback chair, silver-trimmed pipe in hand. Cal Kruger sat on the hull of his speedboat, arm dangling over one knee, wrist decorated by Rolex. In the photos taken by the evidence tech after they'd washed up on the beaches, both wore expressions of ecstasy as had Neil. Both had been as young and virile, but that seemed to be the only thing the three men had in common.

If Sirena was guilty, what had she gained from their deaths?

Then the M.E. report came in. No sign of foul play. No drugs or booze in his system. Another suicide.

"I don't get it," Norelli said. "My gut says murder. All three of them."

Without the M.E. backing up his gut, he had to let it go. At least officially. When you got down to it, Mike Norelli might be impossible sometimes, but he was great at his job. He was like a bulldog, wouldn't let something go until he had the truth.

Which meant I had to beat him to it before he unearthed the truth about Jake.

But for now, I got to leave.

So I was ready when Jake arrived home at eight. Unlike my theatrical twin, I'm a no-fuss kind of woman, who prefers simple clothes, an easy hairstyle and a touch of lipstick. And a Glock holstered to my back. Not that a gun was defense against the supernatural, but carrying it made me feel better. When I opened the door to Jake, his dark eyes glittered, devouring me, sliding over the sheer black dolman-sleeved blouse, stopping at the V at my breasts. I felt myself flush.

"Happy?"

"You decide."

As he kissed me, he took one of my hands and pressed it to the front of his trousers. Despite the cloth barrier, I felt him pulse against my palm. My heart thumped louder. I didn't know whether it was one of those unnatural abilities of his, but he sure could keep a sexual high going. If we started now, he probably wouldn't let me sleep until daybreak.

Moaning, I ripped my lips and hand away. "Let's get out of here while I still can."

In one of his lightning-fast moves, Jake was at the door by the time I turned to it. I patted the cats before leaving. Jake patted them, too. Sarge and Cadet used to be afraid of him—animals feared vampires, even half vampires—but the cats had warmed up to him when they realized he meant them no harm.

We took my red Camaro, top down, but he drove. Soon we were on Lake Shore Drive headed south.

"So what's our destination?" I asked.

"Northerly Island."

Land that used to be home to Chicago's third airport for small planes. Now it was home to restaurants, a concert venue and a casino boat called The Ark.

"Where exactly?"

"Persephone's Den." While I'd heard of the raw bar and seafood restaurant, I'd never been there. I'd never been to Northerly Island other than to investigate a murder at a concert.

We parked and went inside. The sophisticated interior of the place surprised me. Tanks of tropical fish. An aviary with tropical birds. Sea glass tile dressed up the entire back wall. People were dressed up, too. A young man in a tux played a baby grand piano.

Jake took me to the bar where he placed our drink orders—beer for him, seltzer and lime for me.

Already looking around for an exotic blonde, I asked, "So does Sirena work here or is she a regular?"

"Owner. And entertainer. She sings."

His answer immediately put me on edge.

A feeling that intensified a few minutes later when Sirena entered and stopped before the piano. She wore a diaphanous flesh-colored gown, the bodice and sleeves covered with feathers. No introductions. She simply began a low-throated come-hither song.

The noise in the room lowered a notch.

"Does she always wear feathers?" I whispered, remembering Harriet's tale.

Jake didn't answer.

"Jake?"

He frowned. Seemed distracted. "Yeah?"

But he only looked at me for a second before turning back to Sirena.

About to poke him, I stopped when I realized something weird was going on. The hair on the back of my neck rose. The men all seemed mesmerized. Uncomfortable, too. They were shifting in their seats as if they were being seduced. *All* the men, including Jake.

The birds in the aviary had quieted, too. They all seemed focused on the songstress.

The only ones unaffected were the women, most of whom appeared annoyed.

I was simply frightened. A woman with such power over men… displaying it in public. I went on woo-woo warning.

Sirena ended the song with an extended high note that vibrated through me. The whole room went silent as if holding its breath.

With each song, the same thing happened. My head swirled and my gut tightened with the certainty that I was dealing with something beyond human. The men continued to be affected. Enough to send them to their deaths if Sirena so chose? Why? What kind of creature had that power?

I thought about the name of the place—Persephone's Den. I remembered in Greek mythology, Persephone was queen of the underworld and had sirens as her companions. Women who sang to lure sailors to their death.

The sirens…Sirena…

Apparently she wasn't worried about being obvious. How many people, after all, believed in preternatural creatures?

Being one who reluctantly did, I knew I had to stop her.

I pulled out a card and scribbled a note on the back, then asked the bartender to get it to his boss.

Jake gave me a quizzical expression.

"An invite to talk," I said, wondering how Sirena would try to explain what had gone on at Oak Street Beach.

I didn't have long to find out. Shortly after she finished her set, a busboy told us to meet her outside. We went out the back way. The wind had picked up again and rain clouds hid the moon for the second night in a row. A gust tore at Sirena's sheer gown and long hair. She put up her hands to smooth it back in place, and in doing so, her feather-covered arms reminded me of a bird's wings.

"What can I do for you, Detective Caldwell?" Sirena removed a flat gold case from a pocket and took out a cigarette.

She might be speaking to me, but she was giving Jake the once-over as she lit up. Like she was checking him out to see if he was prime victim material. I didn't like it, glanced at Jake for his reaction. Not seeming to notice, he was zeroed in on the cigarette case in her hand.

Watching the woman carefully, I said, "Neil Larson is dead."

Sirena's brow furrowed slightly. She inhaled, asked, "Am I supposed to know who that is?" and blew smoke in my face.

"Neil was a big fan," Jake said.

The other woman laughed. "Just because a man wants me doesn't mean I notice."

"So you didn't know Neil?" I asked.

"That's right, Detective."

"A witness swears that he was with a woman who looked just like you, and that she *sang* him into the lake."

Without missing a beat, Sirena said, "Surely you don't believe such nonsense."

"What kind of creature controls men through the sound of her voice?" I mused, wondering if she would admit it.

"Creature." Sirena laughed. "Dramatic much?"

"Am I? Or maybe I have a sixth sense that recognizes when something is more than human."

Sirena's smile faded. "Maybe you're a wacko."

"Maybe. But I'm definitely a good cop. I always get my man. Or woman."

I only wished I could arrest Sirena and bring her in for a lineup, let Harriet finger her. First I needed proof to make my case that we were dealing with murders, that coincidence was not involved.

Sirena threw down the still-lit cigarette. "Break time is over. I have another set."

"Don't let me stop you."

"Why thank you, Detective. No one *ever* does."

With that, Sirena went back inside and I ground her cigarette into the walkway.

"Did she just challenge me?"

"Yep. And she lied about Neil," Jake added. "The cigarette case belonged to Neil's mother who died of lung cancer. He kept it to remind himself never to smoke. Used it to hold his business cards."

Instincts humming, I said, "Let's go back inside." Entering, I whispered, "I'm going to look around, so go to the bar and keep an eye on her." As a cop, I normally played by the book, but there was nothing in the CPD code that guided me in dealing with the supernatural. I would have to break some rules. "Just be careful."

Jake gave me a quizzical look before leaving my side.

Considering Jake was supernatural, how had Sirena gotten to him on that previous visit?

It had to be the sound of her voice…his hearing was vampire-augmented. Apparently that made him even more susceptible than a normal man. My protective hackles rose, but I was certain Sirena wouldn't try anything now. She might be able to put the men in the room under her spell, but the women were another story.

So how did I stop her?

My real-life supernatural experience was limited, but I'd been reluctantly browsing through Silke's books—my twin had a hard-on for everything supernatural—so I knew all magic had balance, weakness as well as power.

What made Sirena vulnerable?

I sneaked down the rear hall.

Even as I heard Sirena address the audience between songs, I felt Jake probing at my mind.

Find anything?

I haven't even started. I'll let you know when I do.

I shut down station SHELL. Having dealt with my twin all my life, I was well-practiced at closing myself off to psychic interference. As to stopping Sirena, I was a novice. Being human put me at a serious disadvantage.

I found Sirena's office, decorated with sea colors, a fish tank and a cage with colorful birds. I went straight to the desk and her computer. Password protected. I tried *Siren…thethreesirens…Persephone…*every variation I could think of. None worked. Then I remembered the Persephone myth.

Underworld let me in.

The computer desktop photo was that of a yacht called *Siren's Song.*

To my disappointment, I found no files on any of the three drowning victims. About to log off, I hesitated, then opened the browser, clicked on *History* and chose *Last 7 Days.*

And there it was: LarsonGallery.com.

I clicked on the link.

And there *he* was: Neil Larson in his art gallery.

I could still hear Sirena's voice carry through the closed door.

I figured I had a few minutes before she finished. Hoping to find some way to stop her *now*, I typed *siren* into a search engine for references on the preternatural creature who apparently wasn't myth, after all. I quickly scanned several articles.

With her voice she enchants, with her beauty she takes a man's reason and deals destruction and death...

...her irresistible song catches a man in her net until she bathes in his life force...

...sirens combine women and birds in various ways...

And then I found it.

A siren is fated to live only until a man who hears her song can free himself of her spell.

That was it—Sirena's Achilles heel.

How did I make that happen?

Closing the browser, I stared at the photo of *Siren's Song*. Sirena living on the water seemed logical. I could see The Ark in the background, so her yacht was docked in the lakeside harbor halfway between the casino boat and the beach. Perhaps there, I would find the proof I needed and a way to end this before another man fell victim to her charms.

I practically flew out of the office. Sirena's voice held on one of those weird high notes that made the room go silent.

The sound Harriet had described.

A sustained high note that had gone on and on as Neil walked out into the water with her, ending only when they'd disappeared below the waves.

I exited the back way, fought the rising wind and ran along the path to the harbor.

Who was next?

Remembering how Sirena had looked at Jake with such interest, I told myself he would be all right. She wouldn't try anything with so many witnesses.

Once at the harbor, it took a few minutes to find the right slip.

Siren's Song bobbed in the water, its interior dark. Praying there would be no terrible surprises waiting for me, I boarded her and lightly jumped down to the deck. The cabin door was locked. I didn't have a search warrant, but these were supernatural circumstances, and what judge would believe me? I reached into a pocket for my picks. The yacht lurched with a gust of wind and I had to steady my stomach from heaving. The lock took only a minute to open.

I slipped inside, closed the door behind me and turned on the light.

The sound of flapping wings startled me.

Across the open salon, a giant cage held back an owl, two small hawks and a vulture. Predators.

I shuddered. Maybe my coming here alone wasn't such a great idea. Intending to search the place and get out fast, I avoided their beady eyes.

The elegant salon's walls and surfaces held decorative and military artifacts that looked real. My attention was caught by an old, beat-up wooden chest.

Ignoring the squawks and rustling, I stooped before the trunk and opened the lid. The sparkle of gems and precious metal was muted by less costly treasure. All personal items. Two on top caught my attention—a watch and a pipe with silver trim. Using the hem of my blouse to pick up the Rolex, I turned it over. Inscribed on the back were the initials CK. Cal Kruger. The pipe looked like the one that belonged to Bobby Russo.

Proof that Sirena was connected to the three supposed suicides.

Taking out my cell phone, I photographed the open trunk's contents. Souvenirs? Did each item represent one of Sirena's victims, possibly going back centuries? As if the birds could read my mind, they chattered and flapped their wings. I straightened and closed the trunk lid and snapped photos of the salon. Only when I made a one-eighty did I realize I wasn't alone.

"Sirena."

Gown swirling around her, blond hair seeming to stand on end, features twisted into displeasure, she blocked the only exit. She muttered something under her breath and I jumped when the cage door slammed open. A small hawk flew by me and landed on Sirena's shoulder. The other hawk followed. Then the owl and the vulture.

My stomach knotted and I had to remind myself to breathe. I had to get out of there and she was blocking the way. Focusing on her, on the danger, I reopened station SHELL to Jake and transmitted my desperation.

Siren's Song, *Northerly Harbor. I need you now!*

I only hoped he heard.

"How many men, Sirena?" I needed to keep her talking until the cavalry arrived, "And why?"

"Thousands…because their life force kept me alive through the centuries. This time you won't get your man, Detective. I warned you that no one ever stopped me."

With that, she signaled the birds to fly back across the room, me their target. I picked up what looked like a metal and leather shield from the coffee table to protect myself. A hawk smacked into it, the impact sending me reeling backward. When I got my breath, I reached for the Glock holstered at the small of my back.

Sirena laughed. "As if a gun would do you any good against me." With that, she backed out of the room and slammed the door.

I frantically called out to Jake. *Sirena's trying to kill me!*

Too bad I objected to shooting animals of any kind. If a bullet would stop them, that is.

So I shot at the ceiling twice. That scared the birds into flapping away. By the time I got to the door, they came for me. A sharp beak tore at my arm, ripping the blouse. I felt talons dig into my shoulder and hit the bird with the shield. The damn door wouldn't open, so I backed into a corner and tried to use the shield for cover.

Hang on, Shelley!

Where are you?

I released a couple more bullets to the ceiling, but this time they had no effect on the birds.

Right here!

Jake's foot crashed through the door and his body followed even as the birds were inches from attacking me again. Jake hissed at them and showed them his elongated canines. One of the hawks smacked into the owl. All four predators retreated to their cell. Apparently vampires terrified even them.

"You're all right." He grabbed me up in his arms and for a moment I clung to him like I would never let him go.

"Thanks to you," I said into his neck and then pushed away from him. "Sirena murdered them all, Jake. I can't let her go."

I was already out the door, holstering my gun and looking for her when I heard her song coming from the beach to the north. Another victim? I started running, Jake beside me.

"Jake! Stop!" He would be susceptible to her. "You have to go back."

There was barely enough light from the harbor lights for me to see his face. His eyes were glazed over. Sirena's voice carried on the wind, seducing him. I could see it happening.

I ran faster. I had to stop Sirena, but how?

She already told me the gun wouldn't work on her. What then? Jake was running at vampire speed to get to the woman who would end him. As I fell behind, my mind whirled and I focused on the information I'd picked up earlier on the internet.

A siren is fated to live only until a man who hears her song can free himself of her spell.

But Jake wasn't trying to free himself. I could see him jogging straight from the beach into the lake after Sirena.

My feet hit sand and I screamed, "Jake, stop!"

The siren's song drowned my words just as she would drown the man I loved. Up to her waist in the lake, she backed toward deeper waters. Her feathered arms stretched toward him.

I plunged into the water after them. "Jake, please, she'll kill you!" He didn't seem to hear so I yelled louder. "Jake, I need you!"

He glanced back, and I could see his brow pull in confusion, but as if drawn to a magnet, he continued toward Sirena. No matter how hard I tried, I couldn't catch up to him.

I had to stop him, but how? Could he even hear my pleas over Sirena's voice?

I concentrated on getting through to him psychically, tried to make him respond to the desperation I was feeling.

I don't want to lose you, Jake. Please listen to me.

He suddenly stopped, giving me hope.

Until Sirena raised her voice, going for that shattering hot note no man could resist. He continued on, away from me.

My chest squeezed tight. As a cop, I'd seen so many terrible things that tears didn't come easily, but my eyes stung at the thought of losing him this way.

I'm yours, Jake. Hear me, please. I thought about my gun, about shooting Sirena if I had to. It might not kill her, but maybe I could temporarily put off her siren's song. *You* are *my life.*

He stopped moving. *Shelley?*

I'm here, Jake, behind you!

I was fighting against the water to get to him as fast as I could. I could feel him fighting Sirena's influence.

Jake, don't leave me. Don't let her take you from me. I can't imagine going on without you.

My plea got to him and he turned as I caught up to him. I threw myself at him and his arms pulled me up against him where he held me tight.

Suddenly the night was still but for the sound of waves lapping at the shore and a rumble of thunder in the distance. The siren's song had gone silent.

A siren is fated to live only until a man who hears her song can free himself of her spell.

Lightning lit up the lake as Sirena plunged backward into a big wave and with a scream that scraped up my spine, was sucked under.

With my arms and legs wrapped around him, Jake carried me to shore.

Watching the water, I didn't see any sign of the murderess.

Jake set me down on the sand, crashed next to me and held me tight as if he would never let me go. "Do you think she'll wash up here tomorrow morning?"

I was already thinking about how I could explain this to Norelli: I'd called Sirena on the murders and she'd committed suicide.

"One way to find out."

We huddled together on the beach to wait for a new dawn.

LAST SHOT

JON LAND & JEFF AYERS

*This is a be-careful-what-you-wish-for story that has
just the right mix of eeriness and emotion. —SB*

"How long have you known me, Frank?" Molly Wagner asked the banker seated at the desk before her.

"We went to high school together, Molly."

"Right. So you know when I promise something I mean it."

Frank, fellow member of the Class of '93, wrinkled his nose, the reflection of his bald scalp shining in the cubicle's glass walls. "This is different. It's corporate. My hands are tied by the policy."

"Of throwing people out of their homes."

"Only when they're seriously delinquent on their mortgages." He paused long enough to take a deep breath and fold his hands together on the blotter. "I've done everything I can."

Molly started to speak, then stopped. She'd come up with folders full of financial proof she and her husband, Bob, would get through this, but there seemed no reason to produce them.

Frank rose, a clear sign it was time for Molly to take her leave. "You've still got a few months to get current. If you think of anything…"

"I will," she said, rising. "I will think of something. And I'll get another job. Maybe this place. I hear they may be hiring."

Frank looked as if he found that funny. "Here? What makes you think you're qualified?"

"I was about to ask you the same question."

Molly left the bank with file folders tucked under arm, fighting back tears. It was over, done. Time to put their house on the market. No sense delaying the issue any further, so her next stop was the local Rexall to copy a picture of their home taken when upkeep had not been an issue. It had been a fixer-upper when they'd bought it, so she and Bob, no experts at home improvement, had slaved over manuals and videos, adding molding, fresh paint, refinished floors, railings—the list went on. Fifteen years of labor and unwise refinancing all about to go into the Dumpster.

Inside the Rexall, Molly located the photo scanner in the back and thumbed through a shoe box full of old photos, most taken when she and Bob had been mere kids and newlyweds before their son was even a thought. There were prom pictures and high school homecoming, Frank the banker with hair, the picture of which she promptly tore in two, the state college where Bob had proposed near a statue of the school's bear mascot that creaked in the wind, Molly afraid the whole time the thing was going to fall on them. She flipped past wedding shots and baby pictures of Matthew, the family captured back when foreclosure was something that happened to other people.

She finally dug out a picture of a simple shot of her home taken before the fence posts had rotted out and the house paint had dulled and started to peel. Molly laid the shot on the glass and touched the scan button but nothing happened.

"Excuse me, could you help me out here?"

The photo clerk slid out from behind the counter where she'd been balancing her lunch.

"I can't get this to work," Molly said, lifting the scanner top to reveal the snapshot she'd laid on the glass.

That glass was deeply scratched, stained and sun-bleached from years of being left open, contrary to the posted instructions. "That's 'cause you can't use this side," the clerk, whose name tag identified her as Jasmine, was saying. Her voice had an impatient tone to it, bred of helping too many customers befuddled by the machine's finicky workings.

Jasmine repositioned the four-by-six snapshot on the other end of the glass, and Molly caught a glimpse of her own reflection until the picture covered it. Her hair hung limply. Her eyes drooped and seemed drained of life. But at least the weight loss she'd managed gave her a more youthful appearance in spite of everything else, and she resolved to never put it back on again.

"There you go," Jasmine said.

Molly closed the scanner top and started from scratch with the controls. She heard a whirring sound riddled with a few clanks that actually rocked the old scanner from left to right and then back again.

It was a Kodak 470 model, capable of doing nothing more than making halfway decent copies of existing photographs. The process took an interminable time by today's standards but copies here at Rexall Drug were only ninety-nine cents. Price was a prime consideration these days for the Wagner household, ever since Molly had lost her job as a dental assistant. She had thought the dental business to be recession proof, but everything from cosmetic procedures to fillings were down enough to necessitate cutbacks in the nonprofessional staff among which Molly was unfortunately included.

Molly finally hit Print and the Kodak 470 rocked slightly sideways again as a squeaky fan belched heat exhaust from a vent in the rear. A vinegar odor rose from somewhere deep in the old machine's guts. It rattled, wheezed and clanked one last time before spitting out the final product.

Molly knelt into the heart of the chemical stench and retrieved the copied picture of her house and yard. The paper was hot to the touch, still vaguely moist, and curling a bit at the edges.

"We're getting a new one, you know," Jasmine was saying.

"What?"

"Scanner. We're getting a new scanner. It's due in any day. About time, right?"

Molly thanked her and headed back out into the parking lot, a bit chilled by the crisp fall air. The town was laden with maple and elm trees that shed their leaves into brilliant pools of sunlight collecting on the sidewalk. She drove home past the array of For Sale signs and pulled into her driveway. Rexall bag in hand, Molly started for the house only to notice that the paint seemed much brighter than it had just a few hours before. Molly realized she'd left her pocketbook in the car and turned to find herself facing a split rail fence that didn't look dilapidated anymore, the posts and rotting rails having been replaced, as well. Molly was left wondering where the money to pay the bill for her husband Bob's well-placed efforts would come from, as she opened the front door to find old, trusty Sherman lying stiff and still in the hallway making no move to greet or even acknowledge her.

"Oh, no…"

She felt a profound sadness, worse than anything spawned by greedy bankers or unfeeling dentists. A loyal friend she could always rely on was gone and, unlike a job, couldn't be replaced. She felt through her bag for her cell phone.

"Bob," she said, after fumbling her cell phone to her ear, "it's Sherman. He's…gone."

She knew her husband; he'd sob the entire way home. He was always the crier in the house, losing it at movies most men dreaded. Chick flicks had been their one indulgence until Molly had begged off out of a purported lack of interest when lack of discretionary income was truly to blame. But it was strange how absenting themselves from movies about falling in love left them both feeling that they were falling out of it.

Next thing Molly knew she was kneeling by Sherman's body, and stayed there until she heard the familiar rumble of Bob's Volvo pulling into the driveway, stroking his fur which felt strangely cold. Molly swabbed at her eyes with a sleeve, sniffling back her tears, and opened the door to find Bob standing there.

She felt him hug her and she didn't want him to let go, as if his embrace could make everything right as it had when they were mere kids themselves. But they were far from kids now and it couldn't. His grasp felt flaccid, his hands cold from the poor circulation he'd inherited from his father. A paunch had grown over his once-flat stomach, pushing his white dress shirt forward, and his trousers sagged below his hips.

Bob eased her away and she realized how much his brown hair had thinned and gone gray at the temples. His eyes looked like hers had in the scanner's glass, only sadder.

"How are we gonna tell Matt?" he asked, his voice childlike. Then, before she could answer, "Wait, what are you doing home?"

Molly tensed. "I just…had this feeling," she told him, even more anxious at nearly being caught in the truth she'd yet to share with him.

Bob ran his hand through her hair, the gesture comforting in the fond memories it evoked of the days when they'd been truly in love.

"I'll take care of this," Molly said. "You can get back to work."

Bob nodded, having trouble taking his eyes off the dog. "Thirteen years is a lot for a dog, but it's not enough, is it?"

"It's never enough."

He spotted the shoe box full of snapshots on the foyer table and shuffled through them. "Where'd these come from?"

"The closet."

His smile grew sadder as he continued to peruse the box's contents just as Molly had in the Rexall.

"You're right, Molly, it's never enough. But we'll get through this. You know we will."

• • •

The next morning she kissed Bob on the cheek and got Matt settled in his car seat for the drive to day care. The boy was holding a picture of Sherman romping in the front yard a few years before Matt was born; clutching it so hard it was crinkled and dog-eared by the time they got to the school.

"Have a good day at work, Mommy," Matt said, hugging her after she led him up to the front door.

Molly pushed back the lump in her throat and kissed him on the forehead. She watched him grab his small backpack and dash into the building, obsessed for some reason with never being the last kid to class. She saw the teacher wave and she waved back, smiling.

Then Molly remembered the picture of Sherman, twisted and tattered by Matt's tiny hands, now lying on the passenger seat. She'd take it to the Rexall and blow it up to eight by ten. Spring for a decent frame as well so Matt could hold fast to it long into the night, keeping the only pet he'd ever known close to his heart and mind.

She drove to the store and immediately headed for the back of the building where the Kodak 470 was kept, drawn to it like an old friend, equally battered and beaten down by life.

"Hello, again," Jasmine said when she saw her.

Molly nodded and positioned the photo of Sherman on the working side of the scanner. She hit the scan button and the machine started clanking and rocking again, even worse than yesterday. And when she was finally ready to print, the vinegar smell was stronger and laced with something that reminded her of something smoldering on a hot stove.

The machine groaned and Molly could see the first of her print pushing out from the feeder slot in one lurch after another, only to be sucked back in with a sound like an angry cat screech. The final product emerged slightly blackened along the top and bottom edges, but otherwise a perfect shot of a younger, romping Sherman.

Molly spent the next four hours in a coffee shop featuring free Wi-Fi and refills, scouring the internet job sites for something remotely connected to her field. There was nothing, not just in the dental assistant field, but anything she felt qualified for period. Time crawled and the coffee kept sending her to the bathroom.

Finally she went to pick up Matt, already composing the day's workplace lies to share with Bob. She was reciting them out loud, softly so as not to disturb her napping son, when she pulled into the driveway and screeched to a halt.

Because Sherman was standing there waiting. Younger, romping Sherman with tail wagging waiting to greet her. Matt was snoring in the backseat when Molly climbed out and approached the dog.

"Sherman," Molly said, the name nearly catching in the back of her throat.

The dog came and greeted her just as Sherman had a million times. She nuzzled his mane and located his tag, craning her neck to better read it. Lost a breath and felt her heart skip a beat.

Because the dog's name was indeed Sherman, and this was the address to which he should be returned.

"It's Sherman, Mommy! He's back!"

The new Sherman knew where his dog bed was and recalled the hiding place of his favorite rawhide bone, half-chewed under the couch. Then Molly remembered the Rexall bag she'd left in the car. She rushed out to retrieve it and studied the slightly grainy enlargement against the dog waiting upon her return, right down to the collar and dangling dog license.

Identical.

Next she grabbed the shot of the front yard, repaired fence posts and all, copied on the Kodak 470 at Rexall yesterday. Compared it with the same scene pictured through the front bay window.

Identical, too.

Sherman, or whoever he was, loped into the kitchen and pawed at the door to the cabinet holding his food. Molly looked at him, then at the picture again.

Could this be happening? Was she losing her mind?

No, the scanner had done this. It had clanked and clunked and reproduced the photographs in reality as well as on glossy paper.

She filled the new Sherman's bowl with food and watched him dig in, surrounding the bowl with his big paws as he always did.

Incredible, Molly thought, turning to find Bob standing halfway between her and Matt curled up on the couch watching Nickelodeon.

"We need to talk," he said.

● ● ●

"You shouldn't have bought this dog."

"Well, I…"

"Why didn't you tell me you lost your job?"

"How did you—"

"I called the office."

"I just couldn't tell you." Molly felt the tears coming, but pushed them back, not wanting to make a scene in front of Matt. "And I didn't buy the dog, Bob."

"So, what, you got it from the pound or something?"

"Something," Molly said, hesitating. "You said we'd get through this. You remember saying that?"

"I suppose," he shrugged.

"Then let me do it. Let me get us through this."

Molly wanted to hug him, wanted to feel him hug her back reassuringly. But the time for gestures was gone, and they stood facing each other with the few feet separating them feeling like a valley.

"Bob? Please, trust me."

Bob shrugged again and nodded, his own eyes moistening.

• • •

That night, as soon as Bob drifted off to sleep Molly padded back downstairs to the computer, quickly locating an image of real piles of money with the caption, *Did you ever wonder what a million dollars looked like?*

No sense getting greedy. A million dollars would change their lives plenty.

Molly saved the image and then opened the real estate website that had posted the listing of their home. She found a picture of the bedroom and saved it to the desktop.

She tweaked the images with Photoshop until she felt it looked perfect. It depicted the money sitting on top of the bed, the piles looking exactly as they had over the *Did you ever...* caption. Except the same piles now appeared atop their covers and neatly folded afghan, promising a better and happier life.

Molly hit the print key and waited for the HP to roll out the resulting product. Her mind wandered while she waited, drifting back to the honeymoon they'd taken. Finances didn't allow for the typical week in the tropics, so they'd opted to go white-water rafting, something neither of them had ever experienced. Pictures of them framed amid the rapids was part of the package, only once the photos arrived Bob's face wasn't visible in any of the shots. At her wits' end, Molly had labored with paste and tape in the pre-Photoshop days to repair the omission, before finally coming up with something acceptable, Bob displayed clearly now alongside her.

In creating it Molly had the sense that if she made things right on paper, they would remain just as right in life. Even though that had hardly been the case, the picture had remained her favorite of the two of them together for all this time. How often she had stared at it displayed on their family room wall as if to will such unrestrained happiness back into reality and how foolish that had made her feel.

But maybe not so foolish anymore.

The Photoshop effort of the money stacked atop their bed emerged from the HP looking even better than it had on screen. Molly trimmed the edges to make sure it would fit on the Kodak 470, stealing a glance toward the rafting shot hanging on an adjacent wall.

Just one last time, she promised herself.

• • •

Molly was there minutes after the Rexall opened, Bob having offered to drop Matt off at day care after she told him she had an important job interview.

"Back again?" Jasmine said from behind the counter, blowing a bubble. "Can you wait until tomorrow?"

"Tomorrow?"

Jasmine tilted her eyes toward the Kodak 1000, a state-of-the-art scanner pressed up against the wall currently with protective plastic wrapped around its shiny frame in stark contrast to the 470's worn and faded casing.

"We're installing it later today, matter of fact," Jasmine told her.

"No, the old one will do just fine."

With that, Molly positioned the Photoshop shot of a million dollars on the glass and hit Scan. The stench from the Kodak 470 was worse than ever, the thing rattling up a storm as soon as she hit Print, threatening to burst from its bonds and rampage through the store spewing chemicals in its wake. The machine's corrosive smell assaulted her, blackening smoke now rising in thin wisps from its innards.

Please, let it work. Just this one last time....

The copied picture emerged from the slot in a series of fits and starts, much too hot to touch at first, but looking even better than the original she'd created.

Thank God, she thought, brimming with hope and expectation for the first time in longer than she could remember as she moved to the counter.

"Anybody ever have, you know, any strange stories about that scanner?" Molly asked Jasmine.

"I don't know about stories, but we've had plenty of complaints, especially in the last month or so."

"Like what?"

"I don't know, like people saying their pictures were gone by the time they got home."

"Gone?"

"Washed out, colors all bleeding together, something like that. I called the company, but customer support doesn't support the 470 anymore. That'll be a dollar six with tax."

● ● ●

Molly rushed straight home, breathless with expectation, the Kodak 470's parting gift to her hopefully lying on the bedcovers. But she couldn't stop from wondering why the machine, and the magic behind it, had chosen her of all people instead of the multitude of others who had seen their memories dissolve in a mishmash of blended colors. Certainly there was a reason and whatever the reason was, it stopped her from questioning the moral implications of what she had done. Besides, was it any different from praying in church for the impossible to come true.

But what if this time it didn't?

She stepped into the bedroom with eyes closed, terrified she was about to learn she'd played herself for a fool. That it would turn out Bob really had hired someone to brush up the house's exterior and the new Sherman was no more than a look-alike stray. She realized in those final moments between breaths that the machine had taken her hostage, enslaved her in hope. But what if that hope were false?

Molly opened her eyes.

And saw the money, big heaping piles of it stacked atop her bed exactly as it had been in the picture. The scale was identical, the denominations, she was certain, identical, as well.

Molly reached out and touched the cash, half expecting it to be no more than an illustration set atop the spread. But, no, it was real. Smelled real, felt real, fanned like real. An assortment of neatly wrapped twenties, fifties. A million dollars.

A million dollars!

Molly sat on the bed and tossed packet after packet into the air, enjoying the *thump* when each one smacked the pile. Her family's problems solved, the house to remain theirs. No For Sale sign added to the endless collection dotting their suburban world.

Then a different *thump,* one car door and then another slamming closed, brought her to the window.

A pair of police officers was heading up the walk, having exited their cruiser parked in the street. They looked dour, purposeful. Molly shrank away from the window so they couldn't see her, heard the doorbell ring.

Were they here to arrest her? Did they somehow know what she'd done? Surely this couldn't qualify as counterfeiting; she hadn't printed the money, she'd just, well, brought it to life. Was that a crime? Was she going to have to explain this miracle to Bob from a jail cell?

Molly debated briefly about not letting them in, then figured they'd get her sooner or later anyway. So after the second ring she went downstairs and opened the door.

"Good afternoon, Officers," she said, forcing a smile. "Is there a problem?"

The cops removed their caps in eerie unison. Molly saw the look in their eyes and knew.

● ● ●

An 18-wheeler had run a red light and obliterated Bob's Volvo, while he was on his way to drop Matt off at day care. Both Bob and Matt had been pronounced dead at the scene. Of course, if she hadn't made up the lie about the job interview, so she could be at the Rexall when it opened, they'd both be alive now. Bob never would have been behind the wheel at that exact place and time. So this was all her fault, the scanner's fault. Not a blessing, after all, but a terrible curse. A gift from hell, not heaven.

"Ma'am," one of the cops was saying, as Molly sat in a chair with broken springs that felt ready to swallow her. "Ma'am?"

She wanted to wake up, wake up and find the fence posts still broken, Sherman still dead, and no million dollars upstairs in her bedroom. Because then Bob and Matt would still be alive. She was fresh out of miracles. There was no magic that could bring them back to life.

"Is there someone we can call for you, ma'am?" the cop was asking now.

Unless…

Might the scanner, could it possibly…

"Is there someone you can be with, someplace we can take you?"

"Yes!" Molly blurted out, hoping against hope. "The Rexall! Please take me to the Rexall!"

The cops did, both eyeing her strangely but not bothering to question a grieving woman. Molly wished only they'd drive with siren screaming and lights flashing the whole way, praying it wasn't too late. But he drove at a modest clip and it turned out it was too late indeed.

The Kodak 470 was gone, having already been replaced by the 1000 that glistened beneath the harsh fluorescent lighting in the Rexall.

Molly grabbed the clerk Jasmine by the white jacket. *"Where is it?"*

"Where's what?"

"The scanner, the old scanner!"

"Out back," Jasmine said. "With the trash."

Molly bolted for the back, nearly crashing through the automatic doors before they had a chance to open. There it was, the Kodak 470 leaning up against a fence surrounding the Rexall Dumpster. The smell of garbage assaulted her as she rushed up to it, already tearing her wallet from her handbag and a picture of Bob and Matt together from her wallet. The top that covered the scanner's glass had been broken off in the move and was resting against the bottom of the sun-faded frame. Molly laid the small picture down on the clearest portion of the glass and wedged the cover over it, reaching up for the scanning controls to the chilling realization that the machine was no longer plugged in.

Since even the 470's magic extended only so far, Molly ran back into the Rexall and yanked three extension cords from the home electronics shelf.

"Where's the nearest power outlet?" she screamed at Jasmine, already unraveling and connecting them.

Jasmine pointed to a wall featuring the store's ATM machine.

Molly had to snake a hand behind it to plug in the strung-together extension cords and then burst back outside with the cords strung like a white snake in her wake. The store alarm began to wail, a surprisingly polite female voice advising her to please return inside because the store had failed to deactivate the security sensor. So now she was a shoplifter on top of everything else.

Outside a garbage truck was backing its way toward the Dumpster and the scanner.

Beep, beep, beep...

"No!" Molly screamed, daring the truck to hit her as she found the 470's power cord and plugged it into her assemblage of extensions.

She hit the on button and the machine coughed to life, black fluid seeping out from its front, more with each spit and rumble.

"What the hell?" one of trash men asked, approaching warily as if afraid of what the crazed woman operating a junked scanner with patched together extension cords might do next.

Molly hit Scan.

Nothing happened.

She pushed it three more times and still nothing, not even a wheeze. She pushed and held the button down and finally the old-fashioned grid that charted the scan's progress popped up and began filling in, each lurch accompanied by a burning smell that reminded her of a blown-out tire. The scanner's steel casing grew so hot it burned her fingers and forced her to shrink away.

The screen flashed Scan Complete in scratchy letters that were dissolving before her eyes. Molly hit Print.

Black smoke wafted outward, the machine's insides grinding, seizing up. Fluids colored red and green and blue flowed outward from the slot where finished pictures were retrieved, the screen now flashing Paper Out.

Paper! She hadn't even thought to check if the machine had any left in its feeder!

The trash men were grabbing hold of her, pulling.

"Get away from the machine!" one wailed. "It's catching fire!"

"No, please! It's not finished! *Please!*"

She tried to grab hold of the scanner's lip but it singed her fingers and she felt herself being yanked backward. Her hands flailed for the Kodak 470 as more colored fluids leaked from the retrieval slot and the Scan Complete message dissolved into nothing. She saw flames peeking out from the machine's underside before bursting out its feeder slot. Then the glass screen blew out and smoke swallowed the scanner in a thick black cloud that looked like a monstrous specter with a mouth formed of crackling flames laughing at her.

● ● ●

The same cops who dropped Molly at the Rexall brought her back home and escorted her up to the door, exchanging no words because there was nothing to say. Molly entered to find the new Sherman wagging his tail to greet her, oblivious to the scanner's failure to right this terrible wrong. A life so filled with hope barely twelve hours ago now lost to tragedy and guilt. Was it so wrong what she'd done? Was it so wrong to want to preserve her family's life and happiness?

She heard the cops slam their doors closed and drive off, leaving her alone as she'd be for the rest of her life.

Then she saw the tiny football flash by the window looking out into the backyard and, after a brief pause, flash by again in the opposite direction. Molly moved out into the backyard through the sliding glass door off the kitchen, gasping for air as if she'd forgotten how to breathe. Time slowed, then froze.

"Where you been?" Bob asked. "I was worried. The school called when you didn't pick up Matt."

Molly finally found her breath, but not words. Then Matt hugged her tightly and she knew it was real, all of it.

"We made a photo book in school today, Mommy."

Scan Complete, the machine had said. The lack of paper must not have mattered....

She pictured the remains of the Kodak 470 being hauled away to some junkyard, compressed and sold for scrap.

"A photo book," Molly managed to echo. "Wow."

"Wanna see it?"

"Later, Matty, later," she told her son, taking her husband's hand in hers. "We've got plenty of time now."

GRAVE DANGER
HEATHER GRAHAM

Spooky…and then some! Action-packed…and then some! Trust it to Heather Graham to plot so many twists into one short story. —SB

The shuffling sound of footsteps had brought her here.

A leg lay on the floor, burned and scorched, blood pooled and congealed along the severed flesh at the kneecap area. In the shadows, Ali MacGregor stepped carefully by it. She blinked and saw the enormous monster beyond the leg. Fanged teeth appeared to drip saliva; the eyes were red, as if within them, all the fires and brutal evil of hell could be found.

Ali stood still, her heart thundering. She heard the noise again, the shuffling sound that had brought her here. She moved as silently as she could. Another step brought her face-to-face with the decaying skeleton of a one-eyed zombie.

Tattered flesh fell from the bones. The jaw bare, the tongue and teeth looked truly macabre. Now, its head hung in a parody of sadness, creating something even more horrible about its appearance—a touch of humanity, eaten away.

On screen, it had been one of the most terrifying creatures ever.

She was proud of the zombie. She'd had a part in the creation, and she thought it was one of her best pieces. The one eye was brilliantly blue, and it seemed to watch her as she listened again to the shuffling sound that had come from the storage room at the production facilities of *Fantasmic Effects*.

It was strange. She was accustomed to the horrific and the bizarre; without it, she wouldn't make a living. But it was one thing when she was here during the day, when the rhythmic churn of sewing machines could be heard, when buzz saws roared, and there were people at every different workstation.

How different it was by night....

She was there alone for the first time. Of course, she wasn't supposed to be alone. Victor Brill was supposed to be working with her. They were finishing up the last of the half-eaten zombies for tomorrow night's shoot in the "graveyard."

The ironic thing, of course, was that the fake "graveyard" lay just beyond a real graveyard. A small plot in back fell under the jurisdiction of the Catholic Church. The land had been purchased and donated by Blake Richards, the brilliant man who had founded *Fantasmic Studios*. Despite his love of horror and the occult, Blake had been a devout Catholic, and a boy who had almost gone wrong, except for the intervention of a priest. Now, Blake Richards was buried in the plot that immediately bordered the brick-walled parking lot of the studios, and the fake cemetery had been established nearby.

The cemetery had never frightened her. Not the real one, certainly. She'd loved Blake Richards; he'd hired her. He'd been the kindest man in the world, and the first to give a young artist a chance. *So why was she so frightened tonight?*

Victor. The jerk.

Victor had headed out to buy them both some fast food to get them through the next few hours. He'd left at five, when it had still been light. Now the sun had set, and the world around her was dark. *Fantasmic Effects* was out of the city, away from the congestion that seemed a part of all of Los Angeles County. Still, there were other studios and businesses not that far away. Enough so that there were scattered streetlights here and there.

The werewolf still seemed to be looking at her.

Hungrily.

I could call Greg. If he wasn't working, he'd come. He'd come save me...just as he had been determined to save Cassandra.

That sudden thought made her wince. Maybe Greg was with his ex-girlfriend now. Or, maybe, Ali had thrown away her happiness because she'd never really grasped his sense of responsibility. He'd told her once that as a homicide detective, he'd learned that it was only the living he could really help. Sure, the dead did deserve justice, and he could help get that justice for them. But it was those still in danger—whether from a perp or themselves—who still really needed help.

Thinking about Greg wasn't going to help her now. Realizing that she'd only gone on a few half-witted dates since she'd left their apartment that night certainly wasn't exactly good for her mind, either. Remembering the ruggedly handsome and rough-hewn sculpture of his face, and thinking that she'd never been frightened of anything with him around was not going to get her through the night. And, certainly, thinking about being in bed with him on a lazy day, his naked flesh next to hers, even the scent of him intoxicating, would not stop the shuffling sound from terrifying her now....

She gave herself a mental shake. Oddly enough, thinking about Greg was helpful. She felt stronger, remembering his strength and determination, coupled with an even temper that always seemed to allow him to go forward.

What would Greg say now? she wondered.

She smiled to herself. Well, in all honesty, Greg would tell her to get out and get away, and call a cop. But then, he might also smile and remind her that her imagination was truly *fantasmic,* and that sometimes she had to live in the real world. Lord, there had been that one time when she had been working on the gauntlets for *Knights and Aliens* when he had stood behind her, fingers in her hair, knuckles brushing down over her cheeks while his whisper teased her ear, reminding her that the knights weren't real, but he was, and he only had a few hours left before heading out for his shift.

They'd made love for hours then, and she had laughed and suggested they should actually make a movie: *Homicide Cop and Prop Girl.* Naturally, he'd be Supercop, and she'd have extra powers, and of course, he told her, she did have extra powers—what her lips did to his flesh was superhuman....

That was then. This was now.

Yes, it was just that it was dark, and she was alone. What was benign by day seemed frightening by night.

So, the werewolf had the appearance of being about to pounce at any given second. And the damned zombie seemed to be watching her, too, as if it was about to salivate any minute. She'd had a part in creating them; they were damned good effects!

She heard the shuffling sound coming from the rear of the storage room again.

She was an idiot. She needed to get downstairs and get the hell out.

She couldn't just run out; she had to finish work tonight—if she still wanted to have a job tomorrow. She could imagine trying to explain herself to Dustin Avery, her boss. "The zombie and the werewolf were freaking me out, Dustin, and I kept hearing this shuffling sound...so, let's just put that umpteen-million-dollar shoot off a day. It's Victor's fault. He didn't come back with dinner."

For a moment, she was almost overwhelmed by the impulse to call Greg. No. She stood still, trying to turn every muscle in her body into steel with her mind; she couldn't call Greg. Not now. Not ever.

He'd been the love of her life at one time. But she'd left him the night he'd left her—because his crazy ex had been hospitalized and arrested on another drug charge. She'd tried so hard to tell him that he couldn't keep bailing Cassandra out; he'd assured her that it didn't mean anything. He felt responsible. Cassandra had a little boy—*not his*—but he still had to hope that she could get straight and care for the child. Once Ali had left him, she couldn't talk to him again. And she couldn't just call him casually now. "Hey, sorry, how are you? Yes, I know I've ignored your calls. But I'm alone at the studios, and I think a coworker is trying to scare me into getting fired."

No, she couldn't do it. She *had* to be rational.

She heard the shuffling sound again, but when she felt the chills race along her spine again, she straightened, gritting her teeth.

Victor was a jerk and a prankster. When he'd left, the place had supposedly been locked. He'd had a key to get back in, and she'd been so busy sewing the last zombie shirt, she probably hadn't heard him return. And now…Victor was trying to freak her out.

She wasn't going to run. She was going to turn the tables on him.

She gave the werewolf a pat on the chest. "Work with me, okay?" she whispered. She smiled grimly, and, using the creatures and mechanics to hide her, she began to tiptoe back toward the rear of the storage room.

● ● ●

Not at all far away, Greg Austin was on a case.

"Jesus, Mary and Joseph!" Tony Martini whispered.

Something similar almost escaped Greg Austin; he managed to remain silent as he surveyed the scene.

Gravestones. Opalescent in the moonlight, some full of lichen and appearing so worn by time that those buried beneath them must have been long forgotten, some bearing funerary art that drew the eye with its sheer beauty. Angels with folded wings wept over freestanding crypts, and cherubs holding crosses looked up to the skies. The ground seemed overgrown, as if the cemetery had long been neglected, completely lost in time.

And then, of course, there was the dead man. The newly dead man.

At first, he must have been hard to see, even for film director Howard Engel.

Because there were corpses lying everywhere. Some were missing limbs. Most had decaying flesh, and bone jutted from torn shirts and worn pants.

They weren't real. They had been set two days ago for the scheduled shoot in the graveyard. The graveyard, of course, wasn't real, either. It had been put together by the wizards of *Fantasmic Effects*. Thing is, filmmakers never planned for a real corpse showing up in the middle of their zombie shoot. It was understandable that Tony was spooked by the fake graveyard. He wasn't as familiar with special effects as Greg. And, of course, Greg was familiar. He had lived with Ali for a year; he had loved to see the flash of emerald in her eyes when she'd had an idea for a superhero costume, or an evil elf, or some other being of fantasy or horror.

He winced, looking back at the studio building where she worked. Well, she'd be off for a few days now. There would definitely be no filming here by tomorrow's light.

He felt the same dull ache he always felt when he thought about Ali, and he winced, and forced the pain down. He was working.

"Do you think it might be the work of the Slasher?" Tony asked. Over the past year, four women had been found in a similar position, torsos bent over on top of their beds, as if they'd died saying their nightly prayers, throats cut ear to ear.

"This is a man. So far, the Slasher only kills women. And in their homes," Greg said. "I'm not saying that it might not be, but we can't come to any real conclusions right now."

Was it the Slasher? He'd been following clues. They'd questioned dozens of suspects, but the killer used gloves, and he seemed to know exactly what he was doing, studying police procedure, evidence…hell, he didn't leave a hair, a drop of fluid—anything.

Greg hunkered down by the real corpse. The man lay half in and half out of a hole that had been dug in the ground—not a true six-foot depth, but maybe three and half or four feet. He'd been wearing a pair of jeans and a T-shirt sporting a ravenous shark on the back. That seemed an irony now, because the slashes just lower than the gaping jaws made it appear that a shark had taken a bite out of the man. But Greg doubted the slashes on the back had killed him; it was the fact that his head had nearly been severed by a ragged blade and lay at an odd twisted angle on the ground, along with his torso, while his legs dangled over the dark pit of the grave. *He could so easily have been a part of the set!*

Greg slipped a gloved hand into the man's pocket and found his wallet. His California driver's license identified him as Victor Brill of Topanga Canyon. In his wallet, Victor also carried nearly two hundred dollars, an ATM card and a Platinum American Express. Robbery didn't seem to be the motive. But then, overkill was seldom in play when the motive was robbery.

Overkill was usually the work of a psycho.

Still hunched down, Greg looked around the area again. He shook his head. The crime scene units were going to groan aloud when they arrived on the scene what with the body parts everywhere, and fake blood spattered across the "zombie" areas where the creatures had apparently just dined on unwary mourners. He'd checked the ground for impressions in the fake landscape himself; footprints, telltale signs indicating the killer's path. There was such a hodgepodge of horror on the set that it was almost impossible to tell anything.

Greg motioned to the police photographer hovering back at the edge of the fake graveyard. "Come on over. M.E. will be here soon, and I want a good photo record before we move anything else."

The police photographer, a grim young woman, started snapping even as she made her way over.

Overkill.

It was actually not an easy feat to nearly sever a man's head. The throat and neck were vulnerable, of course, but to slice through all the flesh, muscle and ligaments down to the bone, well, that took some effort. And anger.

What had Victor Brill done to have received such wrath? Or had he done anything at all? Was this the work of the Slasher?

Greg stood; old Doc Mabry was carefully maneuvering his way to the site.

"That's the real goner?" Mabry asked him.

Greg nodded. "Old" Doc Mabry wasn't that old. But, recently, a series of retirements had left him, at fifty, the oldest M.E. working in the area. He was tall, straight, fit, and could have easily passed for an aging character actor.

"Well?" Greg asked.

"I may puke," Tony Martini said.

Puke would really foul up the scene.

"Tony, go over to Durfey, there. He was the first to arrive, and I think that's Howard Engel, the director standing with him. Find out what Engel was doing out here alone this late, and how he stumbled on the real body. Ask him about this fellow, Victor Brill. He might work here with the special effects people."

Tony nodded and moved away. Greg watched while Doc Mabry hunkered down himself, investigating the corpse.

"How long has he been here?" Greg asked him.

Mabry looked up at him, looked around the "graveyard," and then back to Greg. "Less than an hour. The guy is still warm and pliable, Greg. Hell, he must have died two minutes before he was found."

Greg wasn't sure what suddenly caused such a sharp pain in his gut. He nodded at Mabry, and left him, walking over to the side of the lot where Tony was now interviewing the director, Howard Engel.

"Mr. Engel, I'm Detective Austin," Greg said.

Engel nodded abstractedly, looking past him to the body.

"Sir, what brought you out here tonight?" Greg asked.

"Huh?" The director looked at him, obviously shaken and barely registering anything. He was a slim, ordinary-looking man. He'd directed some of the biggest moneymaking films in the business. Not great epics with amazing acting, but rather, low budget films that had made his studio a fortune.

"Sir," Greg repeated, "what brought you out here? Were you worried about a shoot?" Greg asked, trying to be patient, but feeling a growing sense of unease.

"I…no," Engel said, blinking and then focusing on Greg at last. Greg's steady gaze seemed to make him snap to the present, and still, the man flushed. "I—I came to visit the graveyard."

"Yes, the set," Greg said. "Was there a rea—"

"No, not the set," Engel said, pointing over the brick wall that led to the back and the parking lot of the studios.

The effects studio, where, by day, Ali worked, creating monsters—and sometimes, things of beauty. Ali had such a talent, and such a smile. She'd laugh when she was talking, and she'd snuggle against him. Sometimes he would think about the real monsters he came across when he worked, but she was always his refuge. He'd feel her against him, they'd make love, and he'd know again why life was worth living, and why his life's work mattered, as well.

"The real graveyard. The cemetery, actually. I think it's a grave-yard when it's next to a church, and a cemetery—"

"Mr. Engel," Greg interrupted. He'd forgotten there was a little cemetery right in back of the studios.

"Why were you visiting it?" he asked.

"Stupid of me, I guess. I came out tonight because of Blake Rich-ards."

"Blake Richards—founder of the effects studio?" Greg asked.

Engel nodded. He swallowed and looked at Greg sheepishly. "I felt like he wanted me to visit him. I don't know. It sounds crazy. I came out to visit his grave. He worked with me on the first movie I ever did. I hadn't been out to the grave in a while, and we were going to be shooting here, tomorrow, so... It felt like he was calling me." He paused, flushing again. "Well, I guess this is really going to make me look like a murder suspect, but I came out to say a little something at his grave."

The odd thing was, it sure as hell sounded as if the guy was tell-ing the truth. Greg had gotten pretty good, through the years, at sifting truth from lies.

"Hey! Detective!" Mabry called to him, standing by the corpse. "All right if I get him out of here now?"

"Yes, you may bring Mr. Brill to the morgue," Greg told Mabry.

"Brill?" Engel said.

"The dead man, Mr. Engel."

Engel shook his head. "That's not Victor Brill. I think Brill is still working, up over in the studios."

"The studio is closed," Greg said. The knifing pain in his gut suddenly seemed more vicious.

"No, they, uh, needed to finish up a few of the zombies for to-morrow." He looked at Greg, his face as ashen as Tony's. "Victor Brill is their top finisher on the creatures."

"I'm sorry, we found his ID. That was Victor Brill," Greg said.

Engel shook his head. "Brill is a dark-eyed fellow of about thirty."

"So, he'd be in the studios?" Greg asked.

"Yeah." Engel smiled. "Working with Alison. She's going places, you know. Great girl. I—"

Greg didn't hear more. He felt so gut-stabbed that he nearly bent double.

Ali.

A killer called the Slasher was loose in the area, and Ali was in that building. Working with Victor Brill, whose ID had been found on the corpse.

He left Engel standing there openmouthed, raced to the brick wall, and leaped over it. Going through the cemetery was the fastest way to reach Ali. He vaulted over the fence and landed hard in the grass. It would only take a minute to dial his cell. Noticing the tremor in his hands, he grabbed a nearby vault to steady himself. Yet as he did so, he felt a hand on his back, steadying him. There was no one there.

In large, embossed letters on the iron grating of the tomb were two words, one name.

Blake Richards.

Greg stared at the tomb. "She's got to be all right!" he whispered.

The cell phone was ringing.

"Answer, Ali, answer!" he prayed aloud.

● ● ●

Dolls.

Ali suddenly felt as if she'd been pitched into a remake of *Indiana Jones,* except that she was the explorer, and the bane of her life was dolls, not snakes. *Fantasmic Effects* created amazing dolls. Dolls as real as life, large or small. Sexy Suzie, the doll that had come alive in the thriller *Real Doll* was standing in front of Bobo, the mock-up for Emil Lasher, the actor in *Death by Clown.*

She heard the noise again. She almost laughed aloud. The sound was coming from Bobo's feet; his motor was on, and he was trying to move, but he was blocked in by Suzie and another doll, one that was covered by a large sheet. She started to reach around Bobo to find the machination cord, but before she could do so, her phone rang. She hit the reply key. "Hello?"

"Ali?"

It was Greg's voice. She knew it, of course, the moment she heard it. Her blood seemed to run instantly like molten lava and her knees felt weak. Had she willed him to call her? she wondered. No, such things didn't happen.

"Ali, its Greg."

"I know. Hey, nice to hear from you." Casual, she warned herself. Don't tell the guy you've been eating your heart out for him since you packed up and left.

"Get out of there," Greg said.

"What?"

"Get the hell out of there," he told her.

"Greg, I'm working. I'm at the studio."

"Yes, get the hell out."

She'd started to jerk the sheet off the life-size doll next to Bobo. It fell away as she frowned, thinking that Greg had to be far away, that something had happened near her apartment in Burbank.

"Ali!"

She didn't answer him. At first, she stared in surprise. The doll next to Bobo seemed to be that of a Mexican Day of the Dead skeleton. Then she realized that it was clad in black, with the skeleton painted on the fabric. She couldn't remember a film in which they'd used such a doll, but....

"I'm here, Greg," she said, puzzling over the doll.

And then it moved. It didn't click, whine, or whirr. It moved, raising its arm and its hand, and in the hand was a knife, blood dripping from it....

The arm lashed out suddenly, sending the phone flying from her hand.

"Victor, stop it!" Ali cried out angrily. "You're not going to scare me off this job!"

"No?" he asked, cocking his black-and-skull-clad head to an angle. "Then I'll just kill you," he said cheerfully.

• • •

Greg told himself he was a rational man, a trained cop. He had a gun; he knew what he was doing. He'd call for backup, but first, he'd get to the studios. He was already at the brick wall that lined the back parking lot. He set his arms on the ledge of the wall and hiked himself up; his arms were shaking and he fell back. Cursing, he hiked up again.

And as he struggled to get a solid grasp, he felt something again. Something. As if someone were there, pushing him up the wall.

Tony. Tony had gotten it together and followed.

"Thanks!" he said huskily, and looked back as he gained the top of the brick. But no one was there. No one. No one had touched him.

He was cracking under the strain.

His feet hit the asphalt of the parking lot and he ran to the rear door of the effects studio. It was locked. He stood back, pulled his gun and shot out the lock. He burst through into the shadowed realm of zombies, bugs, gnomes and superheroes.

• • •

Ali ran back through the prop storage, knocking down a wall of helmets and a carton of costume-grade vampire teeth. As she neared the werewolf, she let out a terrified scream; a massive spiderweb—actually, excellent nylon webbing that she'd designed herself—fell upon her. Screaming, she tore at the netting.

And she heard the shuffling sound of his footsteps.

"Victor, you bastard! Where do you think this will get you? Let me go, you ass! Stop this!" she cried.

"Ali!"

She heard her name shouted. It came from far away; it had to be her imagination. It wasn't. It was Greg.

"Greg!"

She didn't hear the shuffling sound anymore. Instead, she heard a chuckle. "He's coming, Ali. How sweet. The script is complete. The detective is coming to save the maiden in distress. Ah, but not all horror movies have happy endings these days!"

"Greg, no!" she cried. "No…!"

● ● ●

Ali! He'd heard her; she was on the second floor. He raced past the shelves of props toward the stairs. There was something coming down for him. Big, enormous…coming out of the shadows.

"Stop!" he roared.

The thing kept coming. He shot.

It fell.

He raced up the stairs to it.

Laughter seemed to sound all around him. "Congratulations, cop. You just killed a dead werewolf. Watch out—the zombies are coming next."

Greg stepped over the fallen beast. The bastard, Brill, had gotten on to some kind of a microphone. His voice would sound as if it was coming from everywhere, no matter where the guy was. He eased down the hall and looked into a conference room. Nothing there but a bunch of models for fairies in little glass domes. He hurried on, past one conference room, then another, and another.…

He looked in the last conference room. Even in his panic, he paused. There was a life-size statue or mannequin of Blake Richards. He was affable-looking, a smiling and white-haired man with kind brown eyes.

"For the love of God, help me!" Greg pleaded.

He hurried out of the conference room and to the last door. The door to the storage room.

"Ali!" he shouted her name.

"No, Greg!"

He shoved the door open, and there she was. His Ali. She was tied up in a cocoon of white, and at her side was a skeleton with a raised knife. A knife that dripped blood. The blood of the man who had so recently perished in the graveyard.

Greg took aim at the skeleton. "Get the hell away from her!" he ordered.

The skeleton just started to laugh. And, as Greg stepped into the room, both hands on his gun in regulatory stance, Ali screamed.

A second web came crashing down, entangling him instantly. The fall of the web wrenched the gun from his hand, knocking it down near his knee. Tension and fury filled him; he refrained from instantly reaching for the gun.

If he wasn't careful, it would fall through the mesh....

"Oh, Greg, I'm so sorry!" Ali said.

He couldn't think of anything else to say. "I love you," he told her. "I always have."

"This is so sweet! So, so sweet!" Victor said. "Do go on."

"Victor is the Slasher," Ali said.

"Yeah, well, we've been trying to catch him, night and day, for a year," Greg said.

"Of course. And you would have gotten him. You're a great cop, Greg. Dedicated—to everyone. A little late, but I'm seeing that now." He could hear the regret in her voice; she was looking at him through all the mesh that tangled them both. Ali was beautiful. Even now, there was strength and pride in her eyes.

"Yes, but...."

"Greg, forgive me. My timing sucks on this, but…we may die. I love you. I was wrong," she said.

"No, no, I just…there was a kid. I couldn't turn my back on a child."

"Oh, such drama, I love it. But enough," Victor said. "I'd only imagined the pleasure of slicing up my dear coworker, the beloved Ali! But, now, I get to cut her up in front of you. A cop! A big old cop who fell right into my trap."

"Well," Greg said, trying to maintain calm; it was their only chance. He had to reach the gun. "You are an ass, Victor—as well as being a true psychopath, of course. I understand that this place may have a lot of soundproofing, but you must have heard some of the sirens tonight. The place is crawling with cops. Every psycho eventually makes a mistake. You made yours tonight."

"I don't think so. By the time the cops actually get here, I'll be tangled in mesh, too. And they'll think I'm the victim who survived when they scared away the real perp!" Victor said.

"You worked with this idiot, for real?" Greg asked Ali. Slowly, slowly, he stretched his fingers toward the gun. The nylon strained, tearing into his flesh.

"Good jobs are not easy to come by in the film industry, even in special effects," Ali told him.

"Ali, precious Ali! Oh, yeah, everyone loves Ali. Old Blake Richards loved you. You were a suck-up. Always with the blond hair falling over your eyes. And you dressed to be provocative, trying to seduce the old bastard!" Victor accused her.

"In T-shirts and sweats?" Ali asked. "He thought of me as a daughter, Victor."

"Well, you can go and join your old man, then," Victor said. His voice sounded unreal, like the evil whisper of a—a movie picture.

Victor started slashing the webbing that held Ali. He was coming closer and closer to her. Desperate, Greg strained harder to reach the gun.

Slash. Slash. He could hear the nylon ripping away with each dreadful fall of the knife.

No, God, no! The gun was just out of reach. Greg screamed in fear that the blade would touch flesh at any minute. Real flesh. Ali's flesh.

Slash. Slash. Slash.

And then, miraculously, it seemed that although he couldn't reach any farther, the gun was moving—*on its own*—toward his hand.

His fingers twined around the grip. He ignored the pain of the tensing nylon, twisted and took aim.

He started to give fair warning.

But the knife was over Ali's trapped form, right over her throat....

"Die, you bastard!" Greg roared.

He fired.

For a moment, skeletal and eerie, Victor Brill still stood, the knife aimed toward Ali's throat.

And then...

He stumbled backward.

The room was suddenly riddled with shots.

Greg twisted around. Good old Tony. He'd followed, and he'd finished off the Slasher.

• • •

Naturally, soon the whole building was abuzz with police. Ali still couldn't believe that she was alive. She couldn't believe that Greg had come. It had all happened so quickly, except, of course, for the terrifying moments when she had been in the net—strong, unbreakable threaded nylon. Hey, she was good at her work.

But now it was over. And though she had been a victim and a witness, and long through with what the police needed from her, she waited in the conference room for Greg to tie up all the loose ends that a detective had to tie up.

At last, he came back. She was seated at the conference table, next to the superb figure of Blake Richards. For a moment, he paused in the doorway, looking at her. He was impossibly wonderful, she thought. His dark hair was in total disarray over his forehead; his eyes fell upon her with naked longing. He was ever strong and steady.

And he had saved her life.

He hurried from the door to fall on a knee before her. He caught her face between his hands—studying her as if he had to reassure himself over and over again that she was all right, studying her as if she were his world.

"Ali," he whispered, and his voice choked. "The things you said—"

"Were real."

He swallowed and nodded. She touched his dark hair, wanting to find the right words. "Let's go home," was all she could manage, and her words were thick.

He nodded. Then he smiled crookedly. "Yours or mine?"

"Yours—and I'd like it to be mine again," she said softly.

He stood and looked back. Tony was in the room. "I got it, Greg. I'm on the crime scene unit, the M.E., you name it. You get out of here."

Greg nodded. He took Ali's hand and drew her to her feet. She was still shaky. She leaned against him. She loved the feel of him and the smell of him, and she trembled, thinking how lucky she was; she had almost died to find out that pride and fear were ridiculous.

And that monsters *were* real.

"Home," Greg whispered to her. He clapped a hand on Tony's shoulder giving him a gruff, "Thank you."

He looked back into the room for a minute. She realized that he was looking at the wax figure of Blake Richards.

"He was a wonderful man," Ali said. "I almost feel as if he was watching over me tonight."

"A great man," Greg agreed. He was still staring at the wax figure. He smiled. She thought he winked.

She blinked hard herself. She could have sworn that, for just a minute, the wax figure was alive, that Blake Richards smiled in return.

And winked.

"Home," Greg said.

Ali nodded. And still, she wondered, had Blake Richards helped save her life that night?

Yes, quite possibly, because Greg spoke up then, after clearing his throat.

"Thank you, sir. Thank you," he said quietly.

Yes, she thought. *Yes, he had helped save her.*

Her life. And her love. The way that Greg had looked at the wax figure…

"Thank you!" she whispered. A foolish thing to do? She'd probably never know.

She turned, her hand tightly held in Greg's, and they left.

They were going home.

WITHOUT MERCY
MARIAH STEWART

*This story is as real and emotionally gripping as
a current headline. Surely nothing strikes more fear
in us than the report of a missing child.* —SB

Mallory Russo stood and eased the kinks from her back. She'd spent most of the afternoon sitting in the same spot, reading résumés that had flooded in to her employer, the Mercy Street Foundation. Ever since her boss, megamogul Robert Magellan, announced that he was funding an organization to investigate unsolved missing persons cases and needed to hire the best law enforcement personnel he could find, the flow of résumés had been nonstop.

The foundation was a private investigative firm with a unique twist: once a case was selected, their services were free. So now, they needed staff to handle the number of cases that were coming in. Mallory was wavering between two hopefuls—a retired detective from Miami and an FBI profiler who was looking for some new challenges—when the phone in her pocket rang.

"Hey, Charlie." She swiveled her chair around to look out the window. It was already dark. She stole a glance at her watch. It was almost seven. "Are you already home?"

Charlie Wanamaker, the detective who'd been hired by the local police force to replace Mallory when she left the job two years ago was also her fiancé. "I'm on my way. Thought I'd stop and pick up something for dinner. You call it—Chinese or Italian."

"What kind of detective asks a girl whose last name is *Russo* if she wants Chinese or Italian?"

He laughed softly. "Lasagna or ravioli?"

"Surprise me."

"I'll see you at home."

The reports and résumés lost their appeal. They would still be there in the morning. Mallory tucked the files into neat stacks, piled them onto the corner of her desk and left for the night.

● ● ●

"Mal, does the name Karen Ralston ring any bells?" Charlie reached into the cupboard for wineglasses.

"Ralston." Mallory paused, a serving spoon in one hand. "There was an old case of the chief's, must be ten or so years old by now. Thirteen-year-old girl went missing on her way home from school. Her mother used to stop at the station to see if there'd been any developments, but there never were." She walked to the table and spooned ravioli onto Charlie's plate. "Donna Ralston, the mother, was a waitress at the Conroy Diner. Joe wasn't chief when the girl first disappeared, so he handled the case from day one. He always had time for Donna whenever she stopped in, no matter how busy he was."

Mallory served dinner in silence, then asked, "Has Donna Ralston called the department?"

Charlie nodded. "She called this morning. I let Joe know when he checked in. He asked if you'd be willing to give the woman a few minutes, just as a favor."

He poured wine into both their glasses. "You don't have to, of course. You don't work for the department anymore."

"Of course I'll call her, if that's what Joe wants."

Joe Drabyak had been more than Mallory's chief: he'd been her

mentor, her friend and the father she'd never had. She'd never refuse a request of his.

"Joe thought you might want to look through the file," Charlie
said, nodding toward the folder he'd placed on the counter. "He
was hoping you'd stop in at the diner and just have a word with
her, if you weren't too busy."

"Oh. Sure." Mallory nodded. "I'll just let Robert know I'll be a
little late tomorrow…"

● ● ●

It was just before eight the next morning when Mallory walked
into the Blue Moon Diner and scanned the counter for Donna
Ralston. She found the waitress at the far end, where she was handing a check to a diner who had already risen to leave. Mallory
walked to the end and took the seat that had just been vacated.

"Hey, Detective." The waitress's weary face brightened a bit when
she recognized Mallory. "Haven't seen you in a dog's age."

"It has been a while," Mallory agreed. "But I'm not a detective
anymore, remember?"

"You'll always be Detective Russo to me." Donna finished clearing the place for Mallory, then leaned on the counter. "The guy I
spoke with yesterday said the chief was in an accident but he was
going to be okay."

"He has some mending to do, but he'll be fine."

"Good, good." Donna reached behind her for a white porcelain
mug. "Coffee?"

"Please." Mallory waited until the mug was filled before asking,
"Was there something you wanted to tell Joe? Something about
Karen?"

"I don't know if it means squat, but the chief always said to let
him know anything I heard, even if it seemed unimportant." She
glanced at the clock. "I'm on break in ten minutes. Do you have a
little time?"

"Of course," Mallory assured her.

Ten minutes later, Donna was back to refill Mallory's mug, then led the way toward an empty booth.

Donna took a thin leather case from the pocket of her apron and opened it flat onto the table. "This is Karen when she was a toddler. And here she is the year she disappeared."

Mallory picked up the photos and studied them, even though she'd seen them in the file. As a three-year-old, Karen had been the picture of innocence. She wore her blond hair in ponytails. Her yellow dress had a green collar and her hands clutched a stuffed animal. As a young teen, Karen's hair hung straight past her shoulders in soft curls, and she wore a pink cardigan sweater over a sundress. She'd matured in the ten-year span between the pictures, but the smile had never changed.

"Why don't you tell me what's going on?" Mallory asked.

"Over the weekend, a couple came in, used to live here. Virginia and Don Greeley. They were back last week for a family reunion and stopped in for breakfast on their way out of town. Virginia was saying how she thought about my Karen from time to time, that sort of thing, but later, it hit me that something she said seemed off."

"What was that?"

"She said, 'I can still see Karen walking past my house with the Tripp girl on their way across that cornfield sometimes after school.'"

"What was strange about that?" Mal asked.

"Far as I knew, Karen hadn't been friendly with anyone named Tripp. And there's no cornfield she'd have to walk through on her way from school to our house. So I asked Virginia what cornfield was that, and she said the one out on County Line Road."

"Any chance she and this girl were friends and you just weren't aware of it? Maybe they studied together at the other girl's house."

"The rule was straight home from school unless she needed to stop at the library if she had homework. She wasn't supposed to go to anyone else's house after school. That was the rule."

"Donna, even really good kids stretch the rules every chance they get."

"I suppose. She just never said…" Donna sighed heavily. "Anyway, here I am, eleven years later, just finding out she had a friend I didn't even know about."

"Why do you think this is significant?"

"I just can't help but wonder, maybe that girl knew something. Maybe there was someone who tried to pick them up on their way home, or maybe followed them." Donna was close to tears. "After Karen disappeared, Joe asked me to give him a list of all of Karen's friends, everyone she hung out with, talked on the phone with, walked home from school with, so he could talk to them all." She looked at Mallory from across the table. "I don't know if the Tripp girl knew anything about the day Karen disappeared, but I do know that her name wasn't on that list because I created the list, and I didn't know they were friends."

"Donna, I'll go through the file again. There's a good chance that Joe or someone else in the department spoke with this girl back then but you weren't aware of it."

"Thank you. I know it's probably nothing, but I can't let it rest."

"I understand." Mallory drained her mug of coffee. "Where did the Greeley's live in Conroy, do you remember?"

Donna nodded. "On Wister Road, the second to the last house before you come to County Line Road. There's a farm across the street. I'm guessing that's the field Virginia was referring to."

"Did the Greeleys leave a contact number?"

Donna nodded. "I wrote it on the back of my pad." She took the pad from her apron pocket and copied the number onto a napkin, which she handed to Mallory. "Thank you, Detective Russo."

It was on the tip of Mallory's tongue to remind her that she wasn't *detective* anymore, but she let it go.

She paused outside the door of the diner, then speed-dialed a call as she made her way to her car.

"Robert," she said when her boss picked up, "I need to talk to you about a case...."

• • •

Thirty minutes later Mallory was seated at her kitchen table, going through Karen Ralston's file looking for the folder that held the witness statements. It took her all day, but by late afternoon, she'd read every report in the file. Nowhere did the name Tripp appear. So how to find this girl, whose first name she didn't even know?

She called Virginia Greeley and explained that she was following up at Donna Ralston's request. Did she recall when she saw Karen Ralston with the Tripp girl? And did she know the girl's first name?

"It was pretty close to the time Karen disappeared," Virginia Greeley told her. "I remember telling my husband right after we heard the news that I'd just seen the two girls walking off across the back field. I don't recall the girl's first name, sorry. Don't know for sure where they were headed or where the other girl lived."

"Did you mention this to the police at the time?" Mallory asked.

"No. Should I have?" Virginia paused. "It didn't seem unusual. I mean, it was just two girls walking home from school. Why would I have told the police that?"

Because Joe would have talked to the other girl at the time and filled in that blank and I wouldn't be trying to do it now, eleven years later.

"Thank you for your time, Mrs. Greeley. If you remember anything else, would you please give me a call?"

Mallory hung up, then grabbed her bag and headed for the local library, where she scanned shelves of the local school's yearbooks.

Mallory found Elizabeth Tripp in the same eighth grade book in which she found Karen.

The city directory had one listing for *Tripp*. She jotted down the address and phone number. It wasn't likely that Elizabeth Tripp would answer the phone after all this time, but stranger things have happened. She dialed the number, but no one picked up, and the call never went to voice mail.

Maybe just a quick drive-by.

The Tripp home was located in a rural neighborhood of small farms. Mallory counted off the house numbers and stopped when she got to the mailbox that bore the one she was looking for. She paused at the entrance to a long driveway.

The farmhouse at the end of the lane was small and in need of fresh paint. A shiny new black pickup was parked in front of a barn, behind which a stockade fence enclosed an area that appeared to stretch all the way to the back of the house. Mallory continued up the drive slowly and parked behind the truck. She was just about to open the door when a man appeared from behind her car. He was tall with shoulder-length dark hair, a dark beard and piercing dark eyes—and he looked as if he meant business.

"Help you?" he asked before she could get the door open.

"I hope so." Mallory flashed her best smile. "Is this the Tripp home?"

"Maybe."

"My name is Mallory Russo. I work for the Mercy Street Foundation." Mallory had to suck in her stomach to slip out of the car, the man stood so close.

"That's that place that looks for missing people."

"Right." Mallory took a few steps back. She felt ill at ease with him so close. "I'm looking for Elizabeth Tripp."

"Lizzie?" He frowned. "Last I heard, she wasn't missing."

"Are you a relative? Do you know where I could find her?"

"I'm her brother," he replied. "What's this about?"

"I just wanted to ask her a few questions about someone she went to school with."

"Far as I know, Lizzie doesn't keep in touch with anyone from around here, but if you leave me a card, I can ask her to give you a call."

Mallory was about to protest when a child of three or four came running around the corner of the barn. Her pale blond hair was cut short, and she wore a too-long sundress. She froze when she saw Mallory.

"Hi," Mallory called to her and waved.

The man turned to the child. "How'd you get out?"

Shrinking back, the little girl pointed to an open gate.

"Get on back inside."

The child tilted her head slightly, then smiled tentatively, a sweet little smile that turned up on one side. Mallory's breath caught in her throat.

"I said back inside," the man growled. "And close that gate."

The little girl fled through the opening in the fence.

"If there's nothing else…" the man said flatly.

"I was going to give you my card…"

"Right."

Mallory dug in her bag until she found one. He didn't bother to look at it before putting it into his shirt pocket.

"If you could ask your sister to call me, I'd appreciate it."

"I'll be sure to do that," he said. "But don't be surprised if she doesn't."

"Why wouldn't she?" *Assuming you gave her my card, which you clearly have no intention of doing.*

He shrugged. "Lizzie's just like that sometimes."

"Thanks."

It had been on the tip of her tongue to ask him about Karen

Ralston, but something about him sent a chill right through her. Mallory could feel his eyes on her as she got back into her car. Shaking it off, she put the key in the ignition and looked up to see a young boy peer over the top of the fence near where the back door of the house must have been. Seconds later, a woman appeared momentarily in a side window, her hand holding back the curtain. Following Mallory's gaze, the man turned, but the boy and the woman were gone.

Mallory's hands shook as she secured her seat belt. When she raised her hand to wave, the stony-faced man didn't bother to wave back.

The woman had been at the window for only a second and she was too far away for Mallory to get a good look at her. But Mallory had seen the smile on the face of the little girl, and she was pretty sure she'd seen that smile before.

What if…?

Don't let your imagination run away with you, she cautioned herself. *Don't be looking for something that isn't there. The idea is too preposterous for words.*

● ● ●

Mallory tried to process what she'd just seen logically, rationally, but the thought bubbled up inside her like hot tar on a late August road. She knew that jumping to unfounded conclusions had landed many a cop in hot water—but, she reminded herself, she wasn't a cop anymore. Still, she'd seen the child plainly, and the resemblance to the little girl in the photo Donna Ralston had shown her that morning was uncanny—the tilt of the head, the smile that turned up just slightly to the left. Mallory hadn't imagined that.

What if…?

Joe had always said that her instincts were her best qualities as a cop, and he'd taught her to trust herself, but this time, she wasn't so sure. If she was wrong, the error would be more than embarrassing. But dear God, if she were right…

She had to see the child again, and she had to see the woman in the window up close.

The first thing she did when she got home was make a phone call to Lilly Mack, the computer wizard Robert had recently hired. While the call went through, Mallory went through the file until she found what she was looking for.

"Lilly, did you get all your new software programs installed?" Mallory asked.

"Everything's up and running. What do you need?"

"Could you age-progress a photo for me?"

"Is that all?" Lilly pretended to scoff. "Piece of cake."

"I'm scanning it to you right now."

"I'll do my thing and send it back."

"Perfect. Thanks, Lilly."

"That's what I'm here for."

While she waited, she called Charlie to bring him up to date and feel him out.

"I'd say you're reaching, Mal," Charlie said. "Walk through what you actually saw."

"I saw the brother of a girl Karen was seen with close to the time she went missing. I saw a little girl who was a dead ringer for Karen Ralston at about the same age. I saw that the entire back of the Tripp property is enclosed by a tall stockade fence. I saw a little boy of maybe eight or nine over the top of the fence, and I saw a young woman peeking through the window curtains."

"So what do you really have?"

"A gut reaction to a little girl who bears a striking resemblance to a missing child." She sighed. "Technically, I got nothin'."

"So having nothing other than a wild suspicion, what are you planning to do?"

"I sent a photo of Karen from the file to Lily to age-progress it."

"Then what? You don't have anything to compare it with."

"Well, not now I don't. But I was thinking, maybe if I went back out and knocked on the door, she'd open it and I'd see if…"

"Mallory." Charliespeak for, *think about what you just said.*

"Yeah, I know. Long shot. But it's bugging me. I have to see if it's her. What if it's her, Charlie?"

"Surely other people have seen this woman before, Mal. You can't hide someone for eleven years, babe."

"Two words, my love. Jaycee Dugard."

"The woman who'd been kidnapped in California when she was eleven and found eighteen years later," he said thoughtfully.

"Living in a compound in the backyard of a house that was in an actual neighborhood, and no one saw her all that time," she reminded him. "The Tripp place isn't even in a neighborhood, and the house is set way back off the road. You should see the fence. It has to be ten, twelve feet high, and it looks like it goes entirely around the property."

"You get this guy's first name?"

"No. I didn't ask and he didn't offer."

"Let me see what I can find out about him. Sit tight."

No sooner had the call disconnected when her phone rang again.

"I just sent that photo," Lilly told her. "Check your email."

"Thanks, Lilly. That was fast."

"Technology rocks. Let me know if you need anything else."

"Will do." Mallory waited impatiently for Lilly's email. When it finally arrived, she opened it and stared at the image, then printed it out quickly and tucked it into her purse.

• • •

It was almost five in the afternoon when Mallory drove slowly past the Tripp farm. She tried to look up the driveway, but there was a car behind her and she had to keep moving. She decided to park off the road that ran behind the house, then walk along the fence to get a little closer without being seen. There was a really good chance that she was ridiculously off base, in which case, being caught poking around—trespassing—could prove embarrassing.

She studied the photo once more, then followed the fence around the property. She made her way as quietly as she could to the side of the house, where she stood directly under the window, and looked up.

Startled to see the curtain pulled back, and the face of a young woman staring down at her, Mallory's heart all but stopped beating. It was the face from Lilly's age-progression.

"Karen," she said softly. "Karen Ralston."

The woman's eyes grew large and round and her mouth fell open slightly.

"Karen," Mallory repeated. "We've been looking for you. Your mother has never stopped looking for you."

"My mother is dead. Go away," the woman whispered through the screen and began to close the window.

"She's very much alive. I saw her this morning."

The woman turned sharply and looked over her shoulder.

She turned back to Mallory and she mouthed the word, "Run" before dropping the curtain.

Mallory ducked and pressed her body against the side of the house.

From inside she heard a man's voice. "What are you doing at the window? Someone out there?"

Inside her pocket, Mallory's phone vibrated. She opened it and read Charlie's text message.

Subject ID'd as Lonnie Tripp. History of violence. Charged as adult at 16 for assault/kidnapping/rape but charges dropped, victim recanted. No record of employment, no record of anyone living with him at that address. DO NOT APPROACH. Heading home, wait for me.

Too late, Charlie.

The front door slammed, and heavy footsteps started toward the corner of the house. Mallory took off for the fence, hoping that maybe Lonnie Tripp would think she'd ducked into the hedge of evergreens and would waste time enough to permit her to make it back to her car. She ran as quickly as she could along the fence line and rounded the back corner, where she ran face-first into Lonnie's chest.

Without a word, he spun her around, and pinning her arms tightly behind her, forced her through a gate into the backyard.

"Some people," he whispered in her ear, "just don't know when to leave things alone."

"Listen, Lonnie…"

"Shut. Up." He latched the gate behind them.

Mallory did her best to take in as much as she could as they crossed the yard in the direction of the barn. Along the far side of the fence stood a row of stark white crosses. Around each one, flowering vines had been draped. A chill went up Mallory's spine. Graves of the last curious visitors?

The back door slammed and the woman Mallory now knew was Karen Ralston came down the steps.

"What are you going to do?" Karen asked.

"Get back into the house and stay there."

"She said my mother was alive."

"She's a liar. You know where your mother is." Lonnie jerked his head in the direction of the makeshift graveyard.

"She said she saw my mother this morning."

"And I said she's lying." Lonnie stopped abruptly.

"In that picture, the one you said my mother showed you, what was I wearing?" Karen called to Mallory.

"A yellow dress with a big green collar," Mallory called back. "You were holding a stuffed green frog."

"My mother always carried that picture with her," Karen told Lonnie.

"Then she saw it someplace else." Lonnie pushed Mallory forward.

"If Donna Ralston isn't in that grave back there, then who is?" Mallory asked loudly enough for Karen to hear.

He shoved her toward the front gate.

"Who else is buried back there, Karen?" Mallory called to her.

"My babies," Karen told her. "All the ones that died."

Lonnie opened the gate and dragged Mallory though, then across the dirt driveway where he shoved her into his truck.

Pick your moment, she told herself. *You may only get one shot at him.*

He'd just begun to bind her hands behind her with a length of rope when she landed a kick to his gut, but a second kick bounced off his knee. He grabbed her by the throat, cutting off her air.

"You saw that little girl this morning? You keep it up and she'll be joining the others out back underneath the crosses. Understand?"

Mallory's eyes widened and she nodded, her stomach twisting with fear and frustration as he bound her wrists tightly. In a clean fight, she could probably take him down. With her arms tied behind her back and the well-being of a child at stake, she wasn't sure the risk would be worth it. Damn. She should have called Charlie when she first got here.

Lonnie released the pressure and she slumped back on the seat, gulping for air while he tied her legs together at the ankles. He reached under her seat and pulled out a handgun wrapped in a dirty rag. He shoved the disgusting rag into Mallory's mouth and pushed the gun back under the seat. She gagged, and he laughed all the way around the front of the truck.

Lonnie climbed into the cab and jammed the key into the ignition.

"Stupid goddamned people can't mind their own business. Gotta poke around and poke around…"

He slammed the truck into Reverse and backed halfway across the yard before shifting into Drive, hitting the gas and flinging stones and dirt in his wake. He got as far as the end of the lane when three black-and-whites pulled in to block his exit.

"Goddamn," he muttered as he hit the brakes. The truck fishtailed and came to a stop. He reached for his gun just as the driver's side door opened and an arm reached in and yanked him out.

"Don't even think about moving. I am not a very happy man right now."

Charlie shoved Lonnie up against the side panel of the truck.

"He's all yours." Charlie handed Lonnie over to the uniforms who'd followed him.

Seconds later, Mallory's door opened.

"You okay?" Charlie's face appeared before her.

"Errrrrrrr," she replied, rolling her eyes.

"Oh. Right." He carefully removed the rag from her mouth.

"Thank you." She grimaced. "That was disgusting and smelled like…you don't want to know what it smelled like."

While he untied her hands and feet, she asked, "How'd you know I was here?"

"Please. You insult me." He lifted her from the cab.

"Karen Ralston is in there with two kids. Well, two that I know of."

She started off toward the fence.

"I think you'd better let us take it from here." Charlie grabbed her by the arm. "This whole place is a crime scene now, and I don't want there to be any questions later on."

She got it. She was not only the fiancée of the investigating detective, but she was also an intended victim of the suspect.

Mallory backed off.

Charlie waved over one of the other officers. "Take Mallory's statement, then make sure she gets home."

"Be really easy with her, Charlie," Mallory told him. "Lonnie had her convinced that her mother was dead and buried in the yard. Karen said her babies were buried there, too."

"If they're there, we'll find them," he promised.

● ● ●

"Tell me everything," Mallory demanded when Charlie finally got home late that night. She'd been sitting on the sofa watching the door for what had seemed like an eternity. "Don't leave a thing out."

"Karen came home with Lizzie one day after school. Lonnie said he waited until his sister went into the house for something and left Karen alone. He told her to come into the barn to see their kittens. Then he grabbed her, tied her up, gagged her, hid her in the hayloft."

"What did he tell his sister?"

"He told her that Karen had to leave to get home and that she'd see her around. Then he says he put something in Lizzie's food to make her sick so she couldn't go to school the next day and hear about Karen missing because he didn't want her telling anyone that Karen had been at their house. Says he must have put too much in by accident because she started breathing funny, then she just stopped."

"He killed his sister?"

"He said it was an accident," Charlie said dryly.

"What did he do with her body? And where were their parents during all this?"

"The mother died when Lizzie was five, and the father was a long-haul trucker. He was in a bad crash ten years ago and has been in a nursing home ever since. Lizzie's buried in the backyard.

When the school called to ask about his sister, he said he was their father, and that he was taking Lizzie to stay with her grandparents in Maine because she was so upset about Karen's disappearance."

Mallory frowned, remembering all the other crosses. "What about all those other graves where Karen said her babies were buried?"

"They're all empty," he told her, "but it explains where Lonnie's money was coming from."

"What are you talking about?"

"Karen had a child almost every other year since she's been captive. Lonnie told her they all died and he buried them in the backyard so she wouldn't have to see them."

"Oh, my God." Mallory's jaw dropped. "Were they all stillborn?"

"Nope. They were all nice healthy babies. Lonnie sold them. After she fell asleep, he'd take the baby to a contact he had in Reading and handed it over for cash. Healthy white newborns are worth their weight in gold. Literally."

"I can't believe this." Mallory's mind was a jumble of questions. "Why didn't she leave? Why didn't she run away?"

"He'd already told her he'd killed her mother, said he'd kill her, too. He'd let her keep two of the babies because she'd gotten so depressed, but he told her if she tried to run away or tried to alert anyone, one of those babies would join the others in the backyard."

"But what about the babies that he sold? Can Karen get them back?" She thought about the parents—the children themselves—whose lives would be turned inside out.

"So far he's refused to give any information about that, but we'll keep working on him."

"Has Karen seen her mother?"

Charlie nodded. "Donna was at the hospital with Karen and the kids."

"I wonder how her kids are going to cope. I'm guessing they've never been to school."

"They'll work it out." Charlie sat next to her and rested her against his chest, her head on his shoulder. "I stopped in the hospital to see Joe. He said to tell you he's really proud of you for not letting your instincts get rusty since you left the force." Charlie paused. "So am I. And I'm sorry I doubted you."

"You'll pay later for your lapse in judgment."

"I can hardly wait." Charlie smiled and reached into his pocket for his phone. "So what's it going to be tonight? Chinese or Italian?"

Mallory turned slightly to snuggle into the crook of his arm.

"Surprise me."

EVEN STEVEN

D. P. LYLE

*Putting a heart-wrenching spin on the vigilante theme,
Lyle strains and sustains the tension to the last
paragraph, last sentence, last word. —SB*

"I can still smell him." Martha Foster inhaled deeply and closed her eyes.

Tim stood just inside the doorway and looked down at his wife. She sat on the edge of their son's bed, eyes moist, chin trembling, as were the fingers that clutched the navy blue Tommy Hilfiger sweatshirt to her chest.

Behind her, a dozen photos of Steven lay scattered across the blue comforter. A proud Steven in his first baseball uniform. A seven-year-old Steven, grinning, upper left front tooth missing, soft freckles over his nose, buzz-cut hair, a blue swimming ribbon dangling around his neck. A playful Steven, sitting next to Martha at the backyard picnic table, face screwed into a goofy expression, smoke from the Weber BBQ rising behind them. Tim remembered the day he snapped the picture. Labor Day weekend. Just six months before…that day. He squeezed back his own tears and swallowed hard.

Martha shifted her weight and twisted toward the photos. She reached out and lightly touched an image of Steven's face. The trembling of her delicate fingers increased. She said nothing for a moment and then, "I'm taking these."

Tim knelt and pulled her to him, her cheek nestling against his chest, her tears soaking through his shirt. He kissed the top of her head.

"He's gone," Martha said. "Everything's gone. Or will be."

Tim smoothed her hair as details from a room frozen in time raced toward him. A Derek Jeter poster, a photo of Steven's Little League team, and his Student-of-the-Month certificate hung on the wall above his small desk. A crooked-neck lamp spotlighted a history text, opened to the stern face of Thomas Jefferson. His baseball uniform draped over the chair back, sneakers haphazard on the floor. Exactly as it had been the day their lives jumped the track.

They had been through this dozens of times. What they could safely take. What must be abandoned. What could be traced back here. They had scrutinized everything they owned. Their marriage license, birth certificates, engraved wedding bands, the calligraphed family tree Martha had painstakingly drawn and framed, and boxes of family keepsakes. Any photo that showed their home, cars, neighbors, family, Steven's friends, teammates, or school, had to be abandoned. As did Steven's Little League uniform. Each of these could undo everything if seen by a curious eye.

Tim had always won these what-to-take-what-to-leave arguments, but now, with the end so close, he knew he could no longer resist her.

"It's okay," he said.

"Thirty-six hours." She eased from his embrace and looked up at him, swiped the back of her hand across her nose. "I can't believe it's here."

"We can back out. Stay and risk it."

She shook her head. "No. We can't. Not with him around."

"He might've just been blowing off steam."

"You don't believe that."

No, he didn't. He knew better.

"Besides, that's just part of it. We can't let that animal…" She screwed her face down tightly, suppressing another sob.

Tim touched her cheek, catching a stray tear with his thumb. "It'll be okay. Keep the pictures." He stood, walked to Steven's desk, lifted the uniform from the back of the chair and tossed it onto the bed. "The uniform, too."

"His uniform?" A sob escaped her throat. "He was so proud of it." She swallowed, looked up toward him and dabbed her eyes with her shirtsleeve. Her voice broke when she said, "Are you sure?"

"I'm sure."

"Thank you," she whispered.

"But nothing else. Nothing that leads back here. This life is over. Finished. Tomorrow night Tim and Martha Foster no longer exist. But Robert Beckwith and Cindy Strunk will get a chance to live again."

She shook her head, uncertainty lingering in her eyes. "What if they find out Robert and Cindy have been dead for a couple of decades?"

"Not likely."

"Still…"

"It'll work. We're not the first to rummage through old obituaries and cemeteries. Lots of people have done it before us."

"Most get caught."

"Only the ones you hear about. Most just move on. Become someone else."

"Let's hope."

He brushed a wayward strand of hair from her face and lifted her chin with a finger. "You'll make a perfect Cindy."

She smiled, weak and tentative, her face tear streaked, her nose reddened, but it was still a smile. There hadn't been many of those lately.

"It's not like we have another option," Tim said. "We can't simply move. We have to disappear. Become completely untraceable. Be reborn."

She took a deep breath and let it out slowly. "It will be like dying."

"Except that we'll have another chance. A new life." He looked down at her. "And Steven will live on in our memories."

"It's not fair." She hugged the sweatshirt again.

"Can you live with this? What we're doing?"

She sat silently for a moment as if considering his question. The question that had plagued them for the past six months. Even as they pressed ahead with the planning, with getting the documents in order, with building their new life, their new identities, the question hung out there on the horizon. A horizon whose sharp edge dropped into an abyss. A horizon that rapidly approached. Could they do this? Could they really leave everything and everyone behind?

She sighed. "I'll have to."

"We'll both have to."

She swallowed against another burst of tears. "What now?"

He retrieved his to-do list from his shirt pocket and unfolded it. "You have the new passports and the North Carolina driver's licenses. Right?"

"In my purse."

"The money from the house sale and our accounts is in the bank in Boone."

They'd luckily found a buyer willing to pay cash for the house. At a big discount. He bought the story about them needing to sell quickly and head west to Arizona. Ailing mother. That was lucky but also easy. The hard part was closing down all their accounts, selling the bonds and emptying his pension plan without raising too much suspicion. You can't simply take a couple of hundred thousand in cash from a bank without triggering scrutiny. Shutting down a pension plan is even more difficult. Tim had managed to move the money around to several banks and investment houses, each time bleeding off a chunk of cash.

"The rental house there is ready," Tim said. "Tomorrow we'll empty the last bank account."

She stood. "I'll finish packing and then we can take all this over to the new car."

● ● ●

Tim turned the SUV into the mall's parking deck and wound up to the roof of the structure. At 11:00 p.m. only a handful of cars remained on that level. He pulled into the space next to a blue sedan. The one owned by the newly minted Robert Beckwith.

While Martha rechecked the boxes in the back of the SUV, making sure each was securely closed and taped, Tim stepped into the lazy night air where thousands of stars peppered the clear sky. A perfect Alabama spring night. May was a good month here. The damp chill of winter gone and the heat and humidity of summer still a couple of months away. He would miss this. He'd never lived anywhere else. Neither had Martha. This was home. For another day anyway.

Tim popped the SUV's rear hatch. He and Martha loaded the four suitcases into the sedan's trunk and then wedged the three cardboard banker's boxes into the backseat. Amazing that an entire life could fit into one car. But when cutting loose everything that came before, that's the way it was.

● ● ●

Tim and Martha held hands while they waited for Anne Marie Bridges to finish helping another customer. When she waved a goodbye to the elderly lady and turned her smile toward them, they walked up to the teller's window.

"How're you two doing today?" Anne Marie asked.

"Fine," Martha said. "You?"

"Other than my arthritic knee acting up, I suspect okay."

"Time to close the last account," Tim said.

"Is it May already?"

"Afraid so."

"We're so sorry to be losing you as customers," Anne Marie said. "How long has it been? Ten years?"

"At least," Tim said. "We'll miss you and everyone else here."

"You're moving out West? California?"

"Arizona," Martha said. "Phoenix."

"I hear it's hot there."

Martha smiled. "They have air-conditioning."

"And ice cream," Tim added.

Anne Marie laughed. "Your balance is seven thousand six hundred thirty-two dollars and forty-four cents. You want a cashier's check?"

"Cash," Tim said. "Need some traveling money."

"That's a lot to carry around."

"We'll be okay."

"I don't have that much in my drawer. I'll have to run to the vault. It'll take a few minutes. Why don't you have some coffee?" Anne Marie pointed toward the corner table that held a large coffeepot and a stack of foam cups.

Tim nodded and they moved that way. He poured two cups, handed one to Martha, added a pack of creamer to his and stirred it to a caramel brown. He took a sip. Not bad.

"Mr. and Mrs. Foster."

Tim turned. "Detective."

Detective Bruce McGill, today dressed in jeans and an open-collar blue shirt beneath a gray sport coat, had been the lead investigator into the evils of Walter Allen Whitiker. The animal that had taken Steven. He'd helped lock the bastard up. Not nearly long enough, but as long as the corrupt judge would allow.

"I understand you're moving away," McGill said. A statement, not a question.

"We have to," Martha said. "We can't stay in a community with that…that…"

McGill shoved his hands into his pockets, the butt of the gun strapped to his belt now visible. "Because he threatened you?"

"That's part of it," Tim said.

"You don't think we can protect you?"

Tim shrugged. "Maybe. Maybe not. It's the *not* that's the problem."

"It's mostly talk," McGill said. "Just messing with your head. Doubt he'll actually do anything."

"He killed our son," Martha said. "And got away with it. Why wouldn't he try to kill us?"

"He hasn't been exactly repentant," Tim added.

McGill rattled what sounded like keys inside one pocket and rocked back on his heels a little. "When you heading out?"

"Tomorrow."

"I take it that's because he's being released in the morning?"

"We don't want to breathe the same air he does," Martha said.

"Can't say I blame you." Again the keys rattled. "Where you going?"

"Phoenix," Tim said.

"Been there once. Nice place." When Tim didn't respond he went on. "Anything I can do for you, just give me call."

● ● ●

Tim and Martha spent the remainder of the day making final preparations. Loading what they would need into the SUV. Repeatedly going back over everything. Playing the "what-if" game. They decided that they'd done all they could. Planned for all the contingencies. Now with a little luck everything would work out.

They ordered pizza and ate at the kitchen counter. Both quiet now, knowing this was their last night in the only house they had ever lived in together. There was the apartment when they first married, but this was their home.

Tim remembered the day they had moved in. Eleven years ago. Martha had been three months into her pregnancy, barely showing. He'd carried her across the threshold. They'd laughed and made love on the new carpet in the furniture-free living room.

The lump in his throat made swallowing the pizza difficult.

After they finished, Tim cleaned the counter and folded the empty pizza box into the trash compactor. He then found Martha, standing at the door to Steven's room. Not an unusual position for her. Over the past three years she'd often stood there. Silently staring. As if waiting for Steven to materialize. Their towheaded son in his baggy pajamas, sitting at his desk doing homework, or sprawled on his bed in exhausted, innocent sleep.

Tonight was different. She was no doubt soaking in memories, knowing that in a few hours they would walk out of here forever. It was as if she wanted to burn the room's image into her mind. The lump in his throat grew.

He went out back and walked around the yard, making a couple of laps. Smelling the flowers and touching the thick shrubbery that they had planted together. He could still see her dirt-smudged face, glistening with sweat. Could still hear six-month-old Steven squealing in his nearby playpen.

He migrated to the swing set. Steven's fifth birthday present. He'd put it together with his own hands. Took twice as long as it should have, but he managed. He sat on one of the swings and began a slow to-and-fro motion. The rusty chain creaked in protest. He could almost hear Steven begging to go higher and higher as he pushed him from behind. Tears blurred his vision.

Martha came out. He stood and they hugged tightly. Her tears fell against his neck. God, he hated this feeling. His life ripped apart again. As it had been three years ago. A wound that would never heal.

• • •

"You look hot," Tim said.

Martha turned from the mirror. "You like it?" Her shoulder-length blond hair was now clipped short and dyed a deep black. The transition from Martha to Cindy. She laughed. "Look at you. I love the military cut."

He ran a hand over his nearly shaved head. "It'll take a bit of getting used to."

She handed him a plastic trash bag, filled with empty dye bottles and wads of her hair. "Put this by the gym bags. Don't want to forget and leave it here." She began scrubbing her hair with a towel.

"Will do. Then we need to get some sleep. Big day tomorrow."

• • •

The 4:00 a.m. alarm startled Tim. He rolled toward Martha. She wasn't there. Then he heard the shower running. He joined her.

Thirty minutes later they were on the road. Out of the city, into the wooded hills south of town, off on a rarely used gravel road. Tim pulled the SUV into the trees, no longer visible from the road. He parked near the clearing he had found months earlier.

He set up the tent. Not exactly set it up since it was one of those self-contained jobs. Floor, walls, ceiling, support cables all in one. He simply removed it from its flat storage sleeve and dropped it on the ground. The cables unwound and a tent appeared.

He crawled inside and, using his Swiss Army knife, cut two dinner-plate-size holes in one end. About eighteen inches from the bottom. He then piled three pillows near each hole.

It was 5:00 a.m. Two hours to wait. Then they could get this done, stuff the tent and everything else into plastic trash bags and drop them into the industrial Dumpster over by the packing plant where they would ultimately disappear into a landfill. Then back to the mall parking deck, pick up the new car and finally curb the SUV on the east side. Keys inside of course. Easy for the crack dealers to snatch and chop. After that, goodbye. The transformation of Tim and Martha Foster into Robert Beckwith and Cindy Strunk would be complete. He smiled. He actually looked forward to Robert and Cindy getting married. She would make a great North Carolina blushing bride.

He looked at her. She lay on her back, eyes blank, staring at the tent's roof. "You okay?" he asked.

"Nervous."

"Me, too."

"Look." She held up a trembling hand.

"You'll do fine. You have to. We both have to." He rolled onto his side and looked into her face. "For Steven."

● ● ●

Tabitha Martin stood near the prison entrance, a rolling chain-link gate behind her, and a hundred feet beyond that the metal double doors that led to the facility's interior. Inside you could find the worst of the worst. Rapists, murderers, child molesters, you name it. And, of course, Walter Allen Whitiker.

A big day for Tabitha. Her first real hard news story. Not her usual new cub at the zoo, tornado uprooted tree, or Labor Day Parade fluff piece. An honest-to-God story about the city's most controversial trial.

She stood, facing the Channel 16 News camera, and waited for the signal. The cameraman gave her a countdown, finger after finger folding from sight, until only his fist remained.

"This is Tabitha Martin reporting live from Stone Gate Prison. We are just minutes from the release of Walter Allen Whitiker.

Three years ago he was arrested for the murder of eight-year-old Steven Foster, whose body was found six months after he went missing in a wooded area just five miles from where I now stand. Murder charges were brought based on DNA evidence obtained from what were believed to be tearstains in the back of Whitiker's van.

"The murder charges were dropped when Judge Ben Kleinman disallowed this evidence on a technicality. Walter Allen Whitiker was then tried and convicted for obstructing a police investigation and perjury. He received a three-year sentence, and now, nineteen months later, he is being released for good behavior."

She turned and looked back toward the prison, where several guards had gathered near the metal doors.

"I see some activity, so Whitiker might come through that door very soon." She turned back to the camera. "As we have reported here in the past, Whitiker remained in the public eye for making what many believe were not so subtle threats toward Martha Foster, young Steven's mother. Whitiker has repeatedly stated that she lied about seeing him cruising their neighborhood on the day Steven disappeared. Many feel that these threats should preclude Whitiker's early parole, but the parole board ruled that he was safe for release and Judge Kleinman agreed."

● ● ●

The scope was a Bushnell 30x50. It pulled the image of Tabitha Martin into full view. As if she were standing right in front of him. Tim could clearly see the Channel 16 pin she wore on her sweater. She was looking directly at the cameraman who aimed his shoulder-balanced camera at her.

Tim and Martha lay prone on the plastic floor of the tent. Tim had snapped off a few branches of the brush, allowing a clear view down the gentle slope and across the road, to where Tabitha and a small group of curiosity seekers had gathered. He could almost hear what she was saying. How Whitiker had been charged with murder and wiggled free by the machinations of his slick lawyer and a corrupt judge. How he had been a model prisoner. How his threats to Martha weren't real, just the imagination of distraught parents and a homicide investigator who felt that the judge had trashed his reputation. Which is exactly what that nut-job Kleinman had done. Whitiker a model prisoner? Maybe him saying he would "get even with that lying bitch" and "even the score with those that falsely accused him" weren't really threats. Get real.

He wiped his damp palms with a towel. "You ready?"

"I think so."

Tim worked the bolt action of his 30.06, settling the bullet into the firing chamber. Martha did the same. They each rested their weapons on the stacked pillows. Martha pressed her eye against the scope on her rifle.

"Just do it exactly like you did with all those practice shots. Calm, relaxed, exhale slowly, squeeze."

"What if I miss and hit someone else?"

"You won't."

She glanced over at him. "What if the tent doesn't dampen the noise enough? I have a vision of everyone turning and pointing at us."

"You can't watch *Invasion of the Body Snatchers* anymore."

That got a smile from her. Relaxed her a bit.

"We're three hundred yards away," Tim said. "They couldn't see us even if they knew where to look. The tent will work just fine. If they hear anything, it'll be so soft and nondirectional they'll have no idea where it came from. By the time they figure it out, if they ever do, the Fosters will no longer exist and we'll be halfway to North Carolina."

"I hope so."

"Remember, on three."

They had decided that this was a one-shot deal and would be best if one shot came from each of them. The worst thing would be to miss. Then all of this would be for nothing. Simultaneous shots would also help soften any future guilt. No way to know who released the killing bullet.

He looked through the scope again. Just behind the reporter, he saw the prison doors swing open. With arrogant strides and that permanent smirk on his face Whitiker appeared and walked toward the chain-link gate.

● ● ●

Tabitha heard a commotion behind her and turned.

"Here he comes now," she said into her microphone as she and her cameraman moved forward.

The gate rattled open. Whitiker walked through. A free man. The two officers turned and headed back inside.

Tabitha pushed the microphone forward. "Mr. Whitiker. How does it feel to be out of prison?"

"Should never have been there. I never lied to the police. They lied about me. I never hurt that child. I never done nothing to no one."

"What about the DNA evidence?"

"They set me up. When I wouldn't confess…even after they beat on me…they got their lab folks to plant evidence. Just that simple."

"Isn't it true that the lab results were never questioned? Wasn't it the method by which the evidence was obtained that was the controversy? A probable cause issue?"

"Their probable cause and their corrupt lab are jokes. A waste of taxpayer money. This was a railroad job and you know it." He smiled at her. "What're you doing after this? I'm going to get myself a cheeseburger and a bunch of beers. Want to come along?" He looked her up and down. "Been a long time since I had me some.…"

Whitiker's body jerked. Two crimson blossoms appeared on his chest. His eyes widened, then glazed over. He wavered as if being rocked by a breeze. His legs folded and he crumpled to the ground.

DYING TO SCORE

A Black Ops., Inc. Story

CINDY GERARD

*I'm hooked on Gerard's tough-talkin', straight-shootin'
characters. Her story is exciting, taut, sexy
and just plain fun to read. —SB*

Oh, yeah. Judging by the *chuck, chuck, chuck* of her custom AR-15, Crystal—aka: Tinkerbelle, Johnny Duane Reed's own personal transplant from never-never land—was kicking some serious ass. If help didn't arrive soon, preferably in the form of their Black Ops., Inc. extraction team, not only was he going to die in this snake-infested jungle, Tink was going to take the long goodbye with him.

The thought of losing her redoubled the pain that screamed through his shoulder where an AK round had ripped through flesh and bone.

"Shoulda clipped…your wings, Tink." He shook his head and fought the darkness from the blood loss and the suffocating, wet jungle heat that threatened to drag him under. "Told Nate…this… was a…bad idea. Never shoulda…let you…come along…never shoulda—"

"Shut up. Just shut up," his wife snapped. She popped off another burst of return fire, answering the AK-47 rounds that flew at them from a gully fifty yards away. "You don't get to talk anymore. You don't get to do anything but lie still and put pressure on that damn bleeder."

That's my girl, he thought as he closed his eyes and wrestled with the jolt of fire searing through his shoulder. *She don't take no lip from nobody.* But, damn, he shouldn't have folded when she'd begged to get out from behind the desk again. He should have insisted she stay behind.

"Intel on Luis Reyes, big player in the Zeta Mexican drug cartel," their boss, Nate Black of Black Ops., Inc., had recounted, "tells us Reyes has set up a sophisticated paramilitary training compound for his private army."

The team had been gearing up at the same time as their flat-bottom speedboat delivered them to their infiltration point along the south bank of the Rio Usumacinta in Central Guatemala. An active waterway for drug smuggling, the Rio Usumacinta bisected a wild jungle that was a perfect spot for the cartel to set up camp.

"Not only are they training at the paramilitary compound, they're producing weapons," Nate had continued with a hard look as he ran through their mission one last time. "Your primary objectives are to infiltrate Reyes's camp, conduct a recon to confirm their ability to produce weapons, get a read on their inventory and get out. We need a big score on this op.

"And people," Nate had added, glancing at the four-person BOI team consisting of Luke Colter, aka Doc Holliday; Gabe Jones, aka the Archangel; Johnny and Tink, before the boat had pulled away and left them on the riverbank, "let's make this an easy in, easy out, okay?"

Okay, Johnny thought, biting back another groan.

Easy in—check.

Easy out—not so much.

The team had infiltrated the seven-hundred acre enemy encampment through dense, heavily forested terrain in less than two hours, gotten eyes on and confirmed the intel was accurate. The facility included a firing range, a heavy breaching area, an urban training ground used to build explosives, processing and storage facilities, and a chopper landing pad.

It had been a smooth-sailing, piece-of-cake mission…until a truckload of Reyes's thugs had barreled up, caught them inside a bomb prep building and opened fire.

Doc and Gabe had sprinted one direction, he and Tink the other. And that's when he'd caught the round in his shoulder. He and Tink had made it a hundred yards before the blood loss had forced them to stop and hunker down.

He fought to focus on his wife as she continued to cover Reyes's guns with her rifle fire. Damn. She was still too green for this kind of op…and yet, *she* was keeping *his* sorry ass alive. If the bullet didn't end up killing him, the hit to his ego just might finish the job.

What a world. Two years ago, if anyone had given Reed ten to one odds on his chances of someday bleeding out from an AK round in some Central American shit hole of a jungle, he'd have walked away from the bet. In his line of work, a "good" end just wasn't in the cards. The law of averages said he'd buy the farm in a confrontation exactly like this: pinned down by enemy fire, chance of rescue, nada.

By the same token, if that same anyone had told him that his best chance for survival from said AK round came in the form of a hot, petite redhead who was built like a Vegas showgirl, swore like a Force Recon Marine and flitted around like Tinkerbelle on speed, he'd have told them to go blow smoke up someone else's ass.

If that same farseeing SOB had told him he'd not only fall in love with that sexy little fairy but marry her, he'd have asked them exactly what kind of ganja they were smokin'.

Look at her, he thought with more pride than he'd ever thought he was capable of feeling. Lying on her belly, elbows planted in the dirt, sighting down the barrel of her AR-15 and holding off the baddest of the bad guys while bullets whizzed all around them. She was a pint-size warrior woman, fierce and fearless and ready to take on an entire battalion if she had to, to keep them both alive. And she just might have to if help didn't arrive soon.

"God, do you have…any idea how much…you turn me on… right now?" Blood loss made him slur his words but that didn't stop him. "If you weren't…already my wife, I swear…I'd propose. At the very least…proposition you."

"I said, shut up. Save your strength, Reed, because if you die on me, so help me, I'll make you sorry you were ever born."

"That's…my girl," he ground out around a grimace then cursed his useless right arm. He pressed harder on the compress, gritted his teeth against the ripping pain and prayed to God the quick clot Tink had emptied over the wound would do its thing soon. Best guess—he was well over a pint low. He needed to plug the leak fast. And more grim news—he couldn't feel his hand anymore.

This was bad. This was so freakin' bad.

● ● ●

Crystal Debrowski Reed bit down on her lower lip, wiped a trickle of sweat off her forehead with the back of a grubby arm and slowly swept the jungle through her rifle scope. Several silent minutes had passed since they'd last taken fire. No muzzle flashes. No bang-bangs. All was quiet—for the moment. But the bad guys were still out there. No question about that. She glanced over her shoulder at her husband lying on his back in the damp, decaying leaves and fetid jungle heat. His eyes were closed. His mouth was clamped tight with pain. The pasty pallor of his skin scared her to death. She needed Doc to work his magic and fix Johnny up. But Doc and Gabe were out of radio contact, only God knew where. So it was up to her to keep him alive and keep Reyes's thugs at bay until they could hook up and get the heck out of here.

"Did I…mention," her husband asked with that crooked, arrogant and totally smart-ass grin she'd fallen in love with, "that you…are sooo turning me on right now?"

"Yeah, you mentioned it," she grumbled and kept her head on a swivel, checking 360 degrees around them at all times. "Which just goes to show how much blood you've lost."

Looking like she did, she couldn't "turn on" a lightbulb let alone compel a second glance from this tall, blond and gorgeous elite operative who just happened to be her husband and who had better not, by God, die on her.

Her hair looked like it had been groomed by an orangutan. Hell, it looked like orangutan hair—orange/red, short and spiky—and not in a glitz and glamour way that had originally turned the head of this sweet-talking Texan. Her face and arms were covered with camo paint, bug bites and blood. Johnny's blood.

Oh, God. Her stomach sank as she thought of just how much blood he'd lost. She could not lose this man. *Please, God, do not let me lose him.*

"So…d'ya hear the one…about the mercenary…who walked into the—"

"Damn it, Reed," she sputtered, frustrated and afraid for him. "You do *not* get to make me laugh, either. You need to save your breath, not keep my spirits up. I'm fine."

And she was. Because she had to be. She wasn't going to let her guard down. She was going to hold on until help arrived because Reed could not, and *would* not, die here.

"Gambler, Gambler, this is Tinkerbelle," she whispered, cupping her Micom 3 Pathfinder radio mic close to her mouth. She had to risk raising Doc. "Do you read me, over?"

Several silent seconds ticked off before she gave up on Doc and tried Gabe.

"Angel, Angel, this is Tink. Do you read me, over?"

"Nothing?" Johnny asked after more tense seconds slogged by.

She compressed her lips and shook her head, trying to hide her growing desperation.

"Either they're...out of range," he said, "or they...can't respond."

Which she knew. Which worried her even more. If either Doc or Gabe were down, hit by enemy fire, the chances of any of them making it back to the extraction point were about as good as Reed making it an hour without flirting.

Trouble didn't get any bigger than this. They weren't dealing with run-of-the-mill hired guns. They were dealing with Reyes's mercenaries, men who dealt in money and gold and lead. This was their compound, their ground. They owned it. Anyone who came looking for trouble was going to get a faceful of it.

Or in Johnny's case, a shoulderful.

"How many...left, do you figure?" Johnny asked as his head dropped back heavily onto the dirt. Once again, his eyes were closed; his jaw was clenched tight in agony.

Crystal's chest tightened. "In this group? Three, maybe four. But they're bound to have called in reinforcements from other parts of the camp."

"You need to...get out of here, babe. See if you...can hook up with...Doc and Gabe and...send them...back for me."

"You're delirious if you think I'm leaving you here alone. You can't even shoulder your rifle to defend yourself."

"Cover me...with leaves. They'll blow...right by me."

She shot him a look. "You're over six feet tall. There aren't enough leaves in Guatemala to cover you up. Besides, unless that damn dog finds a rabbit to chase, he's going to sniff you out like rot on rancid meat."

"Nice analogy," he said on a weak laugh.

"You know what I meant."

"I do. And you're right. I forgot about…Fido."

"Fido" was a Rottweiler. A big one. So far the drug runners had kept him on a tight leash because they knew exactly where Tink and Johnny were pinned down: fifty yards from a direct hit.

But Johnny was dead right about one thing. They had to move out while he still could. He was fading fast.

Crystal popped off several quick rounds then crawled backward the yard down the ridge to his side. Keeping low, she quickly exchanged her empty magazine for a full one then helped him sit up. "Come on. We're getting out of here."

"Tink—"

"I'm not leaving you." She cut him off with a sharp look. "And the longer you lay there and argue with me, the more time we waste."

He was going with her if she had to drag him out. Considering he outweighed her by over a hundred pounds, she really did not want to do that.

He muffled a groan at the pain and the effort but with her help, managed to get to his feet. Digging deep for strength, she slung his good arm over her shoulder then reached down for his M-4 and shoved it in his good hand. *He* couldn't fire it but *she* might need it before this was over.

Then feeling like she was carrying roughly a half ton of deadweight, she wrapped her free arm around his waist and headed south. The extraction point was a good quarter of a mile away through pulsing heat, dense undergrowth and rough, uneven terrain.

They didn't make it ten yards before his knees buckled.

They both started to go down.

"Stay with me," she pleaded and calling on reserves she hadn't known she possessed, somehow muscled him upright again.

"Damn, Tink. You're…the *woman*," he gritted out as he fought his rubber legs and managed to stay vertical. Sweat poured down his face. "Your first life…I'm thinkin'…pack mule. *Pretty* pack mule," he amended with what little breath he had.

"Shut up," she grumbled again, fighting tears because she knew from the heavy way he leaned on her that she was losing him. "How many times do I have to tell you to save your brea—"

She stopped short when she saw movement up ahead.

"Company," she whispered and quickly eased him down behind a clump of ferns.

Heart hammering, she knelt in a defensive position in front of him and raised her rifle.

"Tinkerbelle, Tinkerbelle, this is Doc. Do you read me, over?"

Still shouldering her rifle, she reached for the radio in the vest pocket near her throat. "I read you, Doc. What's your twenty, over?"

"About fifteen yards from the end of your rifle barrel. Got eyes on, Tink, darlin'. Hold fire. We're comin' in, over."

"Oh, sweet Jesus, Roger that." She almost wept with relief. "Come on in. Johnny's hit, over."

She glanced at Johnny. Eyes closed. Breath shallow. Face pale. Her heart sank even lower. "Hang on, baby. Dammit, you hang on, do you hear me?"

Just when she thought he'd passed out, he cracked one eye open. "Nag, nag, nag."

And just when she thought she had reason to smile, a barrage of AK fire opened up behind them again.

"How bad?" Doc—the tall, lanky former SEAL and team medic—appeared out of the thick foliage. He dropped to his knees and hunkered over Johnny as Gabe emptied a full magazine toward the shooters.

"No vital organs but he's lost a lot of blood," Crystal said over her shoulder as she continued to lay down cover fire with Gabe.

"Damn showboat." Doc urgently assessed Johnny's injury. "Do anything to impress your lady, right, pretty boy?"

"You know me well," Johnny agreed with a pained grimace. "I'm just dyin' to score with that woman."

Doc turned quickly to Gabe, a former Delta Force lieutenant, who was on his belly beside Crystal, his M-4 hammering away. "He's getting shocky. We've gotta get him out of here."

"Cover me." Gabe scrambled back to Johnny then hauled him to his feet.

Crystal stayed on her knees and laid down more return fire as Doc joined her, making sure that Gabe—who was an even bigger man than Johnny—had a running start.

"You my...free ride?" Johnny managed weakly as Gabe hefted him over his shoulder in a fireman's carry and double-timed it away from the enemy fire.

"Always said that you former Force Recon Marines were nothin' but a bunch of slackers," Gabe grumbled over the concern in his voice. "Just hang on, bud. God knows you're not worth the effort, but we're gettin' your sorry ass outta here."

"Countin' on it, Angel Boy," Johnny mumbled then passed out cold.

"Let's boogie." Doc covered Crystal as she backed away, then quickly turned and followed her.

● ● ●

Johnny hung like a lifeless lump over Gabe's shoulder as the big man pushed his way through the trees, vines and undergrowth. Crystal was hardly aware of the thick, dense foliage slicing tiny cuts in her arms and across her face as they hauled ass through the jungle. All she could think about was her husband as she alternately stopped and took a knee, returned the fire that kept dogging them, then jumped up and pressed on toward the beach.

The terrain was rough; the plants and vines grabbed at her feet.

She tripped over a tree root and went down hard. She was just pushing to her knees when Doc grasped her backpack from behind and lifted her to her feet like she didn't weigh any more than a gnat.

"That boat going to be there when we arrive?" she asked breathlessly as she raced alongside him.

"Ever known the Choirboy to let us down?"

Raphael "Choirboy" Mendoza, a native Colombian and charter member of Black Ops., Inc. like Doc, Gabe and Johnny, was their wheelman—in this case their outboard motor man.

"What? What are you doing?" she asked Doc frantically when he stopped beside her.

"Go," he insisted as he pulled the pin on a frag grenade then winged it as hard as he could behind them.

The grenade had no sooner exploded with a deafening blast than Doc shrugged out of his pack, tore open a pocket and pulled out a Claymore. "Go," he repeated.

"I'm not leaving you." She took a knee again and covered him as he set the mine with a trip wire trigger while AK-47 fire lit up with a vengeance behind them.

"That'll keep 'em guessing," he said after setting a second mine. "Now scoot."

They both took off at a run.

She'd lost sight of Gabe and Johnny and was frantic to catch up with them when the first Claymore exploded. At least one bad guy had bought the farm on that one. The others were either hurt or very wary about running blindly after them.

"They're still on our ass." Doc grabbed her arm as he ran alongside her. "Let's double-time it."

They'd just leaped over a huge, downed tree trunk and, thank God, caught up with Gabe when Crystal heard the roar of an outboard motor.

"Hallelujah!" Doc crowed and peeled ahead of Crystal to help

Gabe maneuver Johnny down a steep, dirt embankment that dropped over twenty feet toward the river at a ninety-degree angle.

Crystal scrambled down behind them, digging in her heels as she half skidded, half ran down the vertical drop that ended in the mud of the riverbank, where a flat-bottom boat with a pair of 200 horse outboards plowed up onto the shore.

Their CO, Nate Black himself, was on his knees in the bow of the boat, manning an M-60 machine gun mounted on a tripod.

"Sight for sore eyes, gentlemen," Gabe yelled above the *chuck-chuck-chuck* of the big gun as Nate peppered the bank with shells to the tune of 550 rounds per minute.

Gabe clambered into the boat and laid Johnny as carefully as he could on the floor. Doc was next aboard. He held out a hand for Crystal and she jumped in. Doc was already on his knees beside Johnny, digging into his medic's kit when Rafe shifted the twin motors into Reverse, backed away from the shore, then fast-shifted into Forward again and shot down the river.

The M-60 had fallen silent and the threat from the AKs was in the far distance before Doc sat back on his heels. He'd done what he could for Johnny. He'd staunched the blood flow, wrapped his arm close to his ribs to immobilize it and hung an IV that dumped antibiotics and fluid into his body.

Crystal could tell by the look on Doc's face that the risk to her husband's life was far from over.

She sat on the floor of the boat, Johnny's head cradled in her lap. He was too pale. His skin was too cool. And she was scared to death because he had not yet regained consciousness.

"How bad?" She had to yell to be heard above the roar of the twin outboards.

Doc shot Gabe a grim look over the top of her head before he met Crystal's eyes. "Bad," he said, knowing he had to level with her. "He needs blood."

"Then he's going to get it." She quickly rolled up her sleeve as the wind whipped her hair around her face and the roar of the outboards tried to drown out her words.

Doc shook his head. "Crystal—"

"He's going to get it!" she shouted, cutting Doc off midprotest. "I'm O negative. Universal donor."

"Darlin', a direct donor to recipient doesn't always—"

"I'm not going to let him die!" Tears welled up as she frantically reached for Doc's kit then shoved it into his hands. "*You* are not going to let him die," she said, pleading, demanding, bargaining for the life of the man she loved.

After a long, hard look, Doc assembled what he needed to attempt the transfusion.

"No promises." He inserted the needle into her vein and started the process.

"No promises," she agreed on a whisper that was swept down river by the wind.

She refused, though, absolutely refused to let her hope be swept away, as well.

• • •

Reed awoke to silence. The kind of silence that magnified every little sound and told him he wasn't alone. The minute scrape of a chair leg on a tile floor. The rustle of clothes. A soft breath close by. The scent of the woman he loved.

Very slowly, he opened his eyes. Closed them against the sharp glare of a white-on-white ceiling, walls and window shades. A monitor blipped softly away beside his bed.

No. Not *his* bed. A hospital bed, he decided, picking up the scent of antiseptic and flowers as he sifted through his memory banks.

Oh, right. He remembered. Just to make certain, he tried to move his shoulder.

Very. Bad. Idea.

Lots of pain. Lots of muzzled, distant pain ached and burned and dug into his flesh like a rusty knife. Hurt like hell…but not as bad as when Gabe had hauled him through the jungle then dumped him into the bottom of the boat.

Safe.

Hot damn.

He'd dodged another bullet—figuratively speaking.

A small, warm hand covered his, squeezed. He let out a deep, contented breath.

He'd know her touch anywhere.

When he opened his eyes again, it was to see his wife's beautiful face. Her soft green eyes were misted with tears.

"Hey, Tink," he croaked and smiled for her because she looked so fragile he was afraid she might break.

"Hey," she whispered back, her own smile tremulous. "You had me worried, cowboy," she confessed.

"I need your mouth," he said, suddenly consumed by a deep, demanding need to touch and taste and assure them both that he was alive.

He watched her eyes warm as she stood up on tiptoe then leaned in and kissed him.

Better. So much better.

He lifted a hand to brush a tear from her cheek. "You remember what you said to me the first time we met?"

"Get lost?" Her grin held as much relief as it did amusement.

"Okay, I think that was the *second* time. The *first* time, you said, 'I'm getting a little tired of you dogging my tail, cowboy.'"

She smiled, lowered the side rail then climbed carefully into the bed beside him. "And you said something to the tune of, 'You're not one of those girl-on-girl types, are you?'"

He lifted his good arm and made room for her to snuggle up close—right where she belonged. "Well, you *did* find me awfully easy to resist. What else was I supposed to think?"

"The fact that I said I didn't like you? *That* didn't do it for you? Or that I told you, you were too vain, too pretty and too annoying?"

"And yet—" contented, he dropped a kiss on the top of her head "—I got you where I wanted you, didn't I?"

She slid her leg across his thighs and careful of his IV, wrapped her arm around his waist. "Yeah. In bed."

He breathed deep, loving the scent of her and the lush softness of her body pressed against his. "You saved my bacon, Tink." He swallowed a knot of emotion that suddenly clogged his throat. "Thought I was done for back there."

"Done?" Her voice was barely a whisper as she snuggled even closer. "Not a chance. I'm so not through with you yet."

"Even though I'm too vain, too pretty and too annoying?"

"Yeah. Even though," she said and he could hear the hours of worry slowly leach out of her voice right along with the tension that eased from her body. "Besides, you've got my blood in your veins now. I have high hopes it'll straighten you out."

He tucked his chin and scowled down at her. "*Your* blood?"

She filled him in on the midriver transfusion that had ultimately saved his life.

He was stunned. And humbled. And…*damn*, he loved this woman.

"Well, I guess that explains why I woke up feeling this driving urge to dye my hair red, get my ears pierced and steal your latest Victoria's Secret catalog."

She laughed. "You *always* steal that catalog."

"True, but I've never had a yen to order from it before."

She levered herself up on an elbow and grinned down at him. "Shut up, Reed," she whispered softly. "Just…shut up."

And then she kissed him with all the love any man could hope for.

THE NUMBER OF MAN

J. T. ELLISON

*Eerie to the max. Hitchcock would have loved the creepy,
delusional, manipulative character of Michael. —SB*

It began in a single moment, the briefest of connections. She, in pigtails, a miniature towheaded autocrat, ruling the playground as if it were her kingdom. He, sitting on the swings, the new boy, watching her cross the playground toward him, shoulders squared, prepared for battle. He was an outsider, an unknown, and therefore dangerous, and she needed to determine his loyalties. Only eight, he had been at the receiving end of this conversation several times; his mother wasn't the most upright woman, had a tendency to follow her latest boyfriend when her previous love discarded her.

Imperious Caitlyn hadn't stopped walking, just drove her shoulder into his and laughed as he lost his grip on the swing and toppled over backward.

"What's your name?"

"Michael."

Caitlyn had looked at him, and he squirmed. He knew he was dirty. It was inside him, and no amount of scrubbing would loosen its hold on his soul.

Her blue eyes pierced him, some ineffable movements behind the lashes as she decided his fate.

At long last, she nodded, curt as a judge.

"Fine. You can stay on the swings. We're going to play kickball." She turned, and her minions followed. He swore he heard Caitlyn whisper, "Keep away from me, Michael."

He tried so very hard to listen.

● ● ●

Twenty years later, Michael stood in another lot, waiting for Caitlyn to notice him. He'd been waiting for a month, ever since he'd bumped into her accidentally. He, on his way to work. She, leaving hers after a hard day. Their footsteps tapped in time, echoing through the still night, sneakers and stilettos crossing the asphalt. Distracted by his earbuds, he'd nearly missed her. A flicker of a shadow caught his attention, he raised his head—and there she was. Their eyes met across the darkened parking lot, this same, perfect expanse. His breath came short. Panic, fear and love all mingled together in his thoughts. She was still perfect. He was lost again.

He waited for her every night after that, from the shadows, not wanting to frighten her. He was shy, so afraid to approach her. If she could only see him like she did when they were eight: just a scared young boy. She was too famous now, too important. She was always on her guard, would never let another being see inside her soul.

The Pixies screamed in his ears, words of numbers, of man and beast and heavens, and the death of all things, and he sang the chorus in his mind, knowing exactly what the song was telling him. The iPod was set to shuffle, and it was beyond fitting that this song, his anthem, had come on when he hit the power button.

Traffic had been a nightmare tonight, aggravated by the teasing rains. He never thought he'd make it, but he did. Breath catching in his chest, heart pounding from the sudden exercise, he waited in the usual spot. Rain trickled down his forehead, running into his mouth, pooling in the collar of his shirt. He removed the earbuds, listened to the staccato snapping grow closer.

She passed right by him, didn't see him hovering in the gloom behind her car. He'd found that spot was ideal for watching. *Do it, Michael. Let her see you. Start your life together.*

He stood, quietly. He didn't want to startle her, send her crashing to her car in a panic. She stopped, realizing she wasn't alone, and he froze. He was still deep in the shadows, unable to be seen, wanting so badly for her to know he was there.

Just talk to her, Michael. Just clear your throat and say hello.

He could see the thoughts run through her mind, could tell when she decided she'd been imagining things. But she covered the rest of the steps to her car quickly and locked the doors of her BMW.

He let her go. She'd be back tomorrow night. He would try again.

● ● ●

"I'm Caitlyn Kennedy, Channel 9 News. Good night, Huntsville."

"And you're smiling, you're smiling, now look at your notes, and…we're out."

Caitlyn Kennedy removed the IFB from her left ear and scratched, pulling on her earlobe, trying to get the underwater sensation to dissipate. Thirty-five minutes plugged into the brain of a disembodied voice was hell on her equilibrium. When her ear finally popped, she set the IFB down on the desk, stood and brushed imaginary lint off her white skirt. The disembodied voice became a series of steps, and a man materialized in front of her. Tom Stryc was their new news director, and she though he was great.

"Hey, Caitie, good job tonight! You're gonna land the weekday anchor job if you're not careful."

"Thank you." She dimpled a smile at him, and he patted her arm before scooting off to his office.

Tom was breathing life into the station, shaking things up, encouraging the anchors and reporters to stretch themselves, to inject a modicum of personality into their live shots and extended reports. It was Huntsville, after all. The focus was on NASA and anything space related. The rest of their stories relied on crime and human interest, typical hometown news.

The weekend crew bustled about, finishing their tasks. Caitlyn looked around, as content as she could be. Her station, her jumping-off point. This is where she'd make her mark. This was her very own launchpad.

"Caitlyn, phone!"

A tech was standing by the anchor desk, where they actually had a working phone for call-ins. He held the receiver, only mildly annoyed at being interrupted from his shutdown duties. Caitlyn smiled at him, took the phone and set it against her good ear.

"Yes?"

"Caitlyn Kennedy?"

The voice was male, deep, raspy.

"Who is this?" she asked.

The man chuckled. "I'm your biggest fan. I just wanted to let you know that I like the nude toenail polish better. That red is too garish for your coloring."

And he was gone. Caitlyn looked at the receiver, as if she could see the caller on the other end. Her brow furrowed in puzzlement. She glanced down, looking at her feet. She had on red toenail polish. She thought back, yes, that was it. She'd gotten a pedicure last night, after she got off work.

Great. She'd better tell Tom there was a whack job out there. But first, she went to her tiny cubbyhole office to see what was on deck for tomorrow's broadcast.

• • •

Twenty years, five months and thirteen days after Michael and Caitie met, they had their first date. It took Michael hours to get up the courage to call, to let Caitlyn know he was in town again, that he wanted to see her. He made a lovely dinner—roast pork tenderloin with a mango chutney, asparagus with a lemon butter reduction and garlic mashed potatoes. He was new to the wine scene, but with some help he'd chosen a Shiraz from Western Australia. The table was set with his grandmother's china, a lovely bone with etched fleur-de-lis. He'd found them at a pawnshop in Austin, Texas. He'd remembered that etched fleur-de-lis and a small, gray woman who'd say, "This plate is fit for a king," on those rare special occasions when they used the fine dishes. Before. Before his father died. Before his mother became a trollop. Before the acrid scent of vodka permeated his world.

Now the dishes were used to serve a queen.

When the table was set, the candles lit, the wine poured into brilliantly clear globes of crystal, the food served, steaming and succulent, they focused on reconnecting. It was as Michael always dreamed. Caitlyn faced him, back straight, legs demurely crossed at the ankle under the table, a starched white linen napkin laid gently across her lap. Her manners were perfection, graceful and composed. She was a dream woman, in every respect. She told him about her day at work, the long hours, her dreams and aspirations.

She confided in him. He could hardly believe his luck.

She left shortly after dinner that night. He plied her with a brandy and she decided she was getting a bit tipsy. Michael was charmed. Reluctantly, he saw her to the door, sad to see her go, but invigorated by the realization that he was well and truly in love.

● ● ●

"Caitlyn, phone."

Caitlyn gritted her teeth. Every bloody night. Every time she anchored, he called. It had been nearly a month now. She was rarely alone in the studio; someone always walked her to her car. The police had been brought in four times, but they couldn't seem to figure it out. Every time she changed her polish, he knew, and the studio phone would ring.

It was beyond an invasion of privacy. She was scared to death.

He'd been acting up lately, too. He became furious on the phone with her. He'd lash out in his displeasure, say cruel words meant to belittle and hurt.

He was getting to know more about her. Where she went on her Friday nights. Who she dined with during the week. That the report she'd done the week before some two hundred miles away from Huntsville was falsely backlit because they'd been unable to get the live shot in front of the setting sun.

She varied her schedule as often as she could, but she couldn't afford the time it would take to drive across town to the other gym. There were two grocery stores she could frequent, so she switched it up. She changed nail salons five times.

She didn't want to be chased out of her life just because some nut job was stalking her.

● ● ●

Michael and Caitlyn had been dating for a month when he decided he needed to tell her the truth. As with all new relationships, there were a few things about her that he had issues with. His hypocrite mother always taught him that a lady was never brash, never put herself out there to grab attention. Caitlyn wasn't following these mandates, so he tried to let her know what he liked. She'd started off so demure and ladylike. Softly Southern, feminine.

He was heartened by her response: Caitlyn was terribly distraught that she'd upset him. Promised to stop wearing those shorts out of the house, for starters. Not that he was jealous, not at all, but it just wasn't ladylike for her to leave those gorgeous long legs out for just anyone to stare at.

Their relationship was progressing slowly. They were still timid with one another, hadn't gotten into anything physical. To be honest, Michael didn't know if he could hold back when they reached that point. He had waited so long, and she was just so lovely—those cherry-ripe lips, that silken hair, the alabaster, swanlike neck. When they did reach the point that Michael thought it was all right to move forward and consummate their love, he wanted it to be perfect. Caitlyn deserved perfection. He waited, patient as a monk, for her to be ready.

• • •

Tom Stryc's eyes were moist when he raised his glass.

"I'd like to propose a toast. To Caitlyn Kennedy, the hardest working, smartest reporter Huntsville has seen in years. You will be sorely missed, in all respects."

"Hear! Hear!" The shouts came from all corners of the room. Glasses clinked, throats were cleared. The station had rented out the Palmas Cantina for the night, closing the place down to outside customers.

Caitlyn felt tears burn in the corners of her eyes.

All this work. She'd risen to the top at the station, worked her butt off to *be* someone. Now she was starting over. A new station, a new crew, a new life. The nameless, faceless bastard who haunted her life for the past three months had driven her to succeed, driven her right out of the Huntsville market to a better job.

Caitlyn closed her eyes and thanked whatever God had decreed that she move to Nashville and be the affiliate's lead reporter, because it got her away from the creep.

• • •

Michael and Caitlyn had their first fight that night. Well, it wasn't a fight, exactly. He was hurt, and angry. Caitlyn admitted she wanted something different, wanted to have a change of scenery. He loved Huntsville, felt attached to its seams.

Caitlyn didn't agree. She wanted out.

They talked long into the night, until the crickets stopped chirping. Arms entwined around each other, lying on a soft fleece blanket on the cold ground, they watched the sun rise. They'd come to a decision. Michael wasn't thrilled to leave his grandmother's house behind, but it was more important to make a new life with Caitlyn in Nashville. So long as he was with her, anything was possible.

They left the following morning, both cars packed to the gills. As they got farther north, the skies filled with billowing gray clouds. The rain enveloped them as they pulled in to their new home. Michael laughed while Caitlyn started to unpack, freer than he'd felt in such a long time.

That first night was different. They shared a bottle of wine, a crisp Pinot Grigio bought at a store down the street. Michael had learned a lot more about wine in the past few months, had developed quite a palate and appreciated many varietals now. Caitlyn stood in the gloaming, sipping the last of her wine, halo hair spilling loosely around her shoulders, her face unlined and carefree. Michael knew, deep in his soul, that they would be happy here.

He watched her standing on the deck and realized the time had finally come. He wanted to be with her, always. He went to her, enveloped her in his arms. Caitlyn melted into him, her lips trailing across his neck, leaving a river of goose bumps in their wake. Her ardor astounded him; for months she'd been so contained, calm and poised. But when it came to actual physical contact, she glowed with passion. Lips bruised and tender, she watched Michael undress with a feral gleam in her eyes. He took his time with her blouse, shy again, fingers shaking, until she reached up, used her hands to guide his fingers. Her skin was so soft, so creamy that he couldn't contain himself anymore. He had to have her, right now.

It didn't take long.

Spent, they lay in front of the fireplace, sated with their love, so long in the making.

Michael told her then. That he loved her.

The words unnerved Caitlyn for some reason. She grew distraught, and he didn't know how to make her better. She yelled at him, told him to go to hell, told him to leave. He was so astonished that he did. Walked right out the door, pulling his shirt over his shoulders. And then, not knowing where to go in the strange new town, he stood in front of the town house for two hours, trying to get up the nerve to go back inside, to ask what he'd done wrong.

The lights went out. She'd gone to bed. Gone to bed mad, always a big mistake.

His heart became hard, a rock in his chest. How could she? How dare she?

• • •

"I'm Caitlyn Kennedy, Channel Two News. Good night, Nashville."

"And you're smiling, you're smiling, now look at your notes, and…we're out."

The cameras shut off, and Caitlyn had that moment of déjà vu she experienced every time she wrapped. New city, new studio, new crew—same old, same old. Reporting the news was the same everywhere.

"Great show, Caitie. You've really got something special behind that desk. The camera goes on and BAM—you are on fire."

She smiled at Kevin Claueswitz, her new news director. He was a good guy, ready to take a chance on her from day one.

"Caitlyn, phone!"

Her heart skipped a beat. Surely not. There was no way… She raised the receiver to her ear.

"I hate the red polish, Caitlyn. I've told you that."

She smashed the phone down, heart so suddenly in her throat that she ran from the room, barely made it to the ladies before she choked up her meager dinner in the toilet. She sat, after, with her head against the cool tiled wall, and cried.

• • •

Michael hadn't seen Caitlyn for a week. He knew she was still upset with him, though he'd apologized a thousand times. He wasn't schooled in the moods of women, couldn't figure out exactly what she wanted from him. Hadn't he declared his love properly? Was he so bad in bed that she wasn't willing to do it again, and didn't want to hurt his feelings by sharing that with him? He couldn't help himself; he loved her too much to just walk away. He wished he could take back that night, undo the passion they shared, start over anew. He racked his brain. How could he unwind the clock?

Flowers. Women loved flowers.

He went to the shop down the street and spent too much money on a multicolored spray of roses. Left them on the front porch without a note. She'd know who they were from. She'd always known.

• • •

Caitlyn sat on the edge of the chair in Kevin's office.

"I know you're scared. But, Caitie, I promise, I'm not going to let anything happen to you."

"Kevin…"

"I talked to a couple of homicide detectives. The laws are ridiculous. Basically he has to hurt you before they can do anything. So here's the name of a guy. He's one of the best private investigators around here. I think he can help. At the very least, he can find ways to keep you safe. I know it's only been a month, but we don't want to lose you, Caitie. You're a great reporter and a fabulous anchor."

Caitlyn took the small beige rectangle from Kevin, holding it gingerly in the palm of her hand. She glanced at the embossing—

William Goldman, Private Detective. She stashed the card in the back pocket of her jeans, feigning nonchalance.

The moment she left Kevin's office, Caitlyn's phone was out. Goldman answered on the first ring.

● ● ●

Michael went by the house with more flowers, irises this time, her favorite, but it was locked, a new gold dead bolt affixed to the door. Defeated, he sat on the front steps, shredding the flowers into bits. He wasn't sure what was happening. Two things he knew for certain—they'd made love, and she'd suddenly turned cold, distant. Like she didn't love him anymore. But that couldn't be true. Michael had seen the look in her eyes as he entered her, watched her pupils dilate in pleasure, saw the tiny vein rise in her left temple, felt her breath quicken and her muscles spasm around him. He may not be well versed in the ways of love, but biological responses were impossible to fake. You can't react like that, so organically, and make it feel like a lie.

Maybe it was too soon. Maybe she wasn't as ready as she told him. Or maybe, just maybe, he was wrong about her.

Maybe she was like his mother after all.

He hardened his heart.

● ● ●

Goldman looked like something out of a comic book. Huge, bulbous eyes, a broad forehead, a cauliflower nose flushed with rosacea. He lumbered when he walked. But his eyes, round blueberries tucked into the folds of his cheeks, were kind, and Caitlyn felt safe with him.

They met for the first time in a dark bar in Printer's Alley, next to a strip club. Goldman arrived late, breathless, covered in a sheen of sweat. Caitlyn wondered if he'd taken the advance payment she'd couriered over the day before and had himself a moment next door.

They went over it all, that first night. How the calls had started. How the caller invariably knew what color toenail polish Caitlyn was wearing. How he expressed his dislike for anything that made her "look like a whore."

How he hadn't stopped calling, for weeks on end. The things he said. Little tidbits shared about her day. A comment about the brand of tomato juice she'd bought. A recommendation that she fill her Beemer at the gas station two blocks from her house, because the prices were better.

He'd noticed when she switched from lattes to green tea because the caffeine coupled with the stress was eating her stomach apart.

"Going through your trash," Goldman said, which made it all worse.

The Huntsville police hadn't been able to do much. He used a disposable cell phone and they couldn't trace the number. They didn't have the personnel to have a constant presence, but they'd watched her at odd times, hoping to catch a glimpse of her stalker. It hadn't worked. And now the Nashville police were saying they couldn't do anything, either.

She was tired of being scared.

Caitlyn started to cry. Goldman reached a meaty hand over and patted her shoulder awkwardly.

"It's gonna be okay. You just wait."

● ● ●

Michael had been patient, and kind. He'd been more understanding than a man could ever be expected to. He sent flowers, he wrote beautiful love notes, he called, he dropped by the house. Caitlyn refused to accept any of his overtures. She wouldn't see him. Damn, he knew having sex so soon into their relationship was a mistake.

He didn't know what to do. And he was rapidly coming to the conclusion that he was losing her.

And he refused to lose her.

• • •

Goldman had a plan. He and Caitlyn met in a coffee shop off Broadway, someplace completely anonymous where she could go in dark glasses and hide from the eyes that bored into the back of her neck at all hours of the day and night.

The detective had found some sort of new 007 device that could trace the calls she was receiving day and night using GPS. Even if the cell number itself wasn't available, the illicit company who made the device could monitor the calls, triangulate the caller's where-abouts using the mapping software. It was cutting edge. That's what he told her. She didn't care. Caitlyn just wanted the damn phone to stop ringing. She wanted her life back.

They decided to try the very next night. She made sure to paint her toes vermilion and wear open-toed shoes. Bait.

Goldman came to the studio, watched her do her bit. He had the device hooked up to the phone.

Like clockwork, the creep called as she wrapped the show. When she answered, he asked why she was meeting strange men for cof-fee during business hours. She felt the fear crawl up her spine. He knew. He knew everything. He was inside her head. Knew what she'd think next, what decisions she'd make, where she would go, what she would do.

She flubbed their planned script. "What do you want?" she screamed into the receiver. He simply hung up. Goldman shook his head. Not enough time for the GPS to react.

"We'll try again tomorrow. At least you know he'll call back," Goldman said.

• • •

It was time. Time for Michael to pull out all the stops. He needed to see her. He dressed carefully, certain to look his best, yet able to blend into the night. He went with black, head to toe, slimming, tasteful. If Caitlyn was going to be this woman—this whore, this slut—then she'd have to answer for it. Michael had turned his entire fucking life upside down for her, and this was the way she repaid him? No. He wouldn't stand for it. She would be made to understand what she'd done.

He stood on the street outside the house and called her cell phone.

• • •

Goldman was right. As soon as the cameras went off the next night, the phone rang.

Caitlyn's hands were shaking. She needed to play this just right. She took a deep breath and answered.

"Hello?"

"Nice show, Caitlyn."

"Thank you." She hesitated for effect. "You've been calling me for months. We know each other so well now. Why don't you tell me your name?"

"I've got him. I've got him." Goldman mouthed to Caitlyn, making a rolling gesture with his hand, silently telling her to keep him talking.

He barked a laugh in her ear. "You don't need to know my name. Just know that I love you. Isn't that enough? I call you all the time, just like a boyfriend should. I compliment you. I give you flowers, write you notes. I make sure you know what I like. I give you advice on your career. We eat and drink and make love, at least, we did until you decided to dump me. After all this time, Caitlyn, you really keep playing this game? Why do you think a name will make any difference?"

"It's not a game. I want to know your name. It means a lot to me." Her voice was small, pleading. Just how Goldman wanted her to play it.

"I'll tell you my name, Caitlyn. My name is—"

There was a click in her ear.

"Oh, shit! I lost him. Goddammit it to hell, Caitie, we had him. Let me see, let me see…"

Goldman's eyes were transfixed on the little LED screen. Caitlyn put the receiver down on the table, a small trickle of sweat slipping between her breasts.

"Gotcha, you son of a bitch."

"You found him?"

Goldman smiled hard, and relief streamed through her body, so overwhelming that she needed to sit down. This, this, freak had ruined her life. Now it was time for payback.

"I got him. I got him. 4679 Old Hickory. Jesus, Caitie, he's calling…"

"From my house."

• • •

Michael walked through the familiar rooms, as strange to him now as if he'd never seen them. He stopped in the living room, where a picture of Caitlyn rested on an end table. She looked so damn happy.

The pain in his chest was crushing. She was happy before he came into her life. How was that possible? Could it be so? Could she have been happy without him? All these months, Michael knew every smile was for him, every hair flip, ear touch, lip compression, tongue lick. It was all for him. Caitlyn had stared out at Michael from that television screen and loved him.

Hadn't she?

• • •

"Are you sure you want to do this?" Goldman whispered as he loaded a fresh magazine in his Glock.

"Just give me the goddamn gun. I'm a big girl."

Goldman handed the weapon to Caitlyn. She hefted its unfamiliar weight in her right hand. A good, solid piece of metal. A life taker. Perfect.

"Caitlyn, we can call the police. They'll be here in less than five minutes."

She faced him, her features softened. "Goldman, you know they won't help until he hurts me—that's why I had to bring you into this. This ends, now. If you don't want to be there, want the deniability, I suggest you leave. Because I'm going into my home and stopping him once and for all. I won't ever be free unless I do this. He'll keep following me, keep calling me, keep stalking me." Her voice shook on the last note and she cleared her throat. "No. I won't let this go on any longer. Are you coming or not?"

Goldman nodded. "Of course I'm coming. Wouldn't want anything bad to happen."

They got out of Goldman's beat-up maroon Thunderbird, shutting the doors quietly behind them. She could feel the caller in the air, that palpable sense of foreboding she always got when he was near.

The house was dark. The light in the living room was off. She never turned it out, kept the switch on the wall taped to the on position so it couldn't be accidentally shut off. That one light kept the darkness at bay, kept him away from her life. He was in there, pawing through her possessions, making himself intimate with her things. How many times had he done that, she wondered? Five? Ten? A hundred?

How many times was the recurring nightmare, that he watched her sleep, real?

She took a deep breath. Felt the metal of the gun hard in her hand.

She was in control now.

Emboldened, she stepped up to the front door. It was unlocked, slightly ajar. If he knew they were coming, he would have shut it behind him. Right?

She eyed Goldman, nodded and pushed open the door with the toe of her boot. It swung wide into the gaping darkness.

She slipped through, waited for her eyes to adjust to the light.

A shadow moved. She turned to face it. Extended the gun toward the outline that was him.

"Don't do that, Caitlyn." The bastard's voice was gravelly. "You don't have to do this. I forgive you. I understand. We can try again. Maybe a new town, less distractions. You don't have to work. I'll provide for us."

"Jesus Christ," Goldman whispered.

The shadow moved to the right and Caitlyn fired. The muzzle flash blinded her for a moment, but she fired again, and again, and finally, when her fingers went numb, she heard Goldman yelling at her to stop.

The lights came on. Caitlyn saw the man who ruined her life, lying on the floor. He stared at her as if she were the only person in the world. He looked vaguely familiar, but she brushed that away. He didn't deserve her concern.

She watched the puddle of blood spread across the hardwood, catching the edge of the carpet, and smiled.

"I like red polish, you son of a bitch."

● ● ●

Michael stared at the face of his love in awe. He'd made her happy at last. He could see it in the manic smile, the fire in her eyes. He'd been forgiven. He knew, now, that she was truly, madly, deeply in love with him. At this moment, she adored him. He was complete.

And so it was done.

He sang himself to death, the words he'd written for her whispered into the ether as the world went black.

"If God is one, and man is six, together they make seven. I loved you, darling, loved you long. I'll wait for you in—"

HARD DRIVE
BILL FLOYD

The cop and the femme fatale theme never loses its appeal…and certainly not in this story. —SB

It was sheer agony, trying to avoid meeting Nadia Yohn's eyes. I knew that if I did, everyone in the room would see the spark and flash. I couldn't believe it wasn't already obvious.

But we were the only ones aware of it.

I sat on our side of the table alongside the senior homicide detective, Carl Stimple, and Lori Wiese from the district attorney's office. Across from us sat Nadia and her attorney, Tyler Beckenridge. It was hard to discern which was more highly polished—the walnut tabletop or Beckenridge's pink scalp.

Normally we'd have used the windowless rooms downstairs, but since Nadia had already lawyered up, everyone was obliged to pretend the whole thing was an interview as opposed to an interrogation. Nadia looked older than twenty-six today, probably owing to the circumstances, but she was still off the charts. Lips that managed to be suggestive without making any *specific* promises, auburn hair like burning leaves and those sparkling eyes. Lori Wiese regarded her with that condescending yet wary look older women sometimes reserve for those they'd have once considered competition—you just knew she'd already judged Nadia as a tart or worse.

Stimple had, for all intents and purposes, been my mentor since I'd graduated up the ladder to homicide from the narcotics squad six months back, and I'd never been happier to let him take the lead.

"Thanks for coming, y'all," Stimple said. The senior detective's face was mostly gray sideburns and droopy eyes, his good-ole-boy mannerisms cloaking a razor-blade intuition and an evangelical fervor for justice. His first lesson to me: *In the absence of direct physical evidence, your best bet is the personal Q & A. Learn to read their faces, the nonverbal communication—the hint of a lie. Walk them down.*

Nadia was avoiding my eyes as diligently as I was hers.

Stimple's tack was to put the interviewee at ease at first, but his long pauses and deliberate manner made them more and more nervous as questioning progressed. "You guys know we found Liam Gregg's body yesterday, right?"

"All we know is what we saw on the news," Beckenridge answered. "My client's relationship with Mr. Gregg ended over a year ago, following his last run-in with the law."

"An eight-month sentence for dealing pharmaceutical-grade narcotics is hardly a 'run-in,'" Lori Wiese interjected.

Beckenridge waved it off. "Nevertheless."

Finally, I couldn't help myself; I flicked my eyes her way, just wanting to see if she'd registered any reaction at all, any hint of grief for the man she'd lived with for nearly a year before his bust. I was the one who'd put Gregg down, back when I was still working the narco squad. That was how we'd met.

Nadia was staring straight ahead, clenching her jaw. If I could see it so plainly, then everyone else could, too—she was keeping her expression blank because she knew that any hint of emotion might betray her, paving that road for Stimple to chase her down.

But those eyes. I felt something inside me shift, and quickly looked down at my laptop, open on the table in front of me. The screen saver was a photo of my son's face. We'd talked on the phone last night, but I hadn't seen him in weeks.

Stimple let the theatrical pause hang just long enough. "This is the second time in less than a month that someone connected to you has been found murdered, Ms. Yohn. Do you know how many murders we had within the Morrisville city limits during all of last year?"

Beckenridge rolled his eyes. "I doubt Ms. Yohn has any interest in being a statistician for the police, Detective Stimple."

"No," Nadia said softly. Beckenridge shot her a quick frown: *Let me do the talking.*

"We had exactly one murder during all of last year," Stimple said. "Now of course Raleigh, Durham, all the surrounding towns, they more than make up for our excess of civility. But this is two men dead within the past three weeks, both of whom had intimate connections with Ms. Yohn."

Beckenridge sighed. "Both of those relationships were defunct long before the past three weeks. And these men had plenty of enemies of their own."

"Were you still in contact with either of them?" Wiese asked Nadia directly.

Nadia looked at Beckenridge and he nodded. She shrugged. "I was still getting checks from Bert. But I hadn't seen Liam since he got out of prison."

"Plenty of people make mistakes in their relationships," Beckenridge began.

I glanced at her again and this time she was looking at me. Spark. Flash.

But Stimple didn't miss a beat. "Ms. Yohn has quite an extensive record in that department, though, doesn't she? Hell, I believe she even dated my son for a few months back when they were seniors in high school."

He'd offered it lightly, jokingly, but the atmosphere in the room turned even more awkward and sour. Nadia stared openmouthed at Stimple, caught off guard. He stared right back.

Beckenridge wasn't having it. "Now, Carl, no disrespect, but I hardly think we can pin what happened to your son on Ms. Yohn, can we?"

Shit. They'd both crossed lines now—Stimple by bringing it up, Beckenridge with his less than measured response. Carl Stimple's son, Ronnie, died in Iraq nearly eight years ago, victim of an IED. The whole town knew the story. We'd all hung flags on our porches when the news came.

I finally jumped in. "I think we can stick to Ms. Yohn's adult relationships. So, when was the last time you saw either of the victims in person?"

● ● ●

Nadia Yohn had married Bertram Everhardt when she was only twenty years old. Everhardt was a junior VP at IBM, which had a headquarters in the Research Triangle Park, adjacent to the Morrisville city limits. Everhardt was in his forties, a well-known figure at the Prestonwood Country Club and in the moneyed circles in Cary and Raleigh. Morrisville had been a small rural sort of town until the mid-eighties, when development and sprawl ensnared us among the northern transplants and newly minted immigrants who worked in the high-tech centers nearby.

Nadia had been taking some classes at NC State and working a weekend gig as a hostess for a catering company when she caught Everhardt's eye. Four months later they were married, and they cruised along for three years together before things went bad.

Bertram Everhardt's body had been found off a local bike path three weeks ago, less than forty-eight hours after his coworkers reported him missing. He'd been shot in the back of the head, double-tapped execution style. Everhardt was high-profile enough that Chief Roberson assigned both Stimple and me—the total manpower of the Morrisville Police Department's homicide unit—to the case, along with a couple of guys from the State Bureau of Investigation to work the forensics. I should've come clean at that point, but I convinced myself I was trying to protect people—Nadia, myself, my ex-wife. I'd already caused such wreckage. I wasn't thinking straight.

We conducted a lot of interviews and the one theme that kept recurring was the friction between Everhardt and his ex-wife. Rumors abounded of wild parties at their McMansion back when they were still married, drug-fueled weekends that caused quite a stir among their mostly conservative peers. Morrisville was now one of those towns where everyone drove pricey SUVs and the kids attended private academies and the typical scrape-and-save cycle of American life was little more than a quaint rumor, so the Everhardts' hedonistic streak stuck out.

The man rumored to have supplied the pharmaceutical fun at these soirees was a local rogue named Liam Gregg. On the cusp of their fourth wedding anniversary, Nadia and Bertram had split, and she'd moved in with Gregg. Her lawyers eventually settled for lower alimony than many local wags had predicted, but still enough to maintain her in style for years to come. The suggestion was that there'd been adultery by both spouses. Everhardt's friends said he'd nursed a grudge.

Within a year of the split my narcotics squad had been given an anonymous tip on Gregg's activities, which included tapping deliveries of Vicodin and OxyContin to local pharmacies. The eventual bust took down behind-the-counter employees of several chain retailers, along with Liam and a couple of lower-level dealers. Nadia was never implicated, but I'd had to interview her as part of the investigation.

Her life had been upended and my own marriage was limping through its final rancorous months, the shell of my relationship with Sherri turning more toxic by the day, our young son, Toby, showing signs of anxiety and aggression even though he was only four years old. God, the things people do to each other.

The first time I'd reached out to touch Nadia's hand, in what I told myself was a comforting way, there it was: that spark, that flash. She'd grabbed my hand and linked her fingers into mine. In that one single entwining, I'd lost my marriage and whatever man Howie Logan had been right up until that very moment. I'd never seen that man again.

I'd made all kinds of excuses. None of them were remotely legit. The truth was we'd just reached for each other, connected. Gregg took a plea deal that netted him eight months and Sherri found out about my fling with Nadia. I got separated and within a matter of weeks Nadia told me she couldn't see me anymore. I'd been spinning in place ever since.

No one bothered to report Gregg missing. He'd been living in a shabby apartment complex near I-40 since his release from state prison. A security guard found his body in the parking lot of a nearby defunct research facility, a cluster of glass-and-steel buildings that had been state-of-the-art until the parent company folded during the most recent recession. Gregg was crumpled near the entrance of the main building, killed in the exact same fashion as Everhardt, a double-tap to the back of the skull. Forensics showed it was the same 9 mm weapon that had killed both men.

Stimple was pissed. Gregg had been our prime suspect for the Bertram Everhardt killing. Now only one common factor remained.

• • •

Beckenridge, still testy about his last exchange with Stimple, addressed himself to me. "Detective Logan, I'd like to remind everyone that we came in voluntarily. If we'd known that my client was being treated as a suspect—"

"I don't believe anyone's used that term," I said. *Don't look at her.*

Stimple broke in. "I would like to clarify something, though. Your client says she didn't have any contact with Mr. Gregg after he was released from prison, correct?"

"She said she hadn't seen him."

Stimple grinned. He'd made his point, and now he pounced. "Because Mr. Gregg's family gave us permission to look at his computer. We found a number of recent emails between your client and Mr. Gregg."

"He was threatening me," Nadia said suddenly, loudly. "He was trying to get money."

Beckenridge laid a hand on her arm.

"That seemed apparent from the content of the messages," Stimple said. "As was your adamant refusal to be coerced. Which I admire. You even told him that he'd be sorry if he didn't leave you alone."

"That—" Nadia began.

"This interview is terminated," Beckenridge announced.

"We'd like permission to look on her computer," Stimple said. "She might have information on there that could be helpful."

Beckenridge laughed at that. He stood and glared at us in turn, smarting from the ambush. "Nadia, let's go."

She looked at me, drowning. I studied my screen saver.

"We won't have much trouble getting a warrant," Stimple said, enjoying himself. "The SBI is helping us out on this one, and they've got some digital forensics guys who do *incredible* work."

● ● ●

I was at home that night, eating leftover pizza and watching ESPN when my cell phone rang. I saw her number come up and thought about not answering it. But if she left a message, that would be even worse. Once my number showed up on her phone records, interested parties might be able to make an argument that my phone should be examined.

And those digital forensics guys really can do some incredible things.

"Are you out of your mind?" I asked her when I picked up.

"Your emails are on my computer," she said. "Going back the whole time we were seeing each other. I erased them but your experts can find them, right?"

I'd been thinking of little else since the meeting. I'd hidden the affair from Stimple and the rest of them because it was Sherri's final request to me, the one I couldn't deny after all the pain I'd caused her. She'd pleaded with me not to humiliate her any further. And if it came out, if Beckenridge discovered that Nadia was involved with a cop, he'd use it any way he could, in the media and in court.

"Did you ever have an off-site backup?" I asked her.

"Just my external drive."

"Where is it? In your house?"

"Right beside the computer. Howie, I—"

God, my name on her lips.

"You shouldn't have called me," I said. But I couldn't keep the emotion out of my voice.

"I didn't have anything to do with what happened to Bertram or Liam," she said, her voice breaking just a little. "You know that, don't you?"

"I was in love with you, Nadia. But I'm still not sure I ever *knew* you."

"You lost a lot because of me. I'm willing to take responsibility for that, Howie. But not for this. And if someone's killing the people I've been with, the men I've loved..." She didn't have to say the rest.

"Did you ever tell anyone about us?" I asked.

"Never. I respected your wishes. Does anyone besides your wife know?"

I stared at the TV. I wanted nothing more than to see her, to touch her. But that wasn't real anymore. Our brief affair had allowed me to live out a consuming fantasy of breathless transgression. She'd nurtured the liar in me, the one who lied to everyone else and to myself, even if I never could lie to her. That fantasy had cost me most of the real world, and now we'd come to a place where it just might cost me the rest.

● ● ●

Stimple wanted me to help execute the warrant the next morning but I had to be in court to testify on one of my old drug cases. By the time I got done with my turn on the stand, my mentor had left no less than five messages on my phone, each more progressively anguished than the last.

"She beat us to the punch," he said on the first one, nearly weeping with frustration. "She's saying her house was broken into last night. Call me as soon as you get this."

The next message: "Bitch says she didn't leave her alarm system on when she went out for drinks with her girlfriends. How stupid does she think we are? I am going to crucify her, Howie, you hear me?"

The next: "Computer's gone, along with the gun that's registered to her—9 mm, just like our shooter. Call me when—"

I called my soon-to-be ex-wife instead. This had gone far enough, and my rationalizations were corroding.

Sherri had taken Toby and unofficially moved to South Carolina, to be closer to her parents. I hadn't seen her for more than a few minutes at a time since the split, and then only when she was handing Toby off for a weekend with me. I could've made a fuss in family court about the arrangement, but I didn't feel like I was in any position to fight her. Toby had been exposed to too much bitterness already.

"God, you sound horrible," she said. She, on the other hand, sounded fine. The further she withdrew from me, the better she felt. "What's up?"

I told her. I could hear it when she went cold on the other end of the line.

"Nadia." She fairly spat the name. "I thought you said it was over with her."

"It was. Is."

"So what are you looking for here?" she asked, sounding exhausted. "You're your own man now. You clean up your own messes."

"In order to clean this one up I'm going to have to tell the chief."

She laughed but there was no humor in it, only a resentful sort of self-pity and an open hostility I hadn't felt from her since she'd noticed my increasingly erratic behavior and tailed me over to Nadia's place one night. She used all the surveillance tactics I'd taught her as a lark when we were first dating, giving her the inside trade secrets I thought were inconsequential. Turned out she'd been a good listener, better than I ever was.

"Well, I guess my humiliation's complete," she surmised. "I'm going to keep Toby with me until you clear this up."

No argument from me there.

"Did I ever tell you that you were the worst mistake I ever made?" she asked.

It was what you'd call a rhetorical question.

• • •

I arranged a meeting in the chief's office with Stimple and Lori Wiese in attendance. The worst part was those first few seconds, all of them staring at me, uneasy but still trusting, giving me the benefit of the doubt.

So I just came right out with it.

"You guys know I got separated last year. You know we chalked it up to irreconcilable differences, the usual cop-spouse burnout syndrome." No one had second-guessed that explanation; police forces worldwide were littered with collateral wreckage. "The truth is Sherri caught me cheating. I was having an affair with Nadia Yohn."

At first Stimple actually cracked up, but within a few breaths his laugh had sputtered into gaping disbelief.

Chief Roberson asked me to repeat what I'd just said.

Lori Wiese was up on her feet, pacing. "And why the hell, exactly, did you not mention this before now? Why did you not pull yourself off the case as soon as Everhardt was reported missing? Why the hell did you attend that meeting yesterday?" Her hands were flying around like she couldn't decide what to do with them.

"My wife asked me to keep the affair a secret," I said quietly. I felt a great deflation coming on, like my bones had turned soft. Like I'd been holding myself rigid for so long I'd forgotten how to unclench. "I knew if the truth came out, the lawyers would use it and, well, Sherri didn't want to feel publicly humiliated."

"You humiliated her when you started screwing around with that—that—!" Wiese finally dropped her hands and stared at me. "I cannot believe I'm having this conversation."

Stimple's reaction was worse. The hurt on his face was apparent, a depth of betrayal I hadn't ever imagined. I started to say something to him but he held up a hand and shook his head. The brief sense of confessional relief I'd felt quickly turned poisonous.

Roberson leaned across his desk. "As of this moment, you are suspended with pay pending an investigation. You are not to speak about this matter to anyone. If we discover that you've jeopardized a murder investigation, your losing your badge will be just the beginning."

"What happened to her computer?" Stimple asked quietly.

"I don't know."

"What about *your* computer?" asked the chief.

"My wife took it when she left."

"Of all the stupid, thinking-with-your-dick screwups—" Wiese continued, livid.

I said, "We still don't know for certain that Nadia is involved in the murders."

They stared at me like I was a foreign life-form, a particularly disgusting one composed mostly of quivering valves and offensive odors. "You're right about that," Stimple finally said. "But now we have to figure out if *you* are."

●　●　●

I still lived in the house Sherri and I'd bought when we were first married; it was my only real asset, in terms of ownership. I didn't know if it would survive the final terms of the divorce.

When the empty upstairs rooms loomed too large, I retreated to the basement to really turn up the Bose speakers loud and blank out all thought. I had my flat-screen down there, all my Drive-By Truckers and Avett Brothers and Bobby Bare, Jr. CDs, none of that radio country crap. Real music. It was the only thing I could disappear into anymore.

Nadia had broken it off with me a few weeks after Sherri left. "I love you," she'd said, "I really do, but you're part of this same damned pattern. The rich guy to the troublemaker to the cop with the heart of gold." She'd smiled then and touched me on my chest.

If I'd died right at that moment I'd have been cool with it. But instead she took her hand away and left me behind.

I couldn't really blame her for what had happened with Sherri. Nadia was a catalyst. I'd given my wife a dozen reasons to leave, some having to do with the job, some with whatever was missing inside me. But now I was on the verge of losing my job, maybe my freedom, and yet all I could think of was those flashing eyes, those whispers, the way she'd clung so tight. I'd let Nadia walk away because I knew she was right, she *was* stuck in a pattern that was leading to worse and worse results. What I wanted for her most of all was for her to break free of the machinations of all the jealous petty dipshits who'd ever fallen for her, myself included.

I'd stowed my service weapon in my locker before I left the station. They wouldn't demand it of me yet, not until Roberson and Wiese's investigation—which I imagined would involve a lot of ass-covering and a concerted effort to keep it an internal affair—was complete. The only guns I kept in the house were a shotgun upstairs and my father's little .22 pistol, an antique that I still fired sometimes on the range, just to keep it in working order. I stored the handgun in a cushioned wooden box down in the basement, in one of the coffee table drawers, right there by the couch.

I slid open the drawer and unlatched the box now, five beers in—bad idea.

The last time I'd taken it out was the day Nadia walked away. I'd just wanted to stop hurting. But I'd eventually put it back in the box and closed the lid on it. It was my son's face that turned things for me then, but thinking of him now made me hurt even worse. I took out the .22 and checked the cylinder—fully loaded, six rounds. Small caliber, you'd have to aim it straight into your eye or your mouth or your heart for it to work.

I stared at the gun a while and then put it back in the drawer, too drunk to latch it back into its box, halfway thinking I might work up the guts sooner rather than later.

• • •

"She's gone," Stimple told me on the phone.

"Gone?" I croaked. It was nearly noon, but I was still entangled in stale sheets, the curtains pulled tight, a spilled beer sticky on the bedside table. I couldn't even remember coming up from the basement.

"Lock on the back door broken, blood on the cabinets. The alarm company called it in this morning at around four. Where were you at that time?"

"I was right here, Carl."

"We're going to need to come out there."

They arrived ten minutes later, Stimple pausing only long enough to sneer at my disheveled appearance before moving past me. One of the officers took note of my breath and handed me a stick of chewing gum. It was sickly sweet and made my mouth even drier.

They checked the place top to bottom and then took off. "Do not go anywhere," Stimple ordered me on his way out.

But she was missing, and I couldn't stand the empty house. I showered and went rogue.

• • •

I rousted Liam Gregg's drug associates. My empty threats were rendered plausible by the madness in my eyes, but they didn't know shit. I lied my way past security at Prestonwood and harassed Bertram Everhardt's old golfing buddies. One of them must've contacted the station, because Stimple was on my phone within minutes of my leaving the country club, demanding that I take my ass back home and plant it there.

The impotent frustration shrunk my lungs down to wheezing knots. I drove to my place on autopilot, a single thought repeating: *Where are you?*

Back home, I took a beer and headed for the dim refuge of the basement. I reached the bottom of the stairs and saw her there on the old ratty couch, face bruised and bloody, hands tied behind her back, eyes wide, a sob trapped behind a strip of gray tape.

I dropped my beer.

Carl Stimple was sitting on the couch with her, but he rose now and aimed a gun I recognized as a 9 mm at me, waving me to take his place beside Nadia. I raised my empty hands high and said, "Please, Carl. Whatever this is, stay calm."

Stimple gestured toward a gray boxy object on the coffee table. "See that hard drive, Howie? Came out of her computer. All kinds of emails between the two of you on here, right?"

"You—?"

"Took it right out of her place. Figured it would complete the scene just about perfectly. You panicked, stole it before you decided to come clean."

"Carl, we can talk about this."

He shook his head ruefully.

"I talk, you listen," Stimple said. "Now. Sit. Down."

I moved onto the couch and Nadia leaned into me.

Stimple sneered. "The perfect couple. Howie, you're an asshole. You know she really did kill my son? She really did. Ditched him as soon as they had their diplomas, traded him in to be the life of the party. Ronnie enlisted right off. Barely eighteen years old. Some of the guys in his unit wrote to me after, you know, told me how he never could quit talking about her, how he was always distracted, reckless, trying to prove himself."

Nadia tried to say something from behind her gag.

"Shut up!" Stimple roared at her. "You might've forgotten about Ronnie but I never did. I kept an eye on you, watching as you milked your rich husband and then traded him in for a drug dealer. I've been planning to put you down for a long time, but I wasn't quite sure how to make it work. When I realized you'd seduced my young protégé here, I knew I had my opening." He saw my face and laughed. "Oh, yeah, I knew. Maybe I wasn't quite certain until our little interview the other day, but I saw what happened when you two looked at each other. No mistaking that electricity."

He was wearing gloves. His eyes were wild.

"Up until then, I was just going to frame her for Everhardt and Gregg. But this, this is so much better. Everyone knows how poor Howie's life's been falling apart these past few months, losing his family and all, buckling under the pressures of a new line of work. A perfect line of work for someone who wants payback on the girl who wrecked his life. A murder/suicide scenario if ever there was one." He waved the 9 mm at us. "Same gun used in all the crimes. You've got the hard drive from her computer with all your secret messages. I want you to know this isn't really about you, though, Howie, okay? This is about my boy."

Nadia moved faster than I'd have ever imagined she could. She was up off the couch and barreling at Stimple with her head down before he could quite believe it. He looked like he wanted to laugh, but instead he fired. I saw the wound opening as the bullet punctured her back just above the shoulder blade. The force of her launch carried her into him and he spun around, deflecting her onto the floor.

I grabbed my father's .22 out of the drawer while Stimple was distracted with Nadia. I knew I had to get closer to get off an effective shot. He was turning back in my direction when I shoved the little gun right up under his jaw. Firing all six rounds might've been overdoing it a bit, but I was kind of going on instinct at that point.

●　●　●

Nadia was in the hospital for a week with a collapsed lung. It was touch and go for a while there.

The day she was released I came to see her. Her parents were there, too, and none too pleased to see a police officer of any kind, especially one whose suspension had been extended while the investigation wound down. But Nadia reached out from her wheelchair and entwined her fingers with my own. I leaned in to kiss her while her folks stood there awkwardly.

Spark. Flash.

AFTER HOURS
WILLIAM BERNHARDT

*There are enough twists in this story to warrant
one of those road signs with a snaky arrow on it.
Buckle up. —SB*

Major Morelli shoved his hands into the pockets of his trench coat. "Damn it all to hell."

Morelli's partner, Lieutenant Baxter, was so stricken she could barely speak. "It's…a tragedy, that's all," she finally spit out in a halting, broken voice. "Just…a tragedy."

The corpse sprawled across the king-size bed was, Morelli thought, perhaps the most luminous woman he had ever seen. Even now, with the color drained from her face, she possessed a spellbinding quality that he rarely observed in the living or the dead. A purity that came only with youth. A feminine dignity that even so much blood could not obscure.

"Must've been a heartbreaker," Morelli added, to no one in particular.

"And so young. Hell, I got a niece about her age." Baxter turned her back on the grisly tableau. "Think of everything she'll miss, everything she'll never know. Just makes me sick."

"Try to keep your emotions out of it," Morelli warned. "We have a job to do."

"You're always in control, right? Always the professional. Even when you're looking at a crime so horrible it makes your stomach turn. Makes you want to give up being a cop and just slit your wrists."

Morelli didn't blink. "Let's interview the boyfriend."

On his way out of the bedroom, Morelli glanced through the still-open sliding door that led to the terrace. The Tulsa skyline beckoned with twinkling lights and an irregular skyline, innocent as a Christmas tree. He loved this town, loved its earnestness and well-meaning naïveté. Working here was like policing feral beast outbreaks in a wildlife preserve. Who would dream that even here, after hours, you could discover a horror like this?

He headed into the main living room where Baxter was already waiting. Dr. Barkley, the county coroner, had arrived. He was younger than Morelli and it showed. He had the expertise of a doctor and the aspect of a surfer dude, a combination Morelli never failed to find disturbing.

"She's in there." Morelli jerked his thumb back the way he'd come. "I'd like to know as much as you can tell me as soon as you can tell me."

Barkley frowned. "Mike, you know I can't reach any final conclusions until I've—"

"Yeah, I know the drill." Morelli placed his finger on the lapel of Barkley's overalls. "Nonetheless, I want to know as much as you can tell me as soon as you can tell me. I'd like a preliminary report in fifteen minutes. Understood?"

"Whatever." Barkley passed wordlessly into the bedroom.

"Bit grumpy tonight, aren't you?" Baxter asked.

"Just reminding the coroner who works for whom."

"No, that girl is getting to you. The corpse. You're totally on edge."

"Don't like having my sleep disturbed."

"That I already knew."

She handed him the photos from the videographers, as always, careful that their hands didn't touch.

The affair started years ago. First it was an unexpected kiss during a stakeout. Now they spent most weekends together. No one knew. Departmental regulations didn't permit intimate relationships between officers. If word got out, one of them would have to quit. Not to mention put up with endless harassment from fellow officers.

Morelli crossed the living room of the penthouse apartment. Baxter followed. They found the boyfriend huddled in the far corner of an elegant white sofa.

He was a delicate, slender man—in some respects as beautiful as his slain companion. His hair had been buzzed down almost to the scalp. Ironically, the extreme crew cut did not give him a hard, military appearance but instead made him seem simple and unadorned, almost childlike. His face was red and swollen to such a degree that Morelli couldn't get a clear impression of his features.

Morelli opened his notepad and checked the name. "You're Terry Farnum?"

The man nodded slightly.

"You knew the girl? Kim Masters?"

His response was more a tremble than a nod.

Times like this Morelli hated his job, absolutely hated it. Farnum was grieving hard, and nothing was worse than trying to pry information out of someone who really needed a comforting arm around the shoulder.

"Could you describe your relationship?"

Farnum pressed his hand against his forehead, obscuring much of his face. "We were in love."

"I see." Damn this job. He had to keep pushing. "How long had you…uh…been together?"

"Almost seven months now." His voice cracked when he spoke. "I met her in this club I own down on Peoria. The Red Parrot. When I first saw Kim, I—I can't explain it. You know how, sometimes, you look back on a particular moment in your life and you realize, that was when everything changed? That's how it was when I connected with Kim. From the very first, I knew this was something special."

"I gather your relationship was—" Morelli coughed into his hand "—sexual in nature."

"It wasn't the most important part of the relationship, but yes. That first night, after I finally worked up the courage to speak to her, she came home with me. But there was nothing cheap or sleazy about it. She may look young, but she's an adult. And so smart. We stayed up all night talking, telling secrets, baring our souls. She had not led an easy life. She was confused, troubled, despondent. Said no one understood her. Felt everyone was judging her, finding her inadequate. She was on the verge of suicide. 'Why can't people just let us be who we are?' she said. 'Why can't we be who we want to be?'"

Farnum closed his eyes. "I told her not to worry. Told her she was safe with me. Told her everyone is entitled to a small measure of happiness. And that included her. I don't know how to explain this but, by the time the sun rose, it was as if—we both knew. Can you understand that? We both knew this was right. It was only natural that we should become lovers. Natural and so very right. She was the great romance of my life. Nothing else came close."

Morelli watched Farnum's face carefully. The police department's initial suspect was always the spouse or significant other. But watching this man's grief-ridden face, hearing his cracked and broken voice, Morelli found it impossible to believe he would do Kim Masters any harm.

"Do you know anyone who might have reason to kill Kim?"

Farnum shook his head. "I can't imagine. She quit her job, after we got together. She lived here with me. Most days, she never even went out, unless it was a brief trip to do some shopping or some such. She had very little contact with other people. I think…I think she liked it that way."

"What about yourself?"

"What do you mean?"

"Does anyone bear a grudge against you? Someone who might try to get to you by killing your girlfriend?"

Farnum's eyes widened, suddenly and horribly. "No. I mean, I can't— It wouldn't— No."

Baxter cut in. "But there is someone with an ax to grind against you? Right?"

Farnum's eyes dropped a notch. "I…owe some money. Business at the club dropped off this year but, unfortunately, my debts didn't. I had to borrow. It's purely a business arrangement."

"With the mob?"

Farnum took a deep breath. "Do you know a man named Albert DeCarlo? Intercontinental Imports?"

Morelli did. DeCarlo was the top mobster in Tulsa Town. Inherited the position from his daddy. Intercontinental Imports was a front for all his illegal operations. "I know him."

"He likes to hang out at my club. Has for years. But only recently did we have occasion to do business together."

"How much do you owe?"

"Half a million."

Morelli whistled. "And DeCarlo wants to be paid."

"He's expressed that desire on repeated occasions, yes."

"Maybe the hit was a warning," Baxter said. "Pay up or you'll be next."

"I don't think so. I mean—well, I know that isn't so."

"What makes you so sure?"

"For one thing, I told DeCarlo yesterday that I'm taking bankruptcy. My assets are all in the control of the receiver now. It wouldn't matter who DeCarlo killed. He'll never get more than ten cents on the dollar."

Baxter flipped her long brown curls behind her shoulders. "That wouldn't deter that bloodsucker. He might've thought that if he pushed you, you might find some more money somewhere. Or maybe the hit was to teach you a lesson. Or to send a message to the other schmucks who owe him money."

"I've known DeCarlo for years. Since he was a lieutenant working under his father. That isn't his style."

"But you said—"

"You asked if I knew anyone who had a grudge against me, and I do. But if DeCarlo wanted to send a message, he would've hit me, not Kim. He fancies himself a respectable businessman, in his own twisted way. He might've had me rubbed out, but he would never murder an innocent third person."

"That's a crock of—"

Morelli stopped her in midsentence. "No. He's right." Morelli was familiar enough with DeCarlo's file to know. The young DeCarlo had been linked to a number of high crimes, including contract killings. But no one had ever suggested that he'd struck against a target's wife or family or loved ones. He considered it a point of honor. He wouldn't ice the woman to get at Farnum, no matter how much money was on the line.

"Okay," Morelli said, "if not DeCarlo, then who was it?"

Farnum shrugged. "If I knew that, don't you think I'd tell you?" He wiped puddles from his eyes. "Maybe a burglar."

"The terrace door was open," Baxter noted. "A burglar with good rappelling gear could have lowered himself from the roof."

"These are very expensive apartments. Most of the tenants here are loaded. We've had a lot of break-ins lately. Maybe Kim caught someone in the act."

Part of that was true—the Malador had a crime rate way above average. "We'll check it out," Morelli promised. He glanced up at Baxter. "Anything else you want to ask?"

"Well—yeah. You haven't asked about the victim's family or friends or bad habits or—"

"I think that's enough for now." True, they hadn't covered all the bases, but he wanted to know more about the crime itself. And he wanted to give poor Farnum a break. "Let's see if the coroner can shed any light on this mystery."

Morelli returned to the bedroom. He stopped just before he entered and pulled his cell phone out.

"You going to pick up DeCarlo?" Baxter asked.

"I don't see the point. But I would like someone to speak with him."

"He'll deny everything."

"But he might tell us something useful, just the same." Morelli snapped his fingers. "Do you know a mug named Ernie Bartello? They call him Bart the Dart."

"DeCarlo's top enforcer, right?"

"Right. If DeCarlo had this done, Bartello's the one who did it. And if I'm not mistaken, Bartello likes to hang out at the Velvet Rose when he's not working." He punched a few buttons. "I'll send someone out to pick him up. You send someone over to visit with DeCarlo."

After they made their respective phone calls, they entered the bedroom.

Barkley was in the process of covering the corpse with a bedsheet. Apparently he had finished his preliminary investigation.

"What've you got for me?" Morelli asked.

"As I said before, it's too soon to—"

"What's the cause of death?"

"There is a bullet wound to the abdomen, near the heart. But I can't say—"

"What about the time of death?"

"Can't say."

"Was she killed here?"

"Can't say."

"Did she know her attacker?"

"Can't say."

Morelli got right up in his face. "Look, *Doctor,* we're investigating a murder here—the murder of a beautiful young woman who, as far as we know, never hurt anyone. Most crimes are solved in the first six hours—if they're solved at all. So we need to know everything you can possibly tell us. Right now."

Barkley batted his eyelashes, as if the pool bully had splashed water in his face. "I guess there's one thing I can tell you about this…beautiful young woman."

"What's that?"

The barest glimmer of a smile flickered across his face. "She's a he."

• • •

Baxter looked as if someone had kicked her in the stomach. "What are you talking about? There's no way—"

"I'm surprised you didn't notice it yourself." Barkley flipped the sheet covering the body up, then replaced it. "I'm going to arrange to have him taken to my office as soon as your forensic teams have finished scouring the crime scene."

Morelli was just as stunned as Baxter, but he would never let it show. "I think we'd better have another talk with Mr. Farnum."

• • •

Major Morelli squared himself in front of Farnum, contemplating how to proceed. He made half a dozen false starts, searching for the right words to broach the elephant now in the room. Farnum had referred to Kim as *her*. Did he think they wouldn't find out? Was he too embarrassed to mention it? Or did he really not know the truth?

Morelli coughed into his hand, clearing his throat. "Mr. Farnum...uh...you say you've known Kim Masters almost seven months?"

"Right. Since that first night I brought her home."

"And that was the first night you spotted Kim in your club?"

"Oh, no. I admired her from afar for weeks before I spoke to her."

"Why did it take you so long?"

"I don't know. I was hesitant. I have some...personal eccentricities. I've learned to choose my companions carefully."

Morelli and Baxter exchanged a glance.

"Is something wrong?" Farnum asked. "Something about Kim? My God—what did they do to her?"

Her.

He didn't know. Morelli was certain of it. No one could keep up a charade this long or this well. Farnum had been with her for months, but he didn't know.

Morelli proceeded. "You did say, didn't you, that you and Kim Masters had a sexual relationship?"

"I don't see that that's any of your concern."

"Believe me, if it didn't matter, I wouldn't ask."

Farnum folded his arms across his chest. "Yes. What of it?"

"And...did you..." Morelli wiped his hand across his brow. "Do you mind if I ask what exactly it was you two did?"

Farnum's face tightened. "Not at all. Right after you tell me what you and your wife did in bed last night."

"I'm divorced."

"All right then. You and your girlfriend. You and your plastic blow-up doll. Whatever."

"You've made your point." Morelli pressed his fingers against his temples. "Look—"

"Major Morelli," Farnum said. "I've lost the only woman I've ever loved. I am not in the mood for games. If you have something you want to tell me—then tell me."

Morelli slowly exhaled. "The only woman you've ever loved…"

"Yes?"

"She's a man."

Farnum's reaction could not have been much different had Morelli hit him in the face with a brick. Many moments passed before he whispered, "What?"

"It's true. The coroner confirmed it. She's a man."

"But—this isn't possible."

"I'm afraid it is. You have to understand—there are a lot of drag queens out on the Peoria strip. I've heard some of the boys in Vice say one person in five in those clubs is a cross-dresser."

"I've had drag queens in my club since the day it opened. No matter how good they were, I could always tell the difference."

"Well, I guess this one fooled even you."

"But it's just so…impossible. I can't—I can't—" And then, all at once, Farnum's expression altered dramatically. He laughed.

This was even more perplexing than everything else that had happened tonight. "I'm sorry," Morelli said, "is something funny?"

"It's all just so…so…" Farnum wiped away the tears crystallizing in the corners of his eyes. "No, not funny exactly. More like ironic."

"I'm afraid I don't follow."

"Irony. The juxtaposition of unexpected circumstances—"

"I know what irony is," Morelli growled. "What I don't understand is why it's ironic that your girlfriend turns out to be a man."

With a quick, fluid motion, Farnum untucked his shirt and pulled it up, exposing the tight binding wrapped around his upper abdomen. "Because I'm really a woman."

• • •

Two hours later, Morelli cradled a foam cup filled with hot black coffee while the forensic teams did their work. There was something comforting about the feel of the coffee. It might not be much, but at least you knew what it was. Exactly what you thought it was.

Baxter came in and poured herself a cup. "What's the word from headquarters?"

"DeCarlo flat out denied that he ordered Bartello to make the hit," Morelli replied.

"Does that surprise you?"

"Actually it does. I thought he would call his lawyer and refuse to talk."

"Apparently he fired his mouthpiece. Maybe you should send over that lawyer buddy of yours."

"No point. Ever since his wife had those twin girls, he can't finish a sentence that doesn't have 'goo-goo' in it." Morelli held the coffee under his nose, drawing in the rich Kona aroma. "Anything else?"

"Yeah. Prescott is picking up Bartello and bringing him here. My informants tell me DeCarlo had a big falling-out with Bart the Dart earlier this week. Don't know why, but DeCarlo totally cut him off. Bart's been coming around to his place every night, trying to worm his way back into favor. But so far, no luck."

"So even if DeCarlo was behind the hit, he wouldn't have used the Dartman."

"Looks that way."

"I still want to talk to him."

"Figured as much. But aren't you forgetting something?"

"What's that?"

"You said it yourself—if DeCarlo was out to get Farnum, he would've gone after Farnum. He wouldn't have gone after Farnum's girlfriend. Boyfriend. Whatever."

"That's a problem." He polished off his coffee. "Thanks for the background info. I can always count on you to come up with the goods."

"Should I be reading in between the lines here?"

"No. Just saying I know I can count on you. That's why I like having you for a…partner."

"I thought it was my stunning good looks."

"That, too."

• • •

A few minutes later, Morelli's nemesis-in-homicide, Major Prescott, arrived at the penthouse apartment bearing Ernie Bartello, aka Bart the Dart. Prescott had a grudge against Morelli that went back years. Prescott had been removed from a high-profile murder investigation and Morelli had taken over. Worse, he'd had the audacity to solve the case. Prescott had never forgiven him.

They put Bartello in a separate bedroom, away from Farnum and the crime scene. Prescott motioned Morelli aside for a few pre-interrogation words.

"So lemme see if I've got this straight," Prescott said. "Masters was really a man, all dolled up like a woman."

"Right."

"And he-she was sleeping with Farnum, who was a woman made up like a man."

"So it seems."

"And neither one knew that their love mate was not what they looked to be."

"That also appears to be the case."

"They were both pretending to be what the other one really was."

"By George, I think you've got it."

"What the hell did they do with each other?"

Morelli didn't know if Prescott was being rhetorical, or if he really expected an answer. "I think…they loved one another. Very much."

"Jeez, what is the world coming to?" Prescott muttered. "Disgusting."

"It's not disgusting," Morelli replied. "It's sad."

"Sad? Those sick perverts?" Prescott grimaced. "I think you must be sick, too."

Morelli did not reply. "If you'll excuse me, I've got a suspect to interrogate."

● ● ●

Bartello was a thin man, wiry and tough, exactly the sort of person no one would want to meet alone unless they were packing a two-megaton rocket launcher. Probably not even then. The Grim Reaper tattoo on his forearm and the small but discernible scar on the left side of his face lent two strong clues to his chosen profession.

Morelli was the good cop while Prescott played the bad. Typecasting, Morelli thought, although Prescott might not see it that way.

"What do you know about this murder, Bartello?"

"Nothin'."

"Did you hit Kim Masters?"

"Don't know what you're talking about."

"Did DeCarlo order you to do it?"

"DeCarlo? Who's that?"

Morelli tried not to clench his teeth. "I want the truth."

"Call the psychic hotline."

"This job looks like your handiwork."

Bartello shrugged. "Imitation is the sincerest form of flattery."

Prescott lurched forward and grabbed the man's collar. "Don't screw with us, Bartello. Or so help me—"

Morelli shook his head. Prescott was so bad at this. Like the man was going to be scared enough to break after twenty seconds of softball questions. "Let's calm down, everybody. We're just having a conversation, okay?" He nudged Prescott out of the way. "Bartello, did you know your buddy DeCarlo was bearing a half-million-dollar grudge?"

"DeCarlo ain't my buddy. I don't work for him no more."

"You know, I heard a rumor to that effect. What'd you do to tick off the boss man?"

"I didn't do nothin'. He's got no business treatin' me like this."

"There must've been something."

"It was just one date."

Morelli eased back. "One date with whom?"

Bartello's voice dropped to a whisper. "Sophia."

"Sophia DeCarlo? The boss's daughter?"

"And what's wrong with that? It ain't like I forced her or nothin'. Hell, all I did was kiss her good-night."

"The boss caught you sucking face with his only daughter and he didn't like it. So he sent you away before things got out of control."

"The man was not rational."

"Because he didn't want his pride and joy hooked up with a two-bit hit man? Imagine."

"He's happy enough to have me around when he needs work done."

"You just don't get it, do you, Bartello? That's how all the DeCarlos in this world are. When they can use you, they'll use you. But it doesn't mean they like you. And it sure as hell doesn't mean you have the slightest chance of making it with his daughter."

"May I go now?"

"What happened tonight when you went to DeCarlo's place?"

"Nothin'."

"Did he give you an assignment?"

"No."

Unfortunately, Morelli got the distinct impression he was telling the truth. "Did he mention Terry Farnum?"

Bartello answered with a shoulder shrug. "Yeah. He was ravin'. Shoutin'. On and on. Talkin' about how Farnum had taken his money and wasn't payin' him back. 'This woman has made me a laughingstock,' he kept sayin'. 'I won't tolerate this. I'm Albert De-Carlo!' But he didn't ask me to do it. No, he wouldn't lower himself to deal with the likes of me anymore."

"So you were—" Morelli snapped his fingers. "Becket."

Prescott's head swiveled around. "What?"

"Thomas Becket. The Archbishop of Canterbury. Buddied around with Henry II."

"Look, *Jeopardy* boy, show off some other—"

"Henry and Becket had a falling-out. Classic conflicts between church and state, each trying to maintain as much power as possible. Henry couldn't have the Archbishop of Canterbury axed, so he endured the aggravation. One night, though, when he'd had a bit too much mead, he cried out, 'Will no one rid me of this turbulent priest?' He was probably just blowing off steam. But four of his knights heard the remark and decided to get in the king's good graces by offing the archbishop. Which they did. On hallowed ground."

"And this has something to do with Albert DeCarlo?" Prescott asked.

"Of course. DeCarlo didn't lie. He didn't order Bartello or anyone else to make the hit. But when he screamed, 'This woman has made me a laughingstock,' a lot of people were listening." He turned his head. "Including Bart here, who was desperate to worm his way back into his boss's favor."

"But you said DeCarlo wouldn't go after Farnum's girlfriend."

"Don't you see? Terry can be a man or a woman's name. So can Kim. DeCarlo had known Farnum for years. He knew Farnum was really a she. But Bart didn't. So he came over here to kill 'this woman—'"

"And he thought Kim Masters was the woman?"

Morelli bent down eye level to his suspect. "You screwed it up, Bartello. DeCarlo wanted Farnum done, not Masters. Farnum will go under police protection now. You screwed up the hit, incriminated your boss and pretty much guaranteed DeCarlo will never be able to get to Farnum. I don't think your boss will be too pleased about this. You can forget about Sophia. You can forget about everything."

Bartello's skin turned icy white. "Oh, my God," he said, and his face told Morelli more than all the confessions in the world. "Oh, my God."

● ● ●

By the time the sun rose, the various forensic teams had finished their work. The newest member of the trace evidence squad found a latent thumbprint on the outer terrace door that appeared to match Bartello's. The pieces were coming together.

Not a bad night's work, Morelli thought, for Tulsa after hours.

Two women from Barkley's office carefully lifted the broken body of Kim Masters onto a stretcher. Morelli and Prescott watched as the silent parade crisscrossed the penthouse apartment and disappeared.

"Sick," Prescott said. "And there you were blabbing on about how sad it was, how beautiful she was."

"Is she any less beautiful," Morelli asked, "because she turned out to be a he?"

"As a matter of fact, yeah. The whole thing's revolting. Dressing up, trying to fool people."

"I don't think Kim Masters was trying to fool anyone. The first night they were together, Farnum said he kept asking, 'Why can't people just let us be who we are?'" Morelli shoved his hands into his coat pockets. "I think he was just doing what he could to find solace. They both were."

Prescott pivoted at the door. "You know what I hate most about you, Morelli?"

"Not yet."

"I think you're just as disgusted by this as I am. But you won't admit it. You've got to be the sophisticated enlightened right-thinking liberal. You've got to pretend you aren't repulsed—even when you are."

"Prescott—"

"Just tell me this, Morelli. And for once—be honest. You were all so upset when you saw that poor pretty girl, cut down in the prime of her life. When you found out she was really some...*freak*...running around pretending to be something he wasn't, didn't you feel just a little relieved?"

"No." Morelli pulled his trench coat belt tight and buttoned all the buttons. "I felt worse."

● ● ●

A cool and welcome morning wind caressed Morelli's brow. Baxter joined him on the terrace.

"Crime scene is locked up tight. Lab work should be finished in a few hours." She stood close, but not too close, to him. "Wanna get breakfast? Village Inn is always open."

"We could do that." He turned slightly toward her. "Or we could drive to Arkansas."

"Got a hankering for a hot spring?"

"Might be a nice drive. Leaves are turning. Weather is cool." He paused. "And we could be married by noon."

"*What?*"

"No waiting period. No blood test. Eureka Springs has lots of ambience, if you like that sort of thing."

"What has gotten into you?"

Her took her by the hands and looked straight into her eyes. "Look, we love each other. Even more importantly, we like being together. We're good friends. People who belong together shouldn't have to hide in a closet. No one should."

"One of us would have to quit their job."

"I'll transfer to the suburbs. Jenks has been trying to get me for years. The point is, we don't go on wasting time we could spend together."

"But I haven't planned—"

"We're not kids, Kate. We don't need a big ceremony with forty-seven bridesmaids and a Vera Wang dress. We just need to do it."

He felt her arms relax. "Are you serious about this?"

"Everyone is entitled to a small measure of happiness. Aren't they?" He led her toward the door. "Let's get some pancakes. Long drives always make me hungry."

BLOOD IN, BLOOD OUT
BRENDA NOVAK

This is a story about loyalty, which life often forces to be divided. When faced with making a split decision, it could come down to who you'd take a bullet for. —SB

As he sat in the run-down bar, brooding over a glass of whiskey, Rex McCready decided that his life was a series of battles in a war that would never end, and he wasn't on the winning side very often.

"Hey, thought I'd find you here."

His best friend, former cell mate and current business partner in Bodyguards R Us, Virgil Skinner, slid onto the bar stool next to him.

"What happened *this* time?" Virgil wanted to know.

"The same thing that happens every time," he grumbled. He and Laurel Hodges, Virgil's sister, just couldn't get along. They loved each other, but they were both too damaged to make the relationship work, and the stress of having recently entered WITSEC—the witness protection program—together with Virgil and his wife, Peyton, only made matters worse. They all had different identities, his own name one he'd chosen himself, but no longer liked.

Even after almost two years, whenever someone called him Perry, he looked behind him to see who the hell they were talking to.

It didn't help that they'd been relocated clear across the country, to Washington, D.C. They'd had to get used to a new place, new names, new backgrounds, all while watching their backs for fear that the people who wanted them dead would find them. Add to that the whiplash effect of his on-again, off-again relationship with Laurel, and it wasn't easy to build a stable life.

Virgil sighed as he pulled a bowl of peanuts toward him. "How bad was it this time?"

Rex had never struck her. He never would. But her husband, ex-husband now, hadn't hesitated to cross that line, and that was part of her problem. She didn't want to trust the wrong man. And by most people's standards, Rex was definitely "the wrong man." Seeing as how *his* problems were too numerous to list, beginning with the loveless childhood that'd led him into gang life and an eight-year prison term, he couldn't really recommend himself. He'd probably still be a member of The Crew, his conscience conveniently anesthetized by drugs, if not for Virgil. Rex had recruited Virgil while they were serving time in Arizona. It wasn't until Virgil was exonerated for the murder of his stepfather that having joined such a violent prison gang became such a problem.

Until then, it was the only way to survive.

After that, it was almost a sure way to die.

Blood in, blood out—or in layman's terms, "Once a member, always a member—or else." In order to save Laurel, Rex had had to kill two of the men he'd once called brothers. Kill two and seriously injure a third...

The Crew would never forget what had gone down in Colorado, which meant he, Laurel and Virgil might never be safe.

"We argued. I walked out. That's it." He drained his glass and asked the bartender, a cute blonde with a Southern accent, for another shot.

"Betty," according to her name tag, glanced at Virgil to see if he wanted one, too, and Virgil nodded. "Laurel will cool off," he said when Betty moved away.

Their anger never lasted long. Already Rex wanted to go back. But he wasn't sure how much more he could take. If they weren't having hot, sweaty, full-throttle sex, they were arguing with equal ferocity. There was no middle ground where Laurel was concerned, and if he couldn't have a positive impact on her life he had no business being part of it at all. She had her children—Jake, seven, and Mia, five—to take care of. They didn't need the stress, the disruptions.

"No, man, I'm done. We're just torturing each other. I have to stay away."

Virgil's gaze jerked to his face. "You mean that?"

Rex didn't bother waiting for his second drink. He didn't want to talk about Laurel, didn't want to deal with their problems, not anymore. "Yeah. I mean it," he said and got up and walked out.

He was so upset he almost didn't see the man lingering in the shadow of the building. Out of the corner of his eye, he caught a glimpse of movement, but when he turned, no one was there.

It's nothing. They'd been living in D.C. for nearly two years, and yet he was still seeing faces he thought he recognized, still feeling as if The Crew was only one step behind him.

Quit being so fucking paranoid.

Despite telling himself that, he tensed, listening closely. He wanted to figure out where the man had gone, get a better look at him. But when Virgil emerged from the bar, Rex took off down the street. He loved Virgil, as much as he loved Laurel, but he'd already said all he had to say.

• • •

"I found 'em."

It was Mose, the man Horse had sent to Washington, D.C. Holding his cell phone to his ear, he stared out at the balmy Los Angeles afternoon visible beyond the window of his illegal club and felt a smile stretch across his face. At last! Horse had been waiting to hear those words for twenty-two months, ever since Virgil had emerged from prison and run out on them. Together with the other Crew leaders, he'd been determined to find and stop Virgil, or Skin as they called him, before he could rat anyone out to the cops. But when Rex, formerly known as Pretty Boy, turned on them, too, this became a personal challenge, something that went far deeper than regular gang business. It was partially thanks to Virgil and Rex that Horse held the power he now did inside The Crew, but that didn't mean he wasn't going to avenge those who'd been killed. "*Who,* exactly?"

"Laurel, for one," Mose said. "And I'm pretty sure I saw Rex leaving her place. I followed a guy I think was him to a bar but I was afraid he'd see me, so I couldn't get a good look at his face."

"What about Virgil?"

"Here in D.C., too. I got a better view of him than Rex. They met up at the bar. I tried to follow Virgil home, see where he lives, but he was on a motorcycle. I couldn't keep up."

The Crew's contact in the Federal Bureau of Prisons had taken a while to deliver the information Horse wanted, but apparently she'd slept with the right U.S. Marshal, one who didn't want the pictures of their time together going home to his wife and kids.

"Virgil, Laurel, Rex. All three of them," Horse mused. "That's good."

"Should I kill the woman tonight?"

"Hell, no! If you do you'll never find Virgil and Rex."

"I just told you, man. They're all here in D.C."

"But you don't know *exactly* where they live. Not yet. You hurt Laurel, they'll pop you and disappear."

"They won't pop me. When I come after them, they won't know what hit 'em."

Tough talk, but Horse wasn't taking any chances. Virgil and Rex were the biggest badasses he'd ever known. "Don't give me that bullshit," he said. "We have to play this smart."

"Which means what?"

He could hear the frustration in Mose's voice. "It means you grab Laurel, since you know where she lives, and use her as bait to bring the men to you."

There was a brief silence as Mose considered his instructions. "You think they'll come?"

"They'll do anything for her."

"What if they call the cops instead?"

"They won't, because they know you'll kill her if they do. As soon as they arrive, shoot 'em all and get the hell out of D.C.," he said and hung up.

● ● ●

Was that man following her?

Laurel Hodges stopped in the snack aisle to see if the heavily muscled man she'd spotted two or three times since entering the grocery store would simply walk past.

He didn't. He moved into the same aisle but paused a few feet away and picked up a bag of chocolate chips as if he wanted to study the nutritional information.

"Mommy, what's wrong?"

Laurel forced a smile. Mia was too big for the grocery cart child's seat, so she was riding in the basket while Jake grabbed one item after another and begged Laurel to buy it.

"Can we get this?"

"No." Laurel didn't even look at his latest find. Lowering her head as though taking stock of the contents of her cart, she peeked at the man with the shaved head and the tattoos covering his forearms and tried once again to call Rex on her cell.

She got his voice mail. Damn it. He was really mad at her this time. She couldn't think of any other reason he wouldn't pick up.

She didn't leave a message. If the man was a member of The Crew, this would all be over before Rex could do a thing about it. The same was true for her brother, Virgil—not that she'd call him. He had Peyton and his new baby to worry about.

Should she contact the police? They could probably respond faster than her WITSEC handler. But what would she tell the emergency operator? She could imagine the call...

Nine-one-one, what is the nature of your emergency?

There's a man where I'm shopping who reminds me of some violent gang members who once tried to kill me.

Reminds you of some violent gang members?

Yes...

Has he actually done anything to threaten or harm you?

Not yet.

God, would the police even come?

She dialed her WITSEC handler instead, but he didn't pick up, either.

"Who are you trying to call, Mommy?" Mia had been playing with the cans in the cart but tuned in long enough to notice Laurel pressing the end-call button.

"The restaurant?" she asked next. "Do you have to go to work today?"

Laurel slipped the phone back into her purse. If she had to make a dash for it, she wanted her hands free so she'd be able to hang on to her kids. "No, not today."

"Who will wait on the people?"

"The other servers."

"Oh." Mia went back to playing as Laurel, hands slick with sweat, propelled the shopping cart forward.

The man who'd been making her so uncomfortable didn't follow, but she was afraid he would once she turned the corner. It'd happened twice already. She'd left him in two different aisles only to bump into him a second and a third time.

Unwilling to abandon the treat section quite so soon, Jake slowed their cart to pick up a bottle of soda. "Mom, can we—"

Completely preoccupied with the stranger, and how much he resembled the type of men who belonged to The Crew, she didn't let Jake finish. "No, that has too much sugar."

"Please?" he persisted. "Come on! Other kids drink soda. Look, it's your favorite kind."

"I said no—or...okay." Taking it away from him, she added it to the cart and grasped his hand so he had no choice except to keep up with them.

"Mommy?"

It was Mia again. "What honey?"

"Are you upset?"

She'd had a hard lump in her stomach ever since Rex left, and this wasn't helping. "I'm just thinking."

"What about these?" Jake scooped a bag of cheese puffs from the closest display. "Can we have these?"

Laurel managed a tremulous smile as they passed another shopper. "No. We have to go."

"But we just got here!"

She kept moving, so fast he dropped the bag of cheese puffs, and she didn't even stop to pick it up.

"Mom!" He almost tripped as she dragged him along.

"Just do as I say," she snapped and risked another glance behind them. The man was nowhere to be seen. Was she freaking out for nothing?

Maybe. As busy as the store was, she'd seen several other shoppers more than once. None of them stood out like this guy did, but maybe the argument she'd had with Rex was making her feel extra vulnerable, making her imagine the stranger was keeping a closer watch on her than he was.

Regardless, she didn't feel safe here and wanted to leave.

Choosing the shortest checkout line, she wheeled her cart into place. The tattooed guy didn't come out of the snack aisle, as she'd expected, but that didn't matter. She was already too worked up to talk herself out of her fear. Suddenly, she couldn't even wait the few minutes it would take to buy the groceries she'd selected. She had to get out of the store.

"Come on," she said, lifting Mia from the cart.

"Where are we going?" her daughter asked in surprise.

"Home."

"Without our soda?" Jake complained.

"I'll get you an ice-cream cone later, I promise. Both of you." *Just cooperate,* she prayed and hurried them out and into the crowded parking lot.

Jake wasn't happy about abandoning their purchases, but he didn't say another word as he climbed into the backseat of her old Volvo and put on his seat belt. He'd read her anxiety; it was so intense she could no longer hide it. The only other time he'd seen her like this was in Colorado, when she'd made him take his sister and climb out a bedroom window to escape what was about to happen in the house. She'd told both her children that what they'd witnessed that night had been playacting, but she often wondered if Jake, at least, knew better.

Her hands shook as she buckled Mia in. The painful memories were coming in a torrent now, memories of finding the U.S. Marshal assigned to protect them in a puddle of blood on the floor, his throat slit. Memories of Ink, The Crew member who'd survived.

Ink, with the devilish tattoos covering his face, breaking into her bedroom. Memories of his hands reaching for her, his nails clawing her legs apart. The deafening blast of the gun. The acrid smell of gunpowder...

They'd *all* almost died. If not for Rex, they would have.

"Not again," she whispered. "Please, not again."

She was coming around the car to get behind the wheel when someone called her name. Fear and adrenaline shot through her, and she stiffened, but then she recognized the voice. It was Rex. He was here. *Somehow* he was here.

Turning, she saw him coming toward her and nearly crumpled to the blacktop in relief.

"*There* you are!" As soon as he was close enough, she threw herself into his arms. "What made you come back?"

He stumbled, surprised by her enthusiastic welcome but caught himself before he could fall, caught them both. "I left my phone at your house, but you have the place locked up so tight I couldn't get in, and I didn't want to scare you by breaking in, so I've been checking all your regular places. You mentioned needing groceries this morning, so...fortunately, I spotted your car."

"That's why you wouldn't answer your phone. You didn't have it. I'm sorry about earlier, Rex. I'm so sorry."

He hesitated, and she feared he wouldn't accept her apology, that he'd continue to be mad. But then his hand went to the back of her head and his body adjusted to hers. "It's okay. I shouldn't have pressured you. We...we were good until I ruined it."

"Last night was special," she admitted. "I've never felt so close to anyone." It wasn't until he'd asked her to marry him that everything had fallen apart. After what she'd been through, she just wasn't ready to make that commitment. She'd told him that before. "So don't give up on me," she whispered. "Not yet."

Chin resting on top of her head, he squeezed her tighter. "We'll work it out, huh? Somehow we'll work it out. Don't cry."

She hadn't even realized she was crying. The man in the store had frightened her, but that wasn't the worst of it. She'd been afraid that this time Rex wouldn't come back, that they were really over, and that had sent her reeling.

"You okay?" He pulled back to see her face.

Should she tell him about the panic attack she'd had in the store?

No, she felt silly about that now. The guy who'd spooked her was probably just some biker who liked tattoos and chocolate chips and hadn't meant her any harm. How would The Crew ever find them here? They were in WITSEC, had brand-new identities. *No one* knew where they were. "Yeah, I'm fine. Let's go home." She didn't even want to go back for her groceries.

But the second he released her, the man she'd seen in the store stepped out from behind the van beside her car.

And this time she knew he was dangerous because he shoved the muzzle of a gun into her back.

● ● ●

It took a second for Rex to realize what was going on. He'd been so caught up in his emotional exchange with Laurel, he'd allowed The Crew to get the drop on them. After the uneasy feeling he'd experienced at the bar, he considered this an inexcusable mistake. But he hadn't really believed The Crew could find them, not after everything they'd done to escape. Prison gangs weren't usually that sophisticated, and The Crew was no exception. But they were determined and deadly and somehow they'd managed to follow them to D.C.

He had no doubt this man would shoot Laurel if he didn't do something. And what about the kids?

"Let her go." He raised his hands to show he was compliant. "I'm the one you want. I'm Rex McCready, Pretty Boy. Horse wants me, not her."

The guy—Mose, according to one tattoo—was six foot, about two hundred pounds and solidly built. His dark eyes focused on Rex, but he had a grip on Laurel. One shot at such close range would almost certainly kill her. "He wants you both. Virgil, too. That's my assignment and I'm gonna do it."

Rex wished he had his own gun. Since he was an ex-con, carrying a firearm or any other weapon violated his parole, but he'd picked up a 9 mm on the black market. It was currently stashed under the seat of his truck, which he'd parked along the perimeter of the lot. He'd thought that was close and handy—until this moment, when it might as well be in another state. "You'd be stupid to get greedy. Take me and leave her to her children. She has no part in this, and neither do they."

"Shut up and get in the car." He jerked his head toward Laurel's Volvo.

The kids stared out at them as if they couldn't understand what was wrong. Rex hoped they wouldn't figure it out. They'd already been through more than any kids should have to face.

"Look, you're in over your head here," he said to Mose. "Just let her take the kids and go, and I'll do whatever the fuck you tell me to."

"Sorry, not good enough."

Another Hanley's Grocery customer passed by, the wheels of her cart rattling against the pavement. Rex prayed she'd glance up, see the gun and scream or cause some other type of diversion so he could wrest the weapon away, but she was too focused on the baby she had in a carrier. She walked right past them without noticing a thing. That was when the real panic set in, when Rex had to accept that he wasn't sure how to save them, not this time.

"Get in." The guy with the gun indicated Laurel's car again. "Or I'll drop her right here."

Shit! If he resisted, Laurel would be shot. They'd all be shot, along with other innocent people. But if he complied, they'd be abandoning the relative safety of this public parking lot, giving their enemy even more power over them. Which didn't seem like the best idea…

In the end, Rex had no choice. He'd do anything to delay Laurel getting hurt. He could only cooperate and hope he'd have a better opportunity to save them later.

Heart slamming against his chest, he opened the back door, slid Jake to the middle and got in. He hoped Laurel would be able to make a break for safety the second the guy left her side, but she wasn't taking any chances. Mose trained the gun on the kids as he moved around the car—first one, then the other—and Rex knew she wouldn't do anything to make him fire. He couldn't blame her.

"Where are we going?" she asked, once they were all in.

The guy kept his gun low so the people around them couldn't see it. Neither could Rex, but he had no doubt it was aimed at Laurel because her eyes kept flicking toward it.

"Let's head to Virgil's." Mose tossed a grin over his shoulder for Rex's benefit. "I think it'll be fun to surprise him, don't you?"

• • •

Laurel had no intention of leading this man to her brother. Virgil had a wife and a new baby at home. He was finally happy, and she planned to do everything possible to keep it that way. She knew he'd do the same for her if their roles were reversed. She only hoped The Crew didn't know where he lived, that the man holding the gun wouldn't realize she'd led him to Rex's house instead.

Would Jake or Mia pipe up? It would be so like them, so like any child to declare that she'd gotten it wrong. They certainly knew one house from the other, but they seemed subdued. They hadn't said a word the entire ride. She wondered if they, too, were reliving what had happened in Colorado....

"Not bad," Mose said, admiring Rex's home as they came to a stop at the curb. "Ratting out your friends must pay well."

Virgil had received nothing from the government for the information he'd provided, except a promise of protection for him and those he loved. He'd been given nearly $700,000 for wrongful imprisonment, however, which he'd insisted on sharing. That money had provided them each with a down payment on a house, but they worked to cover the mortgages. Laurel suspected Rex had bought this house hoping she and the kids would move in with him. Even she'd believed she would live here someday.

She'd never dreamed she'd die here instead.

"Virgil didn't rat anybody out until you tried to kill me," she said. "All he wanted was his life back."

"He swore an oath and then he broke it. That means he pays the price."

"But he should never have gone to prison in the first place!"

"That's *his* problem. We're not gonna sit back while he lives in some fancy-ass house like this. A house he bought with blood money!"

She wasn't going to convince him so she quit trying. She knew what these men were like. "Let my kids go, at least," she said. "Let them walk over to the neighbor's, where they'll be safe." She hoped to win their freedom before he became aware that she'd led him to the wrong house. After that, anything could happen.

Jake whimpered. He was catching on—or what they were saying had confirmed what he'd feared since they left the store.

"Mommy? I want to go home," Mia said and began to cry.

Laurel felt as if she was on fire, burning from the inside out. She'd never experienced such a sensation before—such a mixture of fury, righteous indignation, determination and fear. It was different from before because there was a certain amount of resignation involved, too. She'd been expecting this for so long. "You're going to be fine," she said even though it was probably a lie.

The man with the gun twisted around to face them. "Mommy's right—*if* she and your friend here cooperate."

But she wasn't cooperating. She was doing whatever she could to protect Virgil, Peyton and baby Brady. It didn't make sense to put them at risk, too, but the fact that she was endangering her own children in the process made her clammy with sweat. What would this asshole do when he realized? Shoot them all and go after Virgil on his own?

Even if he did, at least Virgil would have a chance to get away....

No longer hiding his weapon, Mose waved the pistol at her door. "Shall we go in?"

Her eyes met Rex's in the rearview mirror, and she hoped he could read the message inside them: *Do whatever you have to.*

● ● ●

Rex made his move as soon as they got out of the car. He couldn't afford to wait, had no idea what might happen if he let this go on. At least outside, the children had room to scatter and hide, and if the gun went off there'd be a greater chance that a neighbor might hear it and call the police.

But the man was prepared. Dodging Rex's blow, he grabbed Mia by the hair and dragged her up against him. "You try that again, and she'll be the first to die," he snapped.

"Run!" Rex stood in front of Jake and tried to shoo him away. He didn't think this man would kill Mia over the loss of her brother. The kids didn't matter that much to him. This wasn't about them. But Jake wouldn't leave—he sidled over to protect his mother.

"Jake, do as I say!"

"No, Uncle Rex." The boy's chest rose and fell so fast Rex could tell he was terrified, but he was equally resolute. "He'll shoot my sister. Then he'll shoot my mom."

Rex couldn't believe he'd refused to obey. The odds were already stacked against them. He didn't need Jake to get stubborn, even if he couldn't help admiring the boy's courage. "Jake!" He hated the risk he was taking but he had no choice. If they went inside, this man would shoot them all the minute he understood that they weren't giving up Virgil.

Then Jake surprised him. He shoved his mother so hard she stumbled back and fell over the planter behind her, and he started jumping and shouting and waving his arms as if he thought he could force the man to fire at him instead of his sister.

Jake's sudden reversal had taken the bastard off guard. Mose paused for a second. Apparently he couldn't decide whether he should actually fire, or even who he should fire at. He glanced behind him almost as if he feared Virgil was already on his way out of the house and that was what had set Jake off.

That brief hesitation gave Rex the opportunity he'd been looking for. Launching himself forward, he tackled the guy.

Mia fell when they did, which probably hurt, but it wasn't going to kill her. The man had to let her go in order to keep control of the gun he was trying to turn on Rex.

She wiggled out from between them and ran off crying almost as soon as they hit the ground. While he wrestled Mose, trying to subdue him, Rex didn't know where she went. He didn't care as long as she remained safe. He hoped Laurel was taking her kids and getting them the hell out of here—he trusted she was. He knew how much they meant to her. He knew how much they meant to him, too, all of them, because he felt a huge surge of relief even as the gun went off.

• • •

Laurel had a large rock in her hand when she crept toward the two men lying, one atop the other, on the ground. She'd yelled for her children to go next door and call 911, and they'd dashed off, but she hadn't been able to bring herself to leave Rex.

Tears rolled down her cheeks as she drew closer. He'd been shot. She was pretty sure of that. But where?

"Rex?"

He didn't answer. She got the impression he was struggling just to breathe and felt the tears come faster.

"Rex, answer me."

Finally, he rolled off the guy and lay there, gazing up at her. Blood covered his shirt, but it wasn't *his* blood. It belonged to the man who'd come to kill them. The Crew had lost another member. The sightless eyes of their attacker stared skyward as the red staining his shirt seeped farther and farther from where the bullet had entered his chest.

Dropping the rock, she sagged to her knees at Rex's side and buried her face in his neck.

"Are you okay?" he murmured.

A surplus of adrenaline had left him weak and shaky. She could tell by the limp way he lifted his arm to hold her, and because she felt the same. "I am now."

• • •

"I'm glad you changed your mind."

Rex glanced across the table at Virgil, who was watching him with a crooked grin. "What'd you say?" The pizza parlor where they'd met Virgil, Peyton and the baby for dinner was too loud to be able to hear unless he raised his voice a bit more. They were no longer in D.C. Now that The Crew had found them, it wasn't safe anymore. They had to decide on a permanent location but for the time being they were in Little Rock, Arkansas.

"I said I'm glad you changed your mind."

Rex drummed his thumbs on the table. "About…"

Virgil jerked his head toward Laurel, who'd left Rex's side to re-fill her children's glasses. "Staying with Laurel. She loves you, you know."

Leaning back, Rex returned his friend's smile. "I know."

WED TO DEATH
VICKI HINZE

Hinze has penned a heart-stopping story about true commitment. You may need a hanky. —SB

Her mother screamed.

Startled, Sara English paused in the middle of refilling her maid of honor's champagne flute. She shushed her mother and followed her horrified gaze around the table past her groom-to-be, Matthew, to his uncle Paul. Why was he listing in his chair? Paul's skin was as gray as winter sleet. Chills streaked up her spine. "Matthew, what's wrong?"

"I—I don't know—"

Paul crumpled, fell nose down onto his plate.

"Uncle Paul?" Matthew stretched over, checked for a pulse. Horror flitted over his angular face. He dragged his uncle onto the floor and began CPR. Between breaths, he darted a stricken look at Sara. "Call 911."

Her brother Hank, Matthew's best man, whipped out his phone. "On it."

Matthew was fighting valiantly to save his only living relative's life, but his panicked expression made the truth clear. The CPR wasn't working. Ignoring the murmurs, Sara asked, "Is he responding?"

"Not yet." Matthew kept working diligently.

Mayhem ensued across the rehearsal dinner and the din of murmurs grew to a roar.

Paramedics rushed in and took over the CPR. For the next forty minutes, they tried to revive Paul, but finally one told the other, "It's time to call it."

The man working on Paul stopped and looked over to Matthew. "I'm sorry." Pity filled his eyes. "We did all we could do."

Sara's heart clutched. She clasped Matthew's hand. Heard him swallow hard. He blinked fast and nodded. Regret warred with grief and pounded off him in waves that tore at her heart. "Oh, Matthew. I—I'm so sorry."

He gave her hand a gentle squeeze. "Can you get everyone out of here? I've got to stay. The hospital will need information and the coroner…"

"Of course." She released his hand, stroked his forearm, turned and issued the order to vacate to Hank and then Angela, her maid of honor and best friend.

"What about the wedding?" Her mother asked, fishing at her feet for her purse.

Matthew had just lost his only living relative and she was worried about the wedding?

"Don't look at me like that, Sara. People need to know."

Sara cringed, but her mother had a point. "We'll postpone it, of course."

"No." Matthew cleared his throat. "You've been planning this for a year. Uncle Paul wouldn't want that."

The coroner had arrived. Squatting, he examined Paul. Sara looked from him to her fiancé. "Don't worry about that. Things will have to be done. The funeral…" Their rehearsal dinner would forever be marred. Starting over on the planning would be an ordeal, but having their wedding day forever scarred by sadness…

That was a bigger one. Paul had raised Matthew. He was father, mother, uncle and best friend. Tomorrow would just be too soon. "The funeral and settling his estate—all that will be up to you. I think we should wait."

"His funeral won't be tomorrow, but there are things that will have to be done." Matthew touched her face. "Can we compromise? Get married tomorrow and postpone our honeymoon for a while?"

"If that's what you want, yes." She said and meant it. She had loved Matthew St. John from the moment she'd met him. Marrying him mattered. When, and when they honeymooned in Fiji didn't.

"It's what I want." He pressed a quick kiss to her cheek. "You go home now. Your mother will be swearing this is another bad sign and you shouldn't marry me. You'll have to talk her down."

He was so right about that. After their engagement party, they'd had a near-miss car accident. It'd taken three days to get her mother back on an even keel—and she didn't even know some-one had cut Matthew's brake lines. That detail Sara would take to her grave.

She had asked Matthew who would do such a thing. He'd re-sponded with a terse, "Has to be work related," and they hadn't discussed it again. Sara didn't need a hammer to the head to know Matthew's job with the government wasn't reading and reporting on books as he claimed. No one cut anyone's brake lines for reading books. What his job was, or what agency he worked for, she didn't have a clue, but not knowing didn't bother her a bit. Not knowing was safer for them both. "I'd be happy to stay with you."

"No, you go on. I'll see you at the church. Two o'clock." He re-leased her hands. "I'll be the penguin down front who can't wipe the smile off his face because he caught the most beautiful woman in the world in a weak moment and she said yes."

Sara stepped closer, hugged him and whispered. "It was the smartest decision I've ever made."

The coroner's voice lifted, calling out to his men. "Don't touch anything—especially his glass and flatware. And stop everyone at the door. No one enters or leaves."

Matthew frowned, stepped back and swung his gaze to the still-squatting coroner in the rumpled gray suit. "Why not?"

He frowned, his thick brows flat-lining nearly the width of his forehead. "Because unless I'm mistaken, your uncle didn't have a heart attack."

"What are you saying?" Sara couldn't wrap her mind around his comment. Paul hadn't been ill. He had no medical issues. He was, as he put it, disgustingly healthy.

The coroner stood, his knees crackling, and removed his gloves. "I'll get lab tests to confirm, of course, but I've been at this forty years. Every sign I see tells me this man was poisoned."

"Poisoned?" Sara lifted a hand to her chest. "But—but that would mean…" She couldn't say it; shot her gaze to Matthew.

"He was murdered?" Matthew tensed. "Are you sure?"

"Not without the lab results, but I'd be shocked if I'm wrong." He turned to speak to one of his men.

The look on Matthew's face turned dark, forbidding. Sara whispered. "What is it, Matthew?"

"Maybe something, maybe nothing." He locked their gazes. "The waiter passed me a glass of champagne. I passed it to Paul."

Matthew didn't drink. Sara's chest went tight. "You think someone meant to poison you?" Fear rippled through her. *First the brake lines and now this?* "We don't know that it was the champagne."

"No, we don't."

He'd agreed with her but the worry in his voice said all that needed saying. Matthew believed that for the second time, someone had just tried to murder him.

• • •

"You're being selfish."

"I love her." His cell phone at his ear, Matthew stepped out of his building to the curb and then slid into the waiting limousine. "Is it so wrong to want a wife?" His boss should understand. He'd gotten married nearly twenty years ago, and he'd been in the job then.

"Look, the brake lines were one thing, but they got close enough to poison you last night. Your uncle is dead. How many more near misses do you think you'll get before one hits? And what about Sara? Will she be collateral damage? Targeted?"

The thought made him queasy. Matthew shut the door and nodded at the driver. "Was it the champagne?"

"We don't know yet."

"Then we don't know it was them." The driver pulled away from the curb. Matthew checked his watch. One-thirty. He should be at the church in plenty of time. "You can't expect me to walk away from the best thing that's happened to me when I don't know for a fact I have to walk away. You can't."

"We don't know that it was the champagne. But no one else is after you, Matt...or is there something you haven't yet told me?"

"No, nothing." Where was this joker driver going? He should have turned right. "I've got to go. Apparently my driver doesn't know the way to the church." Heading to the industrial part of Destin. The man had to be a plant with the drug cartel.

"Matt, listen to me. Listen. Don't do this. They'll kill you both. If you love Sara, then let her go."

He squeezed his eyes shut. "I can't."

Thumbing off his phone, Matt chose a low-key tactic and banged on the glass separating them. "Hey," he told the driver. "You're going the wrong way. It's St. Andrew's."

The driver glanced back in the rearview mirror and stomped the gas.

Definitely cartel.

Matthew kicked at the glass. Bulletproof. Tried to open the door. No handles or way to unlock them. He darted a glance through the windshield, got his bearings. In two minutes or less, they'd be in the isolated industrial park. Working quickly, he raised the privacy panel, tore down the backseat and then crawled through into the trunk and jerked the safety-release lever. The trunk lid popped open.

A swoosh of wind gushed in; the driver sped up. His hair blowing in his eyes, Matthew shoved at it, gauged their speed. *Forty. Forty-five max.* If he landed right, he could survive. He leaped, reverted to training tactics, tucked and braced for impact with the sandy dirt. Hitting with a thud, he sucked in a sharp breath. Pain shot through his shoulder, arm and right leg. His elbow scraped over a loose rock. Rolling on the soft shoulder, he gained his feet then scanned for somewhere to hide.

The limo screeched to a halt, its tires squealing and churning smoke that filled the street.

Parking lot. DCE Industries. Matthew ran full out for it, then ducked behind a blue Toyota and skimmed the street for the limo. The driver turned around, entered the parking lot and inched down the row, turned and searched another.

Three slots down, a man driving a green pickup parked then got out, carrying a black lunch box. Matthew made his way over. The fiftyish guy saw him coming and took in his wrecked tux. "Tough day, eh?"

"Yeah." The guy looked like a regular Joe. Trusting his instincts, Matthew admitted, "I need help."

The guy took his measure and apparently decided Matthew was okay. "What do you need?"

"To get to St. Andrew's." He was their target. They wouldn't go after Sara unless they couldn't get to him. He'd eluded them. Now he had no choice but to go to the church, make sure she was okay, and make sure they saw him. Then she'd be safe. "I'm supposed to be getting married in fifteen minutes."

The man spotted the creeping vehicle. "That your limo?"

"It was supposed to be." He shrugged. "Not everyone wants us to walk down the aisle."

"Understand." He unlocked his truck. "Get in—and don't linger. He just made the turn onto our row."

"Thanks." Matthew entered through the driver's side and hunched low. The man got in and cranked his engine, put the truck in Reverse, and headed out. "Name's Ray."

"Matthew," he said. "Is he following us?"

"Not yet." Ray made a turn and hit a bump. Turned again and was on smooth pavement. "He's still looking for you." Ray glanced again into his rearview. "Which St. Andrew's?"

There was more than one? He hadn't been in Florida that long. "Highway 98."

"That's my church," the man said. "You marrying Sara English?"

Matthew thought hard. *Was he? Did he dare?* "Two o'clock."

"Best move it then. Don't want to leave that sweet one waiting at the altar."

Matthew's face went hot. Under the circumstances, that would probably be the greatest kindness he could do for her.

Every atom in his body rebelled. He wanted her, a family of his own. He'd waited for this day his whole life. He couldn't just walk away. He…couldn't.

The phone vibrated at his hip. Matthew checked the number. His boss. "Yeah."

"You okay?"

"Still have my head." Not many who went up against the cartel did. "Slight interception incident."

"Fatalities?"

"No."

"Glad to hear it." He sighed. "The labs are back."

Matthew checked the side mirror. No signs of the limo. "And?" He knew, but he had to hear it confirmed.

"Cyanide." He paused, hesitant. "It was in the champagne, Matt."

"No." His chest went tight. He was the target. Uncle Paul was dead, and it was his fault. Guilt swarmed, settled in and suffocated him. He coughed.

"Look, I'm sorry. If I could change it, I would, and I know you would. Neither of us can. All I can do is be straight with you. You're in too deep, Matt. You've got to take the meeting with the drug cartel personally. Otherwise, this whole operation blows up in our faces, and we both know what that means."

The cartel had identified him as an agent. Either it got him or it would do exactly what it swore it would do. Release biological contaminants in multiple locations at once and destroy the entire city. But which one? Destin, Fort Walton Beach, Pensacola. Regardless, it had the means and will to attack, and because it would, a hundred thousand people, maybe more, would be going about their lives just as they did every day, only this day, they'd die.

It also meant that word had come down from on high to his boss. Matthew was the designated sacrificial lamb. If things went south, the agency and brass would be covered. Matthew, who'd argued vehemently against this operation from the start, would be tagged with the blame. And that meant the question confronting Matt had changed. Now it was who would kill him first?

The cartel, or his own?

• • •

Sara stood before the full-length mirror in the church's bridal room, her heart pounding. Her mother and Angela fluffed her dress, adjusted her veil for the twentieth time, and all she could think about was that in minutes—mere minutes—she was going to marry the man she'd loved for three years.

"Matthew's eyes are going to pop out of his head when he sees you in that dress."

Sara smiled. "I hope not."

"What?" Angela looked perplexed.

"His eyes are distinct—the first thing I noticed about him. I hope they stay put in their sockets."

"She's being ridiculous." Her mother slapped the air with a dismissive hand. "You do look lovely, Sara."

"Thank you." She was well pleased. The dress was simple, classic, beautiful, and it fit. That was the best news. All her nightmares of a zipper trying to cinch an extra inch gap were over. She let out a relieved sigh.

"Matthew!" Angela squealed. "What are you doing here? You can't see the bride before the ceremony, it's bad lu— What on earth has happened to you?"

"Sara, I need to talk to you," he said, trying to skirt around the maid of honor bent on blocking him. "It's important."

Her mother took serious objection. "Absolutely not. I don't know what happened to you, but we'll deal with it after the wedding. I've worked a year on this and with your uncle there's been enough upset already. Now close your eyes, turn around and get up to the front of the church where you belong."

"Sara," he insisted. "Please. It's important."

It had to be bad news. His face was drawn in unholy gloom. "Mother, Angela, excuse us."

"But—"

"Go. Can't you see something is wrong, Angela?" Sara waved them out. "Please, take Mom and go wait in the hallway."

The women went, but not without her mother shooting worried daggers at Matthew and Sara. "You will change your clothes, won't you? I mean, you're all right now and you won't go up there to marry my daughter in tatters, will you?"

"Ignore her," Sara told him. "What's wrong?" His tux was in tatters. There must have been another incident. After the last one, he'd warned her danger came with his job. "Are you hurt?"

"No." He stepped over to her, clasped her hands and let her see the truth in his eyes. "I want to marry you more than anything. I love you, Sara. I'll always love you."

"I love you, too." Definitely bad news. It was in his eyes, in his cracking tone. "This feels like goodbye."

"It is, sweetheart." His gray eyes glossed. He blinked hard. "I have an assignment. I can stay here and marry you or take the assignment."

"Can't someone else do it?"

"No." He licked at his lips, holding her gaze. "I can't explain specifics—you know that. But if I don't go, a lot of people are going to die. If I stay, odds are good you'll be one of them."

She stiffened. "It's that dangerous?"

"Yes."

"Will you survive?" She didn't want to ask, but she had to know. Of course she had to know.

"It's doubtful, sweetheart." Pain flashed across his face. "I'm so sorry. The potential for trouble is always present, but we have failsafe measures in place. Layers of them. Unfortunately, this time, they all failed. If I'd considered that possible...I wouldn't have put you in this position. I didn't. No one did."

"Marry me, then." She choked back tears. "If you could die, it's the only way I'll know what happens to you."

"You'll know." He stroked her arms. "I've taken care of that—promise."

She'd fought the battle to restrain her emotions but lost. Tears slipped down her face and she threw every reasonable objection she could think of at him, then started a litany of unreasonable ones. "Don't do this."

"If I don't, who will?"

"I don't know." She sobbed, her heart shattering. "I don't care."

"You care, Sara." He dragged a thumb over her face along the line of her jaw. "It's one of the things I love most about you."

"I love you, too." She stood right beside him, yet sensed him already pulling away. "I'll always love you."

"Me, too." He pulled her close and kissed her hard, letting her feel the love that burned in his heart deeper than death. Pulling back, he said, "I have to go."

"Matthew, wait. Please." Tears streamed down her face. "If you… make it, when will you be back?"

"Three days, maybe four. No more than that."

She hugged him tightly, then looked up into his face. "I'll be waiting. No matter how long it takes."

His eyes shined overly bright. "I'm one lucky man."

"Stay that way." She swallowed hard. "Come home to me, okay?"

"I'll do my best." He turned and left the bridal room.

Sara held it together until the door clicked closed. Then her knees folded. In a heap on the marble floor, she prayed hard. *I've never asked for anything. Not in my whole life. But I'm asking now. I'm begging. Keep him safe. Bring him back to me. Please…*

A heavy feeling settled in her chest. Dread and fear blanketed it. The darkest, most bleak fear she'd ever experienced. Shunning it, she denied it any place. *No. No, that's doubt. That's not real, it's doubt.*

He'd be back. Three days, four at most. He would be back.…

• • •

On the third day, Sara received official notification from sober-faced uniformed authorities.

On the fourth, Matthew returned in a casket that would not be opened. He'd been shot seventeen times at point-blank range, identified by his DNA. The assailants eluded capture.

On day seven, Sara stood in the cemetery next to an ancient oak and buried him beside where she'd buried his uncle Paul. Certain she had run out of tears, she cried anyway. Anger at Matthew for dying and leaving her to battle with the devastation and knowing she'd never again see him. Never again feel his kiss, his arms around her. Never again see that special look he reserved just for her shining in his distinct eyes.

There was only one grave on the right side of his—a woman's. Sara wondered about her. Was she loved? Did she leave someone behind? Had she loved some man enough in her time with him to last him a lifetime?

The service went on. Sara separated, present yet apart from herself, lost behind her black net veil in memories of the first time she and Matthew had met. Chen's Chinese restaurant was crowded and he'd invited her to share his table. She'd taken one look into his eyes and seen something remarkable. Something she'd never before or since seen in any man's eyes. It wasn't a twinkle, it was more significant than that, though she still couldn't describe it—and felt she probably wouldn't be able to when she was old and gray. But oh, she'd felt its magic—she still felt it. The look in his eyes had touched her soul and captivated her. Totally, completely and irrevocably.

Love at first sight. What a miracle. And wonder of wonders, it'd been that way for Matthew, too. A fresh wave of tears rolled from deep inside, burned the back of her nose, stung her eyes. She'd loved him well. He'd loved her well. Maybe one day she'd find peace in that. But not today. Today, there was no peace.

She pulled in a shuddery breath. That kind of love happens to a woman only once, if it happens at all. She was a lucky one. She'd known it. And though she'd never know the feeling again, she'd spend the rest of her life knowing exactly what she was missing. That was both blessing and curse, but she couldn't regret it. She'd never regret it…or stop mourning its loss.

The minister's voice claimed her attention. "Ashes to ashes, dust to dust…"

• • •

Sara stooped down and pulled stray weeds from Matthew's grave.

Happy anniversary, honey. One day bled into another and another and turned into months, and now two years had passed. *Where'd they go?* A tear dripped from the corner of her eye down her face and splashed onto the grass. She placed the fresh flowers near his headstone and began their Sunday-afternoon chat. "I landed the Kramer account," she told him. "It'll subsidize the firm for the next five years all on its own." She snagged a drooping green leaf with her thumbnail. Matthew had loved her talking about her marketing ventures. He'd been such a good listener.…

Movement caught the corner of her eye. Startled, she jumped.

"I'm sorry." A man stood before the woman's headstone.

Sara had seen him from a distance for months. He too visited the graveyard every Sunday afternoon. The woman buried at Matthew's right had died seven years ago, and from this man's dedication, she had indeed loved him enough. That comforted Sara. "No, I'm sorry. I didn't see you there." She'd wondered where he was today; he was typically already here when she arrived.

He walked toward her. "Has it started yet?"

Sara stood up. "What?"

"Everyone telling you it's way past time you moved on?"

"Oh, yes." She smiled, bittersweet. "They just don't understand." Seven years for him; he understood. She dusted her hands. He had brought the woman yellow carnations today. Daisies, carnations, irises, but never roses. Odd…

"What do you say to them?" he asked.

Whether looking for something that could be of use to him or gauging her feelings to compare to his own, she didn't know. But it didn't matter. Talking to a stranger was easier than talking to a friend about this—especially a stranger who had been through it. "Mostly just to leave me alone. It takes what it takes." Sara's purse slipped off her shoulder. Why wouldn't he look at her? He kept his gaze fixed on the woman's grave. Shadows from the afternoon sun slanted across his jaw and chest. "When you love someone with your whole heart, you don't stop loving them because they died. The love stays with you." She shrugged. "They don't understand that."

"I do." He turned and looked directly at her.

The twinkle. Sara bit down a gasp. How could it be? His face— totally different. Surgery? Why—the job. The men who'd shot him… Protection. She checked again. The twinkle remained. *Matthew!* Why hadn't he let her know? Her protection.

Angry? Happy? Feeling both, she wasn't sure what to do or say—and then she understood. He should stay away from her but couldn't. She extended her hand, buying herself time to tamp her emotions, certain if she revealed knowing him, he'd walk away and she'd never see him again. Why so certain of that, she didn't know, but the instinctive nudge rammed her like a shove so she heeded it. "I'm Sara English."

"Adam Davis." He clasped her hand and shook.

The voice. *The voice…the eyes…definitely her Matthew!* Her heart soared and the pain of grief, such a heavy part of her for two years, vanished and fell under a surging wave of joy. Sara smiled.

Adam smiled back, and his stomach growled. "Sorry, I missed lunch."

"I was about to go for Chinese." She squeezed his hand, released it. "Would you care to share my table?"

Relief washed over his new face. She recognized him, eyes to eyes and heart to heart, and now he knew it. His tone dropped, deep and husky. "I'd love to, Sara."

She linked their arms, and together they walked out of the cemetery and into their future.

THE HONEYMOON
JULIE KENNER

*On Elizabeth and Tom's honeymoon, things don't
simply go bad. They go really, really bad. Brace yourself
for several jolts. —SB*

"There," Elizabeth said. "That's the cutoff to Balmorhea, and—oh, shit. Now you've passed it. Turn around, Tom. We need to go back."

Tom kept his hands at the ten- and two-o'clock positions. "Balmorhea's off the highway. We'd have to go out of our way. The interstate goes right through Van Horn."

"Yes, but I'm exhausted. I need sleep." She rubbed her hand along his thigh. "And sex. New brides need lots of sex."

He was tempted, no denying that. But the thought of getting out of Texas and closer to their honeymoon was even more tempting.

"Nap now, have wake-up sex in the morning. Or Van Horn sex in an hour. I promise I'll be up for it."

"Tom…"

"Come on, sweetheart. The whole point of driving to Disneyland was so that we could watch America roll by outside. And trust me when I say that this part of Texas is better in the dark. My dad used to take me hunting in West Texas. It's a whole lot of nothing."

"Hunting?"

"Hey, Texas boy here. Handguns and rifles and an oil well in the backyard."

She laughed. "You're so typical."

"Nah, just lucky. Anyway, if we make it to Van Horn, then most of tomorrow is New Mexico and Arizona. And those deserts are much prettier."

"I'm a Texan now, too, remember?" Her fingers brushed his hair, and when he looked over her irritated expression was gone, replaced by that sweet, vulnerable face he fell in love with. "That means I love every part of your state, even the dusty, dry parts."

"I'm very glad to hear it." He smiled at her, still not quite able to believe she was his wife. *Wife.* Man, his parents were going to shit bricks when they found out. "Let me see it."

She cocked her head. "Tom."

"Please?"

She shook her head, then released an indulgent sigh as she held up her left hand and wiggled her ring finger.

"My mother's going to want a big wedding, you know," he said.

"Seems silly since we're already married."

"Married by a judge in Austin doesn't cut it for her."

"Hey, it's your family's money. If she wants to spend it on a big wedding, then more power to her." She shifted in her seat and frowned.

"What?"

"What if we can't find a room in Van Horn?" she asked, as he gritted his teeth and told himself this was the "for better or for worse" part of the vows.

"Do you really want me to turn around?"

She let out a long sigh, then shifted in her seat, looking out at the stretch of highway lit by their headlights in front and the wall of black behind them. "I guess not. We're already a million miles from the turnoff and we'd have to find someplace to double back."

"On we go, then. Tunes?" He had some classic Lyle Lovett in the CD player and cranked the volume. "Why don't you go online and see if you can book us a room," he suggested, as Lyle crooned about *M.O.N.E.Y.* "You can do that, right? Wasn't that the point of buying that thing?"

She smirked and pulled her new iPad out of her bag. She'd bought it before they set out on the road, her first purchase as his wife. "I guess I don't have to say thanks anymore, do I? I mean, now it's community property."

"Yours, mine and ours. For richer or for poorer, so don't buy too many of those toys or we'll be hitting the poorer side of that equation." Not exactly true. He had his trust-fund money plus the cash he'd got when he'd sold his stock options at the height of the tech boom. He was barely past thirty, had a beautiful wife and never had to work a day again. Life was good.

"Let's see what I can find, then." She tapped on the iPad and the screen illuminated the interior of the car in a glowing blue. A light flashed in his rearview mirror, and he flinched.

"Tom?"

"Sorry. I—" He rubbed his eyes.

"What?"

"I thought I saw a car behind us."

She shifted in her seat. "It's pitch-black back there. Doesn't Texas have the money for a few lights on their highways?"

"Like I said—middle of nowhere. And it must have just been a trick of the light. Any luck with the room?"

"There's no signal. It's a great toy, but it's not connecting to the internet, and we're not making phone calls. So don't get a flat, because there's no way we're getting through to Triple A."

"The car's fine. Don't be paranoid. People drove across the country long before cell phones were invented."

"And iPads and CDs. Can you imagine? Eight-track tapes? I mean, what kind of world was that?"

"My dad had an old eight-track player in the garage," he said. "I used to— *Fuck!*"

Lights flashed on behind him—*right* behind him. Filling his rearview mirror and getting bigger by the second.

Beside him, Elizabeth yelled, reaching out to steady herself with a hand on the door. "What the— *Oh, my god.* He's crazy. He's right on your ass!"

"I know! I know!" His heart was pounding in his chest. He told himself this was no big deal. The guy was drunk. He was being an ass. But all they had to do was let him get by and they'd have the road to themselves again.

He lifted his foot off the accelerator.

"What are you doing?" Her voice was high, terrified.

"I'm slowing down. Letting him pass."

"I don't think—"

Wham!

They both jolted forward as the car behind them—no, it was a truck—tapped the rear bumper.

"Jesus, Jesus," Elizabeth said. "Do you have a gun? A weapon?"

"I don't have shit." He had his knife, like always. A folding blade that was spring-loaded and pretty much lived in his pocket. But that wasn't much good against a crazy pickup truck. "*Fuck.* Call 911."

"There's no cell service! I just told you!"

Wham! Tapped again, and this time from an angle, so that his sweet little Mercedes shifted a bit to the right. "Just fucking try again!"

"All right, all right! You don't have to scream at me!"

"Babe, I'm sorry. I'm freaked is all. Okay, look. I'm going to floor it." He did as he was talking. "We're small and fast, and see? We're already pulling away. So just watch the phone and the second you get a signal, you call. Okay?"

She nodded, and he kept his hands tight on the wheel and his foot flat on the floor.

And for a second—one beautiful, wonderful, fabulous second—he thought it was going to work. And then the gap started closing. Those lights started growing bigger. And soon the truck's headlights consumed the small back window of the Mercedes.

Tom tensed. Waiting to feel another smack against the bumper. But none came. The truck just tailed him. Ten, maybe fifteen inches away from the back of his car, tracking him as they whipped down the highway.

The minutes sagged by.

"Signal?"

Beside him, Elizabeth shook her head, her eyes wide and terrified.

"Restart the phone. Sometimes it finds a network when you restart."

She nodded and rebooted the phone.

"Do you think it's over? He's just going to tail us all the way to Van Horn?"

"It's at least half an hour away," Tom said, which technically didn't answer her question. "But he's stopped hitting us. Maybe he's just drunk."

"I bet he's drunk as a fucking snake. *Bastard*."

"So, we just drive, and we breathe in and out, and we will be fine."

The lights behind them snapped off, leaving a gaping black chasm behind them.

"Is it— Did he—?"

Tom reached over and grabbed her hand. "I don't know."

That's when he heard the sharp *crack*. And at the same time the car skidded.

"What was that?" Elizabeth asked.

"I don't know."

Another crack, and that time Tom figured it out, because the car started to fishtail. He tried to steer into it, which was easier said than done, but they just kept skidding in a circle, right off the road until the car tumbled sideways into a ditch.

His right arm was thrust sideways across Elizabeth's chest, a protective cage. She was breathing hard, her fear filling the car along with his.

"He shot out the tires," he whispered. "The crazy son of a bitch shot out the tires."

"What do we do?"

"Stay here. Maybe he's had his fun. Maybe he'll just go. Is there a signal yet?"

"Oh, God." Panic made her voice rise. "I dropped it. Oh, shit." She bent over and scrabbled on the floorboard. He could hear her murmured, "Please, please, please." Then, "Shit. No signal."

"This is what we're going to do. We're going to stay in the car. Simple. Straightforward."

"Do you see him?"

He twisted in his seat, scouring the darkness behind them. "No, I—"

And there he was.

Not some drugged-out kid, or some bearded, wild-eyed desert survivalist. Just a dude. In a white button-down under a denim jacket and jeans. He had a crooked grin and he didn't look the least bit psychotic.

Tom didn't move a muscle.

"Hey!" the Dude called. "Are you okay? Shit! That fucker blew your back tires right out!"

Tom glanced sideways at Elizabeth, who was staring past him at the Dude, her mouth open as if she couldn't quite believe this.

"You—you saw it?"

"Shit, yeah."

Tom swiveled in his seat, trying to see through the oily darkness. "How?"

"My car," the Dude said, pointing vaguely behind them. "I was sleeping—too much driving, you know—and I saw the crazy bastard rail down on you."

Tom rolled the window down—but only about half an inch.

"You—you saw him? Where—"

"Floored it right on by while you were spinning. Man, he's probably in New Mexico by now."

"Do you have cell service? Can you call a cop? A tow truck?"

"Signal picks up in about five miles. Right now, it's like the Wild, Wild West."

"Could you—I mean, would you drive ahead? Call someone?"

"Sure thing." He took a step back, then stopped. "Or, you know, I could help you change the tires. This ditch ain't so deep, and this car's not even as heavy as my sister."

"I don't know…"

Beside him, Elizabeth shifted. "I don't want to wait here, Tom. What if that freak comes back?"

"Lady's got a point. He lit up my car playing chicken with you two. Wouldn't surprise me at all if he comes back to see if I've done just that—gone off to get help for you guys."

"I only have one spare."

"And I got one. Won't be a perfect fit, but I got tools. We get it on, and it'll hold you to a gas station."

He glanced at Elizabeth, who eyed the Dude with a frown, then nodded. "Yeah. I want to get out of here."

"Right. Okay." He felt the weight of the knife in his pocket as he shifted to turn off the car. He had the keys in his hands, keeping them tight between his fingers. Neither the keys nor the knife would do much good if the gun-toting maniac came back, but it made him feel a little safer.

He shifted the keys to his left hand and grabbed Elizabeth's hand. Her side of the car was sitting at an odd angle, and if she opened that door, she'd tumble out. "Just slide over. I've got you."

He opened the door, and the Dude stepped back, then moved forward again as Elizabeth scrambled to get free. The Dude took her elbow. "Here ya go, ma'am. I got you."

She flashed him one of her rare smiles, almost flirtatious, and Tom swallowed, feeling like an idiot because what the hell was he jealous about? He wasn't. He was just on edge, was all.

"We're newlyweds," he said, showing the Dude his hand and his ring.

"Hell of a thing to happen on your honeymoon," the Dude said. "Come on. My car's a few yards back. We can get my spare and a jack."

They started walking that way, Elizabeth using her phone as a flashlight. It barely cut through the inky black, but Tom could tell they were easing off the shoulder and onto the Texas rock and scrubby bushes. "You're off the road?"

"Shit, yeah. Park on the shoulder and some sleepy-ass truck driver will rear-end you before you know it. There she is," he said as Elizabeth's beam caught the front edge of a truck, its bumper scraped with red paint.

Tom grabbed her hand and took a step backward.

"Aw, dammit. You found me out." The Dude pulled a Rossi revolver from under his jacket. "What a fucking inconvenience."

"Look, just—just let us go. I have money. What do you want? A thousand? Ten thousand?"

"Sounds like a start. But maybe I want the girl."

Tom squeezed her fingers even as an invisible hand clutched at his heart. "You leave her the fuck alone."

The Dude stepped closer. "Yeah? You're telling me what to do? Who's the one with the gun here?"

Tom swallowed. "That would be you."

"And don't you fucking forget it. Walk." He waved the gun toward the darkness farther off the highway.

"No." Tom clutched tight to Elizabeth.

"No?" The Dude thrust the gun out and down. Then *blam!* Rocks and sand went flying at Tom's feet before he even had time to think about it.

"Are you fucking crazy?" Elizabeth screamed.

"Me? Crazy? Hell, no." *Blam!* Another shot.

"Goddammit!" she screamed again.

"Hush." Tom kept his voice low, calm. "Don't provoke him."

"That's right, Liz. Don't provoke me."

A chill shot down Tom's spine. "How do you know her name?"

"I think the more relevant question is what the fuck are you doing married to my girl."

"Your gir—" But that was all he got out. He heard the crack of the gun, felt the push as the bullet hit him in the chest. He stumbled back. And in the soft glow of the light from Elizabeth's phone, he saw her release his hand and pull her fingers free.

He landed on the ground and as he looked up at Elizabeth's scowling face, he parted his lips to ask a question.

But the question didn't come.

• • •

"Are you *insane?*" Liz snapped. "How long have we planned this? How much time did we spend working out every fucking little detail?"

"He pissed me off," Eric said.

God save her from idiot lovers. "He's fucking dead, you moron.

How am I supposed to pull anything from his bank accounts when we don't have his goddamn account numbers and access codes?"

The plan had been to get Tom in a hotel, get him tied up, get the information and *then* kill him. Eric would pistol-whip her, fuck her hard and then get himself gone while she called 911. After that, she could draw from the account without having to wait for all the probate bullshit, bullshit that would undoubtedly leave some of *her* money with *his* pedantic, pain-in-the-butt relatives.

Much nicer to be on her own with cash in her pocket, and his too-nice, I-don't-have-to-work-and-can-stay-home-all-day-and-be-a-pain-in-your-butt body out of her life.

And then the brain trust here had to go and screw it all up.

"You're still married. You'll still get it."

"Think, Eric! Think." She pressed her hands to her temple, then scowled at him again. "And you smell like a damn brewery. Are you drunk? Are we seriously doing this while you're drunk?"

He actually looked sheepish. "I was bored. You guys took your damn time."

"Honestly! And quit waving that thing. You're making me nervous." She held out her hand and he slapped the gun into her palm.

"You got a real bitchy attitude sometimes, Liz. You know that, right? Sometimes you just need to chill. Go with the flow. It's all gonna work out just fine, and we're gonna be soaking in the sun on some foreign beach by the weekend."

She drew in a breath, nodded. "Right. You're right. I'm just a little freaked. I wasn't expecting the backup plan."

"That's why they call it a backup, baby." He'd been waiting in the truck at the turnoff to Balmorhea. She'd known she couldn't push too hard, not and be Tom's adoring little Elizabeth. So Eric had waited, and if they passed the exit, then he was supposed to come after them. Smooth as silk.

And in a lot of ways, so much better.

She smiled. "Sorry. I'm okay. You're right. The account numbers were just to speed things up. No prenup. I'm his little wifey. I'll get my share, easy squeazy. My share, and a lot of sympathy. Carjacked on our honeymoon? How fucking rotten is that?"

Eric spread his hands. "I'm the man."

"That you are."

"So, I need to get out of here," he said. "But you gotta be a little fucked-up. Pistol-whipped and all that shit. Just like we planned at the hotel. Gimme the gun back."

She held it out to him. "Don't hold back. When you hit me, make it look good."

"Shit, Liz," he said, stepping close to take it. "Didn't anybody tell you about not pointing that thing at people?"

Blam!

Even in the dark, she could see the blood spread across the bright white cotton of his shirt. She smiled as she watched him fall. "So sorry, Eric," she said. "Nobody told me a thing."

● ● ●

She realized her mistake right away. She should have let him fuck her, let him whack her on the cheek a few times to raise a huge bruise. Because now she was going to have to do at least a little damage to herself.

She'd tell the cops the carjacking story, but she'd say that when he was trying to rape her, she got the gun from him. Managed to shoot him, and then escaped in his truck.

Nice and neat, except for the fact that she didn't have a mark on her.

She turned the flashlight app on and shined a light around the area. She found a rough rock and used it to rip her jeans, then she sat on her ass and dragged herself along the ground, wincing as the gravel and debris cut at her knees and hands.

She'd had a manicure before they left, but now she clawed at the dirt, fighting a pretend assailant who was dragging her off, ripping her cuticles, breaking her nails. Not really a problem, since she could pay for a lifetime of manicures now.

She wasn't looking forward to messing up her face—much easier to have someone else do it for her. She shined the light at Eric's lifeless body. No help there. And as for her dear, departed husband....

Her light found him, too, his shirt stained red, his eyes open in surprise, blood bubbles forming at his moving lips—

What the fuck?

She stepped closer. It had to be a trick of the light.

"E...za...beth."

"Oh, shit, Tom. Why the fuck aren't you dead?"

His lips moved again, but she couldn't make out the words.

Dammit all, she didn't need this shit. "Look, I'm really sorry. I mean, you're an okay guy and all. But I'd have to slit my throat if I stayed married to you. Nothing personal. Really."

Again, the lips moved. Again, she heard nothing.

Fuck. Fuck, fuck, fuck.

She got closer. "What is it? You want to tell me the account numbers? You're probably in a lot of pain. Tell me, and I can make it all go away."

He nodded. Or she thought he did. Not that easy to tell, really.

She got down close to him, the gun in her hand. She could smell the blood. She'd thought Eric had got him in the heart, but now that she was closer, she could see he missed it. Probably got a lung, though. Poor guy was probably drowning in his own blood.

"Nine...ven...teen."

"Hold on, baby. Say it slower, say it louder. Just say it, and I'll make it all be over." She bent closer, her ear near his mouth.

"*Fuck...you...*"

She jerked away, but it was too late. His arm was already up, that damn knife of his already out, and she gagged on blood as he thrust the blade deep into her throat.

Fucker! She screamed, or she tried to. She was gagging, choking, and with her free hand, she yanked the knife out, tossed it aside and clutched hard at her neck as warm blood pulsed out between her fingers. She was on her knees, swaying, her head like a balloon about to lift off into space.

Dead. He was fucking dead. She lifted the gun, got it right in his face, and pulled the trigger.

Click.

Nothing. Just *click.*

In front of her, through the haze of gray that was fast overtaking her, she saw her husband smile, and this time she heard his weak whisper. "Rossi's a five-shooter, bitch."

And as she tumbled sideways, her blood spilling out onto the warm Texas dust, she heard his voice one last time. The last words she ever heard. "Till death do us part, Elizabeth. Till death do us part."

EXECUTION DOCK

JAMES MACOMBER

Macomber moves the action along at a mile a minute but without any sacrifice to the heart of the story. —SB

"No."

Refusing to look at the woman lawyer seated across from him, Sarnath Dutta addressed his remarks to the male magistrate. "I have a superior order from the Sharia court of Jessore that I, as father, have all rights."

"No, Mr. Dutta." Katherine Price, senior partner with Loring, Matsen and Gould, leaned forward and just as pointedly addressed the dark-skinned Bengali man directly. "You married Mrs. Dutta in the United States. That marriage produced two children, now four and six. The marriage failed and divorce proceedings ensued, also in the United States. For good and valid reasons—we won't get into the issues of abuse unless we have to—that court awarded sole custody to Mrs. Dutta. You received specific and, under the circumstances, generous visitation."

Dutta interrupted. "That order—and that court—mean nothing." He realized he was talking directly to Price and shifted abruptly to the magistrate. "No court can supersede the order of the Sharia court."

Theodore Warrenton, Magistrate of the Inner London Family

Proceedings Court raised his eyebrows but said nothing. He was an elderly man, semiretired from active participation on the bench and meticulously fair in his conduct of this hearing. He transferred his gaze to Price for a response.

"To the contrary," Price countered, "you're the one attempting to set aside existing valid orders. After the divorce proceedings, you flew home to Bangladesh to get that order. Then, under the pretense of availing yourself of your visitation rights under the very orders you seek to declare invalid, you took the children and left the United States. Fortunately, you were intercepted at Heathrow on an Interpol watch issued under the Hague Convention on the Civil Aspects of International Child Abduction."

"Which does not apply to me as a Bengali. Bangladesh is not a signatory to that treaty."

"Precisely!" Price seized on the point, and turned toward Magistrate Warrenton. "Perhaps the court is familiar with the term *chutzpah?*" The judge nodded slightly. Dutta bristled at the reference.

"The classic example of *chutzpah*," Price went on, "is the man who murders his parents and then asks for mercy on the grounds he's an orphan." Warrenton smiled. Dutta didn't. "It's only due to the fact that Bangladesh is not a signatory to the Child Abduction statute that Mr. Dutta isn't facing a warrant for his arrest," Price argued. "He should hardly be allowed to use that loophole to justify his otherwise unlawful actions."

"Unlawful!" Dutta scoffed. "My actions are fully consistent with this order and, most importantly, with Sharia law, which may not be set aside."

"This is not a matter of setting aside Sharia law, Mr. Dutta," Warrenton interjected. "As Ms. Price stated, the earlier orders of the United States court take precedence."

"No!" Dutta remained adamant.

"Yes," insisted the magistrate. "And this court so rules." He began to dictate to the stenographer. "In the matter of—" Warrenton stopped when Dutta abruptly stood, banging his chair loudly against the wall. "Mr. Dutta," the magistrate began forcefully.

But Dutta ignored him and stomped toward the door. The bailiff moved to intercept him but Warrenton waved him off. Dutta yanked the door open and left without closing it behind him.

Warrenton completed dictating his ruling then spoke to Beverly Dutta. "This order will be sent over immediately to Child Protection Service." He looked at his watch. "It's now 3:00 p.m. I know it's difficult to wait another night but arrangements have to be made. I'll set the time for their release to you at, say, 11:00 a.m. tomorrow. I trust that's satisfactory?"

"Thank you." Beverly managed a weak smile as she wiped a tear from the corner of her eye. The magistrate smiled gently back at her, then rose and left.

"And thank you, Katherine," Beverly said, leaning over to hug Price. "I could never stand up to Sar on my own." She looked down. "Maybe that was the problem all along."

Though few would believe it, Katherine was old enough to be Beverly's mother—she certainly didn't look it—and she'd developed a strong maternal feeling for this young woman. She gently pushed Beverly's shoulders back so she could look into her face, and told her firmly, "No, *he* was the problem all along." She waved her hand vaguely to indicate the hearing room. "And if this doesn't count as standing up to him, what does?"

"But I couldn't have done it without you. Thanks."

"My pleasure," Katherine said. And it was. Dutta was despicable—a bully and serial abuser. It had been a pleasure to knock him down.

"Is it really over?"

"Well, he could appeal," Katherine acknowledged. "But the

judge's order made it clear that you're to take custody of the children immediately. Even if he appeals. And," she added with emphasis, "you're free to take them back to the States pending an appeal."

"Will you come with me to pick up Sarah and Josh tomorrow?"

"Absolutely. Wouldn't miss it."

"I'm going over there now." The CPS facility was only a few blocks away from both the court and Beverly's hotel. "Do you want to have dinner later?"

Katherine reached out and squeezed Beverly's hand. "Oh, I wish I could. But John's flying in and I'm picking him up at Heathrow."

"Your fiancé?"

"Yes."

"He's a lawyer in your firm, too?"

"Uh-huh. Also a senior partner."

"Have you known him long?"

"We've been colleagues at the firm for several years, but we just never seemed to get together. I understand it drove the office matchmakers nuts for years." They shared a smile.

"Will he come with us tomorrow?" Beverly began to gather her things.

"I think he'd like that. He's the strongest man I've ever known, but he's got a soft side I just love. He'll probably be as sniffly as we are."

"How nice that must be." Beverly's tone was wistful.

Katherine reached out and took her hand. "Give it time, Beverly. As I said, it's worth the wait."

● ● ●

Katherine had hired a car and driver from an Aston Martin dealership just up Park Lane from the Grosvenor House for the trip to and from the airport to pick up John. As they walked into the hotel lobby upon their return, the striking couple were the object of admiring glances—Katherine tall, auburn-haired and head-turningly beautiful; John handsome, salt-and-pepper hair, a few inches taller than Katherine and a few years older.

They went up to their room and, when the bellman had left, fell into a long embrace.

"Hungry?" Katherine asked after a while.

"Very."

"For food?"

"That, too."

Katherine gave a throaty chuckle and turned away to order some wine and appetizers from room service. They settled onto the couch and turned toward each other, spending the next few minutes in an affectionate chat that sometimes bordered on the goofy. Room service arrived and the server arranged the wine bucket, glasses and food items on the low table in front of the couch and left.

"So," John said after a couple of sips of Pinot Grigio, "the case went well?" He was familiar with the nature of it but they'd not discussed specifics. Katherine filled in the details including Sarnath Dutta.

John shook his head. "A real bastard, hey?"

"Unbelievable, John. Every negative stereotype come to life. He wouldn't even talk to me directly because I'm a woman."

"All the more satisfying to hand him his butt, then." John huffed a laugh.

"Exactly." She grew pensive. "But more than that… You see men like that, relationships like that… I hesitate to call it a relationship even." She reached across the back of the couch to caress John's shoulder. "It makes me appreciate you all the more."

"And I you." He raised his glass to her. "So what's on the agenda for tomorrow?"

"Well, I told Beverly I'd—" Katherine smiled "—well, actually

I said *we'd* go with her when she picks up her kids tomorrow. Is that okay?"

"Sure," John said. "Always love to see a happy ending."

They sat in contented silence for a bit, then John stood. "It's been a long day," he said, stretching.

Katherine got off the couch and crossed to him wrapping her arms around his neck. "No rest for the weary, though," she whispered in his ear.

A smile with just the hint of a leer appeared on John's face. "I thought the saying was 'no rest for the wicked.'"

Katherine looked into his eyes, her lips just an inch away from his. "That'll work."

● ● ●

The phone woke John at nine-thirty the next morning. He hadn't meant to fall back asleep after Katherine had left an hour before to meet Beverly at the Coronet Hotel. Savoring the memory of her goodbye kiss, he reached across the empty bed and picked up the receiver.

"Hello?"

"John. I can't find Beverly."

"Where are you?"

"Her hotel. She didn't answer her door or the house phone. I got the manager to open the room. The bed looks slept in. All her stuff's there."

"Maybe she went over to CPS already? Couldn't wait?"

"I don't think she would, but I called anyway. She's not there. Wasn't at the courthouse, either. She wouldn't miss this for anything. Something's not right."

John had learned time and again to trust Katherine's instincts. He was already out of bed and pulling on his clothes. "Have you called the police?"

"I did. Of course, they said 'she's an adult, maybe went out.' The usual."

"Anybody at the hotel see anything?"

"Not so far. I'm going to see if I can persuade the manager to let me look at their security tapes."

"Okay. You're right down Oxford Street?"

"Yes. Right on Berwick. Just down from there. On the right."

"Fifteen minutes."

"I'll be here."

● ● ●

John made it in twelve. He dashed through the front door of the Coronet Hotel and up to the desk. Met with a blank stare when he inquired after Katherine, he requested the manager. A moment later a tall, slender, dark-haired, thirtysomething woman came out a door behind the desk. She spoke with a slight German accent. "May I help you?"

John asked again for Katherine.

"I know who you're referring to, sir," the manager replied. "I spoke with her earlier, yes. Let her into her client's room. But I haven't seen her since."

"She told me she was going to try to look at your surveillance recordings."

The manager shook her head. "She didn't. As I said I only spoke with her the one time."

Nothing was making sense. "Might I examine your security tapes, then?"

"I'm afraid not, sir. Privacy concerns. You understand."

He did, but…he turned away from the desk, punching a number into his cell phone as he walked around the lobby. The call was answered on the first ring.

"Foster."

"Robbie. It's John Cann."

"Robbie" was Sir Robert Foster, a former colonel in Britain's most elite Special Forces unit, the SAS. Foster had retired from the military and gone on to form one of the premier executive protection firms in the U.K. His lifetime of service to his country as well as his current accomplishments had earned him a knighthood in 2007. Cann had been an honored guest at the ceremony.

"John. How wonderful. Are you in the U.K.? Is the lovely Katherine with you?"

"She is but there's a problem."

Foster turned serious. He'd known John for a very long time, well before Loring, Matsen and Gould. And he knew that John Cann did not lightly characterize something as a "problem." Neither did Katherine. Many of the firm's lawyers were more than attorneys, recruited as much for their operational skills as their legal acumen.

Like John and Katherine.

John's background was military; army straight out of high school, Green Beret and Delta Force, operations with DIA, CIA, NSA, etc. And even the SAS. That's how he knew Robbie. Later he was sent to law school on "Uncle Sam's nickel" to establish a cover for clandestine work and turned out to be an excellent attorney. Just what Loring, Matsen and Gould sought.

As for Katherine, she was an honors graduate of a small private law school and had gone to the Department of Justice upon graduation. Glynco Federal Law Enforcement Training Center—"Fletsy"—was followed by assignments as "legal attaché," the euphemism for U.S. agents on foreign soil, before heading to counterterror at State.

They were both very good at what they did. That's why they were at Loring, Matsen and Gould.

And, Foster knew, they didn't *have* problems. They solved them.

"What kind of problem?" Foster asked.

John explained about the acrimonious custody proceeding,

the abusive Sarnath Dutta, and Katherine's efforts to find Beverly Dutta. And now, Katherine was nowhere to be found. "Nothing would keep Beverly Dutta from those kids, Robbie. Katherine either."

"Yes, well, of course, there may be an explanation," he said. "And Katherine's an extraordinary woman. I don't have to tell you."

"No, you don't."

"But there's clearly cause for concern. The Coronet, you say?"

"Berwick. Just off Oxford."

"I know it. I'll be there in half an hour."

"Thanks, Robbie."

Cann paced the lobby for a few minutes then stepped out the front door, looking up and down the street. For what exactly, even he didn't know.

A few moments later, the manager came out. "Ah, there you are, sir," she said. "Sir Robert just phoned and explained the necessity for you to see our security tapes. If you'll follow me?"

As egalitarian and multicultural as the U.K. had become, a knight was still a knight.

● ● ●

Katherine's first perceptions on awakening were dampness and darkness, the only light in the enclosed space coming from slots near the bottom of the wall to her right. She was seated, hands tied behind her, ropes around her chest and legs binding her to a straight-backed chair. Beverly was seated across from her, similarly bound. Sarnath Dutta stood in front of her.

"Not so arrogant now, lady lawyer, are you?" he sneered.

Katherine glared defiantly into Dutta's eyes. "What's this supposed to accomplish? Do you actually think this will get you your children?"

Dutta shrugged. "*Insh'allah*. If not, I will make more children," he looked at Beverly with contempt, "with a proper wife and mother." His expression hardened. "But you will not see it. You will see nothing once the tide rises." He pointed at the slots in the wall where murky water was already starting to slosh in.

Katherine looked to her right then up at Dutta. "Where are we?"

Dutta savored the moment, his mouth curving to a crooked grin. "This place is called Execution Dock."

• • •

Cann was glaring at the computer as Foster walked in accompanied by two men and a woman. On the screen were two West-Asian men dressed in white coveralls, the Coronet Hotel logo visible on the back. Katherine staggered along between them, either stunned or drugged. As they reached a large canvas laundry basket, Katherine leaned back, resisting. One of the men punched her hard in the face with a closed right fist. Twice. She went limp and they threw her into the basket. Cann's knuckles were white.

Foster turned to one of his men. "Get one of the housekeeping staff," he ordered. In moments, he returned with a young black woman whose eyes darted from face to face as she twisted and un-twisted a cleaning cloth in her hands.

"Do you know these men?" Foster asked. Cann had cropped the image so only the men's faces were shown. The woman put a finger on the one who hadn't punched Katherine.

"That's Kanu Mukherjee. Housekeeping. I don't know the other man."

"Is he here now?"

"I saw him a little while ago."

Foster nodded at his two men and they left. He ordered his female employee to "Run him down." She, too, nodded and left.

"May I go?" the housekeeper asked.

"In a moment." Foster was taking no chance she might, however innocently, reveal their hand.

Moments later, Foster's people reappeared with Mukherjee. The maid was allowed to leave. Mukherjee looked merely cautious at first but when Cann returned the images of him and the other man and Katherine to the screen, he paled and cast his eyes downward refusing to meet the others' eyes.

"Where did you take her?" Cann asked.

"I didn't take her nowhere," the man said sullenly.

Cann grabbed the man by the throat and slammed him up against the wall. "Answer now," he growled.

Mukherjee scrunched his chin into his throat in an effort to pull back. "You can't do this. I got rights."

Foster slammed a hand into the side of the Mukherjee's head then put his face up against the man's ear. "No, lad, you don't have rights. Not with us. Answer. Now."

"I can't. I don't know."

"Then tell us who's this other man and where can we find him?"

Mukherjee chewed his lip.

Foster's female employee came back into the room and handed Foster a sheaf of papers. He looked at them briefly before he started to read from them. "'Kanu Mukherjee. Emigrated to the U.K. July 2006. Married, two children.'" Foster continued to read off the details of Mukherjee's life. "Just one problem, though, Kanu, isn't there?"

Mukherjee now looked concerned. "You two never married. And she's not Bengali. She's Bhutanese." He looked hard into Mukherjee's eyes. "As a citizen of Bangladesh, you have Commonwealth citizenship. Your wife does not and is therefore here illegally. As are your children." He grabbed Mukherjee by the chin. "Look at me, here, in my eyes. Do you see anything that says I won't call the authorities in the next five minutes if you don't tell us what we want to know? Immediately." Even as he spoke he was taking his cell phone out of his pocket.

Mukherjee hesitated only briefly. "The other man is my cousin."

"Name."

Mukherjee licked his lips. "Girish Dutta." Cann and Foster exchanged a look.

"Is Sarnath Dutta your cousin, as well?" Cann asked.

The man nodded.

"Where are they?"

"Please…" Kanu hesitated, then said, "Girish lives in Tower Hamlets but…"

Foster grabbed Mukherjee by the shirt and pushed him ahead of them. "Take us."

• • •

Sarnath Dutta pulled the ladder up after him, slammed the trapdoor shut and rammed the bolt through the hasp. Without standing, he crept a few feet to the side and pulled back a small carpet that covered a small grid in the floor. He peered down into the chamber and was gratified to see the water level had already risen almost to Katherine's and Beverly's knees. Both struggled with their bonds but were limited in how much they could move. If the chair tipped over, they would be on their sides, lashed to the seat and would drown that much sooner.

Katherine knew that. She also knew that at the rate the water was rising it would not be long before they drowned no matter what. She called across to Beverly, "The rope seems to stretch a bit when it gets wet. Work on freeing your legs. Be careful." Beverly nodded.

Above them, Sarnath Dutta smiled. He was going to enjoy this.

• • •

Mukherjee took them to the Wapping District in the borough of Tower Hamlets, so named because of its proximity to the Tower of London. They were in two cars, one driven by one of Foster's men with Cann and Foster in the back, Mukherjee squeezed between them. The other man and the woman from Foster's security firm followed in a separate car.

As they drove down Garnet Street, Mukherjee leaned forward and pointed at a man sauntering self-importantly down the street. "That's him. That's Girish."

They drove by slowly, careful to *not* look at the man as Foster communicated with the car behind. At the next intersection, they turned and stopped right on the corner blocking the crosswalk. The man identified as Girish Dutta slowed and started to look around just as the second car pulled up to his left and behind him. The male operative who'd been in the passenger seat of the second car jumped out to block his retreat. Cann leaped from the backseat of the first car and he and the other man threw Dutta into the back-seat of the trailing vehicle. Cann jumped in beside him and grabbed the man's throat.

"Where did you take her?"

Dutta said nothing. Cann's grip tightened around his windpipe.

"Not here, John," Foster said leaning down into the open door. "We've a better place." Cann clipped him across the chin, stunning him.

● ● ●

Minutes later, they were in a small room at the back of a windowless Tower Hamlets warehouse set amid a large enclosed area filled with construction equipment and materials. Girish Dutta was bound to a chair in the middle of the floor, still wearing a defiant look.

"Where is she?" Cann repeated.

Dutta smirked. "What're ya gonna do wif me, mate, waterboard me?"

Cann turned to Foster. "I don't have time for this." There was a tall cylindrical canister in a corner of the room topped with a shallow ashtray. Cann asked one of the security men to take it and fill its entire three-foot height with soil or sand from one of the piles outside. The man did so and returned struggling with the weight of it. Cann thanked him and turned to Foster. "Maybe you and your people should leave."

Foster flipped his chin at the door directing his team to wait outside. When they were gone, he said simply, "I'll stay."

He and Cann then lashed Dutta's right hand so that it lay face-down, fingers splayed on top of the dirt-filled canister. Cann turned again to Foster. "I need a gun." Foster nodded and reached inside his jacket and took out a black Glock 20. "This one's untraceable," he said. From another pocket, he took out a suppressor and handed that to Cann who screwed it onto the muzzle then pulled back the slide to make sure there was a round in the chamber. Girish Dutta watched in silence, a bemused look on his face.

Cann stepped forward and pressed the muzzle of the pistol straight down on the first knuckle of the man's bound hand. "Where did you take her?"

"Who d'you think you're kiddin', mate. You ain't…"

The weapon jolted in Cann's hand as he fired, the bullet severing the finger and penetrating into the soil beneath. With his left hand, Cann picked up the severed finger and held it in front of Dutta's eyes.

"We ain't kiddin', mate," he said, mocking the accent. He tossed the finger into a corner of the room and asked yet again, "Where is she?"

A choking sound came from Dutta's throat and his eyes went from Cann's face to Foster's and found nothing. Cann moved the muzzle to the man's middle finger and fired again. Again he displayed the result to the horrified prisoner and tossed it away. Dutta's eyes were wide and his lips were moving but nothing was coming out.

Cann looked over at Foster. "You know what? He's got eight

more of those," he said coldly. "That'll take too long." He stepped up close and rammed the muzzle straight down into Dutta's groin. "Where is she?"

Girish Dutta couldn't tell them fast enough.

* * *

"It's called Execution Dock," Foster explained to Cann as they sped down Garnet Street toward the Thames, "because that's where executions took place for admiralty crimes—piracy, mutiny, etc. Most they hanged. Others, depending on the crime, were placed in cells below high tide level and left to drown." He looked over at Cann, who was staring ahead, fists clenched.

They'd brought Girish Dutta to show them exactly where he had taken Katherine and, they now knew, Beverly. Despite Girish Dutta's complaints, medical treatment for his hand consisted of a towel wrapping and nothing more. He'd been told to be thankful for that.

They turned right onto Wapping High Street, a narrow road lined with warehouses that fronted on the street and backed onto the river. The large knife pressed into Girish Dutta's side convinced him to promptly point out the building where Katherine and Beverly were being held. They drove past and stopped down the street. Leaving Dutta guarded by one of the men, Cann and Foster approached the side of the warehouse on foot. The two other members of Foster's team positioned themselves at front and rear corners where they could observe the other three sides of the building.

Foster made quick work of the door locks.

Inside the building, Sarnath Dutta heard the old hinges creak and jumped up and peered through a crack in the wall. Two men carrying guns didn't bode well. He pulled a knife from a sheath at the small of his back and dashed back to the trapdoor and pulled it open. Both Katherine and Beverly had managed to get their legs free and were now on their feet but bent over by the chairs to which they remained bound. The water was up to their hips.

Katherine immediately sensed what was happening. "John," she shouted as loudly as she could. Beverly echoed her. Dutta, hanging from one hand on the edge of the trapdoor opening, dropped into the chamber and slipped on the submerged floor. He regained his footing and leaped at Beverly, grabbing her throat and raising the knife. Behind him, Katherine charged forward and slammed hard into Dutta's side throwing him off balance. The side of his head struck the hard stone of the wall and he slid down it, his face just below the water's surface. Stunned, he struggled to raise himself. As he did, Katherine executed a hard side kick to his head knocking him out. He slid back under the surface and Katherine jammed the sole of her right foot into his chest to make sure he stayed there. Then she turned quickly and straddled his upper torso with the chair legs and sat down hard. Beverly saw what was happening and quickly did the same over Dutta's hips and legs.

Cann reached the opening and immediately swung himself down into the water. For a moment he stood looking around frantically for Sarnath Dutta before he saw the blurred image under the chairs. He reached down and pulled the head up, pressing the muzzle of his weapon against its temple. There was no movement and he let go. The body sank back into the water.

John quickly untied Katherine and they both helped free Beverly of her bonds. Foster's people lowered the ladder and they all scrambled out of the pit and headed for the relative warmth of the sun. Once outside, John wrapped his arms around Katherine and pulled her close. They held each other for a very long moment. "You okay?" he asked after a while.

"I am now." She looked down at herself and then at John. "We need to get out of these wet clothes."

"That'll work," John smiled.

Katherine's laugh was interrupted by Beverly. "Can we get to CPS?" she asked, still stunned by what had just occurred and her role in it. "Will they still let me take the children?" She looked desperately at Katherine. "After this?" She pointed back at the building.

"The less said the better," Sir Robert Foster interjected pointedly. He gestured to his team and they went back inside. "We'll clean this up. You go on." He turned to Beverly. "You must understand. This never happened."

Beverly looked at Katherine, who nodded. After a moment, Beverly did the same.

"You'll get your kids," Katherine reassured her. "But we need to change. We can't go like this." She turned to John. "You don't mind, do you?"

"Yup." He caressed her cheek and smiled. "But only a little. You wouldn't be you otherwise."

"Will you come with us?" Beverly asked sincerely.

"Of course," John answered. "Like I told Katherine," he said, though he was looking at Foster, "I always love a happy ending."

IN ATLANTIS

ALEXANDRA SOKOLOFF

This is a delicious fairy tale, complete with a lady and a prince charming. But its ending is nowhere near the traditional happ'ly ever after. —SB

It was true what they said, the water really was that color, that you see in the books.

Melissa stood on the white sand beach of Paradise Island—real white sand, soft as whipped cream under her feet—and looked out on that dazzling, jewel-like, multihued blue. The winds were gentle, and the sun warm and caressing....

And it made not the slightest bit of difference.

Because it was also true what they said about a broken heart. There was absolutely such a thing. It did feel as if her heart had been shattered like glass, and now the broken pieces were moving around in her chest. Too sudden a move or a breath and the jagged edges cut her flesh, racking her with new pain.

Three weeks ago she'd been counting the days until her wedding. And then, the oldest story in the book—Facebook, to be exact. *No harm in friending that high school crush, oh, no.* She would bet every cent in the resort casino that hers wasn't the first broken marriage, or almost-marriage, in Facebook history.

Her grief came in waves, like the sea.

"I don't think I'm ever going to feel anything again," she'd told her now-ex-bridesmaid, Annette.

Annette had grabbed Melissa's purse and rummaged for a credit card, which she proceeded to use to book an air and hotel package to the Bahamas.

"There. I made it easy, it's the Atlantis. They do everything for you. Just go. Bake in the sun. Have Coco Locos. Have fantasies."

And somehow, here she was.

Tiny Paradise Island was just off the main island of New Providence, and the Royal Towers of Atlantis seemed to take up a good quarter of it, a massive twenty-four-story coral-colored resort complex with "Atlantean" ornamentation: leaping swordfish and whorls of shells and tumbling waterfalls of fountains and 141 acres of water rides with names like "The Surge" and "Serpent Slide." An unlikely cross between the mythical underwater paradise and Disneyland.

In Melissa's present condition, the Atlantis was so overwhelming that the first day she was in danger of never leaving her room, never in fact leaving the bed. But ultimately she decided that even a ten-minute walk around the hotel was better than slow death by HBO, so she forced herself to dress—Annette had even packed for her—and foray out of the room.

The staircase spiraled down to a circular mall of marble, lined by boutiques displaying clothing that would cost her a year's salary per item. She passed Prada, Gucci, the Columbian Emeralds store. No one looked at her; she felt invisible, rather like moving in a dream.

The mall opened onto an opulent mirrored lobby…and the centerpiece stopped her in her tracks: a massive crystalline sculpture that seemed to blend the elemental energies of sun and ice.

A *Chihuly,* she recognized right away, as her eyes followed the lines of silver-white crystals up to the skylight. *What I wouldn't give for that,* she thought, drinking in its beauty at the same time that she was assessing its value at easily two million.

Art history was a terrible background for anyone looking to make an actual living. But she'd managed to parlay her degree and her passion into a job as director of a nicely endowed museum on a state college campus. She had enough of a budget to book shows she really cared about: Egyptian antiquities, photography collections, a fantastic impressionist show just last year.

But a Chihuly was something she could never afford. She stifled a surge of resentment that a glorified mall should end up with a piece of work this fine. No one was even looking at. The casino was even more dazzling; more Atlantis themes with sea monsters and ancient temples prominent in the decor. There were more Chihulys, too, a shining globe of blue and white shells, a fiery burst of orange and red, like lava curling up through water.

She first noticed the man because he was looking up at the art rather than down at the roulette table; he was the only one in the casino besides her who seemed to be aware of the gigantic sculptures suspended above the tables. Everyone else was in that gambling haze, or zone, they probably called it, that hypnotic rhythm of the tables and machines. But the man was gazing up at the brilliant sworls of glass.

And very quickly after she noticed him looking at the Chihuly, she couldn't help noticing how noticeable *he* was. The kind of man that you always hoped would be slanted just that way against a roulette table. Dark curly hair and coolly assessing eyes, tall and elegant in a suit cut so well she was instantly aware of every muscle of the equally cut body inside it.

She watched him, invisibly…until she realized what she was doing and was horrified at herself.

After everything you've just been through—this man? The roulette equivalent of a pool hustler?

A cocktail waitress stopped in front of her with a tray full of drinks, and Melissa reached and drank too fast. The rum made it easier to breathe, and she didn't flee after all. By the end of her second she was indulging in a fantasy of stepping up to a table like an old pro, exuding a sly knowingness as she coolly played her rounds....

And of course, of course, the man at the roulette table would be admiring her play....

Her reckless thoughts turned racing.

And what? What?

This was exactly the problem with Danny, the problem for maybe your whole life, this infallible radar for bad boys. She watched the spinning roulette wheel and was suddenly so dizzy she knew she was going to be sick.

She barely made it out of the casino, barely managed the elevator. In her room she pulled open the French doors and stood swaying on the terrace, hands gripping the railing as she stared down at the black waves below....

She backed suddenly away, through the doors...where she crawled into bed and slept for sixteen hours.

• • •

When she woke up, everything was different. A breeze played gently through the room and she felt a surprising lightness.

She rose up out of the bed, walked to the open doors and stepped onto the terrace.

Bougainvilleas in red and purple and orange grew lushly in stone planters. Turquoise sea stretched to infinity beyond the lagoon. She breathed in the salt and flower scent of the air, and felt a profound calm come over her.

It occurred to her that she could simply stay, never go home, run her credit cards out while she wandered the resort until some new plan evolved or she was arrested, one of those. The thought of just giving up all semblance of responsibility was intoxicating.

What's the percentage in being good, anyway?

And it was clear, as clear as the water of the harbor, that she really didn't care what happened to her anymore. Somehow that made her feel the most alive she'd felt…maybe in years.

Inside she put on one of the more daring dresses Annette had packed for her, a shimmering backless coral sheath. She looked at herself in the mirror and felt expensive and reckless.

When she got off the elevator she made a wrong turn and discovered something wonderful. Down that quiet corridor off the mall was a gallery. And the exhibit was "Lost Treasures of Atlantis."

There was no one else in the gallery; fine art apparently not being quite the draw of the casino or the waterslides. Of course the artifacts inside had nothing really to do with Atlantis, which didn't, after all, actually exist. But whoever had curated the exhibit had created a lovely fantasy of what artifacts might have existed in that oceanic world: rough-cut gems, vaguely Minoan creatures; gold carvings of mermaids and tritons; jeweled sea monsters; chalices.

And one that caught her and held her as if she had always known it: a gold shell, encrusted with diamonds and emeralds and what she thought was topaz but the description card identified as yellow diamonds. The shell opened, like a box, and was lined with velvet, and something opened in her heart, seeing it; it seemed to her the most beautiful thing she had ever encountered.

● ● ●

She daydreamed about the piece while she took her first real walk on the beach that day, and was aware of men noticing her. The shell had given her some of its fire; somehow she was no longer invisible.

That night she dreamed about it, dreamed of a dim, cool underwater palace, where she sat, dressed in silk, on a throne of fire and ice and held the jeweled shell in her hands. The dream was so vivid she felt a physical pain, waking up to the real world.

She dressed and hurried down to the gallery, anxious to see the shell again.

But when she stepped through the door, there was someone else there, standing in front of the glass case.

The man from the casino. This time in a white shirt as elegant as his suit had been, and casual trousers that were equally expensive, equally fine. He was even more attractive in profile, dark, encompassing eyes, aristocratically chiseled features softened by a sensual mouth—

Bad men, remember? Steer away.

She almost turned around right there and headed—anywhere— to the beach, back to her room, even the ferry to Nassau, just *away.*

Almost.

But then she had a thought, a dangerous thought.

What difference does it make?

My life is over. Why not look for trouble? Who cares anyway?

The idea was exhilarating, strangely liberating.

As she watched him, he stopped in front of the case that held the shell. *Her* shell. And he stood looking in on it for the longest moment—not just a moment, but long minutes, circling the case, seeming as mesmerized as she had been. He was so absorbed he didn't see her in the arch of the doorway.

She was fascinated—and angry. She felt violated, that a stranger was taking that kind of interest in something that was so deeply personal to her. She felt he was looking at *her,* into her. It was too intimate.

All right, now, that's just crazy.

Besides, what would a man, a gambler no less, find so fascinating about a jewel box? All this intense attention to the piece...and the way he was standing...

Like someone thinking about stealing it.

She felt a jolt.

He's not looking at the box. He's looking at the jewels.

Immediately she dismissed the thought.

The other night he was a roulette hustler and today he's a jewel thief.

But as she looked harder, it became completely obvious. His rapt attention to the art pieces inside was just a cover for his scrutiny of the case itself—the locks, the infrared light that indicated an alarm, the cameras mounted at the corners of the gallery.

He's casing the exhibit. He is thinking of stealing it.

It was brilliant, really—if the security in the gallery was anywhere near as laid-back as the rest of the Bahamas, it was an ideal place to pull off a heist. She'd noticed the lack of security yesterday, in an offhand way, an occupational hazard of the business.

But I never thought I'd see it—almost in progress.

She ducked out of sight, then, back into the dim and endless corridor. Her heart was pounding so hard she could barely walk, but she forced herself to move into the gift shop next door, browsing the racks just inside so he wouldn't notice her when he came out.

This is crazy. What are the chances that you would just happen to catch him casing the place?

On the other hand she was probably the one person in the whole resort most likely to be able to recognize if someone were casing the gallery. Was it really so outlandish?

It would be so easy to do, she thought, her heart racing as she feigned interest in mermaid glitter-globes. She'd had her hours, days, weeks, of worrying about the angles of possible theft every time she had a new exhibit in her own museum. The gallery was so accessible, off a main corridor of the hotel, elevators within a few steps of the gallery doors. If there were some kind of event that made the corridors more crowded than usual, a noisy distraction, a thief could simply slip into the crowd and be…anywhere.

A bribe to the security guard to take care of the alarms, a good glass cutter—it wouldn't be hard at all.

She saw movement in the corner of her eye and her pulse spiked as she saw him step out of the gallery.

She hesitated…then followed.

He moved at a leisurely pace until he was out of the corridor, then sped up with a purposeful stride, pushing out through the glass-and-metal-scrollwork doors onto the terrace.

Melissa ran quickly, silently behind, and slipped through the door.

The sun was blinding and the tropical warmth startling after the air-conditioned chill of the hotel; it took her eyes a moment to focus.

The terrace overlooked a lagoon of that exquisite water, with a crescent-shaped beach. Melissa stared out, trying to spot the man. A flotilla of deck chairs was arranged in perfect lines on the pristine sand; families played in the water on inner tubes and giant bicycle-like water toys. Beyond the walls of the resort the ocean stretched, more turquoise glory.

It seemed she'd lost him…then she spotted the dark curly head moving down a sloping path of painted concrete, toward a giant domed pavilion next to the lagoon.

She followed, forcing herself to move casually.

The pavilion housed a massive round bar, with a mosaic seascape on the arched ceiling two stories above. The sound of rushing water echoed off the dome, drifting up from somewhere below the floor.

The man was already seated at the bar, long legs slanted against the bar stool legs, sea breeze playing with that curly hair. He was writing in a little notebook…no, sketching…and totally engrossed in his drawing.

She was suddenly rabid to see.

She made her way up to the bar, stopping not too close to him, and the bartender stepped toward her. She gestured to the drink board advertising piña coladas; the bartender smiled and poured.

The man didn't look up from his drawing.

She picked up her drink and turned away from the bar, toward him, glancing down for the briefest second.

Then she moved across the glittering tiles of the floor to a table overlooking the lagoon. She sat and sipped the icy drink, her heart racing out of control.

In that one brief glimpse she'd seen he had sketched the piece, *her* piece, the jewel-encrusted shell box.

It was a scale drawing—remarkable, really, how precise the measurements were.

And measurements of the display cases and gallery, and the cameras mounted above.

Her fantasy hadn't been a fantasy at all.

He's going to steal it.

She sat and gazed over the ocean without looking at him and when he rose from the bar stool she watched him in her peripheral vision. She took her drink off its napkin and let the breeze blow it off the table so she would have to turn.

He was gone.

Then she spotted his dark curly head disappearing down a tiled stairwell leading below the floor that she hadn't noticed until just then.

She drained her drink—she was feeling quite light-headed now—and followed. The marble stairs descended into a dim cavern with an ethereal blue glow. Melissa stopped in the middle of the floor. The water fountain she had been hearing was at the base of the stairs—and across the grotto a glass wall looked out onto the blue water of an enormous aquarium. Groupers the size of large dogs drifted through the underwater reefs; a school of barracudas skimmed past slowly circling seven-foot sharks.

Melissa tore her eyes away and turned, moving after the man. She hurried through cavern after cavern…the place was endless, but deserted—no sign of him. She stopped, looking through the glass at a puffer fish floating blimplike in front of her.

"The art lover," a voice said behind her.

She whirled. And he was there, a dark silhouette in the blue-green light of the grotto.

"I'm sorry," he said, a low, elegant voice. "I hadn't meant to startle you." *On top of everything else, an English accent.* Her mind was racing. Had *he* been following *her?*

"Not at all," she answered. "I thought you were a shark."

He laughed, a warm echo in the cavern. "We keep meeting," he said, although they had not met at all. "The casino, the gallery." He cocked his head, looked at her speculatively. "You seemed especially fond of the Chihulys. Thinking of stealing one?"

Although startled to hear her own suspicion voiced, she had to laugh out loud—any one of the pieces weighed at least a half a ton.

"In a good storm, I might be able to float one out."

"Brilliant. You're a professional, then."

A professional what?

He smiled slightly. "I meant—your interest in the Chihulys, in antiquities. Is art a business interest of yours, or personal?"

"A little of both," she said blithely, surprising herself. She could be as ambiguous as he was being. "And yours?"

"The same," he agreed. "I must say it's a pleasure to see at least someone enjoying the gallery. A shame to see all that beauty go to waste."

She felt herself flush; she was suddenly sure that he was talking about her.

"It's a more subtle pleasure than this." She gestured to the glass walls of the aquarium.

"In a way," he said, with what seemed like a secret amusement. "You haven't even seen the best part." He touched her back—lightly, nothing more than that—guiding her into the next grotto.

As they stepped through the archway, Melissa drew in a breath.

They were entirely underwater now, in a long tunnel made completely of glass, arching over their heads. The tunnel allowed them to walk through the aquarium with sea creatures all around them—beside them, above them, as if they were diving through schools of constantly changing fish: the large colorful tropical ones and the schools of barracudas and the sharks, of course, always the sharks.

She looked up through the glass and saw daylight slanting through the surface of the water, fifteen feet above.

He was watching her, or had never stopped watching her.

Why not? she thought.

A shadow passed over the sun, as above a shark slowly circled.

● ● ●

They had planned to meet in the lobby. On a hunch she went down early and drifted by the gallery. He was there again, in front of that case, as intent on the jeweled shell as ever. And she moved quickly back into the elevator and went up again and down another way, afraid that he had seen her.

He took her to a hotel down the beach, on the other side of the island, overlooking the ocean. Far more rustic and natural than anything at the resort—and more private.

The pompano was creamy, the wine mouthwatering, and the gentle rolling of the waves lulled her, lowering all defenses.

His name was Nick, or so he said, and his business was some

kind of finance, or so he said. But from the beginning, his interest was clearly in art.

He was surprised to learn, or feigned it, that she was a gallery director.

"You *are* a professional, then."

"Professional enough to know the gallery director here might be in for more than he bargained for," she said.

"How do you mean?" He sounded innocently intrigued.

"If I were a thief, I couldn't ask for a more enticing collection—or security system."

He looked at her over his wineglass. "You think the collection is vulnerable."

She shrugged a bare shoulder, and shocked herself with her own daring. "I can see how it might be tempting to someone who was paying attention."

He sipped the wine, his face betraying nothing. "It would be difficult to fence such high-profile pieces."

"The pieces, yes. But not if the thief were planning to take a particular piece apart and sell the individual gems."

He looked startled. "That would be a shame, wouldn't you think?" He asked gravely. "A treasure like that."

Suddenly she felt they were talking about something other than the jewels. She met his gaze. "I would think that, yes. I wouldn't say the same of a thief."

His face tightened. "Not everyone can recognize the exquisite. Not everyone is worthy of it." His voice softened. "Myself, I dislike seeing any sort of treasure in the hands of the wrong people. That's the true crime."

She looked into his eyes, wondering. He smiled enigmatically. "It's a lovely night. Let's walk."

They walked along the shoreline while clouds raced across the moon. The wind was strong, and the waves equally stirred up, swelling and crashing onto the shore in an insistent rhythm. Melissa's dress whipped around her thighs, her hair around her head. And finally he spoke.

"Forgive the cliché, but I can't for the life of me understand..." He paused. "Why a woman like you would be at a place like this alone."

It was not only the wine, but the sea and the wind and that nothing-to-lose recklessness that made her say it.

"Honestly—all those things a person would normally ask? It's pointless. All that is over for me now."

He immediately, tactfully backed off. "So you're starting over," he said lightly, and the way he said it made it sound like an adventure, not an end. "You've come to the right place. The islands have always been a place for reinvention. Their pirate history, you know."

"I don't, actually, not much." It was her first trip to the Bahamas.

"It's the location. Seven hundred islands and cays, with all those complex shoals and channels...right off well-traveled shipping lanes like the Windward Passage. It was easy for pirate ships to lie in wait for cargo ships to plunder, and to hide once the plundering had been done."

They had reached a sea break of piled boulders, no way around but to climb. He mounted the rocks barefoot, clambering up with swift, sure steps, then anchored himself and reached down to her. His hand enclosed hers, warm and strong, and he lifted her as if she weighed nothing, releasing her just a beat slowly as she tested her footing, and he spoke again as they continued over the rocks.

"The islands became a hideout for blockade-runners during the Civil War, and rumrunners during Prohibition."

Funny how danger can sound enticing...especially with a British accent.

"That's quite a criminal history," she said aloud. *Emphasis on "criminal."*

He smiled. "And that history translated to modern banking practices, too. Hidden treasure turned into offshore bank accounts. You can live on a boat, always keep moving—no one asks too many questions. It's easy to disappear, here."

He glanced at her and she felt a frisson of unease. It was late, and there were few people on the beach; the shore on this side of the island was rocky and rough and she suddenly felt very alone. It would take only a second for her to "slip," to hit her head on a rock. No one knew where she had gone and who with.

Yes…so very easy to disappear.

But something made her press on. "So you're advocating the life."

He stopped and looked at her in the moonlight. "Am I?"

"Aren't you?" He was silent, and she glanced out over the ocean, felt it rumbling over the jagged rocks below. "Do you really believe people can start over?"

A cloud passed over the moon and she couldn't see his face. "I believe they must. A life is a terrible thing to waste."

Her entire body was wired and numb; she realized she could die, but there was a sort of peace in it.

As she took a faltering step back, her foot slid, slipping…

He caught her…and kissed her.

At the hotel they moved into the elevator together and she pressed the button for her floor, and felt her stomach sink as the elevator rose, a sensation not unlike flying.

At the door her hands were shaking so badly she could barely hold the key card. He took the card from her gently and opened the door.

Inside he was not so gentle.

She welcomed the violent sweetness of his arms and mouth, the hot and tender force of his body crushing all that was left of her former self from her.

After, she lay inside his thighs, against the warm curve of his stomach. The balcony doors were open and the breeze billowed the curtains and she listened to his breath and the rolling sound of the ocean.

I'm past the point of no return. Whatever happens, at least I will have lived these few days.

And she drifted on the sound of the waves into an uneasy sleep.

● ● ●

She dreamed of being underwater, in underwater halls, so far underwater she began to drown, and she panicked, fighting…and then with her last gasp she realized she could breathe after all.

The halls around her looked vaguely like the hotel halls but as blue-green as the ocean. She moved through cool water as silent as space, past an occasional grouper or shark, but the beasts paid no attention to her. Then at the end of the hall she saw a tall, dark, familiar figure. She knew where he was going and what he was going to do. *It's perfect,* she thought; *he's flooded the hotel with water so he can slip in and out of the gallery and simply float away with the jeweled shell.*

She hurried after him, as much as one could hurry in water, and if there was any need for hurry anyway, which she thought maybe there wasn't.

Far ahead he turned into the gallery and she surged forward and was there—and she saw the case, the gems of the shell sparkling through the water.

The gallery was empty; the guard had been washed away. Nick moved elegantly through the water toward the case and pushed lightly at the glass and it tipped slowly back on the stand, just as easily as opening a book.

The shell floated out into the water, sparkling like fire, and he caught it gently in his outstretched hand.

• • •

She jolted awake to alarms—and PA announcements of an immediate evacuation of the hotel.

She grabbed for her robe and ran out through the door…to find flooded halls. She darted forward under showers of tepid water from the emergency sprinkler system, heading for the stairs. She rounded a corner—and ran into a tall form.

Nick. As soaked to the skin as she was.

She jolted back, unnerved, but he took her arms to steady her, speaking urgently and precisely through the pulsing alarms. "I woke and you were gone—I stepped out to find you and was locked out of the room, and then the alarms began…."

Splashing, running footsteps were coming their way. Two security guards appeared down the hall.

"Hold it there!" One of them shouted ahead.

"We're guests of the hotel," Nick said quickly and his eyes signaled Melissa in a way she couldn't interpret.

The guards strode forward. "Room keys, please," the taller one ordered.

Melissa fumbled her key out of her robe pocket. "Ms. Ballard," the guard said, reading the card with a scanner. "Sir?" He turned to Nick.

"We're traveling together," Melissa said. The lie was so smooth she had not realized she was going to say it until the words were out of her mouth.

The guards looked them over. "Have you been in your room all night?" The tall one demanded.

"Until the alarms started," she said calmly.

"Both of you?"

"Of course," she said. "What's happening?"

"There's been a robbery," the guard said.

There was a long moment. No one moved.

"May we return to our room?" she asked finally. "The alarms have stopped, and we'd like to get back to bed."

The guards looked at each other. "Yes, thank you, ma'am."

The guards moved down the hallway, and Nick looked once, silently, into her eyes. Then they walked down the wet hall in silence.

He used her key, and closed the door behind them.

● ● ●

When she woke, in the big creamy bed, to the sound of the ocean, she was alone.

Alone...

She stood slowly, blinking against the sun. She pulled on her robe and stepped to the open doors...

...to look straight out onto open and endless water. The cruise ship cut its wake far below her; the ocean wind teased her bare skin, lifted her hair.

As Nick slept, she'd risen, silent and invisible as a ghost; had taken the ferry over to the Wharf and boarded the ship at dawn. She was miles away from Nassau by now.

And Nick...

Well, she'd never forget their night.

She breathed in salt air, then moved back to the bed and reached under the blankets for the golden shell, held it up in both palms to watch the jewels catch fire in the sunlight.

Some treasures were meant to be free.

BREAK EVEN
PAMELA CALLOW

*When he crows "Eddie Bent is back!" it seemed
the tide had finally turned for our downtrodden hero.
Not so fast, Mr. Bent. —SB*

Tuesday, 4:58 p.m.

"Elaine, it's me." Eddie Bent cradled the phone to his ear, stubbing his cigarette in the plastic lid from his morning coffee. Ash pebbled the newspaper printouts strewn on his desk. It didn't matter that his wife couldn't actually *see* him smoking while they conversed over the phone, she would just *know*. That's what being married for fifteen years did to you.

"Hi, honey," she said. "I'm on my way home. What's up?" Two years ago, she wouldn't have asked that question—she would have known that if he called at supper time, it meant he'd been held up on another case. At that time, he was the go-to guy for high-profile clients on the wrong side of the criminal justice system.

Eddie knew the exact moment the tide had turned: when Gregory MacIsaac, Halifax's other top criminal defense lawyer, pulled off a coup in securing the acquittal of a politician charged with the murder of his aide—and his coaccused, represented by Eddie, took the fall. Within six months, his big cases had dried up. Eddie found himself ready to leave work by 5:00 p.m.

He didn't like it.

So he headed to the bars. Just a couple of drinks, he'd tell himself, and then he'd go home. He didn't think it was affecting his work, but every time another high-profile case hit the news, MacIsaac had gotten the call. Leaving him with the little shitty ones.

Eight months ago, Elaine put her foot down. Counseling had ensued. Eddie promised to drink less, come home earlier.

It seemed to have finally paid off. MacIsaac could eat his dust— Eddie had landed the Brown case. "I've got a new client coming in, Elaine. I'm going to be late."

There was a slight hesitation.

"It's Molly Brown, Elaine. You know, the girl who has been in the news all week."

"Ohhh…" He heard the relief in her voice. "I'll keep some dinner for you. But come home right afterward. You told Brianna you'd help with her social studies project."

Shit. He'd totally forgotten.

"I'm not sure I'll be home in time."

"Eddie, you promised."

"Elaine, this is a big case. There's a lot of media around this." He fought to keep the excitement from his voice. But the truth was he couldn't wait to sink his teeth into it. The publicity would be huge. Eddie Bent was back. "It'll be good for the firm."

"Please don't tell me you are choosing your firm over your daughter."

"God, Elaine, don't twist the knife." He *needed* this case. "That trip down south we're taking will cost us an arm and a leg. This case could generate a lot of billables."

She exhaled. Heavily. "Fine. But just so you know, they're forecasting another storm tonight. Make sure you get home before the snow starts."

"Another storm? We just had one last week."

"It's February. Remember? That's why we want to go south." He could hear the wry smile in her voice. Anyone in Halifax knew that February was a month to be avoided. Ice, snow, rain, wind. Never ended. "But try not to be too late."

He smiled to himself. "Drive safely. Love you."

"Love you, too." That was said with a pleasing sincerity. He was glad he'd made an effort on Valentine's Day.

He was still smiling when his assistant knocked on his door. "Miss Brown is here." She ushered in a young woman wearing a thin navy blue pea jacket with a backpack hiked on one shoulder.

He stepped around his desk and held out his hand. "Molly, I'm Eddie Bent."

She gave him a hesitant smile and clasped his hand. Her fingers were freezing. "Hi."

"Please, sit down." He sat behind his desk, studying her as she slipped off her coat and settled into the comfy armchair facing him. She had one of those faces that seemed familiar—a "look," as his mother used to say. Pretty. Soft. Attractive. With her honey-brown hair smoothed off a pleasingly high brow, she would attract second glances. He decided that if she had to appear before a jury, she should wear her hair just like that. He skimmed her clothes. The outfit worked, too. Cropped cardigan in a delicate plum color, modest crew neck T-shirt underneath, dark pants. His daughter— whom he realized might resemble this girl in six years or so— always made of fun of him for knowing "girls'" fashion when he had such poor style himself. But knowing what made his clients look good—trustworthy, credible, *innocent*—was his job. "Coffee, tea, a cold drink?"

"I'm fine, thank you." She folded her hands across her knees. Unlike most girls her age, she wore no nail polish. Her nails were neatly trimmed, her only adornment a Celtic ring on her right hand.

"So, Molly, tell me why you need my help. I've read about your case in the paper, but as far as I'm aware, you haven't been charged with anything, right?"

She nodded. "But the police keep calling me. They told me yesterday they wanted me to come for questioning. Again. I've told them everything I know, but they won't leave me alone." Tears pricked her eyes. "Why do they keep bugging me? I'm the *victim*. Not him."

Why indeed? She had been raped, and killed her attacker.

The police must have found evidence to suggest that Dr. Nicholson's death could not be justified as self-defense. Interesting.

"I know what the newspapers say," Eddie tapped the open file folder piled with media printouts. "But I want you to tell me, in your own words, what happened, Molly."

She looked away, a flush radiating across her face. It provided a garish contrast to her blackened right eye. He glanced at the date of birth scrawled on the inside of his file folder. She was eighteen years old. A woman. And yet, the soft wisp of hair curling around her earlobe struck him as poignantly childlike.

Molly cleared her throat. "It happened last Monday. I went to my forensic biology class, like usual. It's an elective. I'm premed," she added. "Dr. Nicholson is—was—" she flushed a bit darker but held on to her composure "—one of the lecturers. He was teaching that night." She glanced at Eddie. He bet she was expecting him to write this down. He knew that if he did, she would become conscious of her words, of how she told the story. So instead, he played with a pen, giving the appearance of relaxed curiosity.

"After the class ended, I left. But I realized I'd forgotten my textbook. So I went back. The classroom is upstairs in the library, in the very far end."

And it was there that you stabbed the good doctor to death.
Were you really carrying a knife like the press says, Molly Brown?

She took a deep breath. "When I walked into the classroom, it was dark. He must have put two and two together and heard me come back, because when I got there, he was standing behind the door. I reached over to flip on the switch...." Her voice was low, husky now. Tears. "I felt an arm hook me around the neck.... He yanked me back and stuffed a sock in my mouth. He kicked the door shut. He called me names. Said I was a slut, said that I was asking for it—" She looked away, shame imprinted on those even features. "Then he punched me in the face. He told me to roll onto my stomach—" Her voice choked off. She tried a weak smile. Apologetic. It made Eddie wince. Rape victims always got under his skin. The shame, the guilt, the burden they carried that they somehow provoked the violence that was perpetrated on them. "It's not like I'm a virgin," she whispered. "But he wanted—" She swallowed.

He wanted to sodomize her.

"He yanked my arm. He flipped me over and twisted my arm behind my back. He kept saying, 'I know exactly how far a joint can handle this pressure before it breaks.'"

Eddie's eyes skimmed her arms, but they were covered with her cardigan.

She had begun shivering now. "I fought him, but I couldn't stop him." She hugged her arms. "I couldn't stop him." She didn't seem to be aware that she repeated herself. Her eyes were bleak. Unreadable. *Like a fog bank concealing the depths of the ocean,* Eddie thought. "The next thing I knew, I was covered in blood. And he was dead."

The police acknowledged that sexual intercourse had occurred. Molly had admitted to the press that she had been sodomized. "Molly," Eddie said, his voice gentle. "Are you sure you can't remember what happened after he raped you? It could help your case."

The look she gave him was the despair of someone who knows there is no going back. No going back to the carefree university student who demurely flirted with the guy seated next to her in class, Eddie thought.

"So my choice is to be imprisoned for not remembering—or remembering and having those memories imprisoned in my mind? I don't want to remember killing him." She buried her face in her hands, then blurted, "The police told me I stabbed him four times."

Eddie blinked. The police hadn't disclosed this to the media. Nor had Dr. Nicholson's widow—on police orders, he was sure. Four times. That was, oh, about three times too many for them to claim self-defense.

"He ruined my life," she whispered.

Eddie pushed back his chair, grabbed the tissue box that perched on the edge of his desk, and placed it on the table next to the girl. She ignored it. Her sobs were quiet, despairing.

The rape was traumatic, but Eddie knew the Crown Prosecutor would focus on the numerous stab wounds on Dr. Nicholson's body.

He sat down next to her. "Molly."

She continued to weep.

"Molly." He held out a tissue to her.

She ignored it.

"Molly, please listen to me."

She sniffled but—thank God—had stopped that pitiful weeping.

"I'm sorry, Mr. Bent." She straightened, took the proffered tissue, wiped her eyes. "I won't do that again."

"It's okay to cry, Molly. And please, call me Eddie." He needed her to trust him, feel she could confide in him. "Mr. Bent" created too much distance.

"I don't usually cry…Eddie." Something in the tilt of her chin made Eddie believe her. "But I don't know…you just make me feel safe…and I have no one else right now."

"Why were you carrying a knife, Molly?"

He deliberately phrased it that way. He didn't know for sure—but the information that the police had "leaked" to the press clearly implied that Dr. Nicholson's death had been premeditated.

Her eyes met his. Again, the deep blue pulled him in, tried to make him understand. "I always carry a knife with me. A lot of my classes are on campus at night." Her lips twisted. "I thought it was dangerous to walk around the university at night. You know, the rapes and assaults and stuff. I never thought I'd get attacked by my professor. In a classroom."

"How long have you been in the habit of carrying a knife for protection?"

She shrugged. "I'm not sure…since classes started, I guess. And when that girl got raped on campus a couple of months ago, I got nervous."

"Did your family and friends know you carried a knife?"

She shrugged again. "My family doesn't live in Halifax." There was the slightest hint of testiness in her voice. "And I'm not sure if I showed it to my friends or not. It's not like I was proud of it, or anything. It was there, just in case I needed it. You know, like a tampon."

Eddie fought a grin. The jury would love that. He could just imagine Miss Molly Brown saying to the judge: "Yes, I carry a knife with my tampons. Every girl should, Your Lordship."

"So it was your habit to carry a knife with you?"

She shot him an irritated look. "I just told you that."

Eddie exhaled. "Molly, don't get your back up. Trust me, the police and the Crown Prosecutor will spend a very long time questioning you about this point."

"Why? Aren't I allowed to carry something to defend myself?"

"Yes. But in this case, the issue is that you defended yourself beyond what is considered reasonable in the circumstances."

Her cheeks flamed bright pink. "Reasonable! The guy raped me, Eddie. He *raped* me. He was going to break my arm."

"But did he ever say he was going to kill you?" Eddie's voice was quiet, but it sliced through the air.

"Yes. He did. Over and over. While he was raping me." Was there a flicker of Molly's eyelid? Eddie wasn't sure.

"So after he finished, what happened?"

"I don't know!" She clenched the tissue in her fist. "Why am I being blamed for this? He's the one who attacked me!"

"Dr. Nicholson's widow told the press that her husband had been stabbed from behind. That he was found fully clothed by the door. They think you attacked him after the danger to you had passed. An act of rage, rather than self-defense."

She shrank before his eyes. "Really?" She twisted the tissue. "They think I just…murdered him? Oh, my God…I would never kill anyone on purpose. Ever. I was the girl who rescued spiders from inside the house."

And carried a knife with your tampon.

"Eddie, please, believe me. I must have been out of my head." She paused. Took a deep hiccuping breath. "Are they sure? Isn't there some other explanation?"

The irony of the situation was not lost on Eddie. He wondered if Molly knew about Dr. Nicholson's professional history. In fact, Eddie had been surprised that the university had kept Dr. Nicholson on as a lecturer after being found guilty by a provincial inquiry of botching numerous forensic pediatric autopsies. Those incompetent autopsies had been the sole reason eight different parents were accused and convicted of infanticide. The cases had spanned decades.

Eddie had, in fact, represented one of those parents on a charge of infanticide. He had been convinced Laura Norris was innocent, but the autopsy findings by Dr. Nicholson had been adamant that the child had died by the mother's hand. Eddie had always thought Dr. Nicholson was too arrogant, too keen to accuse the parents of wrongdoing in the face of unsubstantiated facts. Considered one of the foremost experts in pediatric forensic pathology, no defense lawyer at the time could find anyone to contradict his findings.

Ten years later, there had been too many questionable cases that had turned on his evidence. His findings were challenged, cases were reopened, an inquiry was formed. Dr. Nicholson's medical license was revoked. The pathologist had never faced any criminal charges. Perhaps that was why the university hadn't fired him. Small comfort for the eight parents who had been convicted based on his findings. Several had already served their sentences; the remainder had been released from prison. Most were trying to pick up the pieces of their lives, but a few had run into trouble with the law. He had been sad to learn that his former client had overdosed on drugs.

And now, this young woman was asking him whether the autopsy results for Dr. Nicholson could be wrong.

Good question, Molly.

"That's our job, Molly. To give them another explanation. So they don't lay charges. And if they do, to establish that your actions were reasonable self-defense." A snowflake eddied outside the window. "I'll be straight with you, Molly. If you are charged with murder, we'll have to show that you had a blackout. It's not always an easy thing to get a judge or jury to believe."

Her eyes met his. "But you believe me, don't you?"

"Until you tell me you did it, I believe you are innocent." He handed her his business card. "The best thing for your case is if you remember what happened. You can reach me day or night." He gave her an encouraging smile. "When the police call you again, tell them you are not going to talk to them. When they put pressure on you—and they will—tell them to phone me." He saw doubt flicker in her eyes. "They don't have a right to question you until you are a suspect. And if you are a suspect, you need me present. One way or the other, you won't be alone, Molly."

He glanced at his calendar. "Let's meet next Tuesday at 2:00 p.m. and touch base, unless the police have something they want to share sooner."

"Thank you, Eddie." Molly's eyes shone with gratitude.

His heart twisted. Brianna gave him the exact same look when he did something special for her. He needed to get home.

3:01 a.m.

The phone rang. Eddie was still yanking himself from the deepest undertow of sleep, when his wife murmured, "Hello?"

He heard a woman's voice through the receiver. Elaine's voice lost its grogginess as she thrust the phone at his face. "Eddie! It's a client." This was delivered with her usual mixture of resignation and irritation.

Eddie threw back the covers, his feet seeking his slippers as he muttered, "Eddie Bent here."

"Eddie? It's Molly." Her voice was teary, ragged. Breathless.

He hurried down the stairs toward his study, wishing he hadn't drunk that bottle of wine he'd bought to "celebrate." Or capped it off with a couple of scotches. His head throbbed. His mouth tasted foul. "What is it, Molly?" He glanced at the grandfather clock standing in the corner of the landing—3:03 a.m. Jesus. She better not make a habit of this.

"I'm here, Eddie," she whispered.

Her words stopped him in his tracks. "Where?"

"At your back door."

"Jesus. Molly, you can't come to my home."

"Please, Eddie…" Her voice cracked. "I don't have anyone else. Please let me in. I'm freezing."

He headed through the kitchen to the back door and peered through the windowpane. He blinked. "Fuck." In the space of three hours, a foot of snow had fallen. That was why the night sounded so quiet. Until the roads were clear, no one would be out driving.

Molly stood, huddled against the blowing snow, the collar of her wool peacoat pulled up to her ears. Wet snow clung to her eyelashes, her brows. The bitter February wind whipped her hair into wet strands. She didn't try to shield her face from the onslaught dealt by Mother Nature. The wool-gloved hand clutching the cell phone to her ear was probably numb by now, Eddie guessed.

Her eyes met his through the snow-streaked glass. "I have nowhere to go, Eddie."

"I can't let you in, Molly." He spoke firmly into the phone, his face set, but his heart turned once.

"Please."

"No. I'm sorry. You must leave now."

A gust of wind buffeted her slight frame. He heard her, over the phone connection, suck in her breath. But she didn't flinch.

She gave him one last look. He thought of his twelve-year-old daughter, asleep in her warm, safe bedroom. Where were this girl's parents? Why was she standing on his doorstep on this godforsaken February night with no place to call home?

He pressed the phone closer to his cheek. "Why aren't you at the dorm, Molly?"

"I can't stay there. My roommate says she's terrified of me and they asked me to leave."

"What about your parents?"

"They live in British Columbia. The police told me I can't go home right now."

He pulled his thick fleece robe more tightly around him with one hand, the other hand gripping the phone until his fingers turned numb. "I'm sorry."

Somehow, through the blur of snow, her eyes seemed to be able to see straight into his booze-addled soul. She gave a little nod. "I'll see you next Tuesday." Snow rimmed her lashes in white, coated her soggy hair. "Sorry for waking you." Then she disconnected the phone. She shoved her hands in her pockets and hurried off the porch, her footprints almost immediately covered by blowing snow.

She had reached the side of the house when he caught up with her. "Just for tonight," he said. Elaine would be furious with him, but he'd explain. He couldn't just leave her out in a blizzard.

"How did you know where I lived?" he asked, once they were inside the kitchen.

"I just did reverse lookup of the phone number you gave me."

Shit. His number must be unblocked. Probably had been unblocked since they switched carriers a month ago. New Year's budget cutting and all that. He made a mental note to call the phone company first thing in the morning. "How did you get here?"

"I walked." She bunched her stringy hair over her shoulder, shivering. "Do you have a towel? I'm soaked."

"Wait here."

He ran upstairs to the linen closet, his breathing labored by the time he reached the upstairs landing.

"Eddie?" Elaine stood in the doorway, tying her bathrobe. "What in hell's name is going on?"

He heard the scotch bottle call his name. Shit. Elaine was going to blow a gasket when she heard this.

"Remember that rape victim I told you about when I got home?" he asked, his voice low. He didn't want to wake up his daughter.

"That was her on the phone?"

Eddie nodded. "She's in the kitchen."

"What?" Elaine stared at him. *He knew what she was thinking: you are so desperate that you now give our address to your clients?*

"She found our address on the internet. Bloody phone company. They screwed up blocking our phone number."

Elaine exhaled. "What's she doing down there?"

"She has nowhere to go."

"Oh, for God's sake, Eddie, are you kidding me?"

"Her dorm kicked her out, her parents are in B.C."

"Just give her money to go to a hotel. I've got some cash in my purse."

"Have you looked outside?"

Elaine's gaze darted toward the window. But the blinds had been lowered hours before.

"It's a blizzard out there." Eddie waited.

She sighed. "Jesus, Eddie. You are such a bleeding heart. How the hell did you end up being a defense lawyer?" She brushed by him. "Where is this girl?"

"She's down in the kitchen."

"I'll take care of her."

And he knew she would. That was why he married Elaine: she could protest as much as she liked about not being a pushover, but she had the biggest heart around. He knew that one look at the shivering, frozen girl in their kitchen, and Elaine would have her tucked into bed with a mug of hot chocolate in no time.

He followed his wife downstairs. "Molly, meet my wife, Elaine."

Molly stood where he'd left her in the kitchen—dripping on the doormat. She gave Elaine a tentative smile. "I'm so sorry, Mrs. Bent, to intrude. It's just—" she swallowed "—I had nowhere else to go." Her eyes filled with tears. She wiped them with the back of her hand, furiously, and raised her chin. "I promise it's just for tonight. I'll call my parents tomorrow. See if they can send me some money."

Eddie thought of the three-thousand-dollar check he'd cashed after they met today. *Barbados, here we come,* he'd thought. It must have been her entire savings.

Elaine glanced at the kitchen clock. 3:23 a.m. "Let's try to get some sleep, shall we?" She put her arm around Molly. "Come into the family room. The sofa is pretty comfortable there. I'll get you a pair of jammies and some bedding."

"Thank you," Molly whispered. Her earlier bravado had gone, leaving a glazed exhaustion in her eyes. Eddie handed her the towel. "Dry yourself off. I'll let Elaine bring you the stuff." *Give you some privacy.* "Good night."

He headed upstairs. With each step, his bulk complained. He felt like hell. Just two scotches tomorrow night, he promised himself. Maybe three. *But you are not replacing that bottle of wine. You're too old to handle all that booze on a work night, Bent.*

His bed, with its crumpled covers, looked incredibly inviting. He settled into its warmth. Elaine was still downstairs. He wanted to wait up for her, to thank her for putting up with him and his crazy clients once again.

The quietness soothed him. Sleep pulled at him.

And then he jolted awake. Why was it so quiet?

He should hear the stairs creaking as Elaine came back to bed.

He should hear the whisper of her robe as she slipped it off her body and slid under the covers next to him.

He should hear—

Something.

Christ, how long had Elaine been down there with Molly?

He leaped out of bed and rushed to the hallway, smashing his hip against the door frame as he lunged through it.

She's chatting with Molly.

She fell asleep.

Molly asked her not to leave.

All the calm, rational arguments sped in—and out—of his mind. They were chased away by fear. By instinct.

By the knowledge that he'd missed something today.

Something had gnawed at him.

He took the stairs so quickly, his feet barely skimmed them.

He heard a scream. It was his wife, although he'd never heard her make a sound like that before, not even when she was delivering Brianna.

"Elaine!" he yelled, barging into the family room.

He heard Elaine before he saw her: fast, gulping breaths of pure fear.

"Don't move any closer, Eddie," Molly said. She crouched over Elaine, her knees pinning his wife's arms to the ground. At first glance, Eddie thought that Elaine hadn't moved because she was wedged between the sofa and the large steel-and-glass coffee table that anchored the rug.

But then something glinted.

It was a large carving knife. Molly held it against the arch of his wife's neck.

He knew that knife. It was the one they used for Sunday dinner, the one he flourished with great effect on Thanksgiving.

Elaine's eyes met his.

What have you done, Eddie?

He willed his voice to sound calm and steady, not desperate and terrified. "Molly, don't do this. I can help you."

She snorted. "I don't think so." She pushed the tip of the knife against Elaine's throat. Elaine exhaled, trying to shrink from the blade.

Think, Eddie, think. You can talk her out of this. "Molly, you don't want to do this. Don't throw your life away." *Or Elaine's,* he begged silently. "We can solve this together. There are people who will help you."

She raised a brow. "Oh, really?" She traced the knife blade in a small circle on Elaine's throat. Her eyes met Eddie's. So blue, a raging blue. How could he have missed that? "What people will help me? People like you? A defense lawyer who can't even muster a defense against a forensic pathologist who can't tell an asshole from a prick?"

He stared at her.

"You still don't know who I am. Do you, Eddie?" Her lips twisted. Elaine threw a stunned look at him. *You know her?* "Wait, don't answer that question. I know the answer. You didn't give a fuck about me. Or my mother. All you wanted was your money and your ego stroked. When you lost the case, you just abandoned us."

Those eyes, that honey-brown hair...

"You are Laura's daughter, aren't you?" he whispered.

"Took you long enough," Molly said.

Eddie stepped forward. Molly raised her arm, ready to plunge the knife. Her eyes locked with Elaine's.

"Molly!" He needed to break her focus. "I never believed your mother killed your little brother. But Dr. Nicholson was the expert. No one could beat him."

"But someone did. Someone fought it. How else did he get caught?"

Her words slammed him in the heart. "But it was years later..."

"Years that my mother sat in prison, being called a 'baby killer,' and getting beat up by other inmates. She couldn't take it anymore...." Molly's fingers clenched the knife handle so hard they were white. "She started using drugs. Did you know that? She became an addict. And then she overdosed."

"I'm very sorry, Molly." He took a cautious step closer.

"Yeah, I'll bet you are. You put up a shitty defense of my mother, and who pays the price? Not you. Oh, no, you've got this nice house—" she waved the knife around "—with this nice wife and a nice daughter upstairs."

Elaine threw Eddie a panicked look. *Keep her away from Brianna!*

"What did I have, Eddie? I had a mom everyone teased me about. Child Protection took me away. I lost my mother, my little brother and my home. I ended up living in foster care for the past ten years. And did anyone give a shit? No. I lived for the day that my mom would come home. But she overdosed instead." Her voice caught. "Before I could help her. I never had a chance, Eddie. Not one fucking chance."

Elaine eyes locked with his. *Now, Eddie. Do it.*

He stepped closer, as lightly as he could with his bulk, holding his breath.

The knife moved so quickly, he wasn't sure if his fear had conjured it.

Elaine gurgled. Blood welled from her throat.

With a roar, he vaulted around the coffee table. Molly jumped onto the sofa and brandished the knife at him. "You didn't think I'd do it, did you?" He felt the cold steel of the coffee table frame digging into the back of his knees. He lunged forward, grabbing his client's wrist before she could plunge the knife in his chest.

"Molly, drop the knife."

She gazed down at him. Her eyes were bright. Victorious. "So glad you *believed* in my innocence, Mr. Bent. Just like you *believed* my mother. But I made Dr. Nicholson pay. The bastard wasn't even going to jail! So I tricked him. I let him do his perverted little act on me. And then I killed him." She smiled, but it twisted itself into a snarl. How had he ever thought that Brianna could grow up to be like her? "Why should you be able to have a family when you cost me mine?"

"Just drop the knife, Molly. You don't want to do this."

"Don't tell me what I want. I'm not a fucking child anymore!" She yanked her arm upward, trying to break his grip. He leaped onto the sofa and twisted her wrist.

She went limp.

He staggered sideways, off balance. Just as she intended.

She tore her wrist from his hand with a triumphant glare, raising the knife.

He dived at her, angling his body to prevent her from falling on top of Elaine. Air whooshed past his ears as they went flying off the sofa. He felt Molly's body absorb the impact of their fall onto the glass-topped coffee table, his body skidding over hers as he tumbled, headfirst, toward the ground.

His skull exploded when he hit the rug. For a second, light filled his brain. *Get the knife, Eddie. Get the fucking knife!*

He rolled off Molly.

Her head swayed with his movement.

Cold sweat pricked his skin.

Molly lay on her back, mouth open, her head extended at an unnatural angle over the steel edge of the coffee table.

Jesus. He'd broken her neck when he fell on top of her.

He scrambled to his feet and rushed over to Elaine. Blood seeped steadily from the slash in her throat. Eddie grabbed one of the forgotten bedsheets and pressed it against Elaine's neck.

"Hold on, sweetheart. Please." He ran to the phone on the other side of the room and dialed 911.

The ambulance made it in fourteen minutes. Eddie's hands were white from keeping pressure on Elaine's throat, his throat hoarse from whispering pleas for her to hold on. "She's a fighter," one of the Emergency Response Technicians told him as they rushed her to the hospital.

And fight she did. Several transfusions later, Elaine had stabilized.

But despite the endless bottles of vodka, scotch and wine Eddie imbibed, he never did.

DIRTY LOW DOWN

A Jackie Mercer Story

DEBRA WEBB

Some girls know how to have fun…
Jackie Mercer is one of them. —SB

Temporary Command Center, Houston, July 8, 9:30 p.m.

"This is a bad idea, Jackie."

"You think?" Seriously. Some jerk-off tortures and murders five women in the space of as many months? Yeah, that really was a bad idea. Helping out with the official sting to take him down? A flippin' stellar idea. My partner should just get over it.

"Look." Dawson cast a wary glance at the cops on the other side of the room before huddling close to me. "These guys can't guarantee your protection. This whole operation hinges on dangling *you* as bait. I don't like it."

Dawson was worried. If not for the circumstances, I might have smiled. He really could be sweet at just that moment when a woman needed it most. Like now. Problem was, I had to do this. Yeah, it was risky. But this bastard hadn't left a single piece of evidence. Not a speck of DNA or a solitary hair. He washed the bodies and meticulously cleaned the scene. The cops were convinced the suspect on tonight's agenda was the guy, but they had not one lick of evidence. None. Nada. The only way to nail this guy was to catch him in the act.

I was the one person involved with this operation who had the right connections to do just that. More importantly, as a P.I., I wasn't corralled by those sticky cop rules of engagement. There wasn't a cop on the force, man or woman, who could do what I was about to do—not that anyone on the force would admit as much. The key noncop players involved trusted me, Jackie Mercer. I both understood and fit into Houston's gritty streets where those ladies operated night after night. I could play the part of *Happy Hooker* with the best of them.

The idea gave me pause. Exactly what did that say about me?

Okay…maybe that wasn't the precise analogy I was looking for. Basically, I meant that I'm a woman. I've been down and out, and bottom line, I wasn't letting this son of a bitch get away with what he'd done. My partner and I had been over this twice already.

"You ready, Mercer?"

That voice. I cringed. Like nails scraping across a blackboard—yeah, they still had those when I was in school. Twisting on the heel of my thigh-high hooker boots, I faced the bane of my existence. "I was born that way, Nance."

Detective Walter Nance, his off-the-rack suit wrinkled from the long day, his tie still cinched like a noose around his neck because he was too uptight to dare loosen it, marched over to where my partner and I waited patiently for the rest of this crew to get into gear.

"You sound check your com link?" He stared at my breasts as if he expected one or the other to answer.

Duh. I tapped my left tit. "You betcha." I stared at his crotch. "You check yours?" Considering he thought with his dick more often than not, made sense his communications link would be somewhere down there.

He ignored my barb. "You're not carrying a piece are you?" His gaze slid down my bared midriff, paused on the black micromini before visually measuring the length of my religiously toned legs. Those nondescript beady eyes of his popped back up to tangle with mine and promptly narrowed with suspicion. "You better not be. You're a civilian, Mercer. We can't have you going all Rambo on us out there."

I bellied up to the good old boy just close enough to make him sweat and held my arms up surrender style. "You wanna frisk me, Nance?" I cocked my head, a Marilyn Monroe lock of blond wig hair falling across my cheek. "I got nothing to hide."

Every cop in the place sniggered behind Nance's back.

Fury burned a red path up his thick neck and spread across his face. His nostrils flared. "Good. Let's do this thing. We've wasted enough time."

That's what I thought. Nance liked to rag my ass but he didn't have the cojones to follow through. At least not to my face. He'd been known to do some pretty sneaky crap behind my back. Just another reason I strong-armed my way into this operation. Nance was a decent cop on most days, but when it came to women I just didn't trust his motives. I intended to make sure this one got done.

Powerful fingers wrapped around my arm and tugged me around. "Jackie." My partner's glare proclaimed that he was far from finished with our previous conversation before he said a word. "You gotta listen to me."

I sighed in spite of myself. Over the past year I'd gotten used to that sexy voice of Dawson's. I'd even learned to prevent my jaw from sagging so that my tongue didn't loll out the side of my mouth when looking directly at that Hollywood handsome face. But, with Dawson there was always a *but,* the touching still carried an effect I couldn't quite brace for. I melted a little every damned time. Hey, I was only human. Derrick Dawson was sweet, sincere and protective. That said, his knee-weakening physical assets weren't the reason I'd hired him, albeit reluctantly. In fact, in the beginning, I'd only hired him so that I could annoy him with enough crap assignments to get rid of him. The man had refused to give up. He still had a job at my agency a year later because he possessed fierce investigative instincts. I'd had no choice but to admit just how good he was at solving the most puzzling cases.

The benefits of making the right business decision far outweighed my personal discomfort with having him around. The occasional touch in passing, completely innocent occasions, mind you, wasn't what kept me slightly off balance in Dawson's presence. It was the total package. He was cute as hell and had that sexy-ass voice, punctuated with those dreamy blue bedroom eyes and that thick, perpetually tousled dirty blond hair. Not to mention a body that would make any woman alive stand at attention.

He was my cross to bear.

First day on the job I'd laid down the law. Our relationship would be totally professional. He was fifteen or so years my junior—I didn't know for sure since he refused to give me his full date of birth—and he was a man. Not that I didn't love the hell out of men, but I know my history. Good-looking men are like kryptonite to me. End of story.

"Get with the program, Dawson," I warned. "This isn't the first time I've done this. Stop treating me like a greenhorn."

Did I fail to mention he was stubborn?

His fingers tightened, sending little blasts of heat over my skin in a tantalizing hailstorm. "I don't want you out there unarmed."

There went another chorus, sacred chord included. I rallied my defenses and rolled my eyes. "Who said I was?" I pulled free of those long, blunt-tipped fingers and gave him my back. Time to get this done.

"Pretty Boy can ride with me," Nance shouted over his shoulder as he hit the door.

Behind me Dawson muttered, "One of these days I'm gonna kick his ass."

Now that I would pay good money to see.

• • •

An hour later I was still standing on the corner of Montrose and Taft. It was muggy as hell and my feet were killing me. My companions for the evening were complaining that it was slow for a Friday night. Just went to show that the depressed economy even affected the oldest profession. I guess when push came to shove some guys preferred their Starbucks Venti Double Chocolate Chip Frappuccino over a quick blow job.

"Suspect is headed your way, Mercer."

The warning vibrated across the wireless com link and in my ear just as the black Lexus IS convertible rolled up to the curb. Well, well, 'bout time.

"This one's mine," I murmured to the ladies on either side of me. One was a redhead, the other a brunette. Both did a little body wave and cheered me on with *you-go-girl. Ain't no use in us all going home hungry tonight.*

The bastard behind the wheel looked straight at me and smiled. "You like to take a ride, baby?"

Ten plus years as a private detective had prepared me for most any situation. Trailing cheating spouses, locating missing persons, background searches, you name it. But tonight was different. Tonight I had agreed to work with Houston's elite homicide folks to help lure in the suspect in a string of prostitute murders.

Not exactly my usual fare. But, hey, I considered myself a team player. *I scratch your back, you scratch mine.* Mainly, though, tonight was about Kelli Reese, a seventeen-year-old who'd decided high school was getting in the way of making her dreams come true. Kelli, the starry-eyed senior, and I hadn't ever met when her mother hired my agency to find her. Easy as pie I tracked her down within forty-eight hours. Unfortunately her dramatic journey toward independence and celebritydom led to the city morgue. And this good-looking piece of shit in his thousand-dollar Armani suit was her killer. All I had to do was prove it.

I removed my knockoff Versace sunglasses and tucked them atop my blond head. The lush blond wig was part of my cover. He has a penchant for blondes, all five victims had sported golden manes and pretty blue eyes. Colored contacts turned my unremarkable brown eyes to just the right shade of sapphire blue. While it was true that the only seventeen I'd seen lately was on a calendar or as the balance in my checking account, this guy didn't seem to care about age. His victims ranged in age from sixteen to forty.

I strolled over to the car, the six-inch heels of my thigh-high boots making my legs even longer just for him. I leaned down to his eye level, allowing him a nice view of my cleavage. "I ain't cheap, handsome." I surveyed the luxurious car before settling my gaze back on his expectant one. "Can you afford me and this car, too?"

"Get in." He nodded toward the passenger seat. "I can handle whatever you believe you deserve."

Cocky bastard. I opened the door and settled into the buttery-soft leather seat and turned to him. "I'm all yours." He watched as I crossed my legs. The black spandex mini hiked all the way to my crotch. "Like the preview, sugar?" His gaze zeroed in on mine. "I'll make sure you get exactly what you deserve, too."

The Lexus peeled away from the curb. With the push of a button the top went up, then the windows, closing out the rest of the world. I would be lying if I didn't admit the move rattled me just a little. *Focus, Jackie.*

If he stuck to his usual M.O., he would drive to a remote location, demand rough sex, including ropes and other paraphernalia, then he would pound a stake through my heart. After a freaky cleansing ritual, he would leave me with my hands folded prayer-style and secured to the stake protruding from my chest. A real prince. Off the record, Nance and his crew had dubbed him the *Vamp Slayer*. I didn't find their attempt at humor amusing at all. These were women: daughters, sisters, mothers; they deserved respect the same as any other victim.

My job was to draw out the inevitable for as long as possible and to use my wiles to ply incriminating information from this psycho. Ultimately I needed him to pull out the wood—the stake that is. That element of the murders had been kept under wraps for just this moment. We needed to be able to connect him to the murders if we wanted to take him all the way down.

The cops and my partner were listening to every word via the communications link. Backup would be as close behind the Lexus as feasible and would get into position in time to ensure this ass wipe didn't go too far. The tracking device in my sunglasses supposedly guaranteed there would be no hiccups.

That was all well and good but my daddy didn't raise no fool. He used to say, "Jackie, always keep your wits about you. Never trust anyone to take care of you. *You* take care of you." A good Texas girl always listened to her daddy's advice. That's why I tucked *Shorty* into the top of my right boot while no one was looking. Smith & Wesson .38 Special, three-inch barrel and seven ready rounds. A girl's best friend.

Dawson should know me well enough by now to anticipate that I never went anywhere without Shorty.

"What's your name, handsome?" Might as well get this party started.

He glanced at me, his only answer was to punch the accelerator a little harder, pushing the speed limit without the slightest visible fear. Didn't matter. I knew his name. Scott Gant. Software engineer. Loner. No wife. No kids. No family.

He maneuvered the Lexus quickly and expertly through the dark streets, his goal apparently to escape the city limits in record time. The headlines heralding HPD as being stumped by this case had obviously gone to his head. He wasn't even worried enough to watch his mirrors for a tail. Not surprising. I had watched his one interview with the police. More than a dozen men had been questioned about dealings with one or more of the victims. This guy was the only one who had fessed up to having had sex with three. Still, the police hadn't had one damned thing to connect him or anyone else to the murders. Until they discovered the website. Actually, Max Caldwell, Houston's resident computer guru and friend of my son's, had found the naughty little project. The bastard had promised the victims a part in a documentary on prostitution he'd been commissioned to do by a hotshot producer in Hollywood. The website had been his way of looking legit to his prey.

One of the victims had shown the website to a street sister who had refused to come forward at first. Even with the website, the best forensic experts available couldn't connect the site to the killer. Gant was that good at covering his tracks. The idea that he was the only person of interest in the case who possessed the necessary skills wasn't enough. But we all knew. Nance and his crew had opted to watch him rather than attempt to slip him up in an interview. A good move in my opinion. This one wouldn't be tripped up easily.

I might have breathed a little easier at the idea that his reckless driving indicated he fully believed no one was on to him yet, except that I knew this guy was way too smart to make a stupid move out of an overabundance of confidence. He knew what he was doing. He was in the zone. Most likely he was already picturing me dead.

"My friends call me Jenny." I swung my booted foot and smoothed a hand over my bare thigh. "What kind of games do you like to play, handsome?" I leaned against the headrest and smiled at him. "I like games where I get to pretend I'm someone else."

He slowed and made a turn that took us farther away from the city's lights but he said nothing.

Creep. Undeterred, I reached across the console and trailed a finger through his hair. "I could—"

He jerked away from my touch. "No talking."

I withdrew to my side of the car, pretending to sulk. I couldn't help thinking that this ugly emotional distance must have terrified Kelli. Fury ignited in my veins. Had all his victims been treated as if they weren't worthy of conversation before being brutally murdered?

"Look, mister—" he didn't bother looking, just kept driving "—if you changed your mind you can take me back. It's no big deal."

"Don't blow this, Mercer."

I twitched at the sound of Nance's voice in my ear. Cursed myself for the reaction.

"Take off your clothes."

I snapped back to attention. "Now?" Adrenaline followed the path of the fury, effectively nullifying its bravado-inspiring attributes.

"Now." He shot a look my way. "Everything."

"This is weird. Are we going to do this driving down the road?"

"Shut up and do it."

I untied the simple knot between my breasts and peeled off the skimpy top, revealing my lacy red bra. I wasn't worried about him noticing the com link. It was scarcely bigger than a nickel, paper thin and invisible just like the fancy little earpiece that inserted so deeply into my ear I figured it would take an ENT to remove it. I dropped the blouse onto the console and reached for my skirt.

"Throw it out the window."

My gaze collided with his; before I could argue, he growled, "Do it."

"Whatever you say, handsome." The window lowered far enough for me to shove the blouse out, then I raised my bottom from the seat and dragged the skirt over my butt and down my thighs. The lacy red thong left little to the imagination but that was the least of my worries at the moment. Carefully stretching the skirt over the boots was my focus. If he demanded I take off the boots, I was screwed.

The black mini went out the window.

In my earpiece I could hear Dawson arguing with Nance. Good thing the volume was modulated to ensure sound went into my ear only.

"The boots, too."

Oh, hell.

"Dude," I argued. "These boots cost me a whole night's work." Actually I had borrowed them, but Shorty had cost a shitload. "Maybe you should just pull over and let me out. This is getting a little freaky for me."

He reached into his jacket pocket. I resisted the urge to go for Shorty. I had to ride this out…nail this bastard to the—

The pistol was in my face before I finished the thought.

Awesome.

"Take off the boots."

My hands went up in mock panic. "Please don't shoot me." I had no idea if this guy could hit the broad side of a barn at point-blank range but I also had no desire to find out. More debating over the com link. Dawson was pissed and ranting at Nance to end this now.

"Take off the boots, you stupid bitch," the driver roared.

Hands shaking for his benefit, I started with the left. How the hell would I get the right one off without him spotting Shorty? The left boot went out the window. I held the part of the right boot where

the weapon snugged against my leg with one hand, hoping to keep
it from plopping out, as I dragged the boot off with the other hand.

Didn't work.

Shorty hit the carpet.

"What the hell is that?"

The car swerved dangerously. My heart skipped a beat or two.
Reluctantly, I reached down and picked up the gun, holding it
by the butt with my thumb and forefinger so as not to set off the
wrong chain reaction. He snatched it out of my hand and tossed it
to the floor on his side of the car. More swerving ensued. Damn,
I should have buckled up.

The muzzle of his pistol stabbed into my temple. "Why do you
have a gun?"

I turned my face to him, ignoring the jab of the business end of
his pistol. "For protection from freaks like you."

"Toss the sunglasses." His voice was ice-cold and rock hard. He
was through playing now.

I did as I was told. The fake Versaces went out the window.

I was screwed.

The tracking device was history.

Shit.

"Take off the rest."

No way in hell. I was through playing, too. I crossed my arms
over my middle. "Pay me first." I moved my head resolutely from
side to side. "I ain't showing you the goods until I see the money."

He grabbed my purse and tossed it out the window then pushed
me forward and ran the hand with the gun over my back in a half-
assed attempt to feel for any surprises. Did he suspect that I was
working with the cops? The other victims' clothes had been missing, that was true. Was this the way he made that happen? Did he
retrace his route and pick up the clothes? Or was he just lucky since
not a single article had been found?

His encumbered hand groped around my shoulders and chest.

"What the hell are you doing?" Despite my question, I moved my arms and let him have free reign. The more cooperative I appeared the less suspicious he would grow.

I hoped.

Dawson shouting in my earpiece snagged my attention. *Where the hell is he taking you?* There was a distinct crackle that rendered inaudible whatever he said next.

Fear slammed into my brain.

The tracking device was history.

I glanced at the dash, the increasing speed registered. The communications link would fail if there was too much distance between them and me. Without the tracking device there was no way to locate the Lexus once a visual was lost.

Think, Jackie. Where the hell were we? I blinked. Scanned the landscape flying past in a dark blur. An eerie silence in my ear forced the evacuation of the oxygen in my lungs.

Could they still hear me?

My panicked gaze latched onto a familiar landmark as the bastard slowed for another turn. I knew exactly where he was taking me. *The* cemetery…but was it too late to pass the word to my backup?

"Can you turn up the air?" I fanned myself. "I'm suffocating in here." Dawson and I had *almost* suffocated in this very cemetery not so long ago.

Ass wipe didn't react to my request.

"Please, mister. Can we let the top down again? I'm feeling a little claustrophobic?" Spending those few minutes trapped in a cheap coffin made for one with Dawson had given new meaning to claustrophobia.

What else? Something Dawson would understand for sure…

An epiphany made me smile. "I have a Hispanic friend. His

name is Rocky. We could call him up and arrange a threesome."
The rock and a dead Hispanic man had launched the investigation
that resulted in our little buried-alive experience. I felt fairly confident Dawson hadn't forgotten. I hoped like hell he hadn't.

"Shut your filthy trap."

"What's wrong?" I snapped, bored with his control trip. "Your
mommy do bad things to you when you were a kid? You have to
play big bad boy to work up an erection?"

The back of his hand connected with my face. I rode out the
burn of pain.

The com link was dead. Otherwise I would have heard Dawson
arguing with Nance again.

There was a strong possibility that I would be gone as well in
about fifteen minutes. Images from the crime scene photos I'd
studied flashed in front of my eyes like a bad horror movie.

He roared into the old cemetery and parked beneath one of the
ancient trees.

I stared up at the tree, my throat going dry. Each victim had
been propped against the base of a large tree. Raped then staked.

Sucked to be me right now.

He popped the trunk and got out of the car, his aim never de-
viating from me. He'd gotten good at this. "Get out."

Didn't take a genius to figure out that he had his bag of tricks
in the trunk. The very evidence we needed.

I reached for the door handle and opened the damned door.
Somehow between him knocking the crap out of me and now,
my outrage had gotten its second wind. I emerged from his fancy
car and shoved the door shut. The way I saw it, I had two options
here. I could go with the flow and hope backup got here in time
or I could run like hell the first chance I got.

Couldn't run just yet. I wanted to get this guy.

He rounded the hood, a steady bead on me, and manacled my

arm. When he'd dragged me to the trunk of the fancy car, he ordered, "Pick up the bag."

A black gym bag sat in the trunk. There was other stuff. A bottle of bleach spray cleaner, towels—the kind that didn't leave behind fibers—garbage bags. Evidence. Exactly what was needed to prove he was the killer. Anticipation blasted away any lingering fear. This low-down piece of shit was going down. I just hoped he didn't take me with him.

He poked me with the gun and I picked up the bag. I looked directly into his eyes and prompted mine to go big and round. "I don't want to die, mister." Might as well play the game. Keep him off guard.

He hauled me to the tree and shoved me against it.

"Drop the bag and get on your knees."

Whoa, wait. Not that I wanted to go that route, but wasn't the sex supposed to come first? Serial killers did change their M.O.'s from time to time....

"What's wrong?" I asked. "You can't get it up?" I licked my lips. "I can help."

"Get on your fucking knees!"

This was the moment.

The barrel of the pistol was leveled on my torso.

"Please, mister," I pleaded, summoning tears.

He opened his mouth to snarl something else. I slugged him with the bag and darted around the tree, then ran like hell.

It was dark. Woods flanked this old cemetery. I stayed close to the tree line, zigzagging around trees and headstones. The blast of his weapon echoed in the air, a bullet thwacked into a headstone to my right. Close. Too close.

I dived for the ground. Grunted with the impact, then I scrambled into the woods.

He fired another shot.

My hands fumbling in my haste, I ripped open the bag and searched for a weapon. My fingers closed around the wooden stake. I pulled it from the bag, stared at the sharpened end. A smile spread across my lips. This was the coup de grâce. This asshole was going down.

I pushed to my feet, held the stake in my hands, dagger style. For a second I closed my eyes and cleared my head. Then I braced.

He was coming.

The distinct crunch of dry grass whispered across my senses.

I held my position another moment, listened intently to his approach, then swung around, the stake aimed for any part of him I could hit.

Shoulder.

He howled in pain.

The weapon discharged in the air.

Headlights bobbed in the darkness. Engines roared. Backup?

He hurled me to the ground. Knocked the wind out of me.

I started to get up but his weapon was aimed directly at my head. The moonlight cut right through the trees and backlit his menacing profile. Not exactly the last image I'd hoped to see.

A blast shattered the silence.

For a second I couldn't move.

The bastard dropped his weapon and fell on top of me.

I screamed. Scrambled out from under him.

"You okay?"

Dawson.

He dragged me up, held me at arm's length and looked me over. "You okay?" he demanded a second time.

Before I could answer half a dozen vehicles zoomed onto the scene.

And just like that cops were everywhere.

● ● ●

Later, an hour maybe more. The paramedics had given me a clean bill of health and an ice pack for my puffy cheek. One of the cops had found me a jacket since no one wanted to see my ass.

My legs were still a little rubbery but at least I was alive. The bag and the car held all the elements used in the previous crimes, except the stake. That element was still lodged in the asshole's shoulder only inches above his heart. He wasn't dead. Dawson was a crack shot. He'd made sure he got the guy good but not good and dead. The bastard had at least five murders to answer for. A search warrant had already been executed to search his home and place of business.

Nance stomped around raising hell. He wanted Dawson arrested. The cop had a swollen eye and a crooked nose where Dawson had overtaken him to get control of the car when Nance wouldn't listen. My partner had understood the clues I'd given. I glanced across the old pauper's cemetery. One tended to remember an event like being buried alive.

Looking no worse for the wear, Dawson swaggered over to where I waited near one of HPD's cruisers.

As exhausted and emotionally spent as I was, every part of me perked up to watch his approach and in anticipation of the sound of his voice. I could feel the "Hallelujah Chorus" coming on.

"Since I'm not under arrest, Nance said I could take you home."

I went all hot and gooey inside. Idiot. "Good. I'm beat."

Dawson stared at me with those dreamy eyes, regret weighing heavy in them. "Don't ever do anything like this again, Jackie," he warned.

For about five seconds I considered throwing myself into his arms and just letting him have his way with me. I was that overwhelmed and worn down. I could have died tonight and I recognized that scary fact.

Thank God, good sense kicked in. "Maybe you've forgotten." I went toe-to-toe with him. Held my breath so I didn't have to deal with the usual foolish reactions to his scent. "My name is the one over the door at the office. That makes me the boss. Now—" I squared my shoulders "—take me home, Dawson. I'm done here."

I didn't wait for his answer. I gave him my back and walked away. Sadly I had no idea which car we'd been authorized to use but I refused to let that stop my dramatic exit.

"Maybe Nance has a good point," Dawson called after me.

I should have kept walking but my curiosity got the better of me. I turned around and glared at him. "What?"

"You're pretty hot as a blonde."

I gave him the finger and walked away. Sadly I realized there was just one problem with that, I so, so, so wanted to do exactly what that crude hand gesture alluded to.

But that wasn't going to happen.

Not as long as I was the boss.

And he was too good to fire.

BROKEN HALLELUJAH

TONI McGEE CAUSEY

*There was only one thing wrong with Causey's story.
It wasn't long enough. I wanted it to go on for another
couple hundred pages. —SB*

She should not have been here. It was the worst possible scenario.

He'd caught motion on his periphery—someone threading through the crowds, moving that same fluid way she did—a powerful motion that hit his senses as if a car were about to careen into him.

He worked hard to not jerk around and try to find her. Instead, he sat in the folding chair on the hot sidewalk just below the oak trees and strummed another verse on the battered guitar before he turned his head, turned his supposedly blind eyes hidden behind mirrored sunglasses and scanned across the brightly lit Jackson Square in the Quarter.

Someone dropped change in the hat in front of him, and he nodded a gruff thanks as the coins clinked, but he didn't turn back toward them; as a blind man, no one expected him to. Instead, he bobbed his chin a bit, keeping time with the song, and used the cover motion to sort out the tourists—thick as flies—from the buskers. The girl with the hula hoop was particularly hungover and giving a bad show today, but the mime painted silver with robot costuming was in fine form, entertaining the little kids.

Had he imagined her?

He had to consciously slow down the tune he was playing; his hands shook and people politely looked away from the trembling vet. The sun beamed, brilliant against the white stucco of the rising spires of St. Louis Cathedral, and he resisted the urge to shade his eyes, afraid to find her.

Her laugh caught him in the chest and he saw her flowing—small and lithe and with a dancer's grace—through the crowd as she greeted strangers and smiled at the children chasing the pigeons. She was more beautiful than he remembered. The sunlight caught red waves of silken hair that made his hands ache. His mouth had gone dry with fear that she'd look over and recognize him, see him through the ratty disguise, see what he had become. Years ago, the first time he'd met her, the shock of that instant attraction had been like a shotgun blast through his soul.

This was much, much worse.

Because he knew, now, what it was to be in love with someone who hated you.

"Hey, mister, you okay?" a voice near his elbow asked, and he cocked his ear a little, pretending not to see the curious girl, maybe seven, maybe eight, who stood like a wisp of hope, perched on the balls of her feet as if she were about to run. "How come you stopped playing?" she asked, when he didn't answer her.

He looked down at his hands, still on the guitar, stiff as twigs on the strings. He couldn't even remember what the song had been.

"I'm fine, kid."

She took a step closer, unafraid because she was convinced he didn't see her; her big brown eyes looked into his glasses and she whispered, "People who cry ain't okay."

He felt his face, and it shocked him: there were tears.

"What's your name?" She peered up, and he could see the cookie crumbs on her cheek.

"Phineas." He hadn't revealed that in three years. "I'm okay. Just missing a friend."

"Someone you lost in the war?" she asked, staring at the Navy baseball cap he wore.

"Yeah." He resisted the urge to look to see where Sadie had gone. It wasn't the type of war the kid understood, but it had had its losses.

A mother frantically yelled, "Marjorie Ann Naysmith!" and the kid in front of him glanced rabbit fast over her shoulder, then back at him, chagrined.

"Gotta go." Then she stunned him by leaning in and kissing his cheek. "You play pretty," she said. "I bet your friend liked that."

He nodded and she ran off, and he could hear her mother above the din of techno music coming from a boom box somewhere as she chastised little Marjorie about talking to strangers. It worried him that the Marjories of the world would never believe that advice really applied to them, until it was too late.

Phin set about tapping his pockets as if he'd lost something, rummaging around, using it as an excuse to find Sadie again in the crowd. His body went taut, frozen: she was setting up her easel, facing the building he had under surveillance.

There was no way in hell that was a coincidence.

• • •

This was the fourth day in a row now that she'd tried to get this spot—the damned man had been set up right where she *had* to be. Every day. By dawn. She'd beaten him this morning, though, and was the only person out here in the silence of the square. Big, vast, with shops lining two sides, the huge St. Louis Cathedral on another, the river opposite…this place would be crazy with crowds by midmorning, speaking languages from all over the world.

But right now? It belonged to her. Finally.

Sadie opened her folding chair in the blind vet's spot, shivering in the cool spring air, waiting for the sunrise; she watched the cleaning crews who were only just finishing pressure-washing the sidewalks of the side streets, something they did every morning here in the Quarter. There was an entire silent army keeping the place clean so that the tourists wouldn't see what their debauchery the night before had rendered. An entire silent army, just for trash.

It had been a cleaning crew who'd found Abby.

The first rays of sun peeled back the night sky, and a cacophony of birds sang above Sadie in the magnolia trees, as if all were well in the world, and it was wrong that birds could sing after Abby died. It was wrong that the world could laugh and people could vacation. It was wrong that she still hurt with every breath, wanting the man who'd been supposed to stop her big sister, the undercover cop, from going back in when her cover was blown.

Phin.

She sank her face in her hands. Why did she think of him so much here? It had to be the stress. What she was about to do. Because all she could think of lately was Phin, who'd been her sister's boss on the task force trying to take down human trafficking slime. Phin, who'd taken one look at Sadie when Abby had introduced them and had turned to her sister and said, "I hope like hell we get along, Dawson, because I'm going to be family." And he'd meant it.

Sadie had had no intention of settling down. And then he'd courted her, tugged her along, and she could still feel the heat of his hands, the way he touched her, still feel his breath against the back of her neck, still feel that moment when he'd make her fall apart, sublime, and then put her back together again. He'd made her hope.

He'd been running the show, still, when LaCroix had butchered her sister, cut her from her navel to her neck, sliced her up and laid her out in a dirty alley, laid her out on a heap of trash for the world to see.

Phin had known Abby was in trouble. He hadn't stopped the investigation—and all for nothing. LaCroix managed to disappear, conveniently, just as the police were closing in.

Until now. She forced herself not to glance over at the house, at LaCroix's place.

Three years it had taken to find LaCroix's hideaway. To make this plan.

The *tap tap tapping* of the blind man's cane echoed off the almost-empty square, and she snapped open her easel, letting him know of her presence. She'd tried to talk to him, but he'd studiously ignored her, and she knew he wasn't deaf. He thought if he ignored her, she'd go away.

Too damned bad.

She felt a twinge of guilt. He was blind. He was a vet, if that cap and those patches on his shoulder were his and not something he'd bought from Goodwill. He bothered her, and she couldn't put her finger on why. For four days, she kept thinking of Phin when she saw him, which was ridiculous; he was at least twenty years older than Phin's thirty-six. Phin was tall and broad-shouldered and tan, close-cropped dark hair, hands that played her as well as this man played the guitar. But the hands were the only thing they had in common. This guy curled in on himself, nearly broken, it seemed; he had a long, ratty gray ponytail, plaited with something that looked like it had crawled up in there and died. His fuzzy, bushy eyebrows that sat above those mirrored glasses looked alive, like they would fall off and sprout legs. Where Phin had been lithe, athletic, predatory…this guy was nothing but disarray and vulnerable…and he made her sad.

There were a handful of early-morning tourists, taking advantage of the light breaking over the cathedral for photos, but not another single busker had ventured out here, yet. It was too early for the real crop of tourists to wander out of their hotels, ripe for plucking. And still, there he was, shuffling forward from the shadows on the side of the cathedral.

It wasn't this man's fault he had set up in the only place in the square that had a direct line of sight into LaCroix's home. The. Only. Spot. He probably just liked the shade, the acoustics. He was a blind vet, for God's sake, she told herself. Not Phin, the bastard who was two thousand miles away in San Francisco. He just reminded her of Phin.

She shuddered, remembering his heat, the feel of the length of him pressed against her, skin to skin, and she had to squeeze her eyes shut to stop the tears.

He'd let Abby die, may he rot in whatever hell he'd crawled into.

When the vet reached her, she expected aggravation. Not fury. Even though buskers were territorial, what could one spot possibly matter over another, five feet away, to a blind man? He was being silly.

She would be patient. She would be kind. She would be pleasant. But he was not getting this spot. She was not missing that signal.

● ● ●

He folded his cane, anger showing as he clacked the sections together harder than necessary. He'd spent three nights of determined research and paying bribes, trying to figure out what she had planned. He hadn't slept. Had barely eaten. And as soon as he spoke, she'd recognize him, and his own game would be jeopardized.

Who the hell was he kidding? She probably wouldn't recognize him from his voice. *He* had known when *she* was simply walking on the other side of a crowded fucking square filled with people from all over the world. He'd have known her in the pitch-black. And she'd sat right near him for four agonizing days, had heard him playing and hadn't even begun to suspect. He hated her for that.

"I'm really sorry," she said, coming up out of her chair to stand in front of him, where she barely reached his chin, her face tilted up so close, he could see how weary she was. "I just need this spot for a couple of days, tops, to get the light just right on that building I'm painting. Well, I guess you can't tell which one—but this is the only spot in the whole square with this view." She pushed earnestness hard, like a car salesman who knows he's lying, and she tried smiling brightly and flirting, then remembered he was blind. Her face fell as he didn't answer, and she tried for *cheery*. "And I brought a picnic lunch, to thank you. I hope you don't mind sharing."

"I *mind*," he said, straightening up, crossing his arms at his chest as her eyes narrowed, first at the tone, then the words.

● ● ●

He...*unfurled*.... One moment, he was bent over, looking warworn and haggard and old and blind, and then he straightened up and squared his shoulders, feet planted, arms across his chest and Sadie knew she was in trouble. Something was wrong here, and it took a heartbeat more to really *hear* the voice and ignore what she was seeing.

"Phineas Michael Donnelly. You *bastard*," she snapped, balling her fist, wanting to hit him. "Have you been having fun here? Is this some kind of joke? How'd you know I would be here?"

"I've been here for eight months, Sadie," and his voice dropped to that lethally cold tone she hated. "*Eight months*, and you're not about to waltz in here and screw this up. Go home. Aren't you supposed to be teaching?"

"I can be wherever I want, Phin. I'm on vacation."

"Oh, please. You just happened to be here, painting the building that Louis LaCroix owns? What do you plan to do, Sadie? Confront him? Turn him in? The police know he's here. He's well protected. *Go home.*"

"They'll believe it when I catch him red-handed."

"You're waiting for a signal—a red handkerchief hung on the balcony."

She slanted her eyes at him, livid. "How in the hell did you know that?"

"It's my job to know."

"Why?"

When he didn't answer, she pressed closer, letting all of the anger of his betrayal pour through her. All of the years of dreaming of him at night, wishing…wasted years. Damn her stupid heart. "Who. Are. You. Working. For?"

"LaCroix," he said, his voice as flat as the flagstones where they stood. "I'm telling you, for old time's sake, Sadie. It's a trap."

She felt light-headed. Disconnected. She couldn't believe it.

Was *he* why LaCroix got away from the police three years ago? Had he been lying to her then, too? Was everything they'd had a complete farce? She remembered laughing as she chased him one spring day, not unlike this one. Tackling him while he held her keys out of reach, a gleam in his eye. Kissing him, then. Craving him, all over again.

Even here. Even now.

She itched to take a swing at him, but she remembered how fast he could move and she held still. "I knew you were heartless and ambitious, letting Abby go back in there, but I never dreamed you could be the enemy."

Her heart hurt, so much. How stupid was it to still have hoped?

Something flexed in his jaw, like he was holding on to his temper by extreme determination, but he just leaned forward, smug, and said, "Well, darlin', now you know. Go home."

"How do they know I'm here?" LaCroix had not been there, the times she'd been inside. No one else knew her real name, or how she was connected to LaCroix.

He turned, unfolded his cane and tucked back into himself somehow, suddenly the old, blind vet again, as seamless as air. "Because," he said, as he *tap tap tapped* his way away from her, "I told them."

• • •

He'd walked away. It had taken everything he had, but he'd left her there, tears streaming down her face.

Good.

She'd stay away. She'd be shocked and angry and it would take her maybe a day to recover. She wouldn't get the signal she was waiting for; he'd seen to that.

Phin clicked on a pin light: it was twelve hours after his confrontation with Sadie and he was now beneath LaCroix's house. Underground—a place most people would never have believed existed in the Quarter, given how far below sea level the city was, and how common the flooding, even in light rains. Most people did not know there were vaults below the streets that held all of the electrical and cable conduits which wired everything; city code prohibited any wiring above ground.

There were things about the Quarter that went beyond the eye, and tourists rarely ever saw that side, unless they were unlucky. Instead, they experienced the beautiful hotels, the antique shops, the galleries, loud bars and restaurants. Few were ever invited into the homes that were also a part of the Quarter—buildings which had been a part of the fabric of the Vieux Carré so long, people had forgotten how many times they'd been updated and remodeled. Renovation upon renovations, and often the original floor plan was lost in history. There were even old Underground Railroad passages; it was blasphemy, that LaCroix used some of the hidden passages—buildings connected to buildings in ways that weren't obvious from the street—to move his "merchandise" without anyone on the outside able to hear or see.

It had cost Phin the better part of his cop pension to get his hands on the plans he'd needed.

He slid a makeshift plywood door aside and held quiet a moment, patient. Listening. He'd connected two passages over the past couple of months from two very old tunnels, both left off the later plans LaCroix had used and had based his own renovations on.

LaCroix screamed obscenities at someone three floors up, and then a *slap* echoed and everything went dead silent. Phin tensed, waiting for noise to cover his movements. There were more girls above; some locked in rooms, some shuttled out in the night. He'd tipped off the police, and they claimed their hands were tied without hard evidence, and no one had any intention of getting any, from what he could see. LaCroix had paid off someone fairly powerful to keep the warrants at bay. It was how he'd kept the police at a distance in San Francisco when Abby was murdered.

Phin pinched the bridge of his nose to ward away the memories, and there was more yelling again above him. Chairs shuffled about, then a crashing sound, like a vase hitting a wall. Someone had pissed LaCroix off. He listened, praying Sadie had heeded him, when Abby hadn't.

It took him nearly an hour to move through the vaults and tunnels below the house, to make his way through ancient rooms, cobwebbed over, slick with mold, and up into dingy crawl spaces and finally easing into the dark kitchen, quiet for the night, the cook having been sent home every day at 10:00 p.m. He exited the hidden passage into the pantry, and he had to let his eyes adjust before moving forward, making sure he made not a single sound to betray him.

"So this is why you wanted me to stay away," Sadie whispered in the dark and his heartbeat ratcheted to the sky as panic flooded him with adrenaline. When he got his bearings, he realized she was sitting on the floor of the big pantry, dressed in black, her red hair hidden beneath a black cap. She had night vision goggles. And a gun. *How the hell?*

"You're not here because you work for LaCroix, Phin," she said, quietly, deadly. "You're here to kill him, too."

• • •

This was the Phin she remembered: clean-shaven, cropped hair, murderous expression that she was somewhere she wasn't supposed to be. He held out his hand and Sadie gripped it, letting him help her stand, holstering the FN pistol.

"I nearly killed you, just now," she seethed, the shock of that still sending tremors through her as she stepped so close, she could feel the heat radiating off his body. "You should have told me earlier."

"For the love of God, Sadie." His fury pulsed through the small room. He paused to crack the door and keep a view of the kitchen. "Get the hell out of here before it's too late."

"It's already too late. We're working this together."

A crash sounded above them, in the main salon; LaCroix, unhapy with an answer some male voice had just given him, too muffled for Sadie to hear.

"So what? Now you trust me?"

"I made calls today, Phin. You cashed out your pension. You filed a will. A *will*. Left me everything else. You *ass*. You came here to die."

There was a long silence as he stared at her and she stared right back. He was killing her, here.

"No," he answered finally. "I came to finish the job. I can't get close to him without him recognizing me. I tried getting him away from his men—never works. The odds aren't good." He grabbed her shoulders, squeezed. "I'll finish it, Sadie. I can't handle it if you're here, in danger."

"Those odds are better now." She grinned, and he arched an eyebrow and she pointed up at the ongoing tantrum. "LaCroix thinks all of his victims have escaped—he thinks someone on the other end of the tunnel he usually smuggles them out of left a door open. He's going ballistic because he can't find them."

"His men are looking?"

"Yep. And everyone he can call on for favors. Which means they're spread out throughout the Quarter, right now, chasing ghosts."

He stared at her a moment, soaking it in. Then he grinned, that slow, sexy grin, the one where his eyes danced at the possibilities.

"Which means he's down to what? One or two bodyguards?"

"Two, from what I can tell."

"Good. Now, you can get out that way," he said then, angling his head toward the door.

"No. You don't get a choice about this, Phin."

He went completely still. "You either trust me, Sadie, or you can shoot me now."

"This is *my* fight, Phin. I lost everything when he killed Abby."

"So did I," he said, but he closed his eyes, his face a blank mask.

"I'll just follow you in, anyway. You can't stop me."

He glared at her. "It's extremely dangerous. You were never a good shot."

"I've been practicing," she said, and then sobered. "This is for Abby and all those other girls, Phin. I'm not going to miss."

• • •

She had missed.

That was the fuzzy thought running through her mind as she came to, swimming her way out of a blackness so deep, so complete, it felt like death. She couldn't move, could barely breathe. Something bright shone in her eyes, and something—ammonia—filled her nostrils and she tried to jerk away.

Except that she could not move.

The last thing she remembered was Phin trying to stop her from stepping out of their hidden spot that moment she saw LaCroix and realized: *Now. I have a shot now.*

She'd missed. And now, a hardback chair held her hostage, with her hands tied behind it, her feet to its legs. Blood trickled down her forehead and pain radiated from the back of her head where someone had clubbed her just as she'd aimed at LaCroix.

LaCroix, who now sat across from her, one of her knives in his hand as he slapped it against his thigh, a terrifyingly patient rhythm.

"Good," he said, leaning forward to inspect her. "You're the substitute cook. I almost didn't recognize you. Nicely done."

She glared at him, his perfectly chiseled face that seemed practically made for magazine covers, his expensive Armani suit, tailored to perfection across broad shoulders.

She spat on him and he studied the spittle on his suit; his hazel eyes went feral and he held the knife to her cheek. *Stupid stupid stupid* rattled in her head. She tried to blink away the memory of what a knife had done to Abby.

"Hello, Sadie." When she blanched, surprised, he laughed. "Yes, I remember you, now that you're not in disguise. We're going to get to know each other very very well, soon, but first, where are my girls?"

"I don't know where they are," she answered, frantically worried about Phin. "They were running, the last time I saw them. They're probably all over the Quarter, by now."

"No, they're not." He put the knife back up to her cheek and started slicing…lightly, but it burned from the pain.

Where's Phin?

"Did you know your sister begged me to take her back? She especially loved the coke."

She stared at him and realized he wasn't lying. Abby had been acting strangely. Manic…erratic, almost, but Sadie had put it down to the stress.

LaCroix kept taunting, twitching the knife at her cheek. "She'd do anything for the coke. Went a little too deep undercover, that Abby. Told me all about the investigation. You wouldn't believe what she would do for the coke." His lascivious gaze raked over her and she tried to pull back. "Oh, but you will. When I'm done, you'll be begging, too."

Men shouted from the other room, "Got him, *got him!*" and semiautomatic fire startled her, and then a man screamed, *screamed*—and then another shot and…silence.

"Ah," he said, smiling into her wide eyes, the tang of fear, metallic in her mouth, her heartbeat pounding in her head, "that must've been your partner." He leaned closer. "Nobody's coming for you, Sadie." He *tsked tsked* her. "You didn't think I'd run a business this successful to be stopped by a couple of amateurs, did you? I'll show you his mutilated body in a few minutes. Now, answer the damned question, or I start on your breasts."

He put the tip of the knife at her right breast and she knew he would do it. Blood oozed down her cheek, Phin was dead, and she had not avenged Abby. But there were six girls free right now, in a car on their way to Baton Rouge, and he'd never get his hands on them again. Maybe that counted for something.

Then it really hit her: Phin *was dead*. He hadn't told anyone about Abby turning. He'd tried to protect her. Them. And Sadie hadn't trusted him. She'd accused him and walked away, destroying everything.

Her heart shattered; the blade cut into the thin shirt she wore, slicing into her right breast, but she wept for Phin. The pain was almost welcome. Nothing mattered. Phin was gone.

She barely heard the gunshots through the agony of the blade, her entire being focused on that point of pain. Someone slumped just to her right.

LaCroix looked up, past her, and then a red dot bloomed on his forehead and he jerked away from her, the knife still impaled in her breast where he'd begun carving. The look of surprise on his face, frozen in that moment, had been worth it.

● ● ●

Phin watched her open her eyes in the morning light that filtered in through gauzy curtains. He had the doors open to the balcony of his apartment. She was stitched and bandaged and confused when she finally focused on him. He had not known what to expect: recriminations, for allowing her to get hurt. Hate, for the scars she would have. Disgust...

Instead, her face shone with relief.

"Come here," she said, holding out a hand, and Phin moved from the chair at the foot of the bed to sit by her side. She squeezed his hand hard, tears rolling down her cheeks. "You're real."

"I'm real."

"He said he killed you."

"They thought they had. They actually shot one of their own guards who'd been looking for the girls—he'd found the passage-way you'd used and was following it back into the house."

He felt his own tears now, and he didn't try to stop them. "I'm sorry, Sadie. I should have gotten there faster."

"I botched your job."

"No. Without you, I doubt very seriously I would have gotten out alive. Or that I'd have bothered trying." He looked away, staring out the window onto the rooftop of the building next door. "You'd been in the house before? As the cook?" That one had surprised him when LaCroix had said it.

"Just a few times. Elana told him I was her niece, and could be trusted."

She'd planned it well, even if she'd guessed the number of guards wrong. If she'd not frozen in that moment of face-to-face with La-Croix, she might have succeeded.

She reached up toward the bandages, seeming to just now remember, and she flinched.

"Are you in pain?"

She shook her head. "Just grateful. You got me out of there. In one piece."

"Mostly," he said, bitter with regret. "I'm sorry. I got a doctor in here—a guy I know, does amazing work. But there'll be scars, unless you go in for plastic surgery later. There's a lot they can do."

"Does it matter?"

He whipped his gaze back to her, to understand what she meant, and saw the fear that he would somehow be repulsed.

"God, no," he answered. "Everything you do, everything you are, is beautiful to me, Sadie. It would take a lifetime to show you, though, but I'd like to. If you'd let me."

She got a faraway expression, contemplative, and his heart stuttered, scared as witless as he'd been when LaCroix held that knife to her.

"We can't go back to being those people we were before," she said, and his heart broke. He started to step away from the bed, and she tightened her grip on his hand. "I don't ever want to lose you, Phin, and I'll go and do whatever you want. But I can't—" She turned away, her eyes closed, and whispered, "I can't let the LaCroixs of the world get away."

"Neither can I." Her gaze snapped back to him, and he saw her understand. "If I have you, we can do anything."

She smiled, and he could breathe again.

"I will believe in you," she promised. "I will honor you. I will trust you."

"I will believe in you," he whispered, kissing her hand, then clutching it tightly. "I will honor you. I will trust you."

• • •

Marjorie was ten the summer her family went back to New Orleans, and they strolled through the crowded French Quarter, weaving their way through hordes of people meandering in Jackson Square. It felt huge, with the green park in the center surrounded by wrought-iron fences, with shops ringing that area all putting out goods on their sidewalks. Her mom paused briefly at the tap dancers, but Marjorie tugged her hard. She had to know if her friend was here again this year.

"Phin!" she screeched, from halfway across the square and her mamma laughed, letting her go hug the blind vet. "You're here!"

"I am, indeed," he answered, and she guided his hand so he could pat her on the head. "And you remember my wife, Sadie."

Marjorie waved and smiled at the way Phin squeezed Sadie's hand as she painted children right beside him.

"We went to Austin last summer—not nearly as fun. And they don't have vigilantics!"

"Vigilantes?" he asked, as a man dropped a piece of paper in Phin's hat and Marjorie could have sworn—almost could have sworn—that blind Phin saw it and nodded at the man. But that wasn't possible.

"Yeah, vigilantes. I'm hoping we see them. They're in all the papers. Mama said they're cleaning out the riffraff but good!"

Phin laughed. "Well, there was a lot of riffraff here to clean up, I suspect. If you see them, tell 'em I said good luck!"

"I will! Can I come back tomorrow and you'll play me a special song?"

"Sure," Phin said, and smiled when Marjorie hugged him.

She ran off, and when she looked back, she could have sworn he was watching her go, grinning.

HOLDING MERCY

LORI ARMSTRONG

You gotta love a heroine who wears black patent cowgirl boots. And that's the least daring thing she does! —SB

The bad thing about wearing a tight, sexy little black dress?

No place to put my gun.

Granted, I was supposed to be on a date, and probably didn't need a firearm, or handcuffs, but being armed was a habit ingrained during my twenty-year stint in the army and now as a newly minted G-woman. Legally, I could carry everywhere and I took advantage of that perk without apology. But my belt and holster looked clunky strapped over the clingy black dress. Stowing my weapon in my compact beaded purse didn't feel right, neither did slipping the small handgun in the pocket of my leather trench coat, so I compromised and shoved my Kahr Arms P380 inside my right cowgirl boot. Then I placed my handcuffs between the "Mercy Gunderson, Special Agent, FBI" badge in my purse and my cell phone. All set for my date.

Still seemed ridiculous that Dawson referred to our dinner out as a "date" because we were living together. But I'd recently returned from a four-and-a-half-month training stint at Quantico, so we were trying to carve out couple time between his duties as

Eagle River County Sheriff and my new job with the FBI. Plus, he'd been stuck working the night shift, and I worked the day shift, so he was rolling into bed as I was rolling out, which left us little time to roll around in the sheets together.

Our last attempt at an official date ended before it began due to me being covered in blood and vomit after a routine questioning had turned ugly. The woman had raced out the back door of her house after I showed her my badge. When I caught her, she accidentally smacked her face into her knee and blood poured from her nose. Seeing blood turned her hysterical and she hurled all over me. By the time I'd showered and changed clothes at home, neither Dawson nor I had been in the mood to go out.

I hoped tonight would play out differently. Not being much of a girlie-girl, a fact my man Dawson was well aware of, I'd decided to shock him by taking extra time with my appearance for our romantic rendezvous. Hence the sexy dress, the waves in my normally straight hair, the curled eyelashes, the berry-colored stain on my lips. However, I refused to wear high heels—couldn't run in them—and opted for a dressier pair of black patent leather cowgirl boots. I hadn't taken my fashion inspiration of pairing fancy shit-kickers with a dress from ingenue Taylor Swift, but the grand dame of the West, Dale Evans. She'd worn boots with everything. If it was good enough for Roy Rogers, it was good enough for Dawson.

Day morphed into night as I drove from my ranch to the edge of the Eagle River Indian Reservation. The period between autumn and full-out winter on the high plains of Western South Dakota was the most visually depressing time of the year. The rolling hills, previously lush, boasting a dozen different shades of green, were stuck in monochromatic bleakness. Dead grass, naked trees, dry creek beds, lackluster sky. Even the soil, ranging from brick red to cocoa brown, reflected in dull tones. I secretly wished for snow.

At least a blanket of white would hide the ugliness until spring arrived.

As I stood at the front entrance to the Eagle River Casino, I revisited my plan to circumvent a security check so I could keep my gun hidden. The reservation was one place where normal—in my case federal—rules don't apply.

But I noticed right away my carefully crafted plan was unnecessary, because security was decidedly lax. No metal detector. One unarmed guard who gave me a bored once-over before refocusing her attention on her cell phone. When her walkie-talkie beeped, she turned the volume down. I shoved aside the niggling sense of unease, betting the bulk of the security was done in the back via a bank of computer monitors connected to security cameras.

Air from the vents blasted down on me as if I'd stepped into a wind tunnel when I entered the main part of the casino. First time I'd been in the facility. It'd been constructed in the past five years while I'd been toiling in the world's sandboxes. The decor wasn't Vegas glitzy, or bingo parlor cheesy, but somewhere in between, with Indian themes threaded throughout. The hand-painted murals depicting past Indian life on the Great Plains were amazing. Vibrant. Haunting. Glorious.

A decent-size crowd milled about for a Thursday night. Mostly senior citizens. I'd noticed two tour buses in the parking lot. Had they come to gorge themselves on cheap crab legs like Dawson and I intended? He'd called me en route to a traffic accident to relay the unhappy fact he might be as much as an hour late.

So how was I supposed to entertain myself?

Federal law prohibited alcohol to be served or consumed on reservations so I couldn't cool my heels at the casino bar nursing a beer or knocking back shots.

I wasn't much of a gambler. Slot machines bored me. Indian casinos weren't big on craps or roulette. I'd joined in poker tournaments with fellow soldiers, but it'd been more about camaraderie or blocking out the sounds of incoming mortar rounds, than winning the pot.

Between the stifling air and the crowd, I was overheating. I eased off my coat, draping it over my arm. I wandered through the red-topped gaming tables, which were separated from the slot machines, which were separated from the video lottery machines. Surprised me to see those machines in here. Most tribes didn't want to give a percentage of their intake to the state. Hopefully the monies received from this casino were being used for the benefit of the entire tribe, and not just lining the pockets of a few.

I decided to scope out the perimeter. You can take the girl out of the army, but a little bit of that paranoid patrolling soldier remains.

Both windows in the cash-out station had lines of people, a mix of young, old, Indian, white, affluent and not, anxious to grab their payout. Or waiting to write a check or obtain a credit card cash advance to feed their addiction while their kids starved.

Yeah, I've never been a big fan of gambling.

As I followed the curve of the circular room, I passed one direct exit outside. No guard manned the door. My gaze zoomed to the ceiling expecting to see a camera. But as my focus traversed the entire ceiling, I counted five surveillance cameras. Total.

That was it? The Eagle River Casino was off the beaten path, but lack of visual security feeds from all corners of the facility seemed a bad judgment call, especially since I'd only seen one security guard.

Not your concern, Mercy.

But it would be my concern if the place got robbed, since the tribal police called the FBI on any big case. Then again, I could boast insider knowledge of security problems if it came to that.

My stomach rumbled and I meandered to the restaurant. As I

checked out the menu posted on the wall, the young, good-looking Indian kid manning the host stand said, "I can seat you right away."

I smiled at him. "I'm waiting for someone. But thank you."

He moved to stand in front of me. "At least let me take your coat and hang it up while you're waiting."

"That's not—"

"We have a coat check." Slipping the coat from my arm, he walked to a closet behind the podium. He handed me a claim ticket. "See? Now your hands are free to play the slots, eh?"

Rather than snap at him for his presumptive behavior, I realized the poor kid had just been doing his job. I let it go and wandered off, making another full perimeter sweep, in case Dawson had sneaked in and was trying to earn extra cash to buy our dinner.

Bored, I dug out a dollar and plugged it into the nickel video poker machine. I'd always found it more interesting studying the people around me than watching the cards flashing on the screen. Which is why the skinny white dude caught my eye.

During a perimeter sweep, I'd noticed him talking to the security guard—the only sign of life I'd seen from her. He seemed out of place for a number of reasons, the biggest one being his heavy, bulky army surplus jacket. Although the calendar said November, the air temp outside was a balmy fifty degrees and the thermostat in here was definitely set on roast. Or maybe since I'd involuntarily relinquished my jacket I was more attuned to those patrons who still had theirs.

Something about the guy rubbed me wrong so I watched him. He meandered down the walkway between the rows of machines, stopping to plug a nickel into a slot. But he paid no heed to whether he'd won. His attention stayed on the inattentive folks around him, those who pulled on the one-armed bandit as soon as the reels quit spinning, eyes rapt on the crisscrossed bars, finger ready at the bet button to try their luck again.

An older woman wearing a lavender cardigan that matched her thinning cloud of hair had hung her faux crocodile purse on the back of her chair. As skinny dude strolled past, he reached in, snagged her billfold and smoothly shoved it in his outer jacket pocket. If I hadn't been watching him so closely, I would've missed his sleight of hand.

That greasy little shit was a pickpocket. In rural South Dakota? I'd bet my pension they were as rarely seen around here as mimes.

The guy dropped a coin in here and there, pausing to feign interest in the spinning reels while searching for his next mark. Even I could see the easy pickin's. Purses were left unattended. In most cases those purses were wide-open. Trusting lot, these retirees.

But that didn't give this bastard the right to steal from them.

Finishing the fifth pick, he zipped up his coat and made tracks for the exit.

Dammit. I was supposed to be on a date. I was wearing a freakin' dress and a lacy thong. Following him was the last thing I wanted to do. Being in a round room screwed with my sense of direction.

After I exited outside via the side door, I took a second to get my bearings. No lights, no sidewalk indicated I was on the back side of the building. A chain-link fence stretched to the left about fifty yards, with "high voltage" warnings attached to the posts. Doubtful Mr. Snatch-and-Go had gone that direction. Straight ahead was a forested area. Highly unlikely he'd hoofed it into the pine trees to count his loot. To the right, above the roof, an orange glow denoted the parking lot.

Bingo.

Not ideal, trying to fade into stealth mode wearing boots that made a crunching, grinding sound with each step. I hadn't taken out my gun, which caused a bigger sense of imbalance than the continual shifting shadows in my eye, caused by the retinal de-tachment injury that permanently obscured my vision.

I picked my way along the outside of the building, skirting a Dumpster that sat cockeyed a few feet from the building. As soon as I cleared the short end of it, I realized my mistake. The hair on the back of my neck prickled.

Before I crouched into a defensive position, my scalp burned as I was jerked back by my hair. A knife appeared inches from my nose. My mouth dried. Blood pumped hot and fast with fear. My thoughts flashed to the last time I'd been held at knifepoint by a psycho who'd sliced me, skewered me and choked me until I blacked out.

"Don't move," skinny dude warned.

I stayed still.

He didn't place the knife against my throat. Just kept slowly wav-ing it in front of my face like a reverse pendulum. "Why did you follow me?" he demanded, yanking my hair so hard tears sprang into my eyes.

"I—I wanted to get out of there, back to the parking lot. I saw you leave and thought you might know a shortcut."

"Bullshit."

"Please. Just let me go." He hadn't restricted my hands or my legs, which screamed amateur.

"You saw, didn't you?" he demanded.

"Saw what?"

"You're an even worse liar than you are a snoop. I know you were watching me."

Dammit. I'd been in the midst of the freakin' Taliban and hadn't gotten caught, but this snot-nosed punk busted me? Unreal. "Let me go."

"Who do you think you are, anyway?" the skinny dude sneered. "Nancy Drew?"

"More like Sydney Bristow," I retorted, kicking sideways with the heel of my boot until it connected with his knee. When his stance bobbled, I spun, sweeping his feet out from under him. Rolling him over face-first in the dirt, I wrenched his left arm up his back, pressing my knee into his right wrist until he dropped the knife.

He shrieked, "What the hell are you doing? You're hurting me. Help! Help!"

Oh, for Christsake, really? A screamer? "*You* pulled a knife on *me*, asshole."

But he kept yelling. Surprisingly someone not only heard him, but also came to investigate, which was rare in Indian country.

The man, a cook I assumed from his white garb, cautiously wandered closer. "What's goin' on?"

"She followed me out here and attacked me! I didn't do nothin' to her. She's a psycho bitch! Get her offa me!" When he thrashed, trying to break my hold, I pushed his arm just a little farther up his back.

That set him to wailing again.

"Uh, ma'am?" the cook said. "Maybe you should—"

"Maybe you should fetch your manager." Instead of reaching for my gun, I rooted around in my purse for my badge and flipped it open. "FBI. So maybe in addition to your manager, you oughta get the head of security." I sincerely hoped it wasn't the slug guard from the front entrance.

The cook nodded and left much faster than he'd arrived. Still keeping one hand immobilizing the thief, I fished out my cell phone. I had a bad feeling about this situation, especially since I'd seen this punk ass chatting with the lone security guard. Maybe they were in on this scam together.

Grasping at straws, Mercy. You look for conspiracy in everything these days.

Hazard of working for the FBI.

I dialed 911.

"Emergency services, what's your emergency?"

"Special Agent Mercy Gunderson, FBI, requesting assistance from the tribal police. I'm at the Eagle River Casino and have detained a pickpocket."

Pause. "Roger that, Special Agent Gunderson. I've dispatched an officer."

"Thank you." I dropped the phone back in my purse and debated slapping on the cuffs now or leaving that to the tribal cops.

The punk's head snapped to the left and he glared at me. "You're a fucking fed? I shoulda known since you look like a dyke."

Definitely cuffing this smart-ass.

I reached inside my purse, hooking a finger around the metal chain and eased my body back slightly so I could cuff him quickly. But both my knees slipped and I lost my balance. Immediately the kid bucked, knocking me on my ass before he raced off.

Sonuvabitch.

My gun was in my hand before I leaped to my feet to give chase. The lack of light screwed with my depth perception. It'd be just my luck to catch the toe of my boot in a gopher hole and end up sprawled in the dirt with my dress bunched around my hips and my ass hanging out. But I didn't slow down. I yelled, "Stop! FBI. I'm armed. I will shoot you if you don't stop."

He kept running until he tripped. His body slid across the gravel parking lot as if he was diving for home plate from third base.

After he skidded to a stop, I loomed over him, putting my gun in his direct line of sight. "Hands where I can see them. Now!"

Once again he was howling, gaping with horror at his palms. I let my gaze drop for a second and my stomach turned over. Holy shit. His hands were hamburger. A crisscross of scrapes that'd already begun to bleed. The dirt and gravel imbedded beneath his skin looked like Rice Krispies about to pop out of his flesh.

"Help me. Oh, God, I'm bleeding!" He rolled to his knees.

"Don't fucking move or I will shoot you."

He looked at me.

"Repeat it back to me so there's no confusion." When he hesitated, I barked, "Now!"

"Don'tfuckingmoveoryouwillshootme."

The side of his face had fared worse than his hands. His cheek had deep gouges, like he'd taken a header across broken glass.

I heard murmurs behind me. Evidently this incident had already drawn a crowd. Too soon for the tribal cops to be here, so I had a pretty good idea of who was closing in on me.

"Never a dull moment with you, is there, Sergeant Major?" he drawled.

I stepped aside so I could look at Dawson and keep an eye on shit-for-brains moaning on the ground. "Chasing down a pick-pocket was not part of my evening plans, Sheriff. Besides. You're late."

"Sorry. Deputy Moore dropped me off as soon as we were done. I assume you called this in?"

"Yes. Tribal police are en route."

Dawson crossed his arms over his chest, holding court on the guy's other side. "I'll stick around until they get here, if you don't mind."

I appreciated he didn't assume I needed help, but asked. "That'd be great since I need to request an ambulance." I called 911 again.

A portly man barreled up, the security guard on his heels. "What is going on here?"

"I'm stopping bad guys. Who are you?"

"Welchell Whitetail. I'm the manager. Who are you?"

"Mercy Gunderson, FBI."

Whitetail glared at Dawson. Although Dawson wasn't in uniform, he didn't have to be. Everything about him broadcast *law enforcement.* "And who are you?"

"Eagle River County Sheriff."

"Neither of you has jurisdiction here. So I'd like to know why you're holding one of my customers at gunpoint."

"This customer was picking pockets. When he exited the premises with the stolen goods, I followed him. He jumped me with a knife. I take offense to getting jumped with a knife."

"Do you have proof of his alleged crimes?"

"The knife is on the ground by the Dumpster. Check his pockets. He has five wallets that don't belong to him."

Whitetail puffed up like a prairie grouse. "We could've avoided this if you'd contacted my security team after you witnessed the first incident."

"Your security *team* consists of one guard who was far too busy poking buttons on her cell phone to do her job. So I did mine."

"You have no jurisdiction here," Whitetail snapped again. "Let him go and we will handle it in house."

"Sorry. The tribal police are on their way and I will gladly hand this problem over to them. This might not be my jurisdiction, but it is theirs."

Whitetail fumed. His face turned a mottled purple. He seemed too infuriated to speak, which seemed an over-the-top reaction and set off my warning bells. "You had no need to call them. No right. I don't need the tribal cops in my business."

"Well, Mr. Whitetail, that's where you're wrong. This isn't solely your business—it's the tribe's business. The casino and the police are both under the tribe's purview, but it's your job to watch out for guys like this and report them to the tribal cops, so they can do their job and make an arrest."

Skinny dude yelled, "I'm not goin' to jail, especially not on the goddamned rez!"

"You got caught red-handed," I pointed out.

"You promised you'd handle stuff like this," skinny dude said to Whitetail.

Confused, my gaze winged between them. "What stuff does he handle?"

"I have no idea what he's talking about," Whitetail retorted.

"Bullshit! That's why you get a bigger cut."

Whitetail gave me a greasy smile. "Honestly, I'm relieved to have the tribal police deal with him. We don't need anyone to believe we're ignoring the seriousness of this crime."

"Crime?" skinny dude repeated. "It was your plan."

So my inside job theory had been partially right. Good to know paying attention in FBI school rather than doodling in my notebook had paid off. I faced Whitetail. "Ripping off your customers was your idea?"

"You believe him?" Whitetail sneered. "It's obvious he'll say anything to get out of jail time."

Skinny dude fired off, "Last year he told me how easy it'd be to rip off senior groups and foreign tourists. When a tour bus pulls in, I'm the first one he calls. Check my phone records. *He* called *me* tonight. I'm telling the truth! He's lying." He pointed at the security guard. "She knows. She's paid to look the other way."

Greedy damn people. Preying on the elderly. My gaze caught Dawson's. "Have you heard grumbling from locals about missing money or wallets after they visited here?"

Dawson shrugged. "First I've heard of it."

"Me, too," came from behind me. A craggy-faced Indian wearing the tribal police uniform stepped forward. I recognized him from a case we'd worked last week. Officer Spotted Bear's gaze whipped between the security guard, the manager and his thief for hire. "Guess we'll have to take all three of you in to figure out what's what, eh?"

Whitetail threw his hands in the air. "I have a casino to run! I can't just leave."

"That ain't a request," the other cop, Officer Begly, responded.

"I'm pretty sure you don't wanna be around when the tribal president gets here anyway."

The young man who took my coat stepped forward and held up his phone. "I taped everything and sent it to my uncle, who just happens to be the tribal president." He grinned at the cops. "He's speeding here so I hope he don't get arrested, hey."

I wasn't surprised by the tribal president's immediate attention to this situation. The casino employed lots of people on the reservation. In recent months scandal had broken out at two other Indian casinos in South Dakota, resulting in loss of jobs and revenue because of managerial mismanagement, so keeping this place open was key.

Whitetail shouted obscenities and lunged at the kid. Talk about satisfying—shoving Whitetail's smug face in the dirt while Officer Spotted Bear cuffed him.

An ambulance arrived along with a whole crush of people. Dawson and I got separated. By the time he tracked me down my adrenaline rush had faded. I shivered in the chilly air as I answered Officer Begly's questions and the EMTs patched up the pickpocket.

"Thanks for your help on this, Gunderson."

"No problem. Make sure those bus tour people get their wallets back."

"Will do." He gave me a critical once-over. "No offense, but you look like hell. Go home."

"Oh, and—"

"And…we're leaving." Dawson's big palm was warm against my lower back as he herded me away. "Do I need to have the EMTs look at you?"

I scowled. "Not unless you think they'll sew up the rip in my dress."

"Speaking of dresses…with the way you had your knee on the punk's wrist and the other knee by his shoulder, he had the perfect opportunity to look up your skirt."

"Which is why I never wear dresses," I shot back.

"More's the pity, Sergeant Major."

I couldn't tell if he was being sarcastic. "You saw him knock me on my ass?"

"Uh-huh. But you showed off them super FBI agent recovery skills, so I didn't get a chance to tackle him and grind him into dust. Pity about that, too."

That explained his lousy mood. Dawson wasn't happy about seeing me in danger and being too late to help me out. I tried to make light of it. "The real pity is I lost my appetite."

"So we're just gonna go home?"

I hated he sounded so disappointed. Again. "Yeah." After I climbed in the passenger side of my truck and ditched my gun, I remembered my coat. I hopped out and dug in my purse for the claim ticket.

"Whoa. Where you going?"

"I left my coat. I'll be right back."

Dawson snatched the ticket, snarling, "Would it be too much goddamn trouble to let me do one thing for you tonight after you've been beat to shit?"

I shivered violently, from the cold, the adrenaline crash and his harsh tone.

"Get in the truck and stay there."

I didn't argue.

When Dawson returned, he draped my coat over me. We didn't talk on the drive home, which wasn't necessarily odd, but the mood was definitely altered and not the slightest bit romantic.

And whose fault is that?

Mine. Again.

As soon as Dawson parked at the ranch, my boots hit the dirt and I hustled up the porch steps wanting to put this disastrous night behind me.

But Dawson spun me around and crowded me against the wall. He cradled my face in his hands, forcing me to look at him. "What's wrong now?"

I inhaled and let out a long, slow breath. "I can't even have a simple date with you without somehow royally screwing it up. Now you're pissed off, hungry—"

"Mercy—"

"Look at me. I've got mud on my dress, dirt on my knees and grass in my hair. I'm a mess. I wanted… I tried to be… Just forget it."

"If you haven't noticed, I am looking at you. Christ, woman, I can't look away from you." Dawson covered my mouth with his. Not in a sweet kiss, but a frustrated one. "Yes, you looked sexy tonight in this hot little black number, but I gotta admit, the sexiest part of you isn't ever what you wear, Mercy, it's sexy seeing you in action."

"You were mad at me because I jumped into the action."

"No, I don't expect less than that from you." He rested his forehead on mine. "You are ten kinds of kick ass and you don't need me. Sometimes I wish I could sweep in and rescue you. Even if it's just saving you from getting a rip in your dress."

"I do need you, Dawson. Just not to come in, guns blazing, to save me." I pressed my lips to his. "I need you in ways that scare me." I kissed him again. "And I want you so much it makes me crazy to think about it."

"So don't think. In fact, forget about everything but this."

Any protest died as Dawson kissed me. Languidly. Assuredly.

Touched me in that leisurely manner that warned me he'd keep this slow and easy until slow and easy wasn't enough for either of us.

My baser instincts were screaming for more when his big hands slid my dress up past my hips. Then his hands moved down so his rough-skinned thumbs stroked the skin between my navel and the top of my thong.

He kissed a path down my throat and roughly yanked the top of my dress aside. His wet mouth closed over my right nipple and he bit down softly as the blunt tips of his fingers teased the underside of my breasts.

A noise burst from my mouth, half sigh, half hiss. I untangled my hands from his hair, running them down his broad chest to his belly until I reached his belt buckle. I tugged.

Cheap-ass thing popped loose on the first try.

He inhaled a swift breath when I lowered the zipper and freed him, tracing the hard length from tip to root.

Our eyes met. Words were unnecessary. Unwanted.

Dawson eased back only far enough to drop his Wranglers. Then he hoisted me against the side of the house and held me there. Bending his knees, he thrust inside me, hard and high.

This was what I needed. This man knew exactly how to make my world tilt and at the same time set it right again.

Staring into my eyes, he slowly pumped his hips. "More?"

"God yes."

Dawson angled his head and put his lips on mine, eating at my mouth, destroying me with his voracious kisses. Slamming into my body with finesse that always shocked me. Stroking inside me with precision that robbed me of air and reason.

The tight coiling sensation built. Sweat trickled down my back. In the haze of passion I heard the rhythmic clank of his belt buckle hitting the siding. The harsh mix of our breathing. Holding myself rigid, I pulled away, craving that elusive pulsing rush. When he buried his lips in the curve where my neck met my shoulder, it was over. I unraveled.

When I returned to earth, Dawson watched my face with a hunger that made my belly swoop. He pressed my knees wide and took what he needed. Hard. Fast. Urgently. Then he exploded with a shout, and damn if that didn't send me soaring right over the edge with him again.

Luckily I had something solid holding me up, because I became completely boneless. Mindless. Sated in a way that went beyond hot sex. Then Dawson sweetened the finish, sending new chills across my skin with his every whispered word, with each labored breath against my damp skin, with each soft kiss.

When I felt him smile against my neck, I murmured, "What?"

"I'm thinking for the piss-poor way it started, this was the best date ever."

Relieved, I laughed. "And I haven't even broken out the handcuffs yet."

VACATION INTERRUPTED

A Lucy Kincaid/Sean Rogan Story

ALLISON BRENNAN

Kincaid and Rogan are plunged—literally—into another adventure. Two pairs of lovers, plus one psycho, equals a less-than-ideal getaway. —SB

"No dead bodies, no psychopaths, no one trying to kill us." Sean Rogan leaned back on the blanket spread out on the semi-secluded beach. "Just you and me, princess." He took her hand and closed his eyes.

In five days, Lucy was to report at Quantico to start her twenty-week FBI training. She'd suggested a few weeks ago that she and Sean find a couple days to go away—alone. They'd tried twice since they first started seeing each other six months ago, but each time their vacation plans were ruined by criminal activity. Because they were both so busy—Lucy working at the regional FBI office and Sean at his security company, RCK East—Lucy didn't think they'd have the opportunity.

On Tuesday morning, Sean announced he'd finished his assignment early and asked if she wanted to go to the beach. When Lucy said yes, she hadn't expected to leave an hour later in Sean's plane, landing before noon at a small executive airport on Cape Cod in Massachusetts.

Though early August was the height of the tourist season, Sean finagled a wonderful room at a bed-and-breakfast with a view of the bay. Lucy didn't want to ask how—her boyfriend relied heavily on his charm to get him in and out of tricky situations. If that failed, he used his brains or brawn.

Lucy rarely relaxed, and didn't particularly enjoy sunbathing—ironic considering she had earned many blue ribbons and trophies swimming in high school and for Georgetown University—but she found herself half-asleep under the large umbrella Sean had pitched, the soothing lap of waves rolling up the shore leeching the tension from her muscles.

A scream shattered her peaceful afternoon. Lucy sat up quickly; Sean was already on his feet scanning the horizon. It had come from a young woman standing on the shoreline. "Someone help him!"

The blonde was looking out into the ocean, pointing to a man flailing in the waves about a hundred and fifty yards out. Sean was already running and Lucy followed, searching for a lifeguard tower. The only one she spotted was so far away she couldn't see the person manning the booth.

Lucy had spent her high school summers working as a lifeguard in San Diego, and while she didn't have a tube or float, she spotted a boogie board near the shoreline. She didn't know or care who it belonged to, but strapped the board's leash around her ankle and ran into the ocean. The salt water was cold and itchy against her warm, dry skin. "Sean—get the lifeguard!" she ordered.

She pictured where she last saw the man, then swam toward that spot with long, confident strides. The shore was shallow, but fifty yards out it dropped steeply and the water turned choppy.

Every few seconds Lucy stopped briefly to ensure she was still headed toward the troubled swimmer. Her hundred-yard record in competition was 48:10, but she was fighting the current and waves, and it took three times that long.

When she thought she was close to the man, she stopped and treaded water. She didn't see anyone. Had she passed him? The waves were high enough to thwart her view, so she rode them up and down, looking 360 degrees.

Something brushed by her ankle. She dived, fearing the victim was underwater and unconscious, but didn't find anything. She surfaced, dived again, deeper, and swimming a wider perimeter.

Lucy breached the surface, fearing she was too late. As she began to lose hope, she spotted the man only a few feet away, his face twisted with pain and fear as he slipped under again.

She dived at an angle, kicking with all her strength, making a straight line to where she predicted he'd be if sinking. Her hands made contact with flesh, and she grabbed what she could—his biceps, it turned out—and kicked toward the surface, pulling the added weight with her.

She gasped for air when she broke through the surface. She immediately turned the man to his back because it was easier to help him float if he was lying as flat as possible. He wasn't unconscious, but definitely in distress and noticeably exhausted. He coughed and pushed at her, his eyes unfocused.

"I'm here to help," she said.

"Get away!"

He pushed her down, but Lucy saw it coming. She dunked below the surface so he couldn't hold her down, and then popped up a couple feet away.

Disoriented, he must be on drugs. He tried to swim, but a wave hit him in the face, almost pushing him under. She grabbed him. "I'm a lifeguard. Calm down!"

Lucy put the boogie board under his body to help him stay afloat. "Remain calm," she repeated. She glanced toward the shore and saw the lifeguard swimming swiftly toward her. "Help's coming."

"Someone," he gasped. "Someone here." He coughed up water.

"Calm down or you'll hyperventilate. Slow, deep breaths."

"Kill," he breathed heavily. "Me."

Someone tried to kill him? She scanned the area, but being this far out diminished visibility. The only other swimmers were much closer to the shore, where it was only a few feet deep.

The lifeguard approached on a rescue board. He rolled off, barely glanced at Lucy, his attention focused on the near-drowning victim. "What's your name?" he asked the victim.

"Ted."

"I'm Andrew. I'll get you back to shore." He glanced at Lucy. "You okay?"

"I'm good." She rested a minute while Andrew secured Ted to the rescue board. When he was ready, the lifeguard pulled the board with Ted and she followed at a steady pace.

Was Ted delirious or had someone really tried to kill him?

By the time she got back to the shore, Andrew was assessing Ted's injuries. An EMT unit was coming down the beach.

"Thank you, thank you," the blonde repeated. "What happened?"

The lifeguard said, "Caught in a riptide is my guess." Lucy didn't think so, but before she could question Ted or the lifeguard, the EMT arrived.

Sean pulled Lucy to him and hugged her tightly. His body felt hot against her cold skin. She held on, shaking from the adrenaline spike and cold water, grateful for someone to lean on.

He looked down at her, his dark blue eyes full of both worry and pride. He pushed her long, dark hair out of her face. "You really don't know how to relax, do you?" He kissed her repeatedly. "Let's get you in a hot shower."

"I need it."

He smiled at her, his dimple practically winking. "Me, too."

● ● ●

While Sean and Lucy napped after sharing a long shower, the phone rang. Wendy Potter, Ted's fiancée, insisted on taking them to drinks as a thank-you. "Why'd you give her our number?" Sean moaned. Sean tried to talk Lucy out of agreeing, but Lucy hadn't been able to get Ted's odd comment out of her mind.

Three hours later, just after sunset, they walked into a popular club. "One hour, tops," Lucy assured Sean as they spotted the other couple.

"I'm holding you to that." Sean glanced at his watch.

Lucy smiled as they sat down. "You look much better than you did earlier," she said to Ted. He was of average height and build, with a warm manner and attractive smile, even though he appeared both tired and apprehensive. Lucy's mother would classify Wendy as "cute as a button"—blond-haired, blue-eyed and petite. She, too, looked worried.

"We don't know how to thank you," Wendy said.

"I'm just glad I could help."

"What happened out there?" Sean asked. "The lifeguard said you were caught in a riptide?"

Ted shook his head. "No, and the risk of riptides was low today. I checked before I went out."

"You were out pretty far," Lucy said.

He looked sheepish. "I wasn't paying attention, I'll admit. Then I began to feel light-headed and my heart was racing. I felt high, but I haven't done drugs since college. Then—" he glanced at Wendy.

She said, "It's not like she wouldn't do it!"

Lucy's interest was piqued. "Excuse me?"

"His ex-girlfriend."

Ted took a long drink from his beer. "I broke up with Patty a year ago, and she's made my life a living hell since then."

"You think she drugged you?"

"I think she tried to kill me. I felt something grab my legs. I kicked and thrashed, and it still pulled me down. I know it sounds ludicrous, but she's a diver."

"Did you tell the police?" Lucy asked. They remained silent. "You need to file a report and get a restraining order."

Wendy laughed humorlessly. Ted said, "I can't go to the police. Patty is a cop. The first time she harassed me, it was right after I moved out. She trashed my new apartment. I filed a report, but there was no proof she did it. Then two of her cop friends beat me up when I was walking to my car after work. She then started following me, accidentally bumping into me at a restaurant, or the movies, things like that."

Wendy said, "Six months ago I transferred to Boston for a job and met Ted. On our third date, Patty showed up at the restaurant and made a scene. The manager called the police, and when they arrived, they arrested Ted! If I hadn't been there, I wouldn't have believed it. He didn't *do* anything except try to calm her down."

"A week later," Ted said, "I was arrested for assault. Patty said I'd gone to her house and when she told me to leave I hit her. I was never there!"

"You have other options," Lucy said. "Reporting her to internal affairs, for example. Or to the FBI if you're concerned about police corruption."

"I didn't know I could go to the FBI. I guess that's next." He sighed, defeated. "I just want my life back. I proposed to Wendy on Saturday, and we were enjoying our vacation until today. How did she find us? We even lied to our friends and families, told them we were going to Maine because we didn't want them accidentally telling her where we were."

Lucy had been skeptical when they started their story, but they both had the right body language and verbal responses. Still, while police corruption existed, could a cop get her buddies to participate in such harassment? "Why would her friends help her?"

"She's a liar," Wendy said. "She told me once that Ted left her because she was pregnant, then had a miscarriage. Then she changed her story and said Ted made her have an abortion. *Then* she said she had her tubes tied because Ted didn't want any kids."

"None of that was true," Ted said. "She even called my mother and told her we were engaged! The only reason the assault charges were dropped was because I had a good lawyer, but then *Patty* got a restraining order against *me!*"

Sean spoke up for the first time. "Can I see your cell phone?" Ted handed it over. While inspecting the device, Sean asked, "Have you posted any pictures of your trip on the internet? On Facebook? Emailed anyone?"

Wendy shook her head. "No. We didn't want them to know— God, I hate that she's turned us into liars, too!"

"I know how she found you," Sean said. He powered down the phone and took out the battery. "Don't use your phone until you contact your provider and tell them to wipe your backup files, then have the software reinstalled. You'll lose everything on the phone, but it'll also wipe her GPS tracking program."

"She had us bugged?" Wendy asked, incredulous.

"Close. She knew exactly where the phone was at all times."

"I'll get another phone," Ted said.

Sean shook his head. "Won't do any good. The program is integrated and unless you get a completely new phone number and account, it will be downloaded from your backup files."

"We have friends in law enforcement who might be able to help," Lucy said.

"It's too late," Ted said. "Wendy and I have been talking about leaving Boston and moving to California. My sister lives there and said we can stay with her until we find jobs."

"And you don't think she knows where your sister lives?" Lucy said. "Your ex-girlfriend is obsessed. If she tried to kill you today, moving cross-country isn't going to stop her. If you file charges—" She stopped. "Did you get a drug test this afternoon?" When they shook their heads, she added, "Depending on the drug, it may still be in your system. Go to the hospital first thing in the morning. Or now." Though, even if the test was positive, there would be no proof that his ex-girlfriend had been the person who'd drugged him.

Wendy said, "I thought I saw her yesterday, but dismissed it—I wasn't certain because her hair was much darker and she wore big sunglasses."

"Even if we could prove she was here, that's still not going to help." Sean picked up Ted's phone again. "I have an idea."

Lucy didn't like the plan even before hearing Sean's plan. "I already don't like it."

He grinned as he popped the battery back in the phone. "What do you mean? I haven't even told you."

"I know you, Sean Rogan."

He leaned over and kissed her, then said softly, "You know and I know that Ted's psychotic ex-girlfriend will get caught eventually, but probably not until after they're dead."

Wendy gasped.

"Tactful," Lucy muttered.

Sean turned to the newly engaged couple. "So this is the plan. We're taking your phone and your room. Where are you staying?"

"We have a cottage on the beach," Wendy said. "But I don't understand."

"I also need her full name and address if you have it."

"Why would you help us?"

"It's what I do." Sean slid over his business card. "I'm in the security business. It's clear to me that your stalker has escalated. She's going to kill you unless we stop her. And it's also clear that going through the proper channels at this point will take too long. So what do you say?"

Lucy wanted them to decline, but wasn't surprised when they both nodded their heads. "What do you want us to do?" Ted asked.

Sean explained how they would trade phones and rooms, then wait.

"Do you really think she'll try to kill Ted again?"

"If she's still in town? I guarantee it."

• • •

For well over an hour, Sean and Lucy sat in Ted and Wendy's small cottage, digging up everything they could on the parties involved. It wasn't that they didn't believe Ted and Wendy, but their story did stretch credibility. A cursory background check showed them to be exactly who they said they were.

Because of his P.I. license and RCK connections, Sean could go deep. Because of his computer skills, he could do it faster than most. "Patricia Annette Glover, thirty-two, born in Providence, Rhode Island," he said. "Received an AA from a community college. Joined the Army Reserves when she was eighteen. She went through the police academy and worked for Boston Police Department for seven years, then her Reserves unit was called up for service in Iraq. She volunteered for two more tours. Was honorably discharged three years ago."

"And went back to Boston P.D.?"

"Newton Police Department, not far from Boston."

"Big city to small city." Lucy wondered why the switch. "I don't suppose you can access her records?"

Sean raised an eyebrow. "Legally? No. But it wouldn't be difficult—"

Lucy shook her head rapidly. "Please don't."

He laughed. "You're so much fun to tease."

"What can you *legally* get on her?"

"She and our man Ted lived together for a year. And he moved out fourteen months ago like he said. Here's her photo—very pretty."

Lucy examined the image of the sandy blonde—Patty was attractive at first glance, but her smile was forced and didn't reach her eyes. The picture was taken at a police function, though not everyone was in uniform. While the rest of the group were close together, hands on the arms or shoulders of their colleagues, Patty was distinctly separated, an aura of loneliness surrounding her.

Lucy made up the bed to look like two people were sleeping close together. She eyed her handiwork. In the dark, it would pass.

"Glover has clean credit, pays her bills on time, and stays under the radar. If I had just two days, I could have my brother look at her military record through his contacts—getting it through proper channels would take forever." Sean put his computer to sleep and turned off all the lights. Streetlights illuminated the room just enough to make out shapes and shadows. "On the surface, they're all clean. Even Ted and Wendy's social networking is minimal."

Lucy stood by the front window—the two side windows were too narrow for entry—and Sean had the cottage door covered. They hadn't seen any sign of Ted's ex-girlfriend, but now that the lights were off, they expected if she was going to show, it would be before dawn. Much easier to attack when your prey was asleep.

"This isn't the romantic getaway I'd planned," Sean said.

"We'll do it again."

He didn't say anything for a minute. "You're leaving in a few days. You'll be wrapped up in training."

"I'll still have twenty-four hours off every weekend. Saturday night, I'm yours."

He grinned. "I'm holding you to that, princess."

"They say absence makes the heart grow fonder," Lucy said, "but I already know I'll miss you." She'd been preparing for her FBI training for what seemed like years—everything she'd done since college had been aimed toward this moment. Now, she had something more she cared about, someone she loved, that equaled her passion for her career. And, maybe, if she allowed herself to feel deeply, surpassed it.

"How does love turn so wrong?" Lucy asked.

"Wrong? There's nothing wrong with the way we feel—oh. You're thinking about Ted and Patty."

"I mean, I understand the psychology of stalkers. How they are created, their obsessive need. That it's about control and fear and the inability to allow another to have freedom. The excessive unwarranted jealousy, the doubt, the lack of self-worth, as if all that they are is because of someone else. But when is the switch flipped? What's the trigger? What makes them want to kill someone they profess to love?"

"Because it's not love and it never was," Sean said. "Love is letting go, confident your lover will return. Love is helping make your partner the best that they can be."

"You do that for me," Lucy whispered.

"It goes both ways. That's why we work. Never forget that, Luce."

They remained silent, focused on the sounds outside, waiting.

Sean broke the silence thirty minutes later and said, "We still need a real vacation."

"I get four days off at Thanksgiving."

"Those days are mine."

"It'll be in San Diego. My parents will shoot me if I don't go home this year. But between my parents and brothers and sisters, we won't have much time alone."

"We'll find the time. Provided no one we know has a psycho exgirlfriend."

Lucy almost laughed. She looked at her watch. It was well after midnight; they'd been here over three hours. She called her cell phone, which they'd given to Ted. No answer. "I can't reach Ted."

"Dammit! I should have stayed with them. Let's go."

• • •

Under a broken streetlight, Patty Glover sat on a bench and watched the bed-and-breakfast for three hours. The night was still warm, but a light breeze off the bay cooled her.

She wore all black, her newly darkened hair pulled sharply back from her face, the faint hint of dye surrounding her.

Ted thought he could reject her. He thought he could exchange her for a cuter, less-damaged model.

She'd spent three years of her life with Ted. From the first moment she saw him, she knew he was the only one for her.

She'd come off active duty broken. She'd thought she'd hardened her heart and put the war behind her, but around every corner she saw the dead and dying. Until Ted smiled at her the morning of May 3—three years and three months ago—when she had the gun in her pocket, a fraction of a second from putting it to her chin and pulling the trigger.

"You look like you lost your best friend," he had said. Then he smiled. His smile melted her heart.

"It's been a rough couple months." The gun weighed heavy in her grip.

"I'm Ted Odell. I started working at Boston College last week."
"You're a teacher?"

He laughed, and that's when she fell in love. "I'm an accountant."

"Patty Glover—I don't know what I'm doing."

"Maybe you just need someone to talk it through. How about coffee?"

That day, Ted saved her life.

She'd clung to Ted ever since, knowing when he was drifting away, knowing her need was driving him away. And then he left… but she couldn't let him go. The thought of another woman having Ted's heart, his smile, his optimism—it killed Patty deep inside.

Did they actually think she'd fall for their trick? Did they actually think she was that *stupid?* She'd survived three tours of duty in Iraq, alternating periods of intense boredom with intense action. Her best friend died in her arms. Her commander had his head blown off only inches from hers. She could still taste his blood. It could have been her.

She blinked, and for a split second she forgot where she was. She looked around, her hand in her pocket, clutching the gun.

Cape Cod. Ted. Deceiving her, again.

The lights were off in the bed-and-breakfast, had been for some time, but Patty waited another few minutes before she rose from the bench and disappeared into the house.

She was dead without Ted, and so he would be, as well.

• • •

On the short drive to their bed-and-breakfast, Lucy called the local police. She hung up. "I don't know if they took me seriously after I told them no lights, no sirens. They estimate five to seven minutes."

Sean stopped the rental car around the corner, checked his gun and holstered it. "We can't wait," Sean said.

Sean led the way through the shadows toward the B and B, Lucy right behind him. They unlocked the front door and quietly went upstairs to where their room was located in the back. He motioned for Lucy to turn the knob while he trained his gun on the door.

It was unlocked. On three, she pushed open the door.

Sean came in high while Lucy moved aside. He scanned the room, saw no immediate threat. A body lay motionless on the floor. Wendy.

Sean turned on the lights and searched the room while Lucy checked Wendy's pulse and injuries. "She's alive," Lucy said. "She hit her head—there's some blood, but her pulse is strong and steady."

"Coldcocked, most likely. Glover probably threatened to kill her if Ted didn't go with her." Standard tactic since Wendy wasn't Patty's primary target.

Lucy gently shook Wendy. "Wendy, it's Lucy Kincaid. Wake up."

Wendy stirred, moaning.

"Wendy," Lucy said, "where did Patty take Ted?"

"I—I don't know."

Lucy helped her into a chair and asked, "Did Patty say anything?"

"It happened so fast!" Wendy began to shake and Sean tossed Lucy a blanket, which she wrapped around the traumatized woman. "She had a gun! Please, don't let her kill him."

Sean glanced around. "Where's Lucy's phone?"

Wendy blinked. "I—I don't know."

Sean pulled out his cell phone and thumbed in his code. "Got her, the bitch." The phone was only two blocks away, near the harbor. He woke the B and B owner and told him to call for an ambulance and tell the police where they were headed, then he and Lucy left.

It was faster to run to the beach than backtrack to the car. When they arrived, Patty was maneuvering a small motorboat away from the harbor. Very quickly she disappeared with Ted into the moonless night.

Sean made a beeline to a speedboat docked at the end. "I'm just going to borrow it," he told Lucy as he hot-wired the boat in half a minute, pleased he hadn't lost his touch. "I can get to her in three minutes, but she'll hear us." He turned on the radar and adjusted his course to follow.

"I don't see how we have a choice."

"Luce, I'll admit—I'm at a loss. If she's suicidal, threats aren't going to stop her."

"We're going to have to wing it."

"There's a spotlight on the front of the boat." He pointed to the switch on the dash. "She'll be momentarily blinded when I flip it on."

"She's an army private you said, right?"

"You have a plan?"

"I think we can momentarily confuse her. Soldiers are used to taking orders. Can you be Sergeant Rogan for five minutes?"

"I know what you want." Sean gripped her hand. "A distraction."

"Exactly. As soon as you're close enough, I'll slip into the water. Turn on the light and talk to her. I'll swim over to the boat and—"

Sean shook his head. "Hell, no. I'll swim—"

"She'll be more inclined to take orders from a male officer, and I'm a better swimmer than you." The latter was true, but Sean didn't relish the idea of Lucy in the middle of the bay with a psycho stalker ready to commit murder-suicide. "The waters are calm tonight," she continued. "And I'll have a life vest." She was already pulling it on. "When I get to the boat, if her back is to Ted I'll signal him to jump."

"And if it's not?"

"Plan B."

"Which is?"

"I'll figure it out when I get there."

Sean hated the idea, but he didn't have a better one, and they were out of time. "Don't die on me tonight, princess." He kissed her.

"Not tonight."

He glanced at the radar; the other boat was slowing down. When he was thirty feet away, he slowed the speedboat and nodded to Lucy. She slipped silently into the dark water.

He turned the spotlight on at its brightest setting and picked up the microphone.

"Private Glover!" he commanded in an authoritarian voice. He'd learned well from his brothers.

Patty was sitting in the chair at the wheel. Ted was handcuffed at the stern. They both turned toward the light. Patty held one hand to her eyes and raised her gun hand.

"Glover!" Sean said, the mic making his voice even more powerful. "Stand down, soldier! That's an order!"

Lucy swam just outside the glow of the spotlight. Sean hoped Patty couldn't see her.

"Go away!" Glover shouted, her voice small across the distance. Sean was inching closer; the other boat was at a full stop.

"You don't want to hurt a civilian," Sean said.

Glover raised her gun and fired at the spotlight; the shot dinged the metal framing. She fired again and the light went out.

Now Sean was in the dark. He couldn't see Lucy or the other boat.

Glover yelled at Ted, her voice alternately angry and desperate. "Why did you leave me? You saved my life! I need you. It hurts so much—I need you."

"Patty—I'm sorry," Ted said, his voice cracking. "I'm so sorry."

Frantic to find another distraction, Sean searched the captain's box and picked up a flashlight—not as strong as the spotlight, but it would have to suffice.

He waited just a few seconds until he thought Lucy would be in position.

He turned on the flashlight. He was much closer now, only fifteen feet away, and was pretty certain Glover could see him. He had the flashlight in his left fist so he could steady his gun hand on his wrist. He shined the light directly into Glover's eyes. She put her arm up and aimed at him, but before she fired Ted turned his head to the starboard side. She followed his gaze. Sean couldn't see Lucy, but when Glover turned her gun rapidly toward the water and pressed the trigger, Sean fired three times in rapid succession.

Glover only got off that one shot. Her body jerked as each bullet hit. She stumbled backward, then slumped to the floor.

Sean steered his boat to the edge of the smaller craft. "Lucy!"

he called. He couldn't tell if Glover's bullet had gone wild or been spot-on. He didn't see Lucy.

Fear warred with rage. Losing Lucy was not an option. He wouldn't survive it. She was everything to him.

Pushing back his rising panic, he shone the flashlight in the water next to Glover's boat. At first, he didn't see anything. Then Lucy broke the surface, taking in a deep breath. Relief flooded his body.

"Clear!" he called to her. Lucy pulled herself up into the other boat. She kicked Glover's gun away, then checked for a pulse. She shook her head and covered the body with a tarp.

Sean tethered the boats together, then boarded and assessed Ted. He was bleeding from his nose and mouth, but otherwise appeared unharmed.

"Oh, God, Wendy?" Ted's eyes were frantic.

Sean picked the lock on the handcuffs. "Wendy's okay. Can you get yourself into the other boat?"

Ted nodded. "Thank you so much."

Sean grabbed Lucy and held her close. Her skin was ice-cold. "Lucy—"

"You didn't have a choice."

"When she turned her gun toward you…"

"I'm okay."

He helped her back to his boat, wrapped her in a blanket and in his arms, holding her. His heart still raced from the single minute he'd thought she'd been shot.

"I love you, Luce." He didn't have anything else to say.

She kissed him, then burrowed against his body heat. "I love you, Sean. But I'm ready for a hot bath."

"If I'm in that bath with you, you're reading my mind."

She smiled. "You are."

I HEARD
A ROMANTIC STORY
LEE CHILD

One paragraph, one voice, one story by Lee Child.
Enough said. —SB

I heard a romantic story. It was while I was waiting to kill a guy. And not just a guy, by the way. They were calling this guy a prince, and I guess he was. A lot of those guys over there are princes. Not just one or two a country. Families have princes. All kinds of families. They have princes of their own. There are hundreds of them. They have so many that some of them are twenty-five-year-old assholes. That kind of prince. And he was the target. This young asshole. He was going to show up in a large Mercedes sedan. He was going to get out of the backseat and walk about ten steps to the porch of the house. The porch was supposed to be like they have at a Marriott hotel, but smaller. Where you get out of the shuttle bus. Only they made it too small for cars. I guess it was supposed to keep the sun off people. Maybe animals. Because, by the way, this was India. It was the middle of the day and everything was scorching hot and too bright to look at. But this guy was going to walk to this porch. And the porch was kind of walled in partly. And as soon as I was sure he was moving at a consistent pace, I had to time it right so that I actually pushed the button first, and then he got to the walled part of the porch second, and of course the wall was where the bomb was. So it was just a button job. Easy enough for one guy to do. Except of course, they sent two guys. But then, they always do. No guy is ever alone. You go to the movies and you see the guy all on his own? Obviously he's not all on his own, because there's a cameraman right in his face. Otherwise you wouldn't be seeing him. There would be no movie. That's a minimum of two guys right there. And that's how it was for us. Two guys. If I was a sniper, you'd have to call this other guy the spotter. Except I wasn't a sniper. This was a button job. I didn't need a spotter. But he was there. Probably a CIA guy. He was talking to me. It was like he had to validate the hit and give his permission. Maybe they didn't want any radio snafus. So they put the guy right next to me. Right in my ear. And presumably he knows this Mercedes sedan is some distance away, and therefore some time away, and therefore his validation was not going to be required until some future period. And we could see the road, anyway. Certainly we could see the last hundred yards of it. After the turn. And we'd have seen dust clouds miles away. And we weren't seeing any, which gave this guy time to talk. And he talked about how we'd gotten as far as we had, with this prince. He laid the whole thing out. He told me how it was done, basically. Which was not complicated, by the way. It was just a number of fairly simple things. They all had to work together, and we'd get a positive result. And obviously one of the strands was the old thing with the girl, and that part was working fine. Which is what this other guy was telling me. Because he seemed to be in charge of the whole girl part of the program. He was the chief. He sent the girl. Which was obviously a matter of selection. It's about judging the task and sending the right girl. Which this guy did. I don't think there was a lack of self-confidence in his choice. The problem was the best girl for the job in his professional judgment was also the same girl he was in love with, which obviously placed him in a predicament. He had to send the girl he loved into battle. And not battle with guns and bombs. The weapons his girlfriend was going to use were considerably more personal. It was that sort of game. And the guy knew it, obviously. He was the chief. I'm not saying he invented it, by the way. I'm saying he was currently the world's leading exponent. He was the big dog. It's not a question of second-guessing the guy. He did the right thing. He was a professional. He put his country first. The girl went. And did a fine job obviously. Within two weeks the guy was heading to this house in his Mercedes. That's diligence, right there. Two weeks is a pretty short time. To get a positive result in two weeks is extraordinary. Positive in the sense that I still had to push the button. I was a strand, too. I was the final strand. All I had to do was push the button. If the guy showed up. Which he did, because of this other guy's girlfriend. She must have done all sorts of things. The guy knew that. This is what these girls do. But he's kind of denying it. That's what he's saying to me. He's making it different for her. Maybe she didn't do all these things. Or maybe she did. The guy didn't make it entirely clear to me. But if she did, it was because she was doing it for the mission, of which he was the chief. She knew he knew it was mission critical. So she did it. She delivered the guy, and I'm waiting to push my button, which is on a cell phone, by the way. Cell phones are what we use now. They built a whole network just for us to blow things up. Private capital. Providers who take complaints. With radios you couldn't complain. If something went wrong you shrugged your shoulders and you tried again the next day. But if some guy gets his call dropped, he complains. He complains real loud. Maybe it was some big deal he was doing. So the cell companies keep things working. The only drawback being the time lag. You dial a call, it's a long time before it rings. There are all kinds of towers and computers in the way. All kind of technical management. The delay can be eight whole seconds, which was why it was all about timing. I had to judge his pace so I could push the button eight whole seconds before he got where he was going. After he arrived in the car. Which wasn't happening yet, which gave the guy time to talk, which he did, mostly about this girl. She was living with him. Obviously not for the two weeks she was with the prince, which was the point of the whole conversation, which was actually a monologue on his part in that he was attempting to convince me he was okay with it. And that she was okay with him being okay with it. It was a minefield. But allegedly both of them were okay with it. This is what the guy was trying to persuade me about. While we waited. Which turned out to be for an hour, by the way. For one hour. We were in position one hour early. Which proves the guy planned to use the time talking, because he was the one who drew up the schedule and he was the one who was doing the talking. About this girl. This girl was an angel. Which I was prepared to believe. This was a hard guy to tolerate. But he told me all the stuff they did together and I couldn't help but believe they had several happy years behind them. They weren't doing new-relationship stuff anymore, but they weren't doing old-relationship stuff yet, either. They were doing normal things, happy, maybe still a little experimental, same as some people do for a long time. I was convinced. It was a convincing description. At the time I was sure it was true. Which it was, obviously. Eventually a lot of people saw it for themselves. But it was possible to see it way back. I believed the guy. He sent the girl to the prince. They've both had a great time the weekend before. They're cool with it. He's okay with it, and she's okay with everything. So they do it. Monday morning, off she goes. And that should be it. He's the chief, she's a girl in the field, there should be no contact between them. None at all. Organizationally she's lost to him now. She's gone. She might not be coming back. Because some of them don't. There have been fatalities. Hence the protocols. No personal involvement. Which they've been faking so far, but now they're going to have to do it for real. Except they don't. They sneak visits. Which is a huge off-the-charts no-no professionally. It's going to screw everything up forever. It's a double whammy. She's no longer deniable, and his cover is blown. But they did it. And not just once. They met five times. In two weeks. Five out of fourteen. That's a pretty decent fraction. Not far from one half. Which is a long time to be away. Her performance was miraculous. She got the job done in two weeks, half of which was spent back with her original boyfriend. Who was telling me all about these visits. Which was another breach of discipline right there. I mean, what was I? He should have asked for ID. But he didn't, which means he thought I was just some dumb guy who didn't matter. Which was ironic, because I was just the same as him. In fact I was exactly the same as him. I was a government operator, too. His equal in every way. Except I didn't have a girl. He was the one with the girl. And he was visiting her. The first time she was fine. She'd only just met the prince. They were still in the formal stages. The second time, not so much. They'd moved beyond the formal stages. Twenty-four lousy hours, and the prince was already doing stuff. That was totally clear. But we're talking national security here. The best kind. You blow someone up in India, you save a lot of problems later. Maybe you save the world. Obviously people like this guy and his girl have to believe this stuff. Or maybe they already believe this stuff before they join. Maybe that's why they seek out those jobs. Because they believe certain things. They believe there is something bigger than themselves. That's why the girl goes back to the prince, even after that second visit. We can guess what she's doing, because she's in a bad state when the third visit rolls around. The prince is not hitting her. This is not a physical problem. The prince might not be doing anything at all. He could be totally naive and inexperienced. He could be undemanding. There was a range of possibilities. But she had to supply his needs in a very submissive manner. Whatever they were. She had to smile and curtsey like she was the happiest girl in the world. Which is a strain, psychologically. She was not having a good time. But she went back. She was determined to complete the mission. That's the kind of person she was. Which put the chief in a permanent circular argument, of course. He couldn't stop the girl he loved because if he could he wouldn't have loved her. She would have insisted she go. He would have insisted she go. National security is a very important thing. These people believe that. They have to. So she went. And she kept on going back. She seemed stronger at the fourth visit. Better still at the fifth. She was in control now. She was doing it. She was like a boxer who just won the belt. Sure he hurts, but not much. She was like that. She was going to deliver him. She was the undisputed champion of the world. She was nearly done. She was coming home. Except maybe that boxer's hurting worse than he lets on. Maybe she was. Maybe she's tired, but she's close. So she fakes it with you. She's okay to go back. So she goes back. But part of faking was exaggerating. She's going to deliver him, but it's not going to be easy. Not like she's making out. She's going to have to offer incentives. Which she hasn't mentioned to you. Because she's exaggerating. She's telling you it's better than it is. She's in control, but not all the way. And she conceals it, so you don't know. And then you see the dust cloud miles away, and you wait, and then the Mercedes comes around the turn, the last hundred yards; it's an expensive car, but dusty, and it parks right where it should and the guy gets out of the backseat. And like a prick he leaves the door wide open behind him and just walks away, like he's the king of the world, and I'm already timing him. He's doing that kind of fit-guy hustle, which is actually slower than it looks, but I'm on it and I know exactly when I'm going to push the button. Then the girl bounds out of the car behind him, like she had dropped her pocketbook or something and was delayed for a moment, which is exactly what I think she did, because she's doing a kind of apologetic thing with the body language, a kind of I'm-an-idiot look, and then she catches up to the prince and she takes his arm in a kind of affectionate way. Almost an excited way, to be truthful, and you realize she got him there by promising him something special. In one of the rooms, perhaps. Maybe something he's never done before. They're giggling like schoolkids. They're bounding ahead. They're right there at the point where you have to hit the button. And by now the validation process is seriously screwed up. We're just babbling to each other. But we know one thing. National security is very important. It's bigger than either of us. We believe that stuff. I have to. So I hit the button. My timing was good. No reason why it wouldn't be. I had no lack of self-confidence in my estimate of speed and direction. Eight seconds. They were perfectly level with the wall when it went up. Both of them. And that was the end of the romantic story.

AUTHOR BIOGRAPHIES

LORI ARMSTRONG left the firearms industry in 2000. The first book in her Julie Collins series, *Blood Ties,* was nominated for a 2006 Shamus Award for Best First Novel. *Hallowed Ground* received a 2007 Shamus Award nomination and won the 2007 WILLA Cather Literary Award. *Shallow Grave* was nominated for a 2008 High Plains Book Award and finaled for the 2008 WILLA Cather Literary Award. *Snow Blind* won the 2009 Shamus Award for Best Paperback Original. The first book in the Mercy Gunderson series, *No Mercy,* won the 2011 Shamus Award for Best Hardcover Novel and was a finalist for the WILLA Cather Literary Award. *Mercy Kill* released in January 2011. *Dark Mercy* will release in 2013. Lori serves on the Board of Directors of Mystery Writers of America and lives in Rapid City, South Dakota.

● ● ●

JEFF AYERS is the author of the bestselling *Voyages of Imagination: The Star Trek Fiction Companion.* He reviews for the *Associated Press, Library Journal, Booklist* and *RT Book Reviews.* He has interviewed authors for such publications as *Writer* Magazine, the

Seattle Post-Intelligencer, Author Magazine and *The Big Thrill.*
Jeff lives near Seattle, Washington.

• • •

A born romantic, **BEVERLY BARTON** fell in love with *The Beauty and the Beast* epic at an early age, when her grandfather bought her an illustrated copy of the famous fairy tale. Before she learned to read and write, Beverly's vivid imagination created magical worlds and fabulous characters inside her mind.

Movies fascinated Beverly, and by the time she was seven she was rewriting the movies she saw on television and at the local theater to give them all happy endings. By the age of nine she'd penned her first novel. She wrote short stories, TV scripts, poetry and novels throughout high school and into college.

After her marriage and the births of her children, Beverly continued to be a voracious reader and a devoted moviegoer, but she put her writing aspirations on hold until her children were teenagers.

When Beverly rediscovered an old dream of becoming a published writer, no one was more supportive of her aspirations than her family. After writing over seventy books, receiving numerous awards and becoming a *New York Times* bestselling author, Beverly's career became her dream come true.

• • •

WILLIAM BERNHARDT is the nationally bestselling author of twenty-five novels, including the world-renowned Ben Kincaid series of mystery-thrillers—*Primary Justice, Capitol Betrayal. Library Journal* dubbed him the "master of the courtroom thriller." Other Bernhardt novels include *Nemesis: The Final Case of Eliot Ness, Double Jeopardy,* and the critically acclaimed *Dark Eye.* He has received the H. Louise Cobb Distinguished Author Award (Oklahoma State University) the Royden B. Davis Distinguished Author Award (University of Pennsylvania), and the Southern Writer's

Guild's Gold Medal Award. In addition to his novels, he has edited two anthologies as fundraisers for charitable causes, written two books for children, published essays, short stories and poems, constructed crossword puzzles for the *New York Times*, and written the book, music and lyrics for a musical. He is also one of the nation's most in-demand writing instructors. His renowned small group writing seminars have produced several bestselling authors over the past decade. His instructional DVDs, *The Fundamentals of Fiction*, are used by writing programs across the nation. You can learn more about him at www.williambernhardt.com, or you can email him at willbern@gmail.com.

● ● ●

ALLISON BRENNAN is the *New York Times* and *USA TODAY* bestselling and award-winning author of eighteen romantic thrillers and numerous short stories. *RT Book Reviews* calls Allison "a master of suspense" and her books "haunting," "mesmerizing," "pulse-pounding" and "emotionally complex." Lee Child called the first Lucy Kincaid book "a world-class nail-biter," and Lisa Gardner says, "Brennan knows how to deliver."

Allison lives on two acres outside Sacramento, California, with her husband Dan, their five children and assorted animals. She's often said she has no life outside of writing and kids—though she takes her research seriously by role-playing in SWAT training exercises, practicing at the gun range, and hanging out at the morgue. The fourth book in the Lucy Kincaid series, *Silenced*, was released by Minotaur/St. Martin's Press on April 24, 2012 and will be followed by *Stalked* in the fall. Find her online at www.allisonbrennan.com.

● ● ●

ROBERT BROWNE is an award-winning screenwriter and ITW Thriller Award–nominated author of five critically acclaimed thrillers. His first novel, *Kiss Her Goodbye,* was filmed as a pilot for a CBS television series and his latest, *The Paradise Prophecy,* is in development with Temple Hill Productions. Rob lives in California with his wife, two cats and a dog, and is always at work on the next book…

• • •

Inspired by a U.S. tissue harvesting case, **PAMELA CALLOW** wrote *Damaged* (June 2010), the first installment of her legal thriller series for MIRA Books. Pamela drew on her experience working in a blue-chip corporate environment to create series lead Kate Lange, a struggling thirtysomething lawyer, whom *RT Book Reviews* hailed as, "…a standout character." *Damaged* was chosen by Levy Home Entertainment as a June "Need to Read" Pick, with Top Ten Bestseller placement in Target and Walmart.

Indefensible (MIRA, January 2011), the second book of the Kate Lange thriller series, was described by *Omnimystery Reviews* as, "…a superbly plotted and suspenseful novel with a…riveting, dynamic storyline." *Tattooed,* the series' third installment, will be published in 2012.

Prior to making writing a career, Pamela worked as a strategy consultant for international firm Andersen Consulting. She is a member of the Nova Scotia Bar, and holds a Master's degree in Public Administration.

Pamela lives in Nova Scotia, along with her husband, two children and a pug. She loves to go for walks (unlike her dog), drink coffee, and is currently working on the next installment of the Kate Lange thriller series. Visit her at www.pamelacallow.com or at www. facebook.com/PamelaCallowAuthor.

• • •

Previously a television director, union organizer, theater technician and law student, **LEE CHILD** was fired and on the dole when he hatched a harebrained scheme to write a bestselling novel, thus saving his family from ruin. *Killing Floor* went on to win world-wide acclaim. The hero of his series, Jack Reacher, besides being fictional, is a kindhearted soul who allows Lee lots of spare time for reading, listening to music, the Yankees and Aston Villa. Visit him online at www.leechild.com.

• • •

J. T. ELLISON is the international award-winning author of seven critically acclaimed novels, multiple short stories and has been published in over twenty countries. A former White House staffer, she has worked extensively with the Metro Nashville Police, the FBI and various other law enforcement organizations to research her novels. She lives in Nashville with her husband and a poorly trained cat, and is hard at work on her next novel. Visit www.JTEllison.com for more insight into her wicked imagination, or follow her on Twitter @Thrillerchick.

• • •

BILL FLOYD lives in Hillsborough, North Carolina, with his wife, Amy, and his dog, Max. His first published novel, *The Killer's Wife*, won the Mary Higgins Clark Award for 2009. Floyd can often be found in dark music clubs listening to a variety of underground bands. His taste in fiction runs the gamut from literary to genre, with no apologies for either. He is currently working on a novel about secrets and the costs of keeping them. A sampling of his flash fiction can be found at www.billfloydbooks.com.

• • •

New York Times, Publishers Weekly and *USA TODAY* Bestseller **CINDY GERARD** cut her teeth on the works of Iris Johansan, Tammy Hoag and, of course, Sandra Brown, all of whom wrote romantic fiction before branching into the world of suspense. Cindy also wrote award-winning category romance novels for Bantam, Doubleday, Dell and later for Harlequin Books before coming to the realization that she had bigger, bolder, grittier stories to tell. Her fast-paced, action-packed Bodyguard and Black Ops., Inc. (BOI) series featuring covert paramilitary heroes, quickly became much loved among romantic suspense readers. Cindy's short story, "Dying to Score," showcases BOI fan favorites Johnny Duane Reed and Crystal "Tinkerbelle" Debrowski.

Cindy is a six-time Romance Writers of America RITA finalist and is proud to display two RITAs in her office. She considers herself fortunate to count many military families as both readers and friends. Cindy makes her home in Iowa with her husband, Tom, their Brittany Spaniel, Margaret, and their cats, Buddy and Sly. You can find all of Cindy's books at www.cindygerard.com.

• • •

HEATHER GRAHAM is the *New York Times* and *USA TODAY* bestselling author of over a hundred novels including suspense, paranormal, historical and mainstream Christmas fare. She lives in Miami, Florida, her home, and an easy shot down to the Keys where she can indulge in her passion for diving. Travel, research and ballroom dancing also help keep her sane; she is the mother of five, and also resides with two dogs, a cat and an albino skunk. She is CEO of Slush Pile Productions, a recording company and production house for various charity events. Look her up at www.theoriginalheathergraham.com, www.writersforneworleans. com or www.eheathergraham.com.

• • •

New York Times bestselling author **LAURA GRIFFIN** started her career in journalism before venturing into the world of romantic suspense. Her books have won numerous awards, including a 2010 RITA (*Whisper of Warning*) and a 2010 Daphne du Maurier Award (*Untraceable*). Her debut novel, *One Last Breath*, won the Booksellers Best Award for romantic suspense. Laura currently lives in

Austin where she is working on the next book in her popular Tracers series. Visit her at www.lauragriffin.com or www.facebook.com/LauraGriffinAuthor.

• • •

VICKI HINZE is an award-winning author of twenty-five novels, four nonfiction books and hundreds of articles published in as many as sixty-three countries. She's recognized by *Who's Who in America* and in the world as an author and an educator. Her first published novel, a romantic suspense, was a bestseller that sold in nearly a dozen foreign countries. Since then, she's shifted writing focus several times. After cocreating the first single-title open-ended continuity series, she turned to military life and has been credited with a Career Achievement Award for being one of the first to write military romantic suspense, military romantic intrigue and military romantic thrillers. Three years ago, she shifted her focus to Christian fiction, blending romantic thrillers with spiritual elements. Her willingness to take risks and blaze trails has won her many prestigious nominations and awards, though she does it because she loves the adventure of stretching boundaries. Learn more about Vicki at www.vickihinze.com and visit her Facebook page at www.facebook.com/Vicki.Hinze.Author.

• • •

ANDREA KANE'S psychological thriller *The Girl Who Disappeared Twice* became an instant *New York Times* bestseller, the latest in a long string of smash hits. It introduced Forensic Instincts, an eclectic team of maverick investigators, each with different personalities and talents, all with one common bond: a blatant disregard for authority. *The Line Between Here and Gone* is the next exhilarating installment in the Forensic Instincts series. Armed with skills and talents honed by years in the FBI and Special Forces, and training in behavioral and forensic psychology, the team solves seemingly impossible cases while walking a fine line between assisting and enraging law enforcement.

With a worldwide following and novels published in over twenty languages, Kane is also the author of eight romantic thrillers and fourteen historical romances. She lives in New Jersey with her family, where she is plotting new ways for Forensic Instincts to challenge the status quo.

• • •

Praised by *Publishers Weekly* as an author with a "flair for dialogue and eccentric characterizations," bestselling author **JULIE KENNER'S** books have hit lists as varied as *USA TODAY,* Waldenbooks, Barnes & Noble, and *Locus* Magazine. Julie is also a two-time RITA finalist, the winner of Romantic Times' Reviewer's Choice Award for Best Contemporary Paranormal of 2001, the winner of the Reviewers International Organization's Award for best romantic suspense of 2004 and best paranormal of 2005, and the winner of the National Readers' Choice Award for best mainstream book of 2005. She writes a range of stories including urban fantasy, paranormal romance and paranormal mommy lit, including the popular Demon-Hunting Soccer Mom series, currently in for development as a feature film with 1492 Pictures. Julie also writes the Shadow Keepers series of dark, edgy paranormal romantic suspense as J. K. Beck. Julie lives in central Texas with her husband, two daughters and several cats.

• • •

In the past three years, *New York Times* bestselling author **SHERRILYN KENYON** has claimed the number-one spot sixteen times. This extraordinary bestseller continues to top every genre she writes. With more than twenty-five million copies of her books in print in over one hundred countries, her current series include: *The Dark-Hunters, The League, Chronicles of*

Nick, and *Belador.* Since 2004, she has placed more than fifty novels on the *New York Times* list in all formats including manga. The preeminent voice in paranormal fiction, with more than twenty years of publishing credits in all genres, Kenyon not only helped to pioneer, but define the current paranormal trend that has captivated the world. For more on Sherrilyn visit www.SherrilynKenyon.com.

● ● ●

JON LAND is the acclaimed author of thirty thrillers, including the bestselling Caitlin Strong Texas Ranger series *Strong Enough To Die, Strong Justice, Strong at the Break,* and *Strong Vengeance* (July 2012). There are over seven million copies of his books in print in dozens of countries and six languages. He lives in Providence, Rhode Island, and can be found on the web at www.jonlandbooks.com.

● ● ●

New York Times bestseller **DIANNA LOVE** spent her early years dangling over a hundred feet in the air to create unusual marketing projects for Fortune 500 companies. Now she's released her energetic muse on writing high-octane thrillers and urban fantasy. Her first book won the prestigious RITA Award (as Dianna Love Snell) and she now coauthors with number one *New York Times* bestseller Sherrilyn Kenyon. The latest Kenyon-Love collaboration has resulted in the Belador urban fantasy series that debuted on the *New York Times, USA TODAY, Publishers Weekly* and Walmart bestseller lists in 2010 with *Blood Trinity.* The next Belador novel, *Atlerant,* was released September 2011 and *Cathbad's Curse* will be out September 2012. When not speaking at national and international events throughout the year, Dianna lives in the metro Atlanta area with her motorcycle-instructor husband. For more on Dianna visit www.AuthorDiannaLove.com.

• • •

D. P. LYLE, M.D. is the Macavity Award winning and Edgar® Award nominated author of the nonfiction books, *Murder & Mayhem, Forensics For Dummies, Forensics & Fiction, Forensics & Fiction 2,* and *Howdunnit: Forensics* as well as the Samantha Cody thrillers *Devil's Playground* and *Double Blind,* the Dub Walker Thrillers *Stress Fracture* and *Hot Lights, Cold Steel,* and the media tie-in novels *Royal Pains: First, Do No Harm* and *Royal Pains: Sick Rich* based on the hit TV series. His essay on Jules Verne's *The Mysterious Island* appears in *Thrillers: 100 Must Reads.*

He has worked with many novelists and with the writers of popular television shows such as *Law & Order, CSI: Miami, Diagnosis Murder, Monk, Judging Amy, Peacemakers, Cold Case, House, Medium, Women's Murder Club, 1-800-Missing, The Glades,* and *Pretty Little Liars.*

He is a practicing cardiologist in Orange County, California.
Website: www.dplylemd.com
Blog: http://writersforensicsblog.wordpress.com

• • •

JAMES MACOMBER is the author of the international legal thrillers featuring former Special Forces/NSA/CIA operator, now lawyer, John Cann—whom *Booklist* described as a "strong, multilayered protagonist with the star power to keep this series going for a very long time"—along with an ensemble cast of memorable characters in a Washington, D.C., international law firm with very close ties to the intelligence community.

At one time or another, Macomber has been a serviceman, student, bartender, waiter, salesman, tennis instructor, actor, lawyer, photographer and writer. This eclectic background—or checkered past—is reflected in the range of subject matter for his novels, which include terrorist networks in academia in *Bargained for Exchange,* assassinations in the Netherlands during the trial of the Pan Am 103 Lockerbie bombers in *Art & Part,* atrocities, international crime and human trafficking with the Bosnian war crimes trials as the backdrop in *A Grave Breach* and, in *Sovereign Order,* the horrifying prospect of a catastrophic WMD attack on the "crown jewel of Formula 1 racing", the Monaco Grand Prix.

When he's not hanging out on Siesta Key, Florida, Jim is completing work on his fifth novel, *Extraordinary Rendition.*

Visit his website at www.jamesmacomber.com.

• • •

TONI MCGEE CAUSEY is the author of the critically acclaimed and nationally bestselling "Bobbie Faye" novels—an action/caper series set in south Louisiana; the series was released in back-to-back publications, beginning with *Charmed and Dangerous, Girls Just Wanna Have Guns* and *When a Man Loves a Weapon.* While pursuing an MFA in Screenwriting as well as a Masters in Philosophy, Toni had scripts optioned by prominent studios and, just last year, produced an indie film, *LA-308,* which now has offers of distribution pending. Toni began her career by writing nonfiction for local newspapers, edited *Baton Rouge Magazine,* and sold articles to places like *Redbook* and *Mademoiselle.* She was a contributor to the anthology *Do You Know What It Means To Miss New Orleans,* as well as *Killer Year: Stories to Die For.* She has had several of her blogs syndicated nationally from the group blog, "Murderati," and she can currently be found at "Murder She Writes." In her other life, she and her husband are the owners of a construction company which specializes in civil construction. She and her husband reside in New Orleans.

• • •

New York Times bestselling author **CARLA NEGGERS** is always plotting her next adventure, whether in life or for one of her books. Her fertile imagination and curious nature make her ready for anything.

It is also these qualities that sparked her love of reading as a child and continue to drive her passion for storytelling today. With her compelling blend of action, suspense and down-to-earth, realistic characters caught up in extraordinary circumstances, her novels never fail to take her readers on an exciting journey.

With more than sixty novels published and translations in dozens of languages, Carla most appreciates those moments when she feels she's gotten the story just right—when it all comes together on the pages of her book, exactly the way she's envisioned the tale in her mind. Then, when readers connect with the story, her satisfaction is complete.

When she's not working on her next book, Carla enjoys traveling, hiking, kayaking and spending time with her large extended family. She's always planning the next trip—and the next adventure—either of which just might inspire a new story.

Carla lives with her husband in Vermont on a hilltop not far from picturesque Quechee Gorge.

● ● ●

"When I first got the idea to become a novelist, it took me five years to teach myself the craft and finish my first book," **BRENDA NOVAK** says. "I learned how to write by reading what others have written. The best advice for any would-be author: read, read, *read*...."

Brenda sold her first book, and the rest is history. A *New York Times* and *USA TODAY* bestselling author of forty novels, Brenda Novak has been nominated for a prestigious RITA Award three times and won The National Reader's Choice Award, the Bookbuyer's Best, the Bookseller's Best, the Writer Touch Reader Award, the Golden Quill, the Hold Medallion and the Award of Excellence, among others.

Brenda and her husband, Ted, live in Sacramento and are the proud parents of five children—three girls and two boys. She juggles her writing career with her children's softball and soccer games, field trips, carpool runs and homework sessions. When she's not spending time with her family or writing, Brenda is usually working on her annual fundraiser for diabetes research—an online auction held on her website (www.brendanovak.com) every May. To date, she has raised nearly $1.4 million for this cause.

• • •

With more than six million books in print—eighty-nine novels for Harlequin, Silhouette, HarperCollins, Dell and Del Rey—**PATRICIA ROSEMOOR** still finds new story forms and new characters that excite her.

Detective Shelley Caldwell first appeared in *Hot Case*, a Silhouette Bombshell. Combining her love of thrillers with urban fantasy with romance, Patricia experimented with 1st/3rd person. To her good fortune, she was able to reprise her characters and world in *Hot Trick*, a Carina Press digital first novel, and in the short story *Hot Corpse*, also available in digital formats. She was delighted to continue the series with *Hot Note*.

Patricia has received two Career Achievement Awards and two Reviewers' Choice Best Novel Awards from *RT Book Reviews*. Her career as an author took off when she won a Golden Heart from Romance Writers of America for Best Young Adult Romance. In her other life, she teaches credit courses—Writing Popular Fiction and Suspense Thriller Writing—in the Fiction Writing Department of Columbia College Chicago.

• • •

Since 2002, **WILLIAM SIMON** has been the owner and lead investigator for a licensed firm that handles computer forensics and electronic evidence exclusively. This work has led to a few interesting experiences.

He has a ridiculously broad-range DVD collection, listens to little else but music from the 1950s, still reads Sir Arthur Conan

Doyle, and is proud of the fact that he saw both Frank Sinatra and Dean Martin—live and on stage—in Las Vegas, many years ago.

Earlier works published under the pseudonym "Will Graham" include *Street Heat* and *Sometimes, There Really Are Monsters Under the Bed*, both available in ebook editions. *Spider's Dance*, a full-length novel featuring Nicholas White, is also available.

His website is: www.wmsimon.com

● ● ●

ALEXANDRA SOKOLOFF is the author of the supernatural thrillers *The Harrowing, The Price, The Unseen, Book of Shadows*, and *The Space Between*, the paranormal romance, *The Shifters*, and the paranormal trilogy *Twist of Fate*, and is a coauthor of the paranormal Keepers series, with Heather Graham and Harley Jane Kozak. She is a Thriller Award winner and a Bram Stoker and Anthony Award nominee. The *New York Times* Book Review called her novels "Some of the most original and freshly unnerving work in the genre."

As a screenwriter, Alex has sold original thriller scripts and adapted novels for numerous Hollywood studios, for producers such as Michael Bay, Laura Ziskin, David Heyman and Neal Moritz. She has served on the Board of Directors of the Writers Guild of America, west, and the board of the Mystery Writers of America.

In nonfiction, Alex is the author of *Screenwriting Tricks for Authors (and Screenwriters!)*, and *Writing Love*, workbooks based on her internationally acclaimed blog and workshops.

In her spare time (!) she performs with Heather Graham's all-author Slush Pile Players and dances every chance she gets.

http://alexandrasokoloff.com
http://screenwritingtricks.com

• • •

ROXANNE ST. CLAIRE is a *New York Times* bestselling author of twenty-seven novels of suspense and romance. Her most popular romantic suspense novels feature an elite cadre of bodyguards called The Bullet Catchers. In addition, she has published a trilogy focused on a family-based security firm known as The Guardian Angelinos. In 2012, Roxanne is launching a contemporary romance series set in fictional Barefoot Bay, as well as her first young adult novel, *Don't You Wish*.

In addition to being a five-time RITA nominee and one-time RITA winner, Roxanne's novels have won the National Reader's Choice Award for best romantic suspense for two consecutive years, as well as the Daphne du Maurier Award, the HOLT Medallion, the Maggie, Booksellers Best, Book Buyers Best, and many others. Her books have been translated into dozens of languages and are routinely included as a Doubleday/Rhapsody Book Club Selection of the Month.

Roxanne lives in Florida with her husband and two teens, and can be reached via her website, www.roxannestclaire.com or on her Facebook reader page, www.facebook.com/roxannestclaire.

• • •

MARIAH STEWART is the award-winning *New York Times, USA TODAY* and *Publishers Weekly* bestselling author of thirty novels, three novellas and three short stories, and has been featured in the *Wall Street Journal*. Her books are currently published by both Pocket Books and Ballantine Books. She has the unique distinction of having had the same agent and the same editorial team for every one of her novels.

A native of Hightstown, New Jersey, Stewart is a member of Novelists, Inc, Thriller Writers International, PASIC, the Romance Writers of America, the New Jersey Romance Writers, the Valley

Forge Romance Writers and the Washington Romance Writers. She lives with her husband and their dogs amidst the rolling hills of Chester County, Pennsylvania, where she savors country life, tends her gardens, and tries to avoid running the Amish buggies off the road with her SUV.

She considers herself one lucky son of a gun to have landed the best job in the world: getting paid for making up stories. At home. In sweats and J. Crew flip-flops. Could life be sweeter?

● ● ●

DEBRA WEBB, born in Alabama, wrote her first story at age nine and her first romance at thirteen. It wasn't until she spent three years working for the military behind the Iron Curtain—and a five-year stint with NASA—that she realized her true calling. A collision course between suspense and romance was set. Since then she has penned nearly one hundred novels. Visit her at www.debrawebb.com. ✍